OF BRITAIN QUARTET

'Plunging a broadsword into the heart
of Arthurian legend, Tidhar's novel depicts the Knights
of the Round Table as a bunch of sweary, sweaty thugs.
So much for the glories of a magical, mythical past. Britain,
it seems, has forever been a land of factional infighting,
presided over by a brutal, uncaring elite.'
Financial Times

'The novel is a bloody, bravura performance,
which Tidhar pulls off with graphic imagery and modern
vernacular... *By Force Alone* is Tidhar's scatological
contribution to the field of Arthurian romance, a salutary
antidote to the more romantic glossings
of recent modern fantasy.'
Guardian

'A ferocious and often very funny reinvention of the King
Arthur myth, taking in references from Tolkien to Brexit.'
iNews

'A twisted Arthur retelling mixing the historical
and the magical with a very modern eye. Brutal and vicious,
funny, *Peaky Blinders* of the Round Table.'
Adrian Tchaikovsky

'Tidhar fancies himself an iconoclast, and his incidental
invention reaches impressive levels of delirium.'
The Times

LAVIE TIDHAR

An Ad Astra Book

First published in the UK in 2021 by Head of Zeus Ltd
This paperback edition first published in 2022 by Head of Zeus Ltd,
part of Bloomsbury Publishing Plc

9 7 5 3 1 2 4 6 8

A catalogue record for this book is available
from the British Library.

ISBN (PB): 9781838931339
ISBN (E): 9781838931346

Typeset by Ben Cracknell Studios

Printed and bound in Great Britain by
CPI Group (UK) Ltd, Croydon, CR0 4YY

Head of Zeus Ltd
5–8 Hardwick Street
London EC1R 4RG

WWW.HEADOFZEUS.COM

PART ONE

MAID MARIAN AND THE ELFIN KNIGHT

1

Long ago, in the time when the borders to Faerie were not quite as sealed as they are today, ever before a Norman set foot or took a shit or fucked a goat upon the island of Britannia, there lived a maid named Marian.

It was her who started the whole damn thing.

Or perhaps it started even earlier. The wood had been there since the last ice age. Ancient, impenetrable, hiding a dark and secret heart... Etcetera, etcetera, as the Romans would have said. But they were no longer around.

Anyhow.

Dark ravens came and went between the worlds, and sometimes they assumed the shape of handsome men.

One such man once wandered out of the wood and into the town of Nottingham.

The man strolled, much at his leisure. He did not hurry. He hummed a little nameless tune as he walked. He took in the sights, and breathed in deeply from the rarefied city air. Cooking fires burned and there was rubbish in the streets and horse manure and chickens clucking, children shrieking, mothers cursing, sellers crying out their wares. Oh, how he loved it, did the elfin knight. There is nothing like the sight and smell of humans in such close proximity to stir the blood. Some call it civilization. To the elfin knight, it was a buffet of delights.

A leper, begging by the roadside, raised his head and saw the handsome knight. He shook a bowl in which three sad coins joshed and jingled against one another. The knight knelt and looked into the beggar's eyes and smiled. He reached into the bowl and took a coin, a penny from the reign of Athelstan, then dropped it with a curse on feeling the hot burn of the small cross etched into its centre.

'*That* thing?' he said. For he remembered when a cross meant nothing in this world.

The beggar said not a word, for he was not a stupid man, and on seeing this the knight's good cheer returned.

'Tell me,' he said. 'How go things in the world of mortal men?'

'The harvest was good last year,' the beggar confided. 'The priests now sell forgiveness of all sins for modest fees. Byzantium endures against the Saracens, and it is said they have a ship-destroying weapon called Greek Fire which burns all that it touches. In London they are building grand new palaces and churches, and everyone's complaining of the rising costs of rent. The weather is predicted to stay warm all week, and I have taken a good shit this morning. Lord, what more is it you wish to learn?'

'That's more than ample, leper,' said the elfin knight.

The beggar shook his bowl.

'I'll spare your life instead.'

'... Seems fair.'

The knight smiled. The knight rose. The knight went strolling through the market square.

The leper stared after him thoughtfully. Then he packed up his bowl and legged it out of town as fast as he could, and this is where he makes his exit from our story.

The knight strolled through offerings of fresh farm eggs and bread baked early in the morning, of apples, bacon, cabbages and river fish. He strolled through butchers' stalls and leather workers, candles and embroidery, alabaster figurines and fine jewellery worked in gold and silver; and it was at one such stall that he first saw Maid Marian.

The fae, it's said, have an affinity to sharks, for like them, they are cold-blooded, predatory and possess unsettling eyes that do not blink. The knight saw Marian the way a shark scents blood in water. He had come seeking a wife, as he had done once every century on May Day for the past six hundred years. Now he had found her, he was sure of that. She stood at the jeweller's stall, fingering the hilt of a small iron knife with a practical handle, and she palmed it under her sleeve when the owner wasn't looking. She had brown hair, tanned leather leggings, a short jacket and a copper bracelet on her left arm. Her eyes were black, like the peat bogs of Jutland where the old Danes ritually dumped the corpses of sacrificial victims. Her smile was easy and whole.

The knight was enchanted. He followed Maid Marian on her rounds. He watched her as she nicked an apple here and a piece of smoked fish there, and a length of cloth and a silver brooch and two hard boiled eggs and half a loaf of bread. He approached her at last at a stall selling puppies and said, 'Pardon me, miss, may I have the pleasure of asking your name?'

Maid Marian turned and saw the knight and, in truth, the knight was very pleasing on the eye. She said, 'It is Marian, good sir.'

Her gaze evaluated the knight's clothing and accessories and total worth. Since he was dressed well and wore silver and gold on his person quite openly, and in good taste beside, she figured him an easy mark.

He gave her back a name of his own, though names meant little to his kind. He made small conversation – the weather, and the rents in London, and how about those Vikings raiding up and down the coast?

He held a puppy in his arms and stroked the little creature, and at the end he purchased it to give Maid Marian as a present, and to slow her down. She took the puppy from his arms. He said, quite plainly, 'I am a man in want of a wife.'

'And I am a woman in want of some breakfast,' she told him. Then she departed and left him there.

The knight watched her go. He went to see some horses stabled just nearby. He spoke to a white steed a while and told it what he wanted, and loosened the rope that held the horse tight.

Then the knight sought out two members of the city watch who were dozing near the place where the traders dumped their rubbish. He spoke softly and convincingly to them and told them of the young woman he had seen, describing her precisely, and how he'd witnessed her thieving throughout the course of the morning.

The men of the watch thanked him gruffly, for in truth they were none too keen on carrying out their duties, but now they were obliged. They lifted cudgels and put on scowls and went forth into the market in search of the young woman the knight described.

The knight positioned himself at some distance and waited and watched.

It was not too long after that the confrontation occurred. The men of the watch spotted Maid Marian. Maid Marian spotted the men of the watch. They tried to restrain her. She tossed the puppy into the one's face and kicked him right in the nuts, broke the nose of the other, and made a run for it. The men of the watch, cursing, gave chase. Maid Marian headed for the gates, but more of the armed men gathered to block her way.

The knight whistled.

The white steed he had spoken to earlier neighed and broke free from its bonds. It galloped to the knight, and the knight, in one smooth flowing motion, jumped onto the horse's back. The men of the watch converged by the gate on the now-desperate Maid Marian. She turned and turned, but her expression well told that she knew she was outnumbered.

The knight on his white horse galloped to the rescue. The horse bore down on the men from the watch and they scattered lest they fall under its hooves.

'Quick!' the knight called.

Maid Marian turned and flashed him that easy smile. The knight reached down and Maid Marian clasped his hand. He lifted her onto the horse and she sat behind him and held on to his waist. The knight, with a song in his heart in a dark language no one has spoken in centuries, spurred the horse through the gate. In moments they were out of the town – heading into the woods.

2

I f you go into the woods today, you may not come out tomorrow, and the person who comes out may not be you, as the ancient sages said.

The elfin knight carried Maid Marian into the woods, where oaks of yore made their habitat and jostled with rowan and birch, hawthorn and holly. Soon the twisted trees grew too thick for the horse and they abandoned it to wander back at its leisure.

'It isn't that I'm not grateful,' Maid Marian said. 'But it is getting dark, and it is said many malevolent spirits wander inside Sherwood come the witching hour.'

'It is not far to a place of shelter I know,' said the knight, 'and besides, they will be seeking you outside to punish you.'

Maid Marian shrugged. 'It would only be the loss of a nose or an arm.'

'It would be quite a shame should your face lose its nose,' said the knight, 'for a very attractive face it is.'

Maid Marian said nothing to that. The wood grew thick around them and there were no longer any discernible paths. Far in the distance a wolf howled. Something scaly slithered through the underbrush.

The knight, emboldened, led them on, and Maid Marian followed.

As they went the knight shed some of his earthly countenance. The wood-within is older and more dangerous than the wood-without, and now he seemed taller, and crueller, and his skin shone the way some types of fungus glow with faint luminescence.

Maid Marian made no mention of this fact.

Once, she almost stepped on top of a tiny house under the roots of an oak, and its inhabitants, two tiny pixies with the apparel and tools of shoemakers, came out and shook their fists angrily at her, and shouted in voices too high and small for her to clearly hear.

Once, Maid Marian stumbled, and for a moment she disappeared from the knight's view. She had done it on purpose, for she had seen, there on the ground, a large and perfect acorn, which seemed like a diamond to her. She picked it up very carefully and put it away in her garment before the knight came for her and they continued on.

A crow watched her from a high branch and cawed mournfully. All light faded. From time to time, Maid Marian caught a fleeting glimpse of the moon above the canopy, but too soon it always vanished from sight. The knight, too, dropped any attempt at pleasantries at this point. He looked at her sideways with a hungry sort of look, and it was the sort of hunger that has nought to do with apples or honey or bread.

At last they came to the place.

It was a black pool of water deep in the heart of the wood. Gnarled oaks grew near the bank and in the dark water dark creatures frolicked and swam under the surface, while ravens and crows congregated on the high branches like priests at mass.

'It does not much look like the promised place of shelter which you mentioned,' Marian ventured to the knight.

'Oh, but it is,' he said, and smiled with teeth that, she now noticed, were more like sharpened needles, 'for we will not be disturbed. This is my place.'

He led her to a confluence of three oaks. Ropes were tied to their branches and the ropes ended in noose-like loops – the better, perhaps, to tie a person down.

Then the elfin knight turned fully upon Maid Marian, and she saw what she had already suspected, that this was no man at all but a spectre like a hell-wain or a bugaboo or a Dick-a-Tuesdays.

And the knight said: 'Lie down, lie down, you lily-white wench, and deliver yourself unto me. For six pretty maidens I have drowned here, and the seventh you shall be.'

Maid Marian looked at the ropes and she looked at the knight and she saw what there was to see. And she wondered at the names of those six women, murdered over the centuries, and which are not recorded in song. And who they were, and what they did, and what dreams they had before encountering the elfin knight. And she looked at the black watery grave where they must have lain.

Her shoulders sagged in defeat. For men have murdered women with impunity since the beginning of time. And so she said, 'Since I am standing here, this dismal death awaiting me, I'm sure a kiss from your sweet mouth would really comfort me.'

It is indeed a thing about the fae, or men in general for that matter, that they are susceptible to any suggestion of their power. They are also keen on a rhyme.

So the knight went to Maid Marian, and he laid a proper kiss upon her. She felt his hardness against her pelvis. She engulfed him in her arms, and as they kissed she felt his power and she would not let go.

Under her sleeve, the small, cold, iron knife she'd stolen from the market stall still waited. She drew it out and brought her arm onto his chest. The knight grew ever harder at her touch. She ran her hand lightly down his chest, then stabbed him in the belly.

The knight gasped. His breath and power flowed into Maid Marian as she kissed him, hungrily, passionately. She brought the knife up in a quick, experienced motion, and it was much like gutting a large fish. The knight tried to pull away but she would not let him. As his power flowed into her she lowered him onto the ground and quickly fastened his arms and his legs with the ropes that were there for that very purpose. And only then did she release him from the kiss.

She stood there, above him, as he lay spread-eagled on the floor, tied and trussed and bled like a hog. And his dark intestines spilled out of his open belly, and his dark blood seeped into the dark earth of that place.

And she said, 'Lie there, lie there, you false-hearted man. Lie there instead of me. For if six pretty maidens here you slew, the seventh has done for *you*.'

'This is not… the way… it's supposed to… *be*!' the knight said. 'And your rhymes suck!'

Maid Marian stared down at him without expression. 'Oh, and also, *fuck* you!' she said.

The knight closed his eyes. 'Kill me, then,' he said. 'For in that you will merely release me back into the forest, and I shall kill again.'

'I don't think so,' Maid Marian said. And she reached into her garment and brought out the acorn she had found. She looked at it admiringly in the faint bioluminescence of the dying knight.

'What… What do you think you're *doing*?' the knight said, and this time there was a little undulating shiver in his voice.

Maid Marian knelt beside the knight. She stroked his hair and his very pale skin, for just a moment. Then she set to work.

She reached with both hands into his belly and pulled out his entrails and spread open the folds of skin. The knight screamed, but there was no one to hear him to care.

Marian took a handful of dirt from the earth and put it into the cavity. She took a handful more and a handful again, until she'd lined the hole in the knight's belly. It was good, rich soil, full of decaying plant and animal matter and many nutrients.

Then she planted the acorn into the knight's belly.

The knight wriggled and tried to free himself, but the ropes he had himself fashioned held him tight. Maid Marian smiled, though it was a grim sort of smile, and she looked at her nails, which were short and dirty with soil and blood.

She reached for the folds of skin of the knight's belly. She brought them back together, to cover the cavity, and she fastened them loosely with needle and thread, which she always carried on her person, for she believed in being sensible.

Then she sat down with her back to one of the trees, and ate a piece of salted fish, and half a loaf of bread, and a slice of dry cheese and an apple, for she was very hungry.

'What now?' the elfin knight said. His voice had grown weak and his eyes were closed, and his chest moved up and down in a slow and rhythmic breath.

'Now we wait.'

She watched him as he fell asleep.

In time, she knew, the ropes would fray and rot. The knight's body would sink further into the earth until it vanished deep into the roots below. Inside him, the tiny acorn would grow. In time a tree would rise, and it would be mighty, for it fed on blood.

She washed her hands in the black pool. She no longer had fear of it, nor was it so dark anymore. She could see clearly, and all the hidden things that lived in that place were no longer hidden from her.

She cleaned her cold, iron knife, too. She believed in being tidy, in all things.

Then she wandered off, deep into the heartwood.

Time passed.

Behind, an oak tree slowly grew.

Now...

PART TWO

THE ANARCHY

3

It begins to rain as Will Scarlett wends his way through the narrow city streets. His boots are treated leather and his coat runs down to his feet, and on his head he wears a rather jazzy goatskin helmet to protect his head from rain and wind. He can't get used to being back on this God damned island. Back in the Holy Land they'd bake in summer, he swam nude in the waters of the Med. After two years in that hellhole his skin was tanned as dark as a Saracen's.

Will the Knife, they called him. He never learnt the sword properly, liked to get in close and quiet like – back when he was growing up he was top earner for the gangs in paid-for stab-and-runs. He stomps down the dark alleyway until he sees the single torch burning outside the Pilgrim's Inn.

God bless you, England, on this glorious Year of Our Lord, 1145.

A black cat under an upturned cart watches him and hisses. Will grins, recognising a kindred spirit. 'Here, pussy pussy,' he says. The cat purrs.

One year he's been back already. When he was in the Holy Land he'd dreamed of going home. He never thought he'd make it out alive but when he did at last, it was only to discover that, in his absence, England had gone to shit in a handbasket.

He psss-psss-pssses at the pussycat and dashes the remaining distance to the pub. He stands outside and stomps his boots and shakes his coat and checks his knives and then he enters.

'Our Father who art in heaven, hallowed be thy name. Thy kingdom come. Thy fucking kingdom come. Nobody even knows whose kingdom it is now. Is it Stephen's? Is it Empress Maude's? They say he's hung like a cricket and she has tits like pomegranates. Oh, Will, it's you.'

'You could be executed for this, priest, not just excommunicated.'

'And bless you too, my child. Communion wine?'

'If you're buying.'

The ex-priest leers and motions to the barkeep who pours them drinks in silence. The priest's companion wriggles in his lap. Will thinks she's very pretty. The priest leers more and slaps her backside.

'Take a hike, Joanie, got business to discuss.'

The priest's companion sashays to the jakes, not looking back.

'Where did you find him? Her?'

The priest just shrugs. 'Mind your own damn business, Scarlett.'

Will sips his wine. The pub is dark and there's dark business in the corners that's conducted quietly. A veterans' bar. No civilians allowed. And if either Maude or Stephen's soldiers came to town they'd know better than to come here and make trouble. These men have paid their price. They'd done things in the Holy Land no sane man wishes to remember. And they have been absolved of all their guilt and crimes. They took the cross. They earned their place in heaven.

So why does he feel guilt? Why can't he fall asleep? Why does Will the Knife have trouble with his faith in heaven?

In the Bible of the Hebrews they speak of a place, a garden or a sacred grove, long-lost now, where God and his angels dwelled, where strange trees grew. And the priests say that it was sin that had humanity expelled from that place. And the priests, also, speak of hell, an unfathomable realm where the souls of evil men are tortured for eternity.

Yet Will, for all that he has been upon this earth a mere twenty-seven years, has seen enough of hell to know that it is here, right here upon this earth; whereas of heaven he's seen little sign. He murdered and he saw men murdered; in Acre he saw war ships burn, screaming men engulfed in flames jumping into the sea to try and escape, but even that did not avail them, for the secret weapon of the Byzantines burnt even in the water. It is an awful sight, men burnt even as they drown.

And yet the Church would have it that those perpetrators of mass murder are forgiven souls. It is not the vile act that matters but the intent to which it's put: namely, the liberation of the Holy Land from infidels. And Will had thought he had left the horror behind. He had served his time and gratefully departed on board ship to England, to that green and pleasant land.

He thought.

'You seem moody tonight,' the priest, Father Jonas, says. 'Are you still having problems sleeping?'

Will grunts in reply. Jonas – just Jonas, now, though Will has never dared to ask him what he did to be expelled from service of the Church, it would have had to have been terrible indeed to merit such an action – looks at him almost in affection. 'The poppy tincture I recommended, do you not take it?'

'It makes my thinking addled,' Will says.

'You need to sleep.'

What can he tell the ex-priest? That when he closes his eyes he can still see the corpses piled up in that mass grave in Sidon? Hear the screams of the children in that merchant caravan in the Jezreel Valley? Smell the shit and the piss and sour sweat and semen of crusaders on board ship, too long at sea, all crammed together in the hold?

Worse – the things he sees that simply aren't there.

'Come on, Will. Here, take this instead then. I need you conscious.'

'What's that?'

'Khat.'

'Oh.'

He stuffs it in his mouth. The leaves are bitter, dry. He forces himself to chew through it. Back in the Holy Land they could get the leaves fresh, transported from the east across Arabia. Now they brought the habit home and when the ships dock in the port of London fresh from Outremer they carry back supplies.

He waits for it to kick. The room feels brighter, sharper. He says, 'So what's the job?'

'Rufus wants us to provide protection for his dog fight on Old Fish Street tonight.'

'Alright.'

Will doesn't mind the dog fights. It's steady work, and Rufus, an old Irish pirate with red, now thinning hair, pays promptly and appreciates the service they provide. He always hires veterans, not like some.

'Oh, and there's something else.'

'Sure,' Will says. 'Sure, what is it?'

Jonas scratches at his pate. 'It's nothing much,' he says. 'An errand really.'

Will grins at the former priest. 'A hit?'

'A stab-and-grab. But a quiet one, Will.'

'Alright. You got the details?'

'That I have.'

Will downs his wine. 'Got any more of that khat?'

'That I do.'

'Alright then.'

'Alright.'

He sees her when they leave the bar. This time she's a crone, and made of shadows, standing in the place where the black cat was. She doesn't look at him. She doesn't need to.

'What are you staring at, man?' the ex-priest says irritably.

'Nothing,' Will says.

The crone breaks apart, becomes an unkindness of ravens.

They fly away on silent wings. He sees her. He sees her when nobody else does. Sometimes she is a crone, sometimes a maid, at other times a mother.

He saw things in the Holy Land. Mermaids off Cyprus luring sailors to their death – he saw them with his own eyes. That really happened. And in Jerusalem Will's company was tasked by Queen Melisende to hunt down a particularly powerful yet malevolent Ifrit who preyed on young women in the town – Christian or Saracen or Jew it mattered not to the creature. They tracked it from St. Stephen's Gate, through the Patriarch's Quarter and past the Citadel, until they cornered the Ifrit at last somewhere in the newly created German Quarter. It went for them in earnest then. It turned into a pyre and flung flames and Harold the German caught the full blast and was fried on the spot, he didn't even have time to scream. The creature turned into a wolf and a bear and a mouse that tried to scuttle away. They almost caught it then but it turned into a sandstorm and blinded them.

Then Mad Asmund the Half-Viking screamed, and he dashed into the storm with his sword raised high and a long nail of cold iron in his other fist, and he drove it into the ground, where the Ifrit's shadow fell. The creature howled, and it flayed the skin off of Asmund, but then it stopped. And then it died.

The point *being*, Will has *seen* things.

Only now he's *seeing. Things.*

'What is *with* you tonight?' Jonas says.

Will hops from foot to foot and grins and chews the khat. It's really kicking in now, and the world is fast and bright.

'Nothing,' he says. 'Where are we going?'

'Just follow me.'

They trail through dark and narrow streets with lean-to buildings made of wood and stone and clay and thatch. Will sometimes thinks, Just strike a flint and toss a spark and burn down the whole God damned city – poof, just like that, London in flames.

But somehow it carries on. Rats scuttle underfoot but he ignores them. A raven watches him from high above a wall. Will ignores it.

She comes to him sometimes at night, in his rented room. A cat jumps on the windowsill; a woman enters through. *This is* my *town*, she says. She straddles him, makes use of him, his body. *This will* always *be my town*.

She must be some ancient deity, he thinks. A sort of genius loci or a fae. She must have been powerful once, to still be so *present*. But even as they're making love he can see how faded she really is, even if she can't. Even if she pretends not to notice.

The old world is dying, Will thinks. And there's a new God in town.

And everywhere they go they pass the churches. Will took the cross, so why does he still see her? Why does he see the bogies and the bogglebows on the Strand, the nacks and buckies in the river? Why does he see all manner of these spectres?

You don't believe, *boy*, whispers the voice in his head. It has the raspy voice of the Patriarch of Jerusalem. *You'll go to hell, the same one you no longer believe in.*

But I do believe in hell, Will tries to protest. *It's here, it's right—*

'We're here,' Jonas says.

Oh, shit, Will thinks.

They're in the Hole Bourn area, outside the church-and-office complex of the Knights Templar.

Tough motherfuckers. To be a Templar was to be made for life. They ran protection on the way to Outremer for the pilgrims, then branched out into handling finance. You didn't fuck with the Templars, everybody knew that. Jonas knew that. Fucking Rufus knew that. So what the fuck?

The place is quiet. Stout stone walls. A locked gate. Guards behind, somewhere unseen. The banner of the Order hanging high, a red cross on a black-and-white flag. They called themselves the Poor Fellow-Soldiers of Christ and of the Temple of Solomon, but they were no longer poor, not by a long shot, and the Temple of Solomon was a long way away.

'Don't worry,' Jonas says. 'There.'

There's a gaggle of drinking establishments across the road, leading down the incline that leads towards the river. They're dark and dismal, and quiet at this time of night. Will follows Jonas, until they stand across the road from a place called the Saracen's Head, with the inevitable sign hanging above showing a bloodied severed head. Will winces.

'According to my source he should be in there.'

'Who's your source?'

'Mind your own business, Will.'

So Will does. He checks his knives. He and the ex-priest melt into the shadows. They watch the place. They've done this before. Not all deaths in war are carried out on the battlefield.

Some men leave the pub, laughing, swords at their sides, but the target is not with them and they depart peacefully towards the Convent Garden. A little later a short, stout man leaves with two women, one on either side of him, and Will would have argued to rob him if he wasn't convinced the two women would surely do the same, and he would not be surprised if the man was found floating downriver later in the week. Besides it's not their guy.

When their guy does appear, he is alone. He's old and stooped and moves slowly, but at the same time with a certain regal authority, like the reason he don't move fast is cause he don't need to move for anybody; and Will gets a right bad feeling about all this.

'Come on,' Jonas says. They go softly, cross the dirt road barely making sound, spreading out so one's ahead and one's behind. The man just starts to turn towards the Temple complex when they close in on him.

'What do you—'

Then Will's knife sings the way it's often sung before. It finds the old Templar in the exposed neck. The knife stabs with a soft whoomp and Will steps aside as he pulls the knife and the blood shoots out. He finishes the job with a round neat cut. The old man drops to his knees. Jonas and Will pick him up on either side – like a drunk who's fallen over in the street.

'Come on!'

'He's fucking heavy!'

'You're getting old, priest.'

'Fuck you, Will. Did you have to make it so messy? I can't afford a wash!'

Will thinks of cleanliness. Of the Holy Land, where it was always hot. Where one could wash in the sea or the streams, and the locals smelled pleasantly of soap – which is all but unknown here in London – and men and women both rub their armpits clean with a tincture of bay leaves and hyssop. He misses being clean. He's not felt clean since the Sidon Massacre.

They drag the corpse down into a dark alleyway and lay it down. The former priest goes through the old Templar's belongings. He finds a purse and silver pennies, and some papers and a set of keys and, at last, some form of book of accounts, and he takes them all. Then he says, 'We have to make him disappear.'

This is the part Will doesn't like. Killing is easy. It's what comes after in a case like this that causes trouble. That makes things difficult. Too many opportunities to slip up.

But that's the job.

And a job's a job.

'Alright,' he says. 'So what did you have in mind?'

'Ulfric,' the ex-priest says.

'You've got to be fucking kidding me.'

'You have a better idea?'

'The river?'

'Too easy for him to pop up again.'

'How the fuck are we going to get him there?'

The former priest looks grim. The former priest looks pointedly at Will. The former priest brings out a toughened leather sack.

'You've got to be fucking kidding.'

The former priest shrugs.

A job's a job, he seems to say.

4

They hack the corpse with sword and axe. They *are* professional. They've done this sort of thing before. The head, like on the pub sign, first – into the sack. One arm and then the other. A foot, two feet, a leg below the knee and then the other, then thighs. At last the torso, stuffed into a second bag. It's lucky that the man was old and small, but still – the bags are heavy. And it's dirty work.

'I'm thirsty,' the former priest complains. He takes out a bottle and drinks and passes it to Will, who downs the rest. He feels light-headed. She watches from the shadows then, the Morrigan.

'What are you staring at?'

'Nothing,' Will says. Jonas passes him another helping of khat. They chew, the way they used to do on long campaigns out in the desert. Will's buzzing now. The Morrigan looks at him from the shadows and smiles. She's hungry. She feeds on death and blood, for her this is a sacrifice. She seems more solid.

He shakes his head. Picks up a sack. The former priest picks up the other. The looted papers he keeps safely in a satchel on his person.

They skulk.

Past Rat's Corner and down Death's Way and through Damnation Alley, skirting Piss Street and Whore's Lane and the Place Where The Bloofer Ladies Dance. To the Convent Garden and the fields around there, and at last to Ulfric's Farm.

It's muddy there, and dark, and the pigs are awake and grunting. They smell the coming men. They smell the cargo they are carrying.

Never trust a man who owns a pig farm, as Aristophanes of Athens said. They knock on the gates.

'What? What!'

When Ulfric makes an appearance he's scowling and, as usual, he smells of shit.

'Oh, it's you two.'

They push in and follow him inside. Will dumps the sack with some relief. His arms are sore.

'A big'un or a small?'

'Depends, I guess. He was pretty old and—'

'Big'un,' Ulfric says, with certainty borne of experience. 'Three pennies and they better not be Maude's.'

Will, with some surprise, 'You side with Stephen?'

'Lad, I couldn't give a toss which arsewipe steals the crown. But that coinage what they strike for Maude is well inferior.'

'It's true,' Jonas allows. 'They take Stephen's pennies and just deface his bust and besides, never trust a northerner to mint a coin true. Those coins they make in York or Nottingham are underweight.'

'And don't get me started on the barons,' Ulfric says, 'Ol' Bill o' Gloucester and those Scottish pricks besides. Everyone thinks they can mint their own money nowadays. Well?'

Jonas grumbles but extracts the money.

'And a ha'penny if you got something to drink,' he says. He breaks a coin in half and hands it over.

'Sure, help yourselves. I got some cider round the back.'

Jonas grins and Ulfric hefts the two sacks like they weigh nothing and carries them over to the pigs. The pigs regard the men with small shrewd eyes. Ulfric opens a sack and tosses them an arm.

'Who was he, anyway?'

'Nobody,' the ex-priest says and cuts it short.

Ulfric grins. 'We come as nobodies into the world and as nobodies we return, amen, am I right, priest? Sooner or later, we're all just food for the pigs.'

But Jonas isn't in the mood for the pig farmer's philosophising. He stalks to the back and Will follows, and the ex-priest liberates the cider and pours them both a generous measure.

'He was a Templar,' Will says quietly.

'I fucking know that, Scarlett!'

'They'll look for him.'

'Well they ain't gonna find him, ain't they.'

'*Why* did we kill a Templar?'

'What is it with everyone suddenly asking *questions*!' The ex-priest turns on Will. He glares at him with red, mean eyes. 'In this business, Will, we do not *ask* questions.'

'Nevertheless—'

'You'll know when you need to know. Now get that drink down you and let's go see Rufus.'

'Fuck,' Will says. 'I forgot about the dog fight.'

'Yeah, well, good thing you have me then, innit.'

Will drinks the cider. He slaps Jonas on the back. He chews more khat. He downs another cup. It's hot inside. They walk across the mud to Ulfric and his pigs. One pig's chewing on a hand and fingers, another's got a skinny calf.

'Nice doing business with ya, boys,' the farmer says.

'Be seeing you, Ulfric.'

'Come back, you hear? The pigs are always hungry.' He reaches in the sack, pulls out the bloody torso. He takes a knife and guts the man. The insides spill open. Ulfric reaches in and pulls the liver out. He licks his lips.

'Yum yum,' he says.

5

'That motherfucker *eats* them, doesn't he,' Will says.

'I'm sure it's just a rumour.'

'He practically did it in front of us, Jonas!'

'Times are hard everywhere, Will. People got a right to eat.'

'Jesus.'

'Do not take the Lord's name in vain!'

And the ex-priest boxes him roundly behind the ears.

They wend their way through the dark streets. They may seem deserted, but London never sleeps. Will is hopped up on the khat and cider. Drums go off from some house with boarded-up windows. London never sleeps. Will is light on his feet. Someone screams in the distance and then there's laughter. Something smashes and breaks. London never sleeps. The cats watch them pass. They go through Penitents' Row where the lights burn bright and painted men and painted women strut their flesh, whispering soft promises. Here they are approaching the heart of the matter, so to speak. For fuck Stephen and Maude and their civil war across this island, for this is London, where the merchants come and the money changes hands and the ships dock and the sailors walk and the crusaders return and where the villagers flock and the bright young things burn. This is London. And who has time to fucking *sleep*?

'Come over here, big boy!'

'Blow you like a Saracen's houri!'

'You, tall guy! You can fuck me in the ass for a silver ha'penny!'

'Hello, there's Jonas!'

A rise of cheers. Jonas grins and waves.

'Long time too much!'

'Give us a prayer!'

'Forgive us, Father, for we have sinned...' They burst out laughing. Will grins. Will hops. Will shifts from foot to foot. Will sees the Morrigan in an upstairs window, looking down on him. Will drops the smile.

'Not tonight, maybe later, Jezebels!' the ex-priest says. 'The night is long and there's work yet to be done.'

'The dogs again? Put a coin on Cerberus for me—'

'A shekel on the Golden Hound!'

'What am I, your bookie? Fuck off, idol worshippers!'

'We'll worship *your* tiny idol for a coin, you old lech!'

And they burst into laughter again.

Will grins. Will laughs. Will shakes and shakes.

'Holy mother of God, Will, get a hold of yourself!'

They pass the St. Mary of Egypt. They pass St. Angela's Shelter for Fallen Women. They pass the Serge and Bacchus Baths For Men. They pass the Hippodrome. There are no hippos in London but Will had seen one in a sketch once, when they had stopped for a fortnight in Cyprus. The story goes that one of the bishops, mad for exotic fauna, purchased a dozen of the beasts through a contact in the Fatimid Caliphate, had them shipped across Egypt and then by ship. Supposedly half died en route and one got eaten but a few still made it up the Thames to London, and thence to the bishop's menagerie.

As for St. Mary of Egypt, everyone knows she fucked more pilgrims than there are priests in Rome – before she found Christ, at least.

They come out of Penitent's Row at last and down to the docks, where the *real* party's only just kicking in. Musicians on the fiddle and cittern, percussionists making an ungodly racket, jugglers tossing fire in the air and a crowd of drunken, loud, violent men jostle and push in the cold air from the river as money changes hands, the bookies shout themselves hoarse, dogs bark beyond and there, at the opening of the unmarked warehouse, is Rufus, looking pissed off.

'Where the fuck have you two been!'

'You know that thing?'

'The thing with that guy?'

'Yeah.'

'What about it?'

'It's done.'

'Alright. Why didn't you say so? Now can you get to work?'

'Sure, boss.'

'This lot are gonna start murdering each other if the show don't start.'

'Sure, boss.'

'Get to it then, fuckweasel.'

'Charming,' Jonas mutters, but only when Rufus is out of earshot. Truth is the old Irish pirate, for all that he is small, red, and old, is terrifying. For years he terrorised the coast before retiring. And his idea of retiring is this: running dog fights and prostitutes and gambling, and thieving every fucking thing that moves around the docks.

'Bring it down, bring it down!' Jonas screams. His voice carries – and now he holds a mace, with studded iron nails embedded, which he carries like it weighs nothing. Will has his knives but knives are no good for crowd control, so he's helped himself to one of Rufus's spare axes and he lets it whisper through the air and the men quieten, if only a little.

'Form an orderly line! Show's about to start!'

There's booze circling and painted girls carrying flagons and cups and Will snatches one off a tray and downs it in one. *More!* he thinks. He needs more! A man, quite drunk, takes out his dick and starts pissing everywhere, and Jonas's club comes down and the man drops in the pool of his own urine with his blood mixing into the piss.

'Keep some *fucking* manners, people! You need a piss go piss into the river!'

Then the doors are pulled open, and the punters cheer, and inside the warehouse the dogs, crazed with hunger and taunting, bark mad. Will and Jonas nod to the others Rufus hired – Brother Michael, the Byzantine, and No-Ears Seamus who was in the Siege of Acre – as they try to control the crowd.

The punters stream into warehouse and the dogs bark and the painted girls go on stage and put on a show and the punters go *nuts*, and there's more drink and there's more money changing hands and the dogs bark and Will *hops* and Will chews khat and Will downs ale and Will smells of blood and now *dogs* and wet fur and sour sweat – the whole place stinks, in truth.

Then the first fight begins.

The dogmen approach with the dogs for the fight.

'On the one side – Brutus The Brute!'

The crowd cheers. The dog – an *Alaunt Veantre*, bred by the Alani, brought to Gaul by the Vandals and further bred by the Normans who finally brought it here – growls, but quietly. He looks from side to side, measuring out the crowd as though working out the exact numbers of men that he could kill.

Will knows how he feels.

'And on the other – King Arthur!'

The crowd roars. The dog – a *Canis Pugnaces Britanniae*, or British War Dog, as the Romans called the breed – stalks lightly to the arena. The Romans had been so impressed with Britain's fighting dogs they brought them back to Rome and bred them for the coliseum. The Romans, the Romans. Though they are long-gone and their empire's barely the whisper of a forgotten dream, nevertheless, Rome still exerts its influence upon the world. The Church replaced the Empire, the Holy See the place of emperors, but *still* they rule, and *still* they have the fucking power. For if they once ruled over life and death now they've extended that to hell and heaven, to the afterlife itself. And what sane man would dare defy the priests when they can sentence you to torture in the fires of hell, forever?

Not that men don't commit evil deeds. But that's alright when all you have to do is pay for an indulgence. And the Church needs money to fund its ongoing war against the Caliphates.

Which means only the poor must go to hell. And the poor, Will thinks, already live there.

Brutus growls. Arthur pounces. Teeth flash. Blood sprays. The dogs are intertwined. Brutus gets the better of King Arthur for a moment but then the British war dog gets under and tears a bloody hole in his soft underbelly. Brutus cries – a horrible sound when a dog cries like that – Arthur goes for the neck but Brutus rolls over, flails with his hind legs, rolls again and comes rushing up at Arthur, trying to knock him over.

'Round one!' the umpire cries, and the dogmen step into the arena and beat the dogs with sticks to part them. The crowd, drunk, bloodthirsty, roars. More money changes hands.

Will grins. Will hefts his axe. Will feels the bloodlust.

Will wants to brawl.

'Round two!'

And then the dogs are at each other's throat, all discipline forgotten, desperate, perhaps, for this fight to end. There will be no round three. They yelp and bite, and Arthur's foaming at the mouth and Brutus loses an eye and paints a trail of blood.

Will looks away. Will chews the leaves. Will sees a pickpocket reaching into someone's robe. Will goes berserker like a Norseman on high mushrooms.

In the arena the dogs roll in the dirt. They nip and bite. They're tiring. Will kicks the would-be pickpocket in the nuts. He breaks his nose. He bears down on him. He kicks and kicks. The crowd roars. Will lifts the axe. The man's face gone behind a mask of blood, only his eyes are open, pleading. The crowd roars. One dog barks.

'And the winner is… King Arthur!'

Will brings down the axe.

Later, they drag the man's corpse out to the river. The dogmen are there already, with Brutus's pathetic corpse. It's wrapped in rags. The dogman weeps as he cradles the body.

'The Fall of Rome,' Jonas says, and sniggers.

The other dogman brings along his charge. King Arthur limps. King Arthur's blind.

'He won't be good for further fights,' the ex-priest says. 'You should sell him for stew to the almhouse. His bones will make a tasty treat.'

'Fuck off, you cunt.'

'Language!'

The dogmen stand apart. They console each other. King Arthur howls, a mournful cry. The dogman tosses Brutus in the river.

'You didn't have to kill him, you know,' the ex-priest says to Will.

'I know. I wanted to.'

'You need to get some sleep.'

They toss the nameless man into the river. The river's full of excrement, so what's a little more?

And how could I sleep? he wants to ask the former priest. How could he sleep when even now he sees them? Kelpies in the water like horses made of foam and shit. So hungry for the offering. A dog, a man. They fall on both the corpses and tear them up and swallow chunks and let the juice run down their jaws.

Why can't anybody *see* them?

She's there again, then, his Morrigan. She's never far. He has to leave her. She haunts him like the city does.

'Will? Snap out of it.'

It's almost dawn. They go back to the warehouse. The

crowd's gone. A washerwoman scrubs the blood off the ground, puts down fresh straw. Rufus counts coins and hands them over.

'Nice work,' he says.

'And the other matter?' the ex-priest says.

Rufus and Jonas exchange a look Will can't decipher. Jonas nods.

'Alright.'

They part as dawn breaks. Will goes to his rented room. The cockerels crow. He crawls into his bed. He tosses, turns.

At last he sleeps.

He dreams of butterflies.

In Cyprus as they were waiting for the seas to calm and the ships to ready, Father Jonas took Will one day towards the mountains. They rode donkeys and drank wine and laughed, for the world was still bright and gay then, and they were pilgrims to a Holy Land. Then they came into the Fennel Valley, and Will saw the butterflies.

They are a migratory species, butterflies. In their own way they are pilgrims too, and they pass in their millions each year over Cyprus and the Holy Land.

They filled the air. They filled the sky. There were untold thousands of them, reddish and olive and white spotted and black at the tips of their wings. They landed on the flowers and on the cherry trees that grew there in abundance, and Will's soul was filled with wonder, as though he were a child again, for here was a rare and precious sight, like a glimpse into the heart of God.

They ate cheese and bread, and plucked cherries from the trees, and the priest got Will to indulge in some hand-play, for he swore the sight made him as hard as a gatepost, and he needed a comradely hand. They were both still so innocent then.

He never forgot the butterflies. He looked for them in the Holy Land, in the Jezreel and in the low foothills below Jerusalem. But he never saw that kind of profusion again.

6

The days pass remorselessly. It rains, and London turns into a mud bath. Will runs errands for them what pay for it: he escorts Flemish merchants past the Pool of London to their lands in Woolwich, granted to them by the Princess Aelfthryth; he runs a numbers game in Cripplegate for Rufus; he plays doorman at the Whores of Babylon.

Meanwhile there are rumours that King Stephen has been captured by Maude's forces in Lincoln; that Empress Maude was holed up in Oxford where Stephen's forces lay siege to the town; that Maude's escaped from the castle across the frozen river to freedom; that Robert of Gloucester's been captured and held for ransom, and so on and so forth – oh, who gives a flying shit.

The point is, there's no one in *charge*.

It's an anarchy – from the Greek, a state without a ruler.

So money talks and bullshit walks, as Pliny the Elder said.

And for a while, for Will, things kind of slide. He tries to keep himself busy. He tries not to talk to the tod-lowries and scrats and fiends he sees each night in the witching hours, though more and more, he has the sense they've noticed *him*.

And then, on a night like any other night, about a month after they'd killed that old codger, he meets her.

Joan.

He's playing bouncer at the Maids of Honour, where a party of fifteen German merchants and a smaller contingent of seven mercenaries from Antioch are currently splitting five cases of imported Greek wine between them, as well as the affections of the entire staff (plus several additional hands drafted in from the nearby establishments). Three local musicians play the lute, the harp and the fiddle badly, but nobody cares. The air's thick with the smoke of Egyptian hash, the bodies are naked and writhing, the musicians loud and sweating, and the madam and one of the more elderly merchants from the Principality of Antioch are playing dice in a corner of the room, oblivious.

Then she comes in.

And how had he never seen her before?

And how can he take his eyes off her?

She walks in beauty like the night, as Alcaeus of Mytilene wrote of Sappho.

She steps lightly into the Maids of Honour. She looks around her with a kind, amused smile. It is a smile that says it is a night like any other night. It is agreeable.

'Get me a drink, will you?' she says. Then she registers him, staring. 'Oh, it's you,' she says.

'Lady, I'm...' he stammers. 'Will Scarlett, madam, at your service.'

'I know who you are. We met.'

'Did we? Where?'

'At that shithole you and all the other douchebags back from the Holy Land drink at whenever you have two pence to rub together.'

'The Pilgrim's Inn. Wait—'

The girl or boy who sat in Jonas's lap. He barely registered her that time. He does now. She may have a man's physique under that dress but she is all of her a woman all the same.

Will's smitten.

'A cup of wine?' he says, his voice a little hoarse.

She pats him on the arm. 'That would be a start.'

He brings her the wine. She takes it from him. Her hands are soft. Her face is thin.

She says, 'I'm Joan.'

'I'm Will.'

'I know.'

And just like that he is ensnared by her.

Despite Will's misconceptions, Joan's not a working girl. About the priest, she waves her hand and says, 'Oh, Jonas? We have an understanding.'

'What are you doing here, then?'

'I've got business to discuss with Madam de Orfay. Excuse me.'

She gives him a smile that makes the pit of his stomach all fuzzy and warm. Then she's past him, with a whiff of expensive perfume. The madam is still playing dice with the elderly gentleman, but when she sees Joan she speaks quietly to the old man who nods. The madam gets up, and she and Joan disappear into another room.

Curious.

He never does find out what she does for a living, well, not until the end of their affair. When she comes out with the madam again there is a sense of some sort of a deal having been arranged. Joan perches herself on the bar and watches what's left of the orgy as she drinks her wine.

'What do you think?' Will says.

'Not really my kind of thing.'

'What *is* your kind of thing?'

She smiles at him. Her lips are red and full. He marvels at her figure, the illusion of a swell of breasts under her gown.

'I like fucked-up men,' she says.

Will says, 'I'm pretty fucked-up.'

Her smile widens. 'No shit.'

'Do you want to get out of here?' he asks.

'You got a place in mind?'

He looks up. 'Room three upstairs is free.'

'Not much for foreplay, are you, Will Scarlett?'

He looks at her abashed, then sees she's grinning.

She takes his hand. 'Come on.'

They go upstairs.

The room is theirs.

Joan removes her gown and stands in her chemise. She pushes Will onto the bed. He swallows. She straddles him. His mouth is dry. They kiss. Her lips are warm.

He says in wonder, 'I think I love you.'

She says, 'Love is for suckers.'

Then for a long time they don't say nothing at all.

7

They see each other often after that. And for a time the nightmares ebb, the hobgoblins and puckles he sees in the night become mere shadows, and even the dark lady who watches him mutely becomes a mere apparition. Then one night with the snow falling, a summon arrives in the shape of one of Rufus's chalk boys, a ghostly-pale thing in rags. The kids work for Rufus in the Chislehurst flint and chalk mines outside the city, and when they come into London they thieve for their master, for their eyes have grown keen in the darkness of the caves and they can move in near-total dark.

'What the fuck do you want?' Will says.

'Boss wants to see you.'

'Well he can fuck right off.'

The chalk boy stares at him mutely. He creeps Will out.

'Alright, alright,' he says. The bed is warm and Joan's asleep under the rugs; the boy stares but says nothing.

'Where?' Will says.

'The Nave and Chancel.'

The boy turns and vanishes into the snow. Little creep, Will thinks. He sits on the bed. Strokes Joan's hair. She opens her eyes sleepily and smiles at him.

'Got to go out for a bit, love.'

'I'll miss you...' Joan says. 'Don't get into trouble.' She blows him a kiss, turns over and starts to snore.

Will smiles. Will dresses. Will straps on his knives.

Will goes.

Out into the dark streets. Down along the old Roman road that runs parallel to the river, towards the White Tower, and up through the maze of gnarly streets and alleyways, past church after church and brothel after brothel, until he reaches at last the Nave and Chancel near the Barbican. It is, like most such places in the city, a shitty, dismal place but nonetheless, clergymen and lawyers frequent it, and the men from the various guilds, so that it represents a sort of informal meeting place between the intersecting interests of London. It's owned by Rufus who likes to have this sort of easy access to a certain type of clientele, collecting intel for his business dealings. He has his dirty fingers in more pies than a pork pie salesman, as Seneca the Younger would have said.

It's quiet at this time of night, and Will is ushered to a back room where it's private. Rufus is there, and Jonas, who gives him a nod, and three other men he doesn't know. One of them smells very strongly of dog.

'Sit down, sit down. Can we start?' Rufus says irritably.

Will takes an empty chair. Gives Jonas a querying look. Jonas shakes his head.

'I got a job for you fuckweasels,' Rufus says. 'Jonas?'

'Yes.' The ex-priest stands. He takes out vellum and flattens it on the table.

'These,' he says, 'are the plans for the Inner Temple of the Poor Fellow-Soldiers of Christ. We're going to rob the fuckers.'

Will just stares. So this is what they murdered the old boy down in Hole Bourn for.

'Are you fucking insane, man?' From one of the others. 'You want to rob the *Knights Templar*?'

Rufus says, 'Why the fuck not.'

'Because those motherfuckers are crazy!'

'They're also,' Jonas says, 'very rich.'

There is something unassailable about his logic. The men fall silent, objections, at least for the moment, put aside. Everyone knows the Templars are rich. For them, the crusades are like a licence for greed. If you want to travel to the Holy Land you don't want to carry all your money with you, do you? Enter the Templars, who for a modest fee will take your cash right here in London and give you in its place a letter of credit. Arrive safely in the Kingdom of Jerusalem, and the local Templars will exchange that letter for your cash. It's simple, really.

'The money boxes are stored right in the inner vaults,' Jonas says. He traces lines on the blueprints. 'We go in *here* – there is a passage *here* – we break into the vaults and steal the cash. Are there any questions?'

'Yes, are you fucking insane?'

Jonas smiles. Jonas stares them down. Jonas says, 'Do you *want* to be rich?'

That keeps them quiet. Besides, Jonas must have a plan. When they finally pay attention he begins explaining.

Will nods. Will fidgets. Will listens attentively.

Yes. This can work, he thinks.

Yes, it might just work.

8

There are five of them on the team that eventually pulls the Inner Temple Heist.

Jonas, the ex-priest.

Will the Knife Scarlett.

Then there's Wulf the Dogman, who has no teeth and smells of wet fur; Bertram Six-Fingers, the cutthroat man; and Charles the Ghoul, the Flemish graverobber.

They stand in the dark and watch the temple complex on Hole Bourn, waiting for the signal.

Which comes quickly, as Rufus's chalk boys set fire to the row of shops directly behind the temple on Almoners' Alley.

The fire soon bellows into the sky. Black smoke, red flames, screams of anger and despair.

The Templars are no fools, but all the same, the Temple's on a skeleton staff today: the high muckety mucks all gone to the White Tower to meet with a delegation of northern barons, each eager to secure the Order's support in this time of national crisis. Rufus had picked the date and time carefully. So everyone who's in dashes to the fire before it spreads. Now desperate shopkeepers, grizzled crusaders and curious Londoners always up for a good fire or an execution all rush to the flames.

While Jonas's team quietly scales the walls into the Inner Temple on the other side.

There are still guards on duty, but by the time they realise what's happening it's too late. Bertram the cutthroat man is named for a reason, and as for Will, his knives do the talking for him.

Then come the dogs: nasty starved things, half mad, the real defence. But Wulf the Dogman came prepared, with strips of beef laced with monkshood, and the dogs are distracted, and then they're in pain. Those who don't die Bertram and Will finish off. It ain't nice though. Will likes dogs.

They run through the courtyard. Through the doors ahead and into the building. Jonas traces the path they'd marked on the plans. They only come across one elderly priest and Bertram takes care of him with a sort of unholy delight.

A locked door but Charles the Ghoul, who doesn't only rob graves, unlocks it easily. They go through. A second set of doors that the Ghoul opens and then they're into the vaults.

Will stares.

Three warded locks are set into the heavy door. It's true what they say – monastic orders have the best locksmiths in the business. Charles the Ghoul curses in that Flemish tongue of his, but Jonas smiles, and brings a set of heavy keys out of his robe.

Not for the first time, Will thinks – so *that's* what we robbed the old guy for.

Jonas fits the key into the first lock and it opens with a click. He opens the second, too. But the third sticks. Jonas strains in frustration.

'Charles?'

The Ghoul mutters under his breath. He takes a look. He fiddles with the key. Brings out tools. Says, 'It will take a minute.'

'We don't have a minute.'

'It will take a minute!' He files and blows. Tries once again. Repeats the process. Will's starting to sweat. He's hopped on khat. His nerves are shot. His hands are bloodied with the blood of dogs and men.

At last the key works. The Ghoul turns it and the locking mechanism *clicks*, bolts withdraw, and slowly, slowly, the great heavy doors swing open.

Will stares.

In his imagination the Templars' vaults contained money boxes stuffed with silver pennies, everything good wealthy pilgrims left behind in exchange for a promissory note.

But that's not what's there. That's not it at all.

'Holy fuck,' the Dogman says.

'Shit on it!' The Fleming says.

Will just stares.

Gold Almoravid dinars; Fatimid brooches, bracelets and earrings in gold and topaz; Red Sea pearls as large as fists; Hebrew priestly breastplates of pure silver, and gold candleholders; ornate Abbasid daggers with inlaid diamonds – on and on it goes, more than they had ever imagined, *could* ever imagine exists.

'They stole all *this*?' Jonas says, and Will can hear the greed and envy in his voice. 'In all our time there what did we get, Will? We didn't even get a *pension*!'

'This is your pension, priest,' the dogman says, and smirks. He says, 'We're all going to be fucking *rich*!'

They go at the stuff then, all discipline forgotten. Stuffing coins and priceless heirlooms into their sacks, their faces twisted in unholy desire. There's too much here, too much to take, and from outside Will hears the shouts of men, the barking of more dogs, and he knows that time is running out. They've already taken too long.

'Come on, come *on*!' he says. 'Jonas!'

But the former priest's possessed. He holds aloft an illuminated manuscript, of all things. 'Look at this shit!' he says. 'It's in some sort of very bad code but I deciphered it. It claims Jesus and Mary bumped uglies together and had a dynasty of children, can you believe this codswallop!'

'*Jonas*! We don't have *time* for this shit!'

The priest finally hears the cries growing closer. He grabs the Dogman by the scruff of the neck and hauls him off a pile of Syrian gold and shoves him at the door. The others, bags heavy, turn to follow.

Will hears running footsteps.

Will hears running men, the sound of swords being drawn.

Will runs.

They burst out of the treasure room into the main hall. The returning Templars appear from the back. They scream murder. An arrow whistles through the air. It catches Wulf the Dogman in the neck. He pitches forward with a moan and lies there on his face. The bags of loot drop from his lifeless hands. The Flemish Ghoul makes to grab them. Jonas shoves him – 'Run, you fool!'

They run. Into the courtyard, over the corpses of the dogs and guards, over the wall – 'Just toss the bags!'

'Like fuck I will!' the Ghoul snarls. Will pushes him up, Will pushes Jonas, arrows whistle through the air, for just a moment as he turns he sees her: the woman in black, standing between him and the attacking Templars, her arms raised as though in benediction, smiling with a face that is the absence of light.

Nothing hurts him. The others are over and he's last and over the wall, and he's safe. The chalk boys spirit them away, grab all the loot, disperse to all four corners. They set off a giant cloud of chalk and the world turns white and Will is blind. The kids lead him to safety.

9

'**Y**ou did it! Mother*fuckers*! You pulled it off!'

Back in one of Rufus's warehouses upriver, past Westminster. The remaining members of the gang sit facing the boss. He picks up gold coins and lets them fall.

'The Dogman didn't make it, boss.'

'You lot can split his share.'

'That's generous, boss!'

'I'm in a generous mood tonight. You did good, boys.'

Will just sits there. Will picks his nails with his knife. Will's worried.

'What's up with him?' Rufus says.

Jonas turns to look. 'He's coming down, is all,' he says.

Well, that's a part of it. It is. But it's not all of it.

Will doesn't say much. The others are in a more celebratory mood.

Rufus says, 'Here's a taste, boys. Just a taste, you understand, until I shift the merchandise. Then you get your full share.'

He tosses bundles in their laps. Heavy. Charles the Ghoul opens his and silver pennies rain. 'Let's go get pissed and fuck some whores!' he says.

Rufus says, 'On the house.' He claps his hands. Girls and drinks appear. The others fall on both. Will feels ill. He makes his excuses and leaves.

Alone in the dark away from the city. An enormous

white moon appears in the sky. On its face he can see what seem to be seas. He wonders what it's like to sail the lunar oceans.

He was mostly sick on the ship to the Holy Land, he remembers. He bunches his fingers into fists. Walks, skirting Westminster, too many titled knobs and hangers-on of both the present courts. Maude and Stephen, Stephen and Maude. He hopes someone will try to rob him. But no one does.

He makes it home. Joan isn't there. Out on her secret errands. He stashes the money in a hole in the floor with a false bottom. Collapses on the bed.

He wants to sleep forever.

Then she appears. The lady in black. She looks at him in vast amusement. *You know this won't end well, don't you*, she says.

'Go away,' he mumbles. He reaches for a drink. Anything to numb these days of lawlessness.

The lady looks. The lady shakes her head. She says, *I had such high hopes for you, but I can see now I was wrong. Your path leads elsewhere.*

'Lady,' he says, 'you don't even exist anymore.'

At that she screeches, though there is no sound. And then she nods. And then she turns into a cat, and the cat jumps on the windowsill, looks back only once, and is then gone.

He thinks – she isn't coming back.

So that, somehow, is that.

He falls asleep.

When he wakes up Joan is there, nestled in the bed beside him. He engulfs her in his arms. She wriggles close. Smiles into his chest.

'How did it go?'

He says, 'We did it.'

Night into day and day into night. A robbery in Nine Sisters; a double murder-suicide in Montfichet's Tower; in Aldgate one man goes on a stabbing rampage, taking twelve victims before he is caught and beaten to death by passers-by.

Night into day and day into night. A fire in the St. Mary of Egypt, with seven dead and scores severely burned. In Smoothfield a band of Stephen loyalists meets with a troupe of Maude's to settle scores; by the time the swordplay is over there are more than fifty dead and no one to pay for the carting and burial.

Night into day and day into night, and over and over. Plague breaks out in Cock Lane. Before the outbreak is over three hundred are dead. The plague comes and goes like the tides into London. It is like rain, in that it comes often and there is nothing you can do about it whatsoever.

Nights and days and nights, but Will is happy with Joan. He keeps a low profile and drinks less and waits for Rufus to shift the merchandise. It is the score of a lifetime.

Then, one day, they find Bertram Six-Fingers in the river.

He's washed ashore near London Bridge. Jonas tells Will in the pub later. 'No signs of a struggle, boy. No wounds to the back of the head, no torn nails. By all accounts he drank too much and fell into the water.'

'Alright.'

Will sips his wine.

Jonas says, 'I'm telling you, it's nothing.'

'Where is the profit from the job?' Will says.

'Rufus says he has a buyer from the continent. It's coming, Will. We just gotta be patient.'

'And without Bertram it's an extra share of the profits for us.'

'That's right, my boy. That's right.'

Night into day and day into night. Seven women die in childbirth and then another five and then another eight and then ten more and then ten more again and then three. And little graves are dug for corpses too fleeting on this earth to win a name. Two drunks die falling into the cesspits. Five fishermen drown in the Thames. Two prostitutes are murdered. In Apple Tree Way a family all die at dinner upon ingesting rat poison.

The dark lady stalks the streets of London and feeds on the deaths of its denizens and it gives her a semblance of life. Her story is old and she is not ready to leave it.

In Bermondsey a man is pushed out of a high window and dies on impact with the pavement. In Bermondsey Abbey a bishop is poisoned. Across the city three children die of common infections. In the Jewry a mob of good Christians attack shops and string up seven men. Across the city eighteen people die of the flu. Night into day and day into night.

'Somebody slashed Charles the Ghoul's throat on the south side last night,' the ex-priest tells Will in the pub. They're drinking wine at the Pilgrim's Inn. 'Robbed him, of course. Perfectly normal. You go over to the south side you take your life in your own hands.'

'True,' Will allows.

'He didn't have much on him, from what I understand.'

'So just a robbery?'

'Seems like it.'

'Still, Jonas. You must admit it is a little strange they're both dead.'

Jonas shrugs. 'It's London, boy. Sooner or later she does you in.'

Will nods. He sips his wine. He looks around. Just faces. The ex-priest stands up. 'Got to take a piss,' he says.

'Alright.'

Will watches Jonas waddling to the jakes.

He sips his wine. It's finished, somehow, and he orders another while he waits. He promised Joan he'd be back early. He sips his wine. How long *does* it take the former priest to have a piss?

He looks around. Just faces. He gets up. He walks to the loos, not in a hurry. 'Jonas?'

He opens the door.

The priest lies face down in the deep pool of excrement. There's no one else there. Will pulls him out. He's dead. No signs of injuries. He must have slipped or fell and drowned in the shit and piss.

Will opens the door. He steps into the bar. He closes the door behind him.

'Jakes are clogged,' he says.

The bartender grunts.

Will looks around him. Someone here *must* have gone in after Jonas. Someone *must* have drowned him in the pit. And then come out again. And sat back down. And sipped their drink.

He looks around.

Just faces.

He walks very slowly to the bar. He pays both of their tabs. He walks very slowly to the door. Looks back. No one pays him the slightest attention.

He opens the door. Every moment expecting a knife in the back, an arrow to come flying at him out of the outside darkness.

But nothing happens.

Will steps outside.

Will shuts the door.

Will runs.

'Will? What happened?'

'Get dressed, Joanie. We've got to get out of here.'

He shoves his meagre belongings into a bag. Goes to the hole in the floor, removes the false front. The bag of money. He takes it. He checks his knife.

'Move it!'

'But what happened!'

'Those fucking Knights Templar,' Will says. He thinks. 'Or Rufus, double-crossing us. They're all dead, Joanie! They're all fucking dead. We have to run.'

'But Will, I have a life here! Where would we go? What would we do?'

'I have money. It will carry us a while. We could go anywhere. Lie low for a while. Maybe go home. Back to Nottingham.'

'Nottingham?' Joan says. 'Where the *fuck* is Nottingham!'

He looks at her. Her hair is mussed, her shift's in disarray. He loves every part of her, he realises.

'Please,' he says. 'Come with me.'

She softens. She melts under his gaze.

'Alright.'

She dresses quickly. Does her hair.

'Joanie, come *on*!'

'Don't rush me!'

At last they're ready. They depart. It's early dawn. Nobody stops them. They head north. Will can't think where else to go. Past Smoothfield and onto the ancient road the Romans built. It's still there. It runs straight.

He realises suddenly that his old life's over. He'd been a boy thief and he'd been a crusader and he'd been a London man, but all that's done with. What will he be now?

Rich. In love. He think of Joan and all the money in his bag. They'll manage. Perhaps he could buy a little homestead. They can't have children of their own, of course, but maybe they could adopt a kid or two.

He daydreams as they walk out of the city. Expects an arrow in the back or swordsmen's ambush, but there is nothing – nothing!

Perhaps Jonas was right. He's been too hasty. It could all be naturally explained. People die all the time. He could go back to Rufus, wait for his share of the loot. He'd get the lot now. He almost turns back.

Then he looks at Joan, and she is smiling, and this is enough for him. Will's not a greedy man. And he has love.

They leave the city behind them.

Before nightfall they find a wayfarers' inn on the road and take a room. Will washes briefly in the cold, cold water. Sits by the fire in the common room, sips ale and listens to the travellers' tales.

'They say the Earl of Essex's in rebellion against King Stephen.'

'The Empress has gone back to Normandy.'

'What *is* a pomegranate? I keep hearing tales.'

'I heard the fairies stole two children out in Woolpit.'

'Another bout of plague—'

'Choked on bread, my uncle. Face down in the pond—'

'They say old trouble's got a new face in Sherwood Forest. The outlaws—'

'There is no law!'

'Bad times, indeed.'

'And what's an orange?'

'In Lincoln Greens—'

'Another drink?'

Will stirs. Will shakes his head. 'No, thanks,' he says.

Goes to their room. And there's Joan, hair wet from a wash, and she is smiling. She draws his hands to her. She pulls him to the bed.

Darkness. Voices far away. A cockerel crows. Something wakes him.

Something bad.

The pain in his side is unbelievable.

Blood. There is blood all over the sheets.

Will panics. Will cries. Will says, 'Joanie!'

'I'm right here, Will.'

He opens his eyes. A single candle burns. He cannot move. The pain is awful.

She stands above him. Fully dressed.

He feels relief – she's fine.

'I'm sorry, Will.'

He doesn't understand.

She strokes his hair. He realises that he can't move because his hands are tied to the bed.

And that Joan is holding a knife.

'What,' he says. 'What—'

'It's just business.'

She stands. She has the cash, he sees. The bag of silver pennies.

'A job's a job.'

The knife flashes. She stabs him – once, twice, three times. His body shakes and convulses.

'Goodbye, Will.'

And then she's gone. And then the darkness claims him.

But when he wakes, somehow, he's still alive.

A witch is brought from Epping Forest. She puts poultices on the wounds and gives him something vile to drink that makes him sleepy and takes some of the pain away.

'Someone must really love you,' she says.

'How... so?'

'Whoever stabbed you managed to miss all the vital organs. And such nice knife-work, too.'

'She really did... love me.' He sags, defeated.

'You'll have some pretty scars,' the witch says. 'Now, how will you be paying?'

He has a purse on him – Joan didn't take it. He thinks the innkeeper would have been wiser to just cut his throat and rob him and re-let the room, but people can surprise you.

He pays the witch. She leaves him medical supplies – gnarled roots and forest fungus and a powder he must take. The innkeeper prays for him and the innkeeper's daughter washes his wounds with water that is more or less clean.

They even let him stay a few more days when his money's run out.

Will Scarlett sets off into a cold early dawn one day in November. The civil war still rages. The barons rebel. There's fighting in Normandy. From the Holy Land comes word of the fall of Edessa, and that Imad ad-Din Zengi, the feared Atabeg of Mosul, has been murdered by a Frankish slave. There's a new Pope in Rome, and word is that the call will soon arise for a second crusade.

Will Scarlett sets off in the cold mists of dawn. He travels north. And as he sheds the miles away from London, a strange and fragile peace engulfs him. For he had died and is reborn, and a new life awaits him, elsewhere.

Will Scarlett sets off in the cold mists of dawn; and in this fashion he vanishes from the stage of the world, and into the pages of a play yet unwritten.

PART THREE

REBECCA

10

The shadows cast a mummers' play across the wall.

Rebecca watches by the fire.

The fire dances; shadows form. She sees a wounded man travelling on foot along the road to Nottingham. She sees a boxer in a muddy field, gigantic, fighting with bare hands. He always wins, she thinks.

She sees a dancing laughing, couple, deep within the wood. The woman is so pretty, even in silhouette. The man is handsome but his face is hooded.

Rebecca holds the yarn. The witch pulls on the thread. She weaves.

'The shadows speak to you,' she says. 'Is that allowed, amongst your people?'

Rebecca stares. The shadows show journeys, but they all end in one place. A deep dark pool. An oak tree. Death.

She says, 'The Bible speaks of a woman from Ein Dor, who lived in a cave and conversed with the shadows of the dead. She raised the ghost of the prophet Samuel for King Saul...'

'And what was her fate?' the witch enquires. She spools wool.

'She was spared. I think Saul had a soft spot for the soothsayers.'

'A reasonable man.'

'He fell on his sword,' Rebecca says. 'His enemies mutilated his corpse and chopped off his head. They set his corpse on their walls…'

'So he was a king.'

'I suppose.'

'Kings and witches,' the witch says, 'their stories never end well.'

'The rabbis are divided in opinion over the woman of Ein Dor,' Rebecca says. 'Maimonides says speaking to shades must be simple trickery, combining the ritual and the speaking of easy knowledge as though profound, and giving the impression of the uncanny.'

'Then he is wise,' the witch says, and cackles. 'That is the bulk of it, for sure, and an easier way to make a living than toiling in the fields. I should know.'

Rebecca nods. She knows the witch's methods, serves as her ears among the townsfolk. She brings titbits of knowledge, so that the witch may seem to know the hidden hearts of her clients. They all come to see the witch when they have troubles: of the heart, the marriage bed, an illness – some come for simple comfort found in a willing ear. The witch charges modestly enough. She conjures up the dear departed. She gives advice. She prescribes herbal remedies.

She also does abortions. The witch's medical knowledge is patchy and experimental. She has never heard of Galen, and when Rebecca once mentioned Maimonides's *Treatise on Haemorrhoids,* the witch just snorted in amusement. The barber-surgeons' cure for haemorrhoids is to burn them out with red-hot pokers up the ass. They lance boils and cut hair and they can chop a gangrened foot as easy as you please, though you might die from shock, the bleeding or infection. The local barber, Simeon, cuts lovely hair though.

So people come to the witch with their ills, or else they die on the surgeon's table. And the witch's methods mostly *work.* She even has a herbarium, which is very old and on an assortment of skins. She lets Rebecca study the precious book from time to time, though it is written in multiple hands and some of it in scripts like Ogham and one, Rebecca's sure, in Aramaic, though what vanished Jew or Syriac had visited this land in ancient times long enough to leave a record of this sort she's sure she cannot fathom.

Some of the plants, she knows she's never seen. The drawings are fantastical. The names bewildering: Rose of Titania and Boggleboes' Grass, Hodge-Potcher's Tears, Nymph's Vine.

In the Holy Land, which she has never seen, her father told her they grow the small red flower called the Blood of the Maccabees; for it is said that wherever the blood of their soldiers fell there bloomed the flower. She wonders if it has healing properties.

She's near eighteen years old. She's ripe for marriage and her father speaks of sending her to France to find a husband. There are precious few Jews on this godforsaken island. Rebecca can read and write in Hebrew, Latin, Norman, Greek, as well as Viking runes. She can do her father's accounts. She can draw, but not very well. She is trapped in this God-awful town. She wishes something would *happen*, at last.

'Hold still!' the witch says. 'Now I'll have to start all over again.'

'When will we do real magic?' Rebecca says.

The witch snorts. 'Real magic? You don't want to see *that*, my little novice. No one needs *magic*. What you need is clean water, medicine that works, a way to keep food fresh for longer, decent roads. *Contraception*. Magic is no use to anyone. Look what happened when that Jewish boy of yours got himself crucified and then came back from the dead. Now we're fighting wars half the world away. The dead should stay dead or they'll outnumber the living. And then where would we be?'

The witch is a heretic, which is hardly surprising on account of, well, she's a witch. But this is the thing about Nottingham, with the woods all around it. They all go to the church in the daytime, but at night...

They know the score.

'My father is off to London,' Rebecca says. 'I asked to come but he says the roads are dangerous and wouldn't take me. He's taking two of my brothers instead.'

'You *are* a girl,' the witch points out. The shadows whisper on the wall. They speak to Rebecca of the Thing in the Wildwood. They speak to her of freedom.

'I'm a woman,' Rebecca says. 'And I won't take shit.'

'In this life,' the witch says, 'as in all others, you take the shit you're given, girl.'

That is, if anything, the Jewish position on things, Rebecca reflects. There is only this life. There is only this shit. No wonder people flocked to Christianity, with its promises of a glorious afterlife. So long as you obey the earthly laws you'll find a place in the kingdom of heaven. Only the Jews remain in this land to wander and wonder, and how long can they last? The temple is fallen, its people dispersed in the diaspora, and here as always they are slaves to a foreign king's whimsy.

She is a Jew; she has no answers to provide.

Jews, annoyingly, have only questions.

'I've got some errands for you to run,' the witch says at last. She lays down her weaving. What *is* she weaving, anyway? A tapestry of greenwood figures, lost travellers converging on the Major Oak where it is said the Hood makes his abode. Rebecca's never seen it. She longs to see it. She longs for the freedom that the greenwood represents.

'The monk needs ministrations,' the witch says. 'The alewife needs a top-up of her regular dose. And that Mistress Byrne is ailing with a pox of the genitals again. You will take this ointment to her.'

'What is it?' Rebecca says.

'A paste of fungus.'

Rebecca makes a moue of distaste.

'Does it work?' she says.

The witch says, 'Never underestimate fungus.'

Rebecca says, 'The Mistress Byrne lives in the castle.'

'So?' the witch says. 'You know the secret ways.'

Rebecca smirks. She cannot help it. She's Nottingham-born and she knows the highs and lows of the city, its riverside quays and its grassy farmland, the inns where the sailors and robbers who rob them rub shoulders together; she knows the hidden lovers' lanes and the gallows and where the dice games are and where to find such traders as sell illicit venison under the table, in contravention of the king's law.

There is no significance to Nottingham but that it sits in Sherwood. There is no town without the wood. There are... *accommodations*.

Rebecca knows the hidden exits and the routes the poachers follow and the alcoves where the pirates of the Trent make their abodes. She knows the caves and secret tunnels that riddle Castle Rock and crisscross Nottingham like underground scars.

So, yes. She can make her way into the castle.

'Don't dilly-dally, girl. Go to the mistress first, then do the others. The Mistress Byrne's in pain and also wealthy. The rich don't like to wait.'

Rebecca scrams. She takes the packaged ointments and pulls her hood over her head. She steps out into the murky light of Nottingham at dusk.

The clouds amass overhead and the sun shines through a hole in the sky. The clouds are drawn like the scales of a fish across the heavens. The light produced in this manner is hazy and grey, a murk the local residents call Gloomph. It's in the Gloomph that wood and town can co-exist. It's in the Gloomph that shadows walk that by all rights should be consigned to the rubbish heap of superstition. You could say elves, but what are elves if not the heart's secret desire?

Yet they *are* here.

Make no mistake of that. And watch your step.

Hooded and cloaked Rebecca passes through the narrow twisting streets, avoids a pig who dashes at her from an alley, the mourners outside the Church of the Sainted Sons of Zebedee, the lecherous baker on Furriers' Row and the small crowd outside the barber's where a trickster runs the cups-and-ball routine flawlessly while people bet in vain. She skirts the market and enters the Norman Quarter with the nicer houses there and she climbs a short way, and finally, she sneaks behind a thick rosemary shrub and finds the rough-hewn tunnel entrance hidden there.

It's one of many. Castle Rock is riddled with the things – back in the old days all you had to do to get a home was find a suitable spot and start digging.

She creeps inside. It's dark and cool. There are alcoves in the walls for candles and in one she finds a candle stub. She lights it with flint and steel and carries on. The candle casts her shadow on the sandstone walls. Her shadow beckons, smiling in that way that shadows smile. Her shadow loves the secret tunnels. In here she's free, unseen, unjudged, an agent on a secret mission.

Will I see Much? she wonders. Her heart flutters in her chest. She conjures his face in her mind's eye, his smile, his kindness. They had sworn their love behind the stables, under a wavering moon.

Will she have the time? Will she see him?

Twice she hears low voices, and freezes till they pass. Once she comes across a room viewed through a lunette, in which a shackled bear is sleeping. She creeps past and reaches the shaft she often uses to get into the palace. She climbs the knags set in the wall, dead branches of an ancient tree perhaps. Pushes the trapdoor and slides into the palace, closing it behind her.

Now it's just the floor. Now she's in a service corridor, round from the kitchens. She removes her hood and picks a tray and just like that she's once again invisible. A woman with a tray can go anywhere.

Stout wooden walls. Tapestries showing William the Conqueror slaughtering Harold at the Battle of Hastings. William slaughtering rebels. William slaughtering Danes. Ships sailing across the Channel. Billowing sails. William the Red with four of his sisters and a young man who must have been his bum boy. William the Red imprisoning Odo. William the Red lying dead in the forest, struck with an arrow through the lung.

Kings, Rebecca thinks, should tread softly in the forest. But they are drawn to conquest and dominion, and so declare the woods are theirs and theirs alone, and how they love to hunt there! *Their* boar. *Their* deer.

Their fucking funeral.

She pushes through a set of doors and into Mistress Byrne's abode.

'Ah, the Jew girl,' Mistress Byrne says. 'What took you so long? My cunt hurts worse than a chat with King Stephen. Give it here.'

Rebecca hands over the parcel.

'Now fuck off.'

'Yes, mistress.'

'Unless you want to help me apply it.'

'No, thank you, mistress.'

'Then fuck off. Did I say that already?'

'Yes, mistress.'

Rebecca escapes. She steps out into the corridor but it looks different somehow. The floorboards green, the walls like smooth bark, the tapestries now depict fantastical scenes: Herne the Hunter chasing a giant stag, nine pale women standing in a circle round a cold, cold fire, mermaids rising out of a darkened pool.

It happens, now and then. The castle shifts and changes the way wood breathes. They made a mistake, early on, the Normans when they came. To build the castle they cut down the wood, but in so doing they had simply let the wood inside.

The roots go deep. The roots remember ancient humans and the sacrifice of giant beasts. The roots remember Roman blood and whisper of King Arthur. The roots have tasted Saxons, Vikings, Normans now. The roots are *hungry*.

'Hello?' Rebecca says. 'Hello?'

No cross... the branches whisper. Green faces open in the walls. Their eyes are pools of water. Their hair is ripe with fruit. They do not truly understand what *Jew* is, but they loathe the cross.

Rebecca trespasses down the corridor. It lengthens far ahead. She sees a hint of skies that have no earthly constellations. She knows them all the same: The Swift and the Gibbet, the Baleful Eye, Old Lady Death, The Hummingbird.

It's easy to forget sometimes that Nottingham's *inside* the forest. Rebecca's not gone far. She's still within the castle, it's only that the castle sometimes breaches Fairyland.

She loves it here. The air is thick with vegetation, both cold and humid, the smell of decomposing things. Small creatures scuttle in the undergrowth. Rebecca's hooded. She treads along the corridor towards a giant oak.

'Well, well, what have we here?'

The corridor is gone and she is in a clearing that is also, Rebecca's almost sure, the castle's kitchens.

A fat woman stands over a pot over a fire over the unearthly earth, peeling onions. When each is peeled, she slices perfect rings into the boiling stew. The steam dampens her hair. She has a wart on her nose and weak, watery eyes and with each onion she peels she tosses the skin contemptuously into the wind.

'The little girl who likes to play with nasty witches,' the fat woman says. Every now and then the moon drifts behind a cloud and when it does that the light changes and the woman's appearance shifts like a trick. At times she is old and bent, at times a young girl, at others still she is a glamorous lady dressed in fineries. 'Isaac of York's daughter.'

Rebecca is surprised at this, though she tries to hide it. It does no good, of course. The cook sees it and smirks. 'Tell me, what does a man of York do in a shithole like Nottingham?'

'The king's work,' Rebecca says.

'Ah, yes. This thing, what is it called?'

'Money,' Rebecca says.

'That!' the cook says. 'Yes. But what is money, child?'

Rebecca knows this. Her father's told her often enough. 'It's debt,' she says, 'backed with the threat of violence.'

'Very good!' The cook grins. 'I do so love money.'

She sniffs the air. How many onions has she peeled and chopped by now? The pot's enormous. She doesn't cry. The colour of her eyes keeps changing. The moon's a paper moon, just hanging in the sky. The clouds are like a child's drawing.

'I love what it does and I love what people will do to get it,' the cook says. 'They'll scheme and lie and rob and murder, and all for a thing which is not, in itself, real. Just like us. Isn't it wonderful? Tell me, is this how your father feels? Does he love it, too? The smell of blood and the clash of steel, and that wonderful taste of power?'

Rebecca says, 'No, but it is one of the few jobs that are open to us.'

'Jews,' the cook says.

'Yes.'

'What *is* that?' the cook says. 'We never had... *Jews* here before.'

'You never had lots of fucking things here,' Rebecca says, with a boldness she doesn't quite feel. It is dangerous to speak to fairies, everybody knows that. And she is not in Nottingham anymore. She's deeper into Fairyland than she has ever gone before. But it won't do to show weakness. Not here. Not ever. Not to anyone.

Especially not to *her*.

The cook laughs. She tosses the last of the onion skins into the wind and reaches for a shovel and stirs the pot. Something cries inside the pot. Rebecca cringes. The cook hums to herself as she stirs and stirs. When the thing inside cries too loudly she whacks it with the shovel.

'They say we steal babies, you know,' the cook says. 'What a horrible thing.'

63

'They say that about Jews, too.'

The cook sniffs. 'I do so like a shiny bauble,' she says. 'Perhaps I'll keep you. *Should* I keep you? Can you entertain? Do you know any dirty jokes? Can you sing? Are you good in the sack?'

'Mistress, if it pleases you—' Rebecca starts.

'Pish-posh, pish-posh,' the cook says. 'It's Mrs More-Goose, as well you know.'

'Yes, Mrs More-Goose.'

'I'm but a humble servant woman doing all the castle's cooking.'

'Yes, Mrs More-Goose.'

'This utter fucking shithole,' Mrs More-Goose says. 'Don't you think?'

'Nottingham, missus?'

'England, girly. This whole fucking island. Wouldn't you rather go elsewhere?' She looks at Rebecca shrewdly. 'This Outremer, say. The Holy Land, they call it. Is that where you come from?'

'I was born here.'

'Your people.'

'Everyone comes from somewhere else,' Rebecca says.

'Not us,' the cook says. 'We're stuck here. But then again, we don't really exist.'

'Please, mistress – Mrs More-Goose – what are you, then?'

A moue of distaste on the cook's face. 'Do you always ask so many questions?'

Rebecca says, 'Does it bother you?'

The cook laughs. 'You have a mouth on you, girl. Well, I don't know. We are the fae. Like money, we are only as real as people make us. Which is to say, we're plenty real. And we love power. It tastes so sweet…You know the Chicken of the Wood? Or Alder Bracket? Brittle Cinder? Dryad's Saddle?'

Rebecca, surprised, says, 'Fungus?'

'Never underestimate fungus, girl,' Mrs More-Goose says.

'I don't understand.'

'We're like fungus, maybe. Not plant, nor animal, but something else. And like tree fungus we're parasitic.' She smiles into Rebecca's bemused expression. 'From the Greek, *parasitos*, someone who eats at another's table.'

'You sup on power?'

'So tasty, yum-yum-*yum*!' Mrs More-Goose says. She grins. She stirs the pot. 'Almost ready,' she says.

'What is it?'

'Baby soup.'

The thing inside the pot starts crying again. Or maybe it is laughing. It's hard to say.

'It would be nice to go beyond this island,' the cook says. 'My little cousin-nephew-brother, Merle, he always banged on about the Greek philosophers and all that shit. That fungus theory is his.' She shrugs. 'He's had one of his periodic affairs and subsequent fallouts with my sister Nim, and she locked him up again in some crystal cave, where no doubt he has nothing to do but wank himself half to death. He'll surface eventually, I'm sure, the boring little prick. Ha! But I do go on, and you must soon be going, girly. You took the cream to Mistress Byrne?'

'Yes, mistress.'

'She's a bitch. Do you know she complains about my cooking?'

'That's terrible,' Rebecca says.

'You're damn right it is!'

When Rebecca looks, the trees around her seem more like the beams of a large kitchen. The sky's more like a soot-covered roof. She thinks she can see a window, hear the banging of utensils, the roar of flames, the busy tread of many feet.

Fairyland's receding.

'Please, mistress, why did I come here?'

The cook shrugs. 'Why do you ask me? You chose to come, and I let you. I thought you might be useful.'

'Useful for what?'

The cook shrugs. 'One likes to stock up on ingredients. Just in case.'

'Ingredients for what?'

'We sow the seeds of our own destruction…' The cook looks at Rebecca curiously. 'That's from one of those new testaments, I think,' she says. 'Here, take this. A gift.'

She removes a necklace from her neck (a necklace Rebecca's pretty sure wasn't there a moment earlier) and hands it to Rebecca—

Who takes it, though she knows it's foolish to accept a gift from such as they. And she knows it is no gift. It's debt, set against credit.

'What is it—'

But the world of Faery's gone; she's in the kitchens of the castle, someone knocks against her with a clatter of pans and curses her out; someone sweeps a broom over her feet; and Mrs More-Goose stirs the pot over the fire, humming to herself, and a drop of sweat gathers on the wart upon her nose and slowly, slowly, lengthens… till it falls into the soup.

'Well, fuck off then,' Mrs More-Goose says.

11

The Gloomph envelops Rebecca when she steps out of the castle grounds. She feels the heavy burden of the cook's gift in her palm.

A rough wooden disc, with a hole that has a string through. A green man crudely etched into the wood. Its hair is made of leaves, its eyes are sharp and cruel. It's watching her.

The green man motif repeats all throughout town. It emerges unexpectedly on walls, over doors, in alleyways. The wood is *always* watching. Rebecca closes her fingers on the disc. She blinds the green man. She can feel the wood's warmth.

Oh, *fuck it*! she thinks.

She hangs it round her neck and tucks it out of sight under her cloak. She draws the hood around her head.

She knows what this gift is, what everyone craves, what church and king both sell: protection.

And nobody fucks with the green man in *this* town.

As she walks under the hill her eye is drawn unpleasantly to the town gibbet. It stands alone above the town, a thing of strong wood and industry, stained dark with blood.

Two corpses dangle from their ropes above the town. The breeze moves them. Rebecca sees the Lincoln greens in which they're clad, and something worse, for she is pretty sure that one of them has horns.

Creatures of the wood. *His* creatures.

A Christian would cross herself, perhaps. Rebecca mutters a curse and walks off quickly, making sure her shadow doesn't fall under the shadow of the gallows.

She makes her way to the Antlers, an alehouse on the edge of the English Quarter, near the wall. It's usually frequented by rangers and poachers. The alehouse sign is of a giant stag, its antlers caught in the branches of an oak. The door is oak, too, and heavy. Rebecca steps in and lets her eyes adjust to the gloom.

'No women in here, miss– oh, it's you, Miss Rebecca.'

'Charlie.'

The alehouse keeper's a one-armed, grizzled man with a balding pate like a monk's tonsure. He claims to have lost his arm in the Holy Land, though everyone knows he'd never been three miles out of Nottingham in all his life. He is a former woodsman; and how he lost his arm is his and the wood's business, and neither one is telling.

'Get you something? On the house, like.'

He pulls a cup of ale and plonks it on a table. The alehouse isn't empty but it's hard to make out the clientele. The place is wrapped in shadows; hooded men sit in alcoves where they can watch the door and not be seen. It is that kind of place. Which is to say, it is of Nottingham.

'Thanks, Charlie.'

Rebecca takes a sip. The Antlers brew good ale, whatever else you want to say about the place. It's too close to the wood. The water used for brewing comes from deep within the forest. Well, a drink's a drink. She sips politely.

'She's in the back, like, Miss Rebecca.'

'Alright, Charlie.'

She finishes the cup and puts it down. Goes to the door, aware of eyes on her. She vanishes into the back.

Alewife Aldrich lies in the small bed, hemmed in by casks of ale. The air is thick with the smell of fermentation, and something worse, the sickly sweet scent of gangrene.

Alewife Aldrich is tiny; Rebecca remembers her as a fierce, uncompromising woman who cursed the sellers in the market till they gave in to her demands, and put unholy fear into her customers. She had brewed ale in the Antlers for decades. Charlie is only one of her numerous offspring. She looks like a tiny ill bird in the small bed. She opens bright, pain-filled eyes. She says, 'Oh, it's you.'

Rebecca steals to her. She kneels by the small bed and gently unwraps the bandages. The infection's worse than the last time. The leg is swollen and red. Rebecca cleans the puss as gently as she can. Alewife Aldrich bites down on a piece of leather and utters not a word. They say she killed two men when she was younger. They say she hoards a fortune in gold coins under her floorboards. They say she knows the Lady Marian.

They say a lot of things.

Rebecca applies the poultice that the witch prepared. She wraps clean bandages. Alewife Aldrich doesn't say a goddamned word. She *knows*, Rebecca thinks. She isn't stupid. She could have called the barber-surgeon, but early amputation would have only killed her quicker. She knows she's dying. She just tries to make it go a little more.

Rebecca does it quickly. Alewife Aldrich's bright eyes grow brighter then.

'Do you have it?' she says. It's the only time her voice changes, becomes desperate and needy.

Rebecca nods, unwillingly.

She takes a bottle out of her scrip. Opens it carefully. She measures out a spoon.

Dwale, the witch calls it.

The stuff is rare. Opium and henbane and hemlock. Some other things. The witch guards the exact recipe jealously.

Alewife Aldrich's mouth opens hungrily. She gulps the medicine in one.

'Please,' she says. 'Please, just one more, for the pain.'

Rebecca looks from side to side, but of course, no one can see her. Unless the witch can.

'Please,' Alewife Aldrich says. 'I can pay.'

She pushes a coin into Rebecca's hand. 'I need it,' she says. 'Too much of it and it can—'

'Kill me?' The old woman laughs, but it just turns to coughs of pain. Rebecca's suddenly desperate to escape that awful room, the cloying smell of death and fermentation.

She measures out a spoon. 'No more,' she says.

'Then make it strong—Ahhhh…'

The old woman lies back. She closes her eyes.

'It is well,' she says. 'Now fuck off.'

'See you, Charlie.'

'See you, Miss Rebecca.'

She's happy to escape the Antlers; happy to escape the smell. She emerges back into the Gloomph of Nottingham, but the quality of murk is different. The sun is setting, somewhere behind the clouds, and the air is cooler and there's a sense of menace in the air, like something bad's about to happen.

But something bad is always happening, somewhere.

She shrugs it off. But she can't stop thinking about the way the alewife's lips fastened on that spoonful of dwale so greedily. The coin Rebecca was paid sits heavily in her pocket.

Opium and henbane and hemlock. Some other things.

She quickens her pace. Night falls fast in Sherwood.

At home, her father is waiting.

One last errand to run for the witch…

She makes her way along the wall and down the hill and out of the Kissing Gate onto the grazing field that slopes down to the river. She hears the clash of swords and horse's hooves. A strong hand fastens on her waist and *pulls* and she is lifted in the air.

'Much!'

He sits her on his horse and grins foolishly and she wraps her arms around him and grins back – she cannot help it.

'Much, you idiot!'

'Where are you *going*?' he says. 'Did you come to visit me?'

'How could I? I didn't know you were here!'

'You know, you always know,' he says. He rides them round and round the field. The horse is a war horse, in the middle of the field the sheriff's men practise with swords and arrows. Rebecca wraps her arms around Much's neck.

She covers his face in kisses.

Much, the miller's son, isn't the most handsome of men; his smile is gap-toothed if earnest, his left eye has a prominent squint, his hair is already receding though he's only young. But he is true of heart, and kind, and he is hers: he loves her true.

'I'm to St. Nicks,' Rebecca says, when they part at last to draw air. 'And you?'

Much slows the horse. 'Incursion,' he says.

'Incursion?' Rebecca says, aghast. 'Into the—?'

Much has the good sense to look sheepish. 'The wood, yes,' he says. 'Sheriff's orders.'

'But that's—'

'It's fine. Really. A show of force and all that.'

'I saw the corpses on the hill. Are they—'

'Excursions from the wood into the town. The sheriff's under orders from the king, Rebecca. He cannot let it stand.'

'It's dangerous and foolish.'

'We are king's men. We're trained and armed. It will be fine.'

'Much! What are you doing! Come here at once!'

A booming voice. Rebecca sees the sheriff, a short, stout man with grey and close-cropped hair, armed to the teeth. A Norman knight and proud with it.

'When—'

'We go at nightfall—'

'Much, this is madness!'

He kisses her. His lips are hot. She puts her hand on his cheek. How warm and alive he is.

'Much! To me this instant!' the sheriff bellows.

'My love, I have to go...'

'Then take this,' Rebecca says. Not thinking. She removes the cook's pendant from round her own neck and places it gently over Much's. She tucks it quickly away.

'Now go, my love. You will be safe.'

He grins good-naturedly. 'I will come back,' he says. 'There's nothing to it.'

He helps her off the horse then rides to his commander. The clash of sword on sword. The whistle of the arrows. Rebecca watches as the men prepare. They're hardened soldiers, and the sheriff's seasoned in warfare. The whole *point* of being sheriff's men is that you're the toughest and the nastiest in all the land and, when you show up, it's the *other* fuckers who run.

How else do you keep order?

But this is Sherwood.

Rebecca reaches for the pendant round her neck for reassurance, but of course, it isn't there.

'Mind your step,' Brother Robert says. 'I'm sorry it's so dark. We're saving money...'

He holds a saucer with a fat half-candle. The flame flickers. The candle gives off the smell of rancid fat. The shadows shudder. 'Up the stairs, up the stairs...'

The Benedictine Priory of St. Nicholas the Wonderworker sits outside the town wall, adjacent to the grazing field. It is a stout stronghold of burnt-brick construction, as black as the robes of the monks within. The story of St. Nick, the Greek, is that he once, during a famine, came upon a butcher who slaughtered three small children to be sold as pork. He sliced them into cuts and pickled them in barrels, but Nicholas of Myra saw the lie.

The saint made the sign of the cross. The children were miraculously resurrected. And if you'll believe that, you'll believe anything, as Rebecca's father likes to say, if only in the privacy of their home.

Rebecca doesn't mind. She likes St. Nick's, where the monks grow cabbages and onions, keep a decent garden and bake passable bread. Like all monks, some were cloistered young, while others had a longer journey to the cowl, have served in war and done horrific things before seeking atonement.

Brother Robert is one of the latter kind. They say he served in the Holy Land, and if he did or not he has the scars to prove it. Where he truly got them he doesn't say.

'Not far, not far.'

The stairs twist up and up and up. It's said a spiral staircase stood in the Temple of Solomon. It must have been grand. But whoever built St. Nick's went for practicality, not comfort. The stairs are narrow and the stones are bare and the tower's tall, and Brother Robert's breathing comes out laboured as they trudge to the top.

At last they're there.

They emerge out of the gloom of the stairwell onto a crow's nest of a room that opens out onto night's engulfing silence. This high above the ground the stars seem closer. They shine cold and bright. Rebecca knows the constellations by their Greek and Hebrew names. She sees Leviathan, the Serpent Bearer, the Virgin and the Dragon. From up here the world is hushed. The winds are cold. The dark is vast. Rebecca sees the river and the bridge that crawls atop it on the road to London. She sees the wood. All about her, she sees the wood. It spreads in all directions, it swallows light and sound.

'Here, Birdie, Birdie,' Brother Robert says. His voice is soft and kind. A small, dark figure huddles on the very precipice of the crow's nest.

'Rebecca's here,' the monk says. Coaxing. The little figure

turns its head. He wears monk's black but underneath Rebecca sees the flash of Lincoln green.

No, not cloth, she realises, not for the first time, but it catches her anew.

Feathers.

The monk raises his candle and a small pale face looks startled at the two of them.

His eyes are black, his nose is beaked, and he is trembling, but not from cold.

'Hey, Birdie,' Rebecca says.

The small, shy face breaks into an unexpected smile.

'Becca,' he says.

'Sure,' Rebecca says.

She kneels beside him.

'Can I see?' she says gently.

He blinks at her.

'Please, Birdie.'

'All right, Miss Becca.'

She lifts his robe. Sees the thin body beneath, the plume of bright-green feathers on the taut, white skin, then—

It's worse than before, she thinks.

Three ugly slashes of a knife across his ribs and down his left thigh.

The cuts are deep – too deep, she thinks.

'*Why*, Birdie?' she says.

He shrugs. 'Makes me feel better,' he says. 'Makes me feel in control.'

Rebecca sets to work, for there is nothing she can say. She cleans the cuts and rubs a salve into his skin, applies a poultice. Birdie suffers her ministrations without protest. Then it is done, and Rebecca pulls down his robe. She helps him up.

'He won't come down,' Brother Robert complains.

'I like it up here,' Birdie says in his soft, quiet voice. He gives Rebecca another smile. 'I can feel more up here.'

She joins him at the railings. Their shoulders touch. She

wonders at the wings beneath his robe. St. Nick's where miracles do happen, so they say. Sometimes, they walk in straight out of the woods.

She looks out at the night.

The stars are out over Sherwood Forest. Few lights in town. But out in the wood...

She sees a great bonfire burning merrily. It is so far away yet she can imagine the sound of merriment and music, can almost taste the king's venison turning on a spit...

She wants to be *there*.

But she's here.

'We danced round the flames and the pipes played on and the lord and lady of the greenwood danced under the moonlight as the fae wove silver moonlight in their hair...' Birdie says.

'Don't you *miss* it?' Rebecca says.

Birdie looks at her with his disconcerting bright eyes.

'I have God now,' he says.

12

'Where have you been?' Isaac of York says mildly. He lays down the manuscript he has been studying: Rashi's *Interpretation of the Torah*, copied by hand in some French yeshiva long ago, perhaps even when the rabbi was still living in Troyes. Rashi was a vintner, it's said; and therefore had knowledge of the roots and soil and what they hid. And Rebecca wishes suddenly that she had had the opportunity to meet him, if only to pose a question as to the nature of the miraculous.

Of this, the sages are, as they always are, even dead as they are, in disagreement with each other. They posit, for instance, that the nature of the universe is immutable. God does not intervene. How, then, does one explain such miracles as recorded in the Torah? The sages argue that not all of nature is yet understood. Therefore, a miracle may only appear to be miraculous, until such time as thinking may reveal its inner workings.

But Maimonides asserted that wonders are a *suspension* of nature, and thus a direct intervention into the workings of the natural world.

So which is it?

And why, whatever the inhabitants of Faerie truly are, are they so fucking *weird*?

'I was out,' Rebecca says.

Her father sighs and reaches for the candle flickering on the table. 'Rebecca...'

'What!'

'You're not a little girl anymore.'

'I *know* that!'

'I will not scold you. It does no good anyway... I want you to be careful. It isn't safe outside.'

'For a girl, you mean?'

'For anyone. For a Jew...'

'I won't hide, if that's what you mean,' Rebecca says.

'You need to show *decorum*!'

'I need a husband, is what you mean to say.'

'Rebecca...'

She storms away. The house is so quiet since her mother died, and her brothers are out. She hesitates. Turns back to look. Her father, at the dining table. The candlelight casts little more than gloom.

'It's bad for your eyes,' she says, relenting.

'What?'

'I said, it's bad for your eyes!' she says.

He waves a hand dismissively. 'I'll manage for a while longer.'

'I can help you.'

'With Rashi?'

'With the accounts.'

She sees the book of numbers on the table under Rashi. Her father's work. The kings of England keep their Jews to make them money to fight wars: against each other, against their continental cousins, against the Muslims in the Holy Land... Old William brought his Jews over from Rouen when he conquered England. They are pet Jews, *sicut res propriae nostrae*, the king's own property. So Father keeps accounts of money lent and money borrowed, and writes down numbers in long tidy columns of the profits and the loss.

'I'm fine, Rebecca. Thank you.'

She stomps to her quarters and slams the door.

*

The world is full of *magic*! Mystery, intrigue! She's no desire to pussyfoot around and jump at shadows. Father keeps a permanent travel bag by the door. In case, he always says. In case, in case! For when they come. King Stephen burnt down a Jew's home in Oxford for not paying his dues. In Norwich two decades past a boy was murdered and the Jews were blamed for his death, it was said to be a blood sacrifice.

But *her* blood's warm. *Her* feet are light. She wants to be *in* the world, the world as it is, nasty and rough and full of sharp edges, and so full of promise! She wants to dance, she wants to scream, she wants—

Power… whispers the mocking voice of Mrs More-Goose.

Rebecca thinks of the miraculous and the divine. If God exists then all that is existence emanates from it. Such a supreme being can therefore manipulate space and time, make miracles of the mundane. Such a spirit can make a man rise from the dead in far Jerusalem and make the saints of the Church bring butchered kids back to life from pork or Jewish sages such as Honi the Circle-Drawer summon rain. But before her people fled Egypt and before Abram made his covenant with God, there were many, smaller gods. Maybe the fae are simply the remnants left behind of the old ways of the world.

Or maybe, Rebecca has to conclude, she just doesn't know shit.

She stands at her window. The shadows whisper to her, for the wood is restless tonight. She thinks of the bonfire she had seen from the top of the Benedictines' tower. How merrily it burnt.

And Brother Robert, watching it, said, 'No fire burns forever.'

'Excuse me?' Rebecca said.

The brother shrugged. 'Sooner or later,' he said, 'you run out of wood.'

Rebecca stares out of the window. The night is dark and she

thinks of Much who is the miller's son, only the miller's dead, not even the witch could save him from the cancer that ate him from inside.

She thinks of Much, out there in the dark.

She thinks of bonfires burning.

Out in the wood, the soldiers trespass.

Rebecca sleeps.

Under the watchful moon the soldiers march through leaf and branch, over roots and twigs that crunch, softly, softly.

They are armed with steel-tipped arrows and with swords.

Rebecca sleeps.

Over Nottingham a nervous calm descends. Up on the hill the corpses swing upon their gibbet.

Hooves and antlers, feathers and claws.

A child cries on the English side of town and is quickly silenced. It doesn't do, to bring attention at this time of night.

In the tunnels of Castle Rock two men roll dice, muttering numbers to each other.

In her abode the witch, too, mutters in her sleep. She gnashes teeth. Asleep, she's frail. Upon her bed-stand is a ragdoll made of twigs and cloth and mud.

Above the town and the forest clouds amass but there's no rain. The air is heavy with humidity. On the French side of town a woman cries, is silenced in her turn.

Isaac of York raises his head, stares out of the window. A brewing storm must surely break. But he has lived in Nottingham too long. He knows who owes and who is owed. And not all debts are written down on paper.

In the castle's kitchens the cook scrubs and scrubs an iron pot. She wears thick gloves. She, too, is listening – though this is not her business.

Higher up in the castle the Mistress Byrne applies cream vigorously between her legs and sighs.

Inside St. Nick's, Brother Robert wakes up with a start, guiltily, for he is tasked with guarding the Benedictines' sacred relics. His candle gutters. He does his rounds.

Jesus of Nazareth's left big toe.

The dried earlobe of John the Baptist.

A piece of the True Cross.

The femur bone of the Virgin Mary.

All is well and the relics are safe. Brother Robert goes back to his rest.

High above in the tower, Birdie watches the skies.

There's a crackle in the clouds, like a whisper of lightning…

Birdie takes a deep breath of air. There's a wild scent, what forest folk call the smell-that-follows-lightning. Birdie wants to fly into the brewing storm.

Takes out his knife instead.

Closes his hand on the blade and *pulls* until the pain comes; until his blood drips down from the closed fist onto the ground.

Rebecca sleeps.

Out in the wood, the soldiers trespass.

Softly, so softly.

Till Much steps on a twig and something snaps.

13

The sound of something terribly and irrevocably broken wakes Rebecca up. Thunder cracks beyond the house walls. Water beats down on the paving and bricks of the town. Dirty grey water pools, and a dog trapped outside swims to higher ground.

A loud, insistent knocking on the door beats in rhythm to the pain built up behind Rebecca's eyes.

'Becca, get up, Becca, we're going!'

There's pressure in her ears. She swallows. Sheets of rain beat down on the town. Nottingham, in this Year of Their Lord 1153.

'Becca!'

'I *heard* you!'

She opens her eyes. She steals out of bed. Washes her face in the cold water in the basin, brushes her hair, puts on her cloak and her good boots. Reaches for the talisman that is not round her neck, with a feeling like loss.

'All right already,' she says. When she opens the door it is to see her brother Mordechai grinning at her.

'You forgot?' he said. 'We're going to London.'

'*You're* going,' Rebecca says sourly.

'The roads are full of brigands, Bex.'

'Don't call me that.'

'Are you coming or what? Dad's waiting.'

She follows him out. Down the stairs. A fire burns in the hearth. Bread, cheese and eggs on the table. Watered ale and pottage.

Besides, she thinks. The only roads out of town go *through* the wood.

And the only brigands in *there* are hoods.

She should be going to London. Where they say the river is alive with the colourful sails of a hundred ships.

Where they say the roads are paved with Andalusian gold.

Where Moorish cuisine vies with Jewish garum or fermented fish sauce, with Welsh honey and Norman roasts, and spices from the distant Holy Land, and wine from Italy, and, and...

Where the fashions are direct from Rome and Normandy, where the cloths are dyed a hundred vibrant colours, where every boy is handsome and every woman glamorous...

London.

She longs to go and see it for herself.

Or anywhere but here.

'It is time,' her father says. He breaks the bread. He's dressed for travel. A wide-brimmed hat all but hides his face. 'I will try to keep this trip short. Rebecca... I will miss you.'

She goes to him. She hugs him. Whispers, 'I will miss you too,' into his chest. He pats her back.

She accompanies him outside. Mordechai and Ezra are waiting with the horses. They're eager to go. The rain eases. The clouds shimmer like fish scales. Murky light glints through. Rebecca sees offal float past, pink-red blood eddying in the water, spoiled tripe and spleen.

'I'll walk you,' Rebecca says.

'Only to the gates,' Mordechai says.

'Shut it, Mordy.'

'Don't call me that.'

Their father lets them bicker. They walk together, down narrow cobbled streets, the horses whinnying softly for they do not much like the rain. They're not knights' beasts, no coursers or destriers. They're simple beasts of burden, and used to the indignity of Jews in rain.

Low thunder rumbles overhead. Pressure builds in Rebecca's ears. The shops are shuttered but the bells begin to ring across the town. The bells cough and belch from every tower and every church. They sound like a chorus of ill omens.

The road slopes down to the gates. The guards are huddled in a misery of drowning birds.

'Hey ho, Isaac.'

'Hey ho, Bert.'

'I should let you out?' Bert the guardsman, says.

'If you would be so kind.'

'It's raining cats and dogs,' Bert says.

'It is.'

'You'll be to London, then?'

'If God is willing.'

The guardsman makes the cross. 'They have no God there, in that den of vice.'

'The gates, then, Bert?'

'Aye, aye, hold your horses, man.'

Bert dangles a ring of iron with a set of keys. He fumbles with the locks. The gates are fortified perhaps more than they should be. They're etched with iron crosses, and Latin inscriptions cut deep into the wood: *Vade retro Satana* – Turn back, Satan – and then, repeatedly and in divers hands, *Veto, veto, veto* – I forbid.

Bert turns the key. Bert and the other man, a dour Anglo-Saxon called Ernest, push open the gates. The gates shudder and groan. Ernest and Bert shudder and groan. The gates open. The road ahead is clear. The river's overflowing with the rain. The bridge holds true. A black bird hops under the cover of a yew tree then takes flight into the downpour.

'I guess this is goodbye,' Isaac of York says.

'Hark!' Bert says suddenly. He raises his hand for silence.

'*Hark?*' Mordechai says. 'Hark? Who *talks* like this?'

'Hark!' Bert says.

Silence settles. Rebecca strains to hear. The rain falls. The road's empty. No birds sing. No voices speak. Only the quiet, and the rain. The pitter-patter of raindrops on earth. Pitter-patter, pitter-pat—

Not rain.

Hooves.

And bursting out of a line of trees, out of the *wood*, comes the Sheriff of Nottingham on a giant black destrier, riding like the devil's at his back. The horse gallops at full speed towards them. Rebecca stares. The sheriff's bare-headed, his face is frozen in a rictus of horror. He wears no sword, no chainmail. There are deep cuts on his arms and face; they make Rebecca think of fangs and talons.

She's almost too slow to get out of the way. The sheriff doesn't slow. The horse thunders ahead. The guardsmen scatter and Isaac, startled, just stands there looking at this looming doom. Rebecca comes to her senses just in time. She pushes her father out of the way and they both tumble onto the hard wet ground as the horse gallops past them and bears the sheriff through the open gates.

'Ow,' Isaac says.

'Sorry,' Rebecca says. She gets to her feet and helps him up. He is surprisingly light, her father. 'Are you hurt?'

'I will live. Thank you, Rebecca.'

She marvels at how small he is. There are new lines on his face. His eyebrows, were they always white? He still has all his teeth, his eyes are bright, and yet… She realises with a pang of sudden sadness that her father's old.

'What?' Isaac says. 'What are you looking at me like this for?'

'Nothing,' Rebecca mumbles.

Her father gives her a smile. 'I will endure.'

She nods. Her father wipes rain from the brim of his hat. Behind them, in the town, the black destrier bolts. The sheriff's flung from the horse to the ground. He groans and stands up, and his eyes are wild. He reaches for his sword and it is missing.

'A blade!' he cries. 'Give me a blade!'

'What's the matter with him?' Mordechai says, but quietly. It doesn't do to incur the king's men's wrath.

'I don't... know.'

'Here, lord,' Ernest says. He hands the sheriff a blunt old sword. 'What is the matter? What happened in the wood?'

'The wood...' The sheriff's voice is drawn and lost. 'They were waiting for us, in the dark, in the gloom... Faces in the bark... the panpipes! I saw things then... women in the trees, green as the grass, with luscious hungry lips... Get back! Get back, I said!'

He waves the sword. They pull away.

'My lord, there's no one there,' Bert says.

The sheriff's blind eyes stare.

'I saw,' he says.

And: 'Something is coming,' he says.

A cold fear traps Rebecca's heart in a fist and squeezes. She thinks of Much. But surely Much should be all right. He has protection.

'My lord sheriff,' she says, 'what of your men?'

'Dead, all dead, the branches pierced their hearts and lungs, the roots devoured their livers and their kidneys, yum yum,' the sheriff says and licks his lips. He waves the sword. 'Get back, get back I said!'

'He's mad,' Mordechai says.

Bert shakes his head. 'He has been touched,' he says.

'By what?'

'The wood.'

The rain stops. Thunder rumbles in the distance. Up on the hill the ropes of Hangman's Bluff twist empty in the wind, their cargo gone.

It is so very quiet then.

The sheriff says, 'It's here.'

★

Rebecca turns with the slow dread of inevitability.

And something *does* come out of the wood and down the London road towards the gates. At first Rebecca makes little sense of it. It's like a tree's detached from among all the other trees (and say what you want about trees, they all kinda look alike after a while) and started stalking down the road—

Then she sees that it's human shaped, if a human grew branches for arms and leaves for hair—

It stalks awkwardly, like it hadn't learned how to properly walk yet. It has a strange shambling gait. It's like a—

'Is that a fucking *scarecrow*?' Ezra says.

'Language!' Isaac says.

'Fuck that!' Ezra says. 'Dad, look, it's a fucking *scare*—'

Crow. Rebecca stares in horror, for the creature shambling to the gates is strangely known to her, something about the slender frame that makes her think of being held, of easy laughter, stolen kisses—

And the face that comes at once into a sudden focus, for all that it has black button eyes and is a crude carved wooden mask, and at the end of his arms the fingers are five blackened twigs, and it wears green—

'Oh, no,' she says. 'Oh, no.'

Because she *does* know it. Him. This thing that came out of the wood.

It wears a familiar wooden disc over its neck, hanging with string. A coarse carved talisman of protection.

'Oh, no,' Rebecca says. 'Much...'

Her heart is hollow. The thing on the road stops. It turns its scarecrow's head. Its black button eyes seek her out. Its crude mouth moves without sound. Perhaps it's trying to say Rebecca. Perhaps it's trying to say, My love.

Then it stalks on. It brushes past her. It tears the wooden talisman from round its neck and tosses it to the ground. Rebecca picks it up. The disc is cold and lifeless in her hand. It has no power left. When she closes her fingers round it, it simply breaks apart, into tiny florets that float away into the wind.

'Oh, Much...'

'The miller's son?' her father says, in some surprise.

'Who's there?' the sheriff cries. He turns and turns with his blunt sword. His milky eyes stare into horrors no one else can see. 'I said, who's there!'

It's like a mummers' play. Rebecca can do nothing, only watch as the thing that was once Much the miller's son creeps through the open gates into the town of Nottingham. His arms raised up. Those twigs for fingers are so nasty sharp. The sheriff cries a wordless cry. The sword goes swish. The sword goes swash. The scarecrow weaves. The scarecrow ducks. Its arms reach out. They pull and scratch. They twist and crush. There is an awful, bone-deep *crunch*—

Bert and Ernest make the sign of the cross. Ezra throws up, next to his horse. Mordechai grimly watches, Isaac of York mutters a prayer. High overhead the church bells ring for Lauds.

You foolish girl, you wanted power, yet when I gave you it you squandered it on love?

She hears Mrs More-Goose's mocking voice in her mind.

And you are left with what? A heap of twigs. He'll kill again, you know. He has the taste of it now. Next time don't be so fucking stupid. Consider this a lesson, and my true gift to you, Rebecca of the Holy Land. Choose love, or choose power. And either one will corrupt you in the end.

The scarecrow thing turns. The Sheriff of Nottingham lies on the ground and his blood seeps into the cracks in the stones. The thing walks out and no one tries to stop it. It pauses near Rebecca. She hears the rustling of leaves. She reaches out, gently, strokes a thorny arm.

'Goodbye, Much...'

A leaf falls from his eye like a tear. Then he is gone, back to the wood.

'He a Hood now,' Bert says, quietly.

'The sheriff's dead,' Ernest says. 'Someone should inform the king.'

'I will take word to London,' Isaac offers. He stares at the corpse on the ground. Shakes his head.

'He should have known better than to go into the wood,' he says.

'They never learn,' Bert says, and spits. 'Come on, Ernest, help me lift him.'

The guardsmen pick the corpse up with an ease borne of much practice. Isaac and his sons mount their horses.

'Goodbye, Rebecca. We'll be back as soon as we are able.'

Rebecca waves farewell.

Then she's alone, for all that, all of Nottingham's now hers to do with as she pleases.

PART FOUR

A GEST OF
ROBYN HODE

14

Thursday, 1 November, 1156 Anno Domini

My Lord Bishop,

The road from York is wearying, but I carry the burden you've placed upon me without complaint. Three years have passed since the death of the Sheriff of Nottingham. Yet the circumstances of his demise remain unknown.

The new sheriff, who I am to meet upon my arrival in the town, has assured you, my lord bishop, that all is well. The death arose out of a disagreement over a woman; strong drink was involved. The sheriff was stabbed. His assailant fled to the wood. The new sheriff assigned to the town quickly established order.

He reports no strange occurrences or beings.

So why am I sent there, my lord?

Wood's Ford, on the outskirts of Sherwood, is a shithole of a place but it's the last stop before the forest. With the rain beating down I was glad for the respite.

I took a seat near the fire and studied my companions on this cold, wet night.

Merchants from London and York, speaking a mixture of English and French: lean, hardened men, used to the road and armed. They watched the coin they spent, but spend it they did all the same.

'Hey, you,' one of them said. He stared at me curiously. He was beak-nosed and stooped, and wore a thick, rich cloak effortlessly. 'What's your story, friend?'

I stirred. 'A mere traveller,' I said.

'You have the bearing of a nobleman,' he said. 'If one fallen on hard times.'

'I served under King Henry in my younger days.' I meant the last Henry, of course, son of the Conqueror, not the young king who now sat on the throne.

'You are a knight?'

'I was.'

He gestured to the innkeeper, a straggly man. He hurried over. 'Yes, good sir?'

'Another round of your punch, and a cup for my friend here.' It was good apple punch. It had a real kick to it.

'Thank you,' I said, and meant it.

'It is a cold night. Tell me, where do you travel to? If you don't mind my asking.'

'Nottingham.'

He nodded, as though he had expected as much. I knew men like him in the past. There was little their eyes missed.

'We are going the same way.'

'What do you trade?'

He shrugged. 'This and that,' he said. 'They make religious carvings in Nottingham which we hope to arrange for in bulk.'

'Are they pretty?' I said.

'Hideous,' he said, and laughed. 'But they come with good mark-up.'

'I know very little of trade,' I said. 'Even less of the acquisition of wealth.'

He gestured to me to join them. 'I am Hugh de Grantmesnil.'

'I am Sir Richard at the Lee,' I said.

He pulled a chair for me. 'Tfadel.'

'Atik al arf,' I said. Only then did I realise he had spoken to me in the Saracens' tongue, and unthinkingly I had responded in kind.

His companions talked among themselves. At another table sat a group of blackfriars muttering softly; at another several rough-looking characters, heavily cloaked, with flashes of Lincoln green under the cloth; on a bench near the wall lay a comatose woman holding a metal beaker.

'You took the cross,' Hugh de Grantmesnil said.

'As did you, apparently.'

He inched his head in answer.

'Where?' I said.

'Jerusalem,' he said. 'Then the Siege of Damascus. My God, it seems forever ago. I bummed around the Holy Land for a while after that, then took a ship back home with everything I could carry.'

'What did you bring back?'

'Cloth, wine, honey, olive oil... hashish. God, but I miss the hashish.'

'I was an inquisitor,' I told him.

I saw he was taken aback, but he covered it quickly and well.

'Then it's a good thing we never met before,' he said and smiled.

I smiled back. 'As you say,' I told him. 'It was a lifetime ago.'

Transgressions and infractions, I thought. The thieving and senseless murder our men inflicted on the other side and on each other. Someone had to keep up the pretence of keeping order, no matter how many fucking indulgences were issued by the pope.

But I wasn't exactly popular with the troops.

When I came back from the Holy Land my son was grown. He was restless and wild, and treated me like a stranger. Then he killed a knight of Lancaster in an underground jousting tournament, and to spare his life and cover his gambling debts I had to borrow from your lordship. The Church's coffers are deep, while men die in the gutter of hunger and cold.

I will erase these paragraphs when I post the letter later.

'I could accompany you through the forest,' I said, testing him.

'I may be getting on a bit in years but I am yet proficient with the sword.'

He shook his head.

'We have no need to hire,' he said. 'I'm sorry.'

'It is no matter,' I said.

'No, no,' he said. 'It is simply that...' He lowered his voice then. 'We have an arrangement, you see.'

'An arrangement?' I said.

'With the hoods in the woods.'

At last, unexpectedly, I was getting somewhere.

'How so?' I said.

He shrugged.

'To pass the wood you must pay the tax.'

'These are the king's woods,' I said, and he laughed.

'These woods are Hood's,' he said. And that was that.

On my way out I passed the comatose woman who lay on a bench against the wall. In all this time she hadn't stirred. The beaker was held loosely in her hand. I lifted it gently. There was little liquid left at the bottom.

I sniffed the cup.

A bitter, instantly-recognisable smell.

Opium.

I remembered the festering wound in my thigh on that long-ago escape from Damascus. My comrades abandoned me. 'And who would miss a fucking inquisitor,' my commander said. He sketched the cross in the air.

'Go with God,' he said, and spat, and left me to rot and die.

The Saracens got me. They could have had their fun with me, and it was not kindness that stopped them but a desire for collateral. We had their men and they had ours. A truce and prisoner exchange were not impossible.

A physician of theirs treated me. Poppy juice took away my

pain, but after a while it made me its prisoner just as surely as the Saracens did. I had taken too much, too quickly.

It was strong, and I was weak.

They let me loose then, for I had no use anymore for escape. I spent months with them, doing terrible things to acquire the drug I needed. I will not set those deeds in writing.

Then one morning I woke and the whole camp was gone.

I went on in a daze, searching for them, my body and soul screaming for the medicine I needed.

Instead I stumbled into a Christian camp and was taken in as a hero.

15

My Lord Bishop,

I stole up early and left the inn before the sun ever rose. Nothing moved and nothing stirred as I approached the forest.

The woods start abruptly. At first you barely notice how the landscape changes, how the road subtly twists.

Then you turn a corner and suddenly the light fades and the world is full of fucking trees.

Four carts arrived on the Nottingham road, led by a woman in a hood. They stopped on the demarcation line between wood and world. They were laden with heavy cargo.

I heard the beat of hooves and saw my friends of the previous night arrive from the other direction.

Hugh de Grantmesnil rode a fine horse. He climbed down and met with the woman. She removed her hood and I saw that she was young.

'Sir Hugh,' she said.

'Mistress Rebecca. This is the merchandise?'

She nodded. She had the look of a hidden blade, the sort you don't ever notice until it nicks your lung and then it's too late.

De Grantmesnil went to the back of the cart and lifted the covering. Hideous alabaster statues all crammed together. I saw Jesus and the Virgin Mary and a bunch of saints.

De Grantmesnil inspected them carefully.

'May I?' he said.

The woman, Rebecca, nodded.

He reached for the Virgin Mary's hand. Held her wrist in both his hands and twisted.

What was this sacrilege?

The hand came off in a shower of plaster. The statue was hollow, crammed with a dark substance inside. De Grantmesnil stuck his finger in, then put it to his lips and tasted.

He nodded.

'Good?' Rebecca said.

'Good.'

He tossed her a heavy bag. I could hear the jingle of coins.

Rebecca whistled to her drivers. The carts continued on their way. Hugh de Grantmesnil remounted his horse, spoke briefly to his companions, and they galloped away.

Dawn slowly suffused the sky. Rebecca looked around. Her gaze seemed to fall on me, though I was hidden behind a gorse bush.

She stared intently at the spot, as though she could tell I was there, and it took all my will not to look away.

Then she smiled to herself and departed.

Regular traffic began.

I returned to my horse. When I reached to untie her I was troubled to discover a crude mark etched into the bark of the tree at eye level.

It had not been there before.

I stared at it. Two eyes had been etched into the bark and now stared back at me.

The slash of a sharp knife left a thin curved line of a mouth.

It mocked me with its smile.

The wood soon rose all about me as I went on. The sky was a sodden grey. Everything seemed muted – the sounds, the colours. The air smelled of wet earth and rotting leaves. The horse whinnied softly, then fell silent.

Mostly I saw no one. Even when I did see other travellers the sight was misty from the rain and the sound subdued, so that it felt as though they were not entirely real, if that makes sense: like ghosts passing you by on the other side of a mirror.

It got dark quickly, and the woods were still – too still. It was with some relief that I saw a solid road turn from the main one, and with the sign of the cross to mark the turning. I hurried my horse and we followed the short path until we reached, in the last of the dimming light, a small chapel in the wood.

It is here that I am writing this letter now, in the half-light of a burning candle. My horse is tied up outside.

I shall kneel by this simple altar and pray tonight for my son's life.

16

Saturday, 3 November, 1156 Anno Domini

In the night I woke up for a piss.

There was an earthen brown cup of fresh water near me and without thinking I grabbed it and drained it for I felt very thirsty all of a sudden.

I stepped out of the chapel. My feet trod on wet grass. The air was still. It had rained in the night and now the forest was quiet, and faint silver moonlight fell down, illuminating the mute trunks and twisted branches of the trees.

A faint glow rose over the bark. I pissed against the roots of one ancient oak. All was still and I watched with fascination as the fungus on the bark glowed.

It was when I turned back that I saw there was a scarecrow planted into the ground beside the chapel.

I stared at the scarecrow. It was an unsettling construction, quite detailed, with a crude wooden mask for a face, with a luxurious head of green shoots for hair, stout arms, and black disconcerting twigs for fingers.

'And what's your name?' I said, and laughed.

I was feeling quite strange. I went back into the chapel and saw that it now shone brightly with some inner glow. The cross on the wall was a living rose bush. It grew a profusion of shoots and flowers, and bees buzzed between the petals and the crowns.

I whispered a prayer and made to go back to my bed when I noticed a man sitting quite unconcernedly by the window, one long leg draped over the other. He was clad in forest green.

'I took the liberty of slipping toadstool dust into your drink earlier,' the man said. 'Sorry about that, but it does help, you know.'

'Fungus?' I said. 'You put fungus in my water?'

'Fairy dust,' he said, and smiled. He had an easy smile.

'What?' I said. 'Who the fuck are you?'

'I'm Alan,' he said. 'Alan-a-dale. I'm the harpist.'

'The harpist of what!'

'Just a harpist. Also a juggler. And I'm pretty handy with the garrotte, when it comes to that. Can't shoot for shit, though. This is Much.'

'Who—' Then I screamed as the scarecrow I saw outside materialised silently next to the rosy cross. It moved its head and stared at me out of those empty eyes.

'What the fuck!'

'Much,' Alan-a-dale said patiently. 'You know, the miller's son.'

'I don't know shit!'

'Man, you gotta relax,' Alan-a-dale said. 'This is no place to pass the night, not in the green god's chapel. Come with us, we'll show you a good time.'

'I don't think—'

'Come along, old fellow,' he said. He rose languidly to his feet. His face went in and out of focus, and bright silver moonlight wove in his light-coloured hair. The scarecrow's fingers closed on my wrist with surprising force and I supressed a shudder at the feel of those twigs on my skin.

'Alright, alright,' I said. Not that I had much choice. You ever danced with a scarecrow in the moonlight? It's shit.

Not that we danced, exactly. The scarecrow pulled me along and it was futile to resist. We left the chapel and made our way through narrow woodland paths lit by the same eerie glow; some sort of fungus again.

Or maybe it was something else. I do not rightly know. I was not in the right frame of mind to make rational deductions exactly. I could feel the fairy dust coursing through my veins. My heart beat faster and my mouth felt dry and I kept grinding my teeth. The scarecrow released me then, for where was I to go? I fell into step with it – him? – and the harpist. The moon shone down and when I raised my head I could see it through the canopy, and mark the dark valleys on its face.

It's funny how the moon's always the same, whether above the Holy Land or England. I read a book once by an ancient Greek by name of Lucian. In it he claims to have been blown off course in his ship, to find himself on the moon, which was at war with the sun at the time. The moon was both inhabited and cultivated. It was ruled over by a king named Endymion, and populated by many strange creatures: horse-vultures and giant fleas upon which rode the flea-archers of the moon, and cloud centaurs and stalk-fungi, whose shields were made of mushrooms.

It seemed to me a curious story then, as it does now; yet who's to say what the moon and its inhabitants are truly like, if no human being has yet set foot there? It looks to me like a giant lump of rock, lifeless and serene. But there's magic in rock and stone; there is a magic in everything, in root and branch, in stone and wind—

'Whoa, take it easy there, bud,' Alan-a-dale said, clutching my arm and laughing. 'We're nearly there,' he said.

'The moon?'

He laughed again. 'I may have slipped you a tad too much of the old toady,' he said. 'But never mind. It probably won't kill you. Through here—' and he led me down an avenue of yews and ferns that opened up, the earth beneath us packed as though many feet had trodden it.

Then we came to a great oak.

17

They say the Major Oak of Sherwood Forest is a thousand years old and more. That it is nearly a hundred feet high and as wide as a fortress. They say it grew from the poisoned acorn planted in a murderer's chest, that it is fed with elfin blood, and that the outlaw called Robin Hood makes his abode within its wide expanse of branches and hollows.

But then they do say many things, my lord bishop, and most of them are crap.

I woke up in the morning with my head clearer than it's been for days. I remembered my mission, and my debt to you. I washed my face and said my prayers and mounted my horse. I re-joined the main road, and saw that it was indeed wide and in a good state of repair, and was busy with traffic on this fine Saturday, with many travelling into town, to worship and pray in the many churches that are said to stand there – all within your diocese, all under your lordship's pastoral care.

Whole families together, walking in peace; cheerful monks ferrying freshly-brewed beer; and carpenters and brickmakers who told me with simple folksy happiness of their work enlarging the castle. Prosperous, happy and secure they all were, my lord. The anarchy of Stephen and Maude was over, and a new king reigned.

I took a deep breath of forest air and spurred my horse to make haste. On the way I passed a very large oak indeed, but saw no hoods skulking about it. It was just a very large tree, and trees they have an overabundance of in Sherwood Forest.

'Man, that's a big fucking tree!' I said, swaying in the arms of my new friends of the forest.

The charming harpist laughed. His laughter had the dulcet tones of windpipes and bells. 'Welcome to Sherwood Forest, stranger!' he called, and his voice carried and was amplified through the night, so all who were present turned, and watched me, and smiled.

'Welcome to Hood's manor! Forget your troubles and your cares! The road is long and winding and the world beyond is cold and filled with woes, but here it's warm, and safe, and all who are lost can be found again. All who are weary may rest. And all who seek shelter are granted it. So come, and warm yourself, and eat, and drink, and be merry!'

And with a riotous laugh he vaulted over a large barrel of beer, leapt, grabbed hold of a branch high overhead and somersaulted twice in the air, landed next to a fair-haired man with a quiver of arrows on his back, grabbed and kissed him full on the lips to the crowd's cheers, then cartwheeled to where a dwarf was dishing out beers, grabbed two mugs, tossed one high and drank the other.

The second beer arced across the night and over the heads of the crowd and the burning fires. I reached out instinctively and grabbed it, then took a sip and grinned.

Everyone cheered.

How do I describe this abode of lawlessness and outlaws?

The Major Oak towered into the sky above the forest. It was a castle made of living wood, and I could see ramparts and winding steps that led between the giant branches, and houses constructed in the upper echelons; rope swings from which greenwood men as lithe as dancers swung from one section of the tree to another.

I lowered my gaze and beyond the oak I could just make out a small black pool of water. The sight made me quite uncomfortable, for it seemed to suck all light and joy from the world, that place, and I knew something bad happened there.

But bad things happen everywhere, and all the time. Pull back, and below the giant tree there was a great big feast and party, which seemed to go on all day and all night and forevermore. Torches burnt and tables were set laden with food and drink, and a band of musicians played on, a strange and wild melody of panpipes and chimes, harps and drums.

I felt the wild music take me. Men and women in forest green danced with abandon on the great packed grounds before the Major Oak. A bonfire burnt, fed with whole logs, and over it roasted the entire carcass of one of the king's deer, and the smell of the fat and the meat rose through the air and made my stomach growl, for it had been many days since I had had meat for my supper; for all that this meat was forbidden and belonged to the king.

The dancers swirled and whirled; the music played, intensified; the harpist, Alan-a-dale, juggled burning torches in the air and laughed delightedly; in a square of dirt under the giant tree two men boxed with silent fury, naked from the waist up, sweat glistening on their muscled and scarred bodies.

'Welcome, stranger,' a voice said close in my ear. I turned and beheld a beautiful woman in a green-leaf dress under a long fur coat. She had the most enchanting eyes.

'He wants to see you,' she said, gesturing towards the edge of the gathering, where a man sat on a wooden throne, a woman in a hood behind him with her hand on his shoulder. I thought I could see other faces in the murk between the trees, then: ethereal beings, pale faces with eyes that were not entirely human.

Fairies, a nagging voice in my head said.

'Are you a nymph?' I said in wonder.

The woman laughed. 'No,' she said. 'I'm English.'

She extended her hand and, unthinkingly, I took it.

'I am Lady Rowena,' she said.

'Sir Richard at the Lee,' I said. 'Charmed to meet you.'

I realised I was slurring my words. Lady Rowena leant into me. She felt warm and alive. She smelt of saffron and cloves. Her lips brushed mine and my whole body reacted as though it were hit by a heavenly charge.

I mean to say: my dick got as hard as reading the Book of Ezekiel.

Rowena wove her arm through mine and led me across the dance floor to the place where the king of the greenwood sat on his wooden throne.

In truth, he wasn't much to look at up close. He was just a man in a hood. Youngish, I'd say. Short hair. Calloused hands – you notice that sort of thing. He was dressed in green.

'Welcome, stranger,' he said courteously. 'May I query your name?'

'He's Sir Richard at the Lee!' Lady Rowena said. She squeezed my arm. 'We are already firm friends.'

The man in the hood smiled. 'Ah, Lady Rowena. Always a pleasure. But I prefer to hear the man himself tell me.'

I nodded. 'I am Sir Richard,' I said. 'And you are?'

'I'm Robin.'

He jumped from the throne and landed beside me. Put his hand comradely on my shoulder. 'Come, stay with us a while,' he said. 'Eat, drink and be merry.'

'Your men do seem plenty merry,' I said.

'They're free,' he said simply – as though that meant the world, which perhaps it did.

I thought about freedom. Was such a thing possible? I was one of the lucky ones, a landowner, a knight – and yet all I ever did was serve: the king, the pope, now your lord bishop. Was freedom possible? I doubted it. Life was but a ledger of debts to be paid.

So what price did these people pay, these merry men of Sherwood Forest?

That's what you'd like to know, my lord bishop, I am sure. For one thing at least was certain, even in my drugged state: these were outlaws. They were out of the reach of the king, out of reach of the Church. The land could not suffer them to exist. They were an affront to the moral structure of the world. They paid no dues. Their mere existence was rebellious.

But I had little time for such thoughts, or indeed for this Robin fellow. My gaze went up and stayed where the woman was.

She too was dressed in green, but on her it didn't look like clothes: Her hair was reeds and her eyes were black pools after the rain. Her lips were as red as the blood of a dying fawn.

She was like the spirit of the wood given human form.

They say in Sherwood Forest there live a band of outlaws, and their leader's a man by name of Robyn Hode or Robin Hood.

I've read the dossier you keep, lord bishop. Tall tales and flights of fancy, mostly. So there are poachers in the king's larder, so what? There always have been, there always will be.

I can assure you, my lord bishop. They are of no consequence. I wouldn't give them the steam off your piss.

I no longer recall what she said to me. That, and many other details of my sojourn with the hoods, is frustratingly out of reach in my memory, fading like mist or a morning's boner. Of which I have fewer and fewer these days. I cannot in truth say

Sunday, 4 November, 1156 Anno Domini

how long I even dwelt there. Or what the lady was truly like. She spoke to me and her voice was

Monday, 5 November, 1156 Anno Domini

beautiful.

Tuesday, 6 November, 1156 Anno Domini

She spoke of freedom, and of a place where all the lost things go. Of where the old legends still hold sway. Something to believe in, she said. And she gave me something, something precious.

The taste of opium and belladonna, the lady of the rocks, the lady of situations.

My lord, I...

Thursday, 8 November, 1156 Anno Domini

My lord bishop,

I have now spent a full week in the forest, and all I have seen are fungus and leaves. Once, I saw a pair of wolf hunters in the distance, amid the trees, but they did not see me. And once I saw the footprints of a giant bear, for all that bears have long been reported extinct on this isle. I saw many curious things: the ruins of a Roman fort and Roman soldiers still guarding it; a stone tor stained with ancient blood at the base, and untold bones littering the ground before it, and some were animal and some were human, for sure they were human, and some were old but some were fresh, my lord; and I saw the fairies dance on tiny wings amid the flowers; and once, I swear, I saw a house made of gingerbread, a type of food which was brought to our French masters, so it is said, by the mad Armenian monk, Gregory of Nicopolis; but in truth I think I must have been hallucinating for some time by that point on account of the mushrooms.

Fungus and leaves. The roads are well maintained, on the whole. I woke up on the side of the road with no clear memory of how I got there. I remembered music, and dancing, and the bright gaiety of fairy lights. The forest-keepers are a surly bunch but seem to do a decent job. I saw no poaching, plenty of deer in the distance, and the king's new hunting lodge at Clipstone, deep in the forest, which is under construction. I can report that the builders seemed efficient, and good progress is being made.

I am entrusting this bundle of letters to Alan-a-dale, the assassin and harpist a passing Benedictine who assures me he will seek your lordship in York post-haste upon his arrival.

I shall now proceed immediately to Nottingham to interrogate your new sheriff. Whatever mysteries the town holds they will be no match against your primo inquisitor, my lord!

I remain your humble servant, and considerably in your debt,
Sir Richard

PART FIVE

THE SECOND SHERIFF

18

The Sheriff of Nottingham, that is to say, the king's man in these here parts, being as it were the parish of Nottinghamshire and Sherwood Forest, a man of some standing, a Norman knight, a man of authority, whose word is law, a man who commands the king's soldiers, a man who collects the tax and passes judgement, a man who is, he is the *man* for his time and place, and I'm talking about the Sheriff of Nottingham here, not some bum, not some Anglo-Saxon peasant, not some old timer still going on about the Holy Land or whose side they fought on during the anarchy of Stephen and Maude and, I mean a real man, *the* guy, he has a girl in every port and has killed more men then you could count, and he speaks English and French and he can fucking *knit*, he once had to knit his buddy's belly back together and push the fucking intestines back, I mean the guy died but still, it was a neat stitch and a stitch in time saves nine, this sheriff, the Sheriff of Nottingham, who saw some frankly *horrible* things during his time of service, for King and Country, *that* guy, I mean, he's a fucking *legend*, only he—

The Sheriff of Nottingham can no longer remember his own name.

At first it didn't trouble him. It wasn't like anyone called him by his name anyway. He had a title and titles, in this time and place, are everything. He remembers some things, certainly: he came from landed folk, his progenitors served in Poitiers, they got what's theirs by shedding blood and that's the way you get about in life, and they're devout besides, he does remember that, fear of the Christ and of the place below, where devils live. The sheriff's led a righteous life. He's sure of that.

He remembers, for instance, as clear as day, the Bishop of York, Roger de Pont L'Évêque summoning him into his office one day. The bishop's a wily man, a political *operator*, tight with the king, and not above getting his hands dirty either, when it comes to that. Word is he had himself a young man for a lover in his early days and when the guy went public with it, Roger, gouged his eyes out and had him condemned to death and they put the guy to the rope. The word is he's a greedy fuck, hates monks, and he is tight with Alexander III, the pope what lives in Rome. In *these* lands, he's second only to the Bishop of Canterbury... and doesn't *that* fuck him right off.

So Roger, the most honourable Archbishop of York, summoned him to his office, and said, 'I'm making you Sheriff of Nottingham.'

And he said, 'My lord bishop?'

'The last one's dead.'

'I see.'

'I want you to clean up that nest of vipers – can you do that for me? They worship trees, they have elves and wood nymphs in that forest, abominations that should not exist. Can you do that for me?'

'My lord.'

Roger smiled at him kindly. 'You have heard of Hood?'

At that the man who is now the Sheriff of Nottingham felt uneasy, though he no longer recalls why.

'I have heard rumours of bandits,' he said, 'but those are not uncommon in these troubled times.'

'Well, this one troubles *me*.'

'My lord.' He bowed. 'It is as good as done. The rope will whisper round his neck and sing your glory.'

'They will try to suborn you. They will play you false.'

'I have my sword, and elves hate steel.' He felt so smug, saying that. Why?

'Do not fail me.'

'My lord.'

'Congratulations on your promotion... sheriff. You are dismissed.'

He bowed and left.

What did he do then? Put together a team of trusted men. All seasoned knights, all men he knew and valued. They rode out. Man, they were unstoppable. So dapper, too. Maids gave them their second and third virginity all along the route. Boys ran out to shout in admiration as they thundered past on their battle horses. Elders welcomed them into villages that were now under *his* control. This was *his* domain. All of Nottinghamshire, Idle and Soar, Arkham and Gotham, Eastwood and Mansfield and the Creswell Crags. And he gloried in it.

At least until they came to the forest. They passed the night in a place called Wood's Ford, the last shithole stop on the way to the forest. Oh, they made their presence known! They roughed up the locals and made the merchant men cough up a toll. That's the way it was going to be from now on. His job, when it came right down to it, was to keep the king's law and collect the king's money. It was the fairest system of governance the new sheriff could ever think of. The king issued currency and backed it up with steel. That was called finance. People exchanged those little discs of metal with the king's picture on them because the king and his swords gave them value. People *trusted* the king. Or they trusted his swords. Either way, the system worked, but the king kept needing more of those little discs so he could make people do the things *he* needed, which was to make them fight for him, so he could keep being king and get more places to be king *of*.

It all made sense, even if sometimes the sheriff struggled with exactly how it worked. All he knew was that he was now the sheriff, he had plenty of those funny little discs himself, and he had lots of swords, which meant he, in turn, could do the things *he* wanted to do, like eat and fuck and have a soft bed to sleep on and a castle of his own and men to do his bidding.

It was a nice evening, he remembers that. They drank, but moderately. Somebody played the harp, beautifully. He remembers looking for the harpist but he kept to the shadows, only the melody filled up the room. It was like a lullaby, it made the sheriff think of his mother, who he had not thought about for years. He remembered being a little boy and he was playing with a wooden sword and he hurt himself somehow, and he burst out crying. And his mother hugged him and kissed the tears away. But she died so long ago, and he couldn't even be sure what colour her eyes were.

In the morning the ground was icy and the path to the wood was littered with rotting leaves. The sky was grey and overcast and the air filled with a gloom he'd already learned the locals called Gloomph, and it was a clammy sort of thing, like a corpse drowned for too long in saltwater. Then they went through the trees and the sheriff said, 'Shoot anyone in green,' and the men nodded assent and some smiled.

They rode on and the trees thickened and the sheriff ordered his men to their axes. They stopped and they chopped down the ancient trees, though it was hard work and their eyes filled with sweat and pollen. There was a mighty sound as the trees fell, and after that a deep and tremulous silence, as though the wood were brooding.

Well, let it brood, he remembers thinking. Then he had his men dig a deep pit and into the pit they threw chopped logs of wood and set a fire to them. The wood was fresh and moist and the fire took forever to catch and the black smoke that rose out of it made all the men cough and the sheriff's eyes water, but still – he did it to make a *point*.

Many of the trees had strange fungus growing on their trunks and roots and when it burned, the smoke had a strange funky odour and it clogged the sheriff's nostrils.

They rode on and no one got in their way and they came into Nottingham, reeking of smoke, the wind in their hair and the flames at their back, and that fungal smell still in his nose – he could not seem to get rid of it. The gates to the town opened and he rode through the narrow streets, and the citizens all came out to watch him, but warily, and he saw too many hoods in the crowds. He rode to Castle Rock and claimed Nottingham Castle.

So why can't he remember his name?

And what else can't he remember? Well, he wouldn't know, would he? he thinks.

He's up in the Witching Tower, so called because it commands a view of the wood all around. And far in the distance he sees a bonfire burning. It has burned every night since he got here, but try as he might, when he goes in the wood, he can never find it, and the hoods in the woods are hidden from his sight.

Oh, he *knows* where they are. They're all around him! The city's rife with outlaws, the borders between town and wood are fucking *porous*. He *knows* what really happened to the former sheriff. He *knows* about the woodland creatures and the *thing* like a scarecrow, and he's fucking *terrified* of the cook.

But none of this *matters* anymore.

It was that burning smell. The fungus. This place is so moist and unhealthy and there is mould everywhere. It grows on the walls and gets in the water. At first he suffered from headaches and blurry vision, that sort of thing. But then, you see, the headaches passed and he began to *see*, more clearly than ever before. Even as little bits of his past kept flaking off and away.

This, here, this was *his* kingdom. Not the king's, who couldn't give two fucks about Nottingham. Not Hood's, who was, when it came to it, just some petty fucking outlaw prancing about in the trees. No, this was the sheriff's manor. He could... *mould* it to suit his needs.

He wrote regularly to the bishop. Reporting no strange

sightings, for all that sometimes when he stalked the corridors they lengthened unnaturally, and he thought himself walking in some primordial forest, under an alien sky; sometimes a harpist played out of the darkness, haunting the night, and they could never find the source; sometimes he could hear footsteps when there was no one around, and some of the children born in the town had the scaly green bark of trees. The sheriff wrote that everything was well. The town quietly prosperous. The hoods in the woods were merely a nuisance. He collected the toll and he kept the peace, and that's all that mattered.

In his rooms in the castle, the black mould grew.

'You've got the bush fever,' the witch said to him, and cackled. The sheriff, with his hands shaking, sought her out at last. Strange dreams plagued his nights, the harpist's hated music soared into his nightmares. He had the sweats, he had the shits, he couldn't keep still.

'I am the sheriff!' he yelled at her. 'Master of this domain! Why can't I sleep, woman?'

'You cut down the sacred grove, you set on fire trees even the druids feared when they were here. The spirits of the forest are restless. What will you do to appease them?'

'You can't honestly expect me to buy this bullshit,' he said.

She cackled again.

'Of course not,' she said. 'You're just having withdrawal, you dipshit.'

'You what?' he said. He noticed the witch's assistant, the young Jewish woman, in the corner of the room, weaving – she raised her head sharply when the witch said that last bit.

He doesn't much like Jews, does the sheriff. He doesn't like their stupid faces, and it's said they smell funny when it rains. But they are the king's Jews and, like the sheriff, they serve their purpose. In truth, the sheriff doesn't like too many things: he hates the dumb villeins with their pathetic looks and broken backs and poverty, these fucking slaves in all but name; he hates the woodsmen and the smugglers and the backwoods cunts who make this place their home. It stinks. The whole place stinks. But it is his, and not the wood's, it's his, it's—

'You took in fairy dust,' the witch said. 'Goblin Fruit, Mother Mab's Money Maker, the Toadstool Refreshment, the Gnome's Thirst Quencher, Troll Toddy, Hobgoblin's Nightcap, Pan's Pecker, Nymph's Mischief, the rotten fruit, the hairy powder, the mould they dare not speak its name, the fuzzy wuzzy welcome wagon, the wayward woody, the howdy doody, the how's your father, the—'

'Fuck, don't bother.'

He got it then, he knew it though before. The wood's inside him, the stink of it, the sap: he dreams of the secret Green Place and of river nymphs – they stink of trout with their soft moist flesh – of wood nymphs with their insect honeydew, of fairy frauleins dancing in a meadow – he *needs* it, damn it. It consumes him, who he was, he realised it then but had known it for some time – and on that day he went to see the witch he found the first time that his name was gone.

'My name,' he said, 'what is my *name*?'

'I'm sure I couldn't tell you, duck,' the witch said, and cackled.

'How do I get the cure?'

'There is no cure, ducky, other than to give in to your medicine. It'll calm your nerves, at any rate. Just breathe, and let it go into your lungs and blood.'

'You have—'

She tossed him a bag. He opened it. Dry powder inside.

'How much?'

'First one's always free…'

He sweated, fidgeted; he wouldn't open it, not there. He took it to the castle. He tossed and turned in bed all night. There has to be another way, he thought.

He was a fucking *knight*! This wasn't *Christian*, is what it wasn't!

At cock crow hour, and still wide awake, he took a pinch. He shot it up his nose, and there were heavenly explosions, aurora borealis grade hallucinations, dance of the spirits, all that crap – man, it was good and righteous.

There has to be another way, he thought.

They will try to suborn you, the bishop had warned.

Well. Let them think they succeeded. Let them be *lulled*.

The next day, through the knights he trusted most, he put out a call to London, Leeds, Chichester and Bath: for masons, herbalists and wizards. And he laid his plans.

'What *is* that crazy motherfucker up to?' said the cook, then shrugged. She dropped fresh mushrooms in the stew pot and hummed happily.

She had *her* plans, too.

'What *is* that Norman dingdong doing?' Hood enquired of his merry men.

'He sent for truce,' Will Scarlett said.

'And do we trust him?'

'Like fuck we do,' the harpist said. Alan-a-dale, carrying mail – Hood's eyes and ears beyond the forest.

'I don't know that that's true,' Will said. 'He's being changed from the inside out – he's of the wood now. You have a power over him.'

'The only thing you can trust a bull-baiting dog to do is to bite you in the ass,' Alan-a-dale said with unassailable logic. 'Drug the shit out of it first or not.'

Will inched his head, acknowledging this truth.

'Nevertheless,' he said, 'accommodations must be made.'

Hood lifted bow and arrow. He let one loose. The arrow flew across the skies and hit a target at three hundred feet.

'Then make it so,' he said.

19

What *is* his name? These days he barely wonders anymore. He is the sheriff. This is his domain.

He never met the Hood. The Big Chief. The Pinecone Capo. The Man in Green. The Arrow Tosser. The Arch Archer. The Prince of Thieves. The Hooded Hoodlum. The Righteous Robber. The Cunt in the Hat. The cradle-snatching, rich-folk robbin', cock-a-robin, tax avoiding, goods-a-smuggling, back door stabbing son of a bitch. The Deer Hunter. The hail-fellow-well-met motherfucker who'd shoot you soon as look at you. The fairy feller. The knock-off rebel. The Sherwood Snatcher. The tick-tock taker of the ten-toll tax. The joey juggler. The woodlands looter of the filthy lucre. The roots-a-clutchin', green leaf blowin', fuck-the-king-and-all-his-hoein' freakin' *outlaw*.

That guy.

Total legend.

You know. The Hood.

But there had been an accommodation. And he kept sending letters to the bishop saying, simply, *all is well*.

And so it was. The green folk toed the line, the town stood against the wood. He left them alone and they left him alone.

A sheriff's job is to keep the *peace*.

And the peace held.

And he paid his fees to the witch and got his supply of dust.

And in his rooms in the castle the black mould grew.

He could *feel* himself change from within.

And he *liked* it.

Even as he lost more memories.

Who needed memories, anyway? His mother's hugs, his father's curses, the battles and the men he'd slain, whose ghostly faces sometimes haunted him – who cared? Begone, the past. Begone, his name. That past belonged to mortal men, and mortal men were weak.

There have been fungi on this earth long before human life ever began.

And so he laid his plans. Masons and carpenters had their tongues cut out on arrival so they wouldn't tittle-tattle. Aged wizards with bad teeth and shrivelled cocks and fortune-tellers clad in dirt, with bones wove in their hair, and astrologers with oiled skins and French perfumes, and diviners, augurs, palmists, seers and soothsayers.

'What *is* that motherfucker up to?' said the cook.

In his rooms in the castle, the black mould spread.

PART SIX

THE GRIFT

20

High on her tower Birdie watches the wood. She sees Sir Richard as he emerges, blinking, bleary-eyed, out of the trees. How long has he been lost there, this agent of the Bishop of York? Everybody knows who and what he is. From up on her perch high above the world Birdie catches rumour like a bird breathes air. The knight had been taken in by the wood, and word is that the Robin's tried him and found him to his liking.

So they shall see what he will do.

You can't serve two masters, though. And Birdie knows this better than most. She shudders as she looks out to the wood, its pull on her, its seductive song. She reaches for the cross that lies against her skin and holds it tight. Under her black monk's robe her breasts and her wings both are bound tight. She prays to the Jesusman. Her lips move without sound as she stares out at the wood. Her mother's there, the Green Lady, her and her Robin to rule the wood. Birdie misses moss and twigs to make a nest, she misses the whisper of the leaves and the way they sing when the rain falls. She misses the black pool where the elfin knight lies, feeding the oaken roots. Sometimes the scarecrow, Much, climbs up her tower in the night and brings a tale in grunts and wheezes. Sometimes the harpist, Alan-a-dale, sends a sweet melody her way, but all their stories, whichever way they're told, are filled with death and violence and blood.

Birdie holds the cross and prays to the Jesusman, whose life, if she is to be honest with herself, is much as Hood's: an outlaw who fought across that place called Palestine and died in pain and in betrayal – and this is how she sees Hood's death, far in the distance. With blood soaking the earth much as the Saviour's had. There is no happy ending here, she thinks.

No. She will not heed the call of the wood, and she shivers there on the edge of her tower, afraid of taking flight.

She is afraid of the wood's impossible promise. For it is doomed, she has foreseen it. There is a world beyond the fucking trees, and it is a bad world, of steel and violence and depravity, but it is the world all the same, and she must live in it if she is to survive. The fae just do not know it yet; beyond the ancient barrier of roots Herne still hunts and Titania dances, and Cousin Merle's still looking for the place where his boy won the war...

They're merely shades. They just don't know it yet. And up on her perch Birdie hears of the new university in Oxford, in which they teach logic and arithmetic, geometry, astronomy! She almost laughs. Logic has no place here, in the heart of the old world, though Merle, were he around, would surely disagree. Dream logic's logic all the same, he would have said – but then, isn't he stuck still in some crystal cave? Well, Birdie doesn't know him well; he is her mother's cousin from the witchy side.

The knight, she sees, recovers slowly. He stares around him in some obvious bewilderment. His horse appears from somewhere. It must be a very loyal horse, to have waited for its human all this time. Perhaps this bides well for the knight. She isn't sure. It's hard these days to make Nottingham out clearly. There is a fog of fairy dust and fungal spores. She thinks she should tell Mistress Becca, who is always kind to her, for the knight's business in these parts is not yet done – Birdie can tell. And she watches without much surprise as the knight, this Sir Richard, mounts his horse and turns, not back the way in which he came but to the town.

Oh, yes, she thinks, almost happy in the knowledge – there's going to be trouble.

Rebecca counts money in the cellar of the Goat, one penny, two pennies, three, livres and deniers and pffenigs from the continent, a couple of dinars from the Holy Land, a handful of blackened discs used no doubt for centuries as tokens of exchange by the local villagers, which she thinks might be Roman denarii. For all she knows King Arthur himself might have used them once to pay for a shave or a shit.

She jots down numbers in a book. She'd learned accounts from her father. So much of sales, so much of costs, so much of profits after dealer cuts and incidental losses, bribes and muscle hired for protection, and the exorbitant fees of middlemen.

Her hand cramps and the candle gutters and casts shadows on the walls. The door to the cellar opens and the flame brightens, for a fire's always hungry, and in sashays Rowena, two bags of money in her hands, but looking nonetheless not so well pleased.

'How much?' Rowena says.

'We made a tidy profit,' Rebecca says, smiling at her friend.

'You're back from London, then.'

'As you can see.'

'You made arrangements there?' Rowena says.

'My cousin introduced me to a lady by the name of Joan. She can handle the product. And de Grantmesnil's men already handle the shipping. Rowena… I am reluctant to go beyond the town so fast. The new king's soldiers are alert upon the roads and London's dangerous, they say the revenant Morgana lives there still – she holds some sway.'

'Life's dangerous, princess. A girl's gotta do what a girl's gotta do to survive.'

'If the witch finds out…'

And she feels bad. She's grown the last few years. The witch is older and Rebecca's no longer just an apprentice, and she's learned some tricks. But still.

'Relax, she doesn't know,' Rowena says. 'Besides, what's it to her? She's content to cure warts and carry out abortions. What use is power if you never fucking *use* it?'

And Rebecca thinks of the witch's teachings, how magic is best when it's used the least. How power is dangerous.

'She helped *you*,' she can't help but say, 'when you had your roll in the hay with David of Doncaster.'

'Pish posh,' Rowena says, but fondly. 'There's power and there's power.'

And Rebecca thinks, What use is a magic ring or a magic sword in comparison to the power over one's own body? To decide if you wanted a child or not? The witch does not pray, for she says a prayer never helped a single woman in this fashion, so what power does it have? The witch advocates the study of herbs and smuggles in diagrams of anatomy from Paris, where they study such things, and from old crusaders she gets scraps of medical texts of the Saracens, whose knowledge is much more advanced. She'd go and see the Holy Land, she tells Rebecca often, and cackles, only she's too old and there is war and strife enough right here at home.

In that she isn't wrong, but neither is Rowena. What *is* a girl to do? A Jewish one at that? Life is precarious, and as Rabbi Akiva *might* have said, to stop the rock of the world crushing you under you better get yourself a lever.

Or maybe it was Archimedes, the Greek. Well, regardless, Rebecca's only doing what she must to survive. And so she changes tack and says, 'How goes it in the Green Court?'

'Much the same. The Merry Men are merry but then again, they're men, why wouldn't they be. Bex, I think we have a problem.'

'Oh?' Rebecca's taken aback, though she tries not to show it. Everything has been going on so *well*. 'What is it?'

'The count is short. Someone is shafting us.'

Rebecca stands. A fury of a kind she hasn't known suffuses her so suddenly it's terrifying. But in this time, and in this place, a girl, if she is to survive, has to be fucking *ruthless*.

She says, 'Then get me a big fucking lever.'

Up from the cellar into the Goat proper, the alehouse is now under Rebecca's domain. It was easy enough to do, there was no art to it. The owner of the building, one Wilfred the Dim-Witted as they called him, not because he was but because he spoke slow, this Wilfrid had a business venture up-river stringing up water fowl for sale, the expansion of which led the man to seek credit. Since only Jews could give credit he went to Isaac of York, and was granted a loan – and since the king was sure to come, sooner or later, and claim *Isaac's* share of the funds – for what were Jews for if not to raise funds for their king – then by this line of reasoning this Dim-Witted Wilfrid found himself in debt to the throne.

Which is *not* the place you want to find yourself in if you're coming up short on your payments.

So Rebecca stepped in, quiet-like. She came to this Wilfrid and made him a proposition. Let *her* buy his debt. She would give him the money to be free from the king. In return she asked little enough. All she wanted was the Goat, which is handily situated in an unfashionable part of the English Quarter, far enough from the castle, close enough to the trade. And Wilfrid could well keep his name on the deed to the joint – Rebecca had no need for *attention*.

So Wilfrid remains. And Wilfrid keeps bar. And Wilfrid – a man slow to speak at the best of times – knows well enough to keep his fucking mouth shut.

Now the Goat's hers, and from here she runs the whole operation. This is where the grift's played.

It was the ailing alewife Aldrich what gave her the idea. How she needed solace in her final days. How she needed *medicine*.

Well, there were lots who needed medicine, as it turned out, and many more who didn't but just liked the flavour.

And the nice thing 'bout this medicine is that it keeps you wanting more.

She started small. Mixing her own batches of dwale from over-supplies. She sold to the needy and expanded by referral. Until she, too, needed more.

Rebecca knew that Alewife Aldrich's son Charlie was a poacher, he had dealings with the wood. She cut a deal herself. He brought her over what she needed.

One night two guys in masks jumped her. Stole the gear. That fury that she felt, it had come upon her then. This was *her* shit. This was *her* town. And if it wasn't, she would make it so.

She brought in Rowena. They had come up together. She could trust Rowena, for all that the girl was part-forest. And Rowena brought Elgitha, who was her waiting-woman and also handy with a knife – she had more brawl scars on her than a crusader, and she did wonderful lace work besides. And Elgitha found Ulrica, a girl out from Gotham, where the wise men played fools to avoid paying tax. So Ulrica looked simple, but never missed count, and instead of a knife she favoured a bat. Then there was Penny, and Peggy and Sue, Miranda and Charlotte and Winifred too.

Rebecca expanded, slowly. The girls each had a corner. They had each other's backs. Rebecca kept the local kids on payroll. Fox-face Reynard and his little gang, who went around ignored but heard everything. One night they came and told her of two guys, not local, from up-country in Mansfield, who moved to the town a few months back. They'd been seen round the town flashing cash, and Reynard heard one of the guys bragging how he ripped off the Jew broad, would have fucked her, too, if she wasn't a witch.

That night Rebecca and the girls, armed with knives and clubs, paid a visit to the dosshouse where the two hosers camped. Down by the river docks.

'Should I break down the door?' Ulrica said, waving her club.

Rebecca shook her head. She knocked, gently.

'Fuck off!'

Rebecca smiled. She pushed the door open. It wasn't locked and she went in.

A candle burning on the floor. A rat feasting on an apple by the wall. Two human rats lying on straw, scrambling for knives when they saw her.

She shook her head. Nah-ah.

The girls came in behind her. Their shadows danced on the wall.

'Are you the ones who jumped me?'

'Wasn't us, missus! Wasn't us!'

'Then what was you?'

'Huh?'

'What was you doing?'

'This and that, missus. Not that!'

'So what's that?'

And she pointed to a bag on the floor. Empty now.

But a hint of the smell.

Medicine.

Dwale.

'Got this from some bloke down the pub!'

'From an out-of-towner!'

'Some Norman bloke! Please!'

'It's ours!'

On the threshold of violence, Rebecca hesitated.

Thou shall not kill, God told Moses on Mount Sinai.

But that wasn't entirely true, was it, she thought. God more rightly said, Thou shall not *murder*. There was a difference there. Somewhat lost in translation.

And God also said, *Do not steal.*

And these men stole from her.

She knew she had to send a *message*.

'Shall I, Bex?' said Ulrica.

And still Rebecca hesitated.

The men saw it, too. They reached for their knives. They rose at the women. Their faces twisted then and were feral and ugly. A knife slashed, fast as a snake. Caught Elgitha on the arm. She raised it and smiled. She licked the blood right off the wound.

'Mother*fuckers*,' she said.

Rebecca said, 'Do it.'

Then the clubs came down, and the men screamed as their knuckles broke and their bones smashed and the useless knives fell to the floor. The shadows danced on the wall, two men on their knees, broken hands held in prayer.

Ulrica hefted her club.

'Well?' she said.

Rebecca said, 'Do it.'

The thump of a branch smashing fruit that was rotten. Pips and juice on the wall, pittering pattering. Rebecca's eyes stung. There was blood on her face. She wiped it off with a fine piece of lace.

'We could dump them in the river,' Elgitha said.

'No.'

'No?'

'No.'

'Then what do you want to do with this dead weight?'

The smell was awful and there was still blood on her face, and she could *taste* it, the hot salty tang of it, of blood that only moments ago pumped through the veins of living men. There was blood on the floor, on the walls, on her clothes... The rat in the corner dumped his apple and lapped at the fallen men's blood.

What if she was wrong? What if they were innocent?

The men who robbed her had worn masks, she couldn't tell faces.

Then it *would* be murder, she thought.

Though *is* it still murder if you did it in good faith?

And besides, what if it was? She was no Christian, in fear of Christian hell. Rebecca will die, and lie in the ground until any and all such time as the real messiah comes, and then it will be judgement day. Well, she could wait. And God will judge her in his own good time.

So fuck them, she thought.

'Bring them out,' she said.

The girls dragged the bodies by their feet. They panted in the cold night air and their breath rose like fog. They dragged them to the empty, quiet market square, where it was said that centuries before Maid Marian escaped the Watch and fled into the forest.

'Here,' Rebecca said.

'Here?'

'By the gate. So everyone can see them in the morning.'

The girls grinned at each other.

'Let's get *drunk*,' Penny Red said.

'Let's get *fucked*,' Dagger Deb said and leered. 'If you know what I mean.'

'We *always* know what you mean, Deb.'

Rebecca stood there, only half listening. The corpses leant against each other by the wall. They no longer had faces.

That fury was on her again. This was *her* town. This was *her* shit.

No one was ever going to jump her again.

'Give me a knife,' she said.

'What?'

'Give me a knife!'

'But they're already dead, Bex.'

'It isn't finished.'

Ulrica passed her the knife. Rebecca knelt on the ground. She raised the man's face by the chin. Stared at his blood-crusted eyes.

Stuck in the knife. The eyeball *popped*. Rebecca heaved.

Gritted her teeth. Severed the string that tied it in. Then stuck the knife in again.

The other eye went *plop*.

She did the other man next.

She stood in the empty market square of Nottingham and the forest leant in over the walls and listened. In their homes all across town people huddled together in cold rooms, and only those who sought comfort from the medicine she sold slept soundly and well.

'Hear this,' Rebecca said. 'Declare this in the house of Anjou and proclaim it in all Nottinghamshire: O foolish and senseless people, who have eyes but do not see, who have ears but do not hear. *Do you not fear me?*'

She screamed the last, and the fury came out of her and washed over the city, and dogs barked and babies woke crying in their cradles.

'That's really good, Bex,' Ulrica said admiringly.

'It's Jeremiah,' Rebecca said.

'Who?'

'He's in the B... forget about it.'

She stood there breathing heavily.

'*My* fucking house,' she said.

Now the eyes of her enemies slowly rot in a jar on the counter in the Goat. She assembles her troops. And no one fucking looks and no one fucking speaks her name in this town. *Her* town.

So the very idea someone's trying to screw her again is troubling all by itself.

'Let's go, girls,' she says.

And so, armed with knives and clubs, they march once more into the night.

21

Friday, 9 November, 1156 Anno Domini

My lord bishop,

It rained as I emerged back from the wood.

A thin, cold thing, like bad soup, and it just kept on falling.

The sickness hit me then. The transition back into the world was awful. Everything was grey and I was unsteady on my horse. I felt hot and cold in turns. I missed the deep greens of the wood, and the fairies' music, and the sweet ringing laughter of the Lady Rowena.

It took all my courage just to stay in the world as it was. I shook upon my horse. I felt like a sailor on board a rudderless ship. I was sick with it, I needed it bad.

... He was standing by the side of the road under an oak, and hailed me as I passed.

He was a miserable-looking peasant, nothing more. Anglo-Saxon. Once-golden hair now reduced to a bit of fuzz over a bald scalp. A face that had lines etched into it as though with a carving knife. He had very few teeth.

His cart was under the tree. He seemed to be selling stuff nobody wanted. A few sorry-looking cabbages. A handful of hens' eggs. A trussed-up chicken even thinner than he was. And charms and amulets. Dowdy things, inexpertly made, acorns on a string and twisted roots and dried fungus. Fuck knows where he got them or what use they were to anyone.

I don't know why I stopped. Maybe I took pity on him. Maybe I just needed the rest.

I dismounted and leant against the tree.

'You got anything to drink?'

'Sorry, no.'

He didn't look sorry. But he pushed a hand at me.

'Take these,' he said, not unkindly. 'They'll help.'

Some dry black fungus in his palm. It looked revolting. I took it all the same and chewed and swallowed, though it tasted awful.

'You're the bishop's agent, ain'tcha,' he said.

I was taken aback, and failed not to show it.

He nodded. 'Thought so,' he said. 'Heard you was coming.'

'How?' I said.

He shrugged.

'Everyone knows.'

'How?'

'Someone was bound to come, eventually.'

I gave up. I was waiting for the fungus to kick in. There were faces in the trees, but then, there were always faces in the trees up here.

'What do you want, then?' I said.

I knew he wanted something. He just took his time getting around to it.

'It's my daughter,' he said. 'She's missing.'

'Do I,' I said, annunciating clearly, 'look like I give much of a fuck?'

The words kind of tumbled out of my mouth and then grew wings and flew away. It was kind of funny and I tried not to laugh.

'Listen,' he said. 'I'm a Christian man. And this is the archbishop's diocese. He should care what's been happening here.'

'And what's been happening here?' I said.

'It's this lot up in the castle,' he said. 'They ain't right, mister.'

'The sheriff?' I said.

He shrugged. Unwilling to answer, or he just didn't know. What did I care. He was just some peasant.

'How many sheriffs have you had so far, anyway?' I said.

'This is only the second one.'

'What happened to the last one?'

'He died.'

'I know that,' I said. 'How did he die?'

He shrugged. 'How do you think?'

'I have no fucking idea. They say he was stabbed.'

'You can say that again,' he said and sniggered.

I didn't like him. I didn't like him at all.

'My daughter,' he said again. 'She's gone into the town and she never came out. Listen, mister. As ugly as I am, and I ain't got no illusions, but as ugly as I am she was – she is – beautiful. She lit up the world and everything in it was a little bit greyer in comparison.'

I grinned at him. My headache was gone. I felt great all of a sudden.

'So, what?' I said. 'She didn't want to be a villein all her life so she took the one commodity she had and fucked off into town to find a buyer?'

His face twisted in hate; like he wanted to punch me. Then the fight went out of him all at once and he looked even older.

'Her name's Olivia,' he said. 'I just want to find her. I just want her home again.'

'Did you try to find her?'

I felt sorry for him.

'I did but I am no one, there.'

'Maybe she doesn't want to be found.'

'Please,' he said. 'You are the bishop's man—'

'I am no one's man!'

'Everyone knows you're here to clean house.'

'Fine,' I said. 'Fine.' I felt so tired then. I was up and I was down. I went round and round this town. 'If she pops up I'll send her packing.'

'That's all I ask,' he said. 'Thank you.'

'Whatever, man,' I said. I got back up on my horse. As I rode away I looked back, half expecting him to have vanished, just another mirage conjured by the wood. But he was still there, under the oak, with that table with shit for sale on it that nobody wanted. You had to feel sorry for him.

No wonder the girl took off. In her place I'd have done the same thing.

Two goombahs with the sullen expressions of disappointed lovers stood guard at the gates as I approached the city.

'Halt, who goes there!'

'Just a traveller,' I said. 'Come to admire the sights.'

'Your name, knight?'

'Sir Richard.'

They exchanged glances then.

'Heard you was coming. I'm Bert, this is Ernest. We're the guardsmen.'

'We had nothing to do with it, mister.'

I stared at them both. They didn't look like they could defend a pint of ale, let alone a town.

'Nothing to do with what?' I said.

'Nothing,' Bert mumbled. He gave his friend a dour look.

'Yeah,' Ernest said. 'We weren't even there.'

'Weren't even where—oh, forget it,' I said. 'I don't even care. Are you going to let me in or are we going to stand here chitchatting till the cows come home?'

'The cows are on the west field today,' Bert said. 'They'll be grazing on the out for a couple more days at least.'

'I don't—' I said, and then I gave up again. 'Just move.'

I pushed my horse forwards, only gently, but it was enough for them to scatter. They opened the gates and I rode into Nottingham.

I've been to some pretty impressive cities in my time.

London, where the tower stands. Poitiers with its lofty cathedral. Jerusalem, where the Saviour walked the Way of the Cross.

Grand, ancient seats of power and influence. Places that really made you proud to be human. Places that said, here was civilization. Here was knowledge, learning, faith.

In comparison to those places Nottingham was just a speck of shit in the middle of a goddamned forest.

Twisty dark alleyways that turned and bent and led you nowhere.

All manner of unsavoury cowled folk skulking about.

Shit everywhere.

I was desperate for medicine. All the sobriety I'd kept since leaving the Holy Land abandoned me on entering that forest and I was shaking for a fix again. The fungus didn't help much, it just made me woozy. They had green man faces etched into the walls and I could swear the lips smiled mockingly, the eyes followed me as I passed.

I got lost three times trying to find the fucking castle.

Not that it was hard to find, you understand. The awful thing towered over the city like some sort of a malignant growth, like the infection that sometimes takes over trees; a huge tumour rising over Castle Rock. Yet every time I headed there I got lost in the narrow streets and found myself at another dead-end.

The people of Nottingham were aware of my passing. They stared as I got lost and the men looked hostile and the women shook their heads, and they all drew into the shadows when I came and all I could see were their eyes. Kids played kick-ball in one alleyway and when I got closer I realised it was not an inflated pig's gallbladder they were kicking but a dead, grey rat.

'Get away with you!' I screamed. They stared at me sullenly.

'You ain't from around here, mister.'

'Yeah.'

'Fuck off.'

'Yeah.'

'Fucking ponce.'

I could have taken them easily. I mean, they were just kids. And yet I found myself taking a step back.

There was something mean and unhealthy and vicious about them – like they'd pull a knife and gut you if they had a chance and not even think twice about it.

'Listen, you little wank stains,' I said, changing tack. I pointed at a fox-faced little shit with bright eyes. He looked a little less dumb than the rest. 'I need to get to the castle.'

'So? It's up there.'

They sniggered. The fox-faced one looked up.

'What's in it for me, mister?' he said.

'What do you want?'

'What does anyone want, mister? Lucre, mister! Show me the shine of your shekels! Or fuck off.'

'Listen, you little shit—'

They dropped the dead rat and turned on me, the lot of them. You ever been attacked by a pack of rabid dogs? You could kick each one individually but somehow, when they worked together...

'Alright, alright,' I said. 'Show me the way.'

'Money first,' he said.

'Fuck off. What's your name, anyway, you little twerp?'

He flashed pearl teeth at me.

'Reynard,' he said.

'Then lead the way, Reynard. I'm already sick of this shithole town.'

He slapped palms with his mates and lolled ahead, even moving like a fox.

'Oh, I don't know, mister,' he said. 'It might grow on you.'

22

We finally found the castle, though even the little fox kid struggled towards the end. He kept leading me, confidently at first, down a familiar alley, with a name like Rose Street or Daisy Lane – either way they always smelt of piss – but then a bemused expression would come on his face and he'd change tack suddenly, and try another pathway.

'It's got... more resistance than usual,' he said, panting.

'What the fuck are you talking about, boy?'

'The castle... sometimes it doesn't want you to go there.'

He stared at me. It was no doubt some ignorant peasant superstition, my lord bishop.

'Someone in this town really doesn't like you, mister,' he said.

Which was when three burly shadows emerged out of the entrance of the Fighting Cock Alehouse directly in front of us and started to move in rather an aggressive fashion towards where we stood.

'We should probably let them pass...' I said.

Which was when the biggest of the three rushed forwards and landed a punch on me that threw me sideways.

'See?' Raynard said. 'I told you.'

I hit the wall of a decrepit house and staggered, fresh blood in my mouth, my nerves fully on edge. A slow-building rage, which had been there all along, emerged with a roar.

'I. Don't. Need this!' I screamed. I reached for my sword. 'Die! Die, motherfuckers, die!'

I hacked at them. They were unarmed, and my blade went right through the first one without resistance.

I stared.

There was no blood.

His arm had been sliced clean off. It lay on the ground. The man looked down at the wound. His skin was white and porous. He shrugged. Then he came at me again.

'Die!'

I stabbed him through the heart. My sword went in and out. He looked down at the hole in his chest and shrugged again. Then he came back at me.

'Why won't you die!'

I hacked at him in blind fury. The other two flanked me on either side. They rained down blows but I barely felt them. I was sick, and my malaise had no cure. None that I could get right then, at any rate.

'Prune them!' Reynard whisper-shouted from his hiding place. 'You can't kill them but you can cut them down!'

'What the fuck sort of place is this!' I screamed, and heard him laugh with glee.

'It's Nottingham,' he said.

I hacked and slashed. In the wan light of the gloom of that town – Gloomph, I'd heard it called – I could just about make out their faces. They were ill-formed: crooked noses and runny eyes and a sort of doughy, unformed feel to them. Like they'd been grown, like fungus.

I cut and I cut and they rained down blows until they had no fingers nor arms nor legs to kick with. Then there was just a pile of white mooshy parts on the ground, and I was sick all over them.

'Let it all out, my man,' Reynard said encouragingly. 'Let it all out.'

'What... the fuck... was that,' I said.

'Just, you know... goons,' he said.

'Goons?'

'Somebody up there really doesn't like you,' he said again. He looked quite pleased with the thought. I wiped my mouth with the back of my hand.

'Just take me to the fucking castle,' I said.

'What do you think I've been trying to do all this time, mister?' he said. He plodded on and I followed. I had nothing else to go on right then.

We wended our way up and down passageways, hearing English here, French there, and some sort of woodland pidgin which I realised I'd heard before, back in the... In that green place.

Whatever. I didn't have to learn the natives' fucking tongue.

All I had to do was conclude the inquisition on behalf of your lordship and hightail it out of town.

Debt forgotten.

Adult son freed.

A life of sobriety and abstinence at the Lee awaiting.

Fuck that for a game of conkers, I thought.

At last we reached the gates to the castle. I was perspiring heavily by then.

A gnarly knight materialised out of the Gloomph and regarded me sourly.

'The sheriff will see you now,' he said.

23

Up on her high perch Birdie watches the castle.

The castle had begun as just your average Norman hill fortification. Old Conqueror Bill himself ordered it built, back in the heady days of invasion and sedition, when peasants had to be kept from rebelling, when knights were knights and men were men, and the Anglo-Saxon shitbrains were either trained or slain.

It had been built initially of wood.

But there was the Normans' first mistake. The wood came from the forest. The trees that were felled were old, and their roots ran deep, and some still imprisoned the spirits of the tree-nymphs who dwelt in them. Some of those spirits were well old, proper Brythonic bitches who could still remember when Julius Caesar once took a piss on a rock nearby (or so they claimed). Others were younger, harsh Germanic spirits with a Saxon sense of vengeance and Jutish sympathies, while others still came with the Viking pirates and dreamt in dreams of snow and ice and flashing steel.

But none of them liked to be disturbed, nor did they much like each other.

As a result, the castle was like a bad-tempered, occasionally murderous ancient ancestor at the dinner table. It stretched and shook and grew unfathomable, gross things upon itself. Holes opened unexpectedly and dropped the unwary into deep-down oubliettes. Rooms closed upon their occupants and suffocated them within. The castle, not quite sane, sat upon the spongy crest of Castle Rock and sank its roots into the sandstone.

But for some time now the voices of the nymphs, which Birdie could hear clearly, on account of her witchy ancestry and all, were muted. And the sound of construction could be heard instead, day and night, and the roads were clogged with carts ferrying hewn stone and new timber up to the castle, and builders with dust on their clothes swamped the alehouses and picked fights. And in the nights Birdie could see strange lights burn within the castle, green and gold flames, and she could smell witchery and enchantment – it smelt like ripe, good cheese, a good stink it had.

She knows the Jesusman was a powerful magician too, of course. Was he not a weather worker, who could speak to the elements, who calmed the storm on the Sea of Galilee? And did he not exorcize the powerful demons of Gerasene, and cast them into swine, and then drowned the pigs? He was a mighty big magic man, and did he not rise from the dead, too? And was he not a healer? No wonder Birdie follows him. She knows the old magic's doomed. Fairies and bogarts and things that go bump in the night. The rustle of leaves against a window. Curdled milk and stolen babies, all that shit the fairies like. It's unsustainable.

In time the nymphs will drowse into the sleep from which there's no return. In time the wells will fill with poison. Even a mighty oak must sooner or later fall. And then they will be shadows, little more, barely troubling the sleep of the living.

No, she's picked her side, hard as it is. For no one said that having faith was *easy*.

Her soul will go to *Him*. And *He* doesn't wear a fucking *hood*. *He* being the son of God and all.

So *fuck* Robin. Fuck the lot of them. And whatever the sheriff's up to in that poky castle on the hill, fuck him and all his witchery, too. It's nothing to her. She can smell the foul experiments emanating from that hell house. Fungal spores and fairy dust. The cook must have something to do with it, Birdie thinks.

Now the cook, there's a funny old bird. Mrs More-Goose, she calls herself now. But Birdie knows what she is, doesn't she. Oh yes she does. No one fucks with one of the original nine sisters. They say she fucked Arthur himself, not that she liked him much but they are real suckers for power, the fae – they eat it up like porridge. Diminished now, of course. Word is her sister Morgana's still running London, same as it ever was, and Cailleach's still betting on her Picts. Where Thitis is is anybody's guess, and as for Nimue, she's probably skulking in some lake or river. Same as it ever was.

Only it isn't. With every passing year the old traditions fade, the rituals more rarely re-enacted. The priests of the Jesusman came, and the priests of the Jesusman conquered, for all that they had a hard time of it at first. The Church is powerful, there's real magic in its faith. And even in amid themselves the fairies bicker, and word from Fairyland is that the cook's not happy with the Hood – or with his mistress. For Robin's just a man in a hood, and men in hoods can be replaced at will.

But Marian's a different thing altogether.

But Birdie doesn't want to guess her mother's mind. The Green Lady can be terrible, and she can be kind; she can be loving and cruel as all mothers can be. But she'd chosen her path and Birdie, in turn, chose hers.

So Birdie dismisses the castle and its denizens from her mind and turns her gaze upon the darkening town instead. She had seen the knight ride in, only to get lost in the maze of a city that didn't want him. She saw the foul miasma that drifted down from the castle (*whatever they are doing there*) and the things in the shape of men, who weren't men, who attacked the knight.

But she does not care for the knight and whether he lives or dies by sword or fungus. She looks, until she finds the Goat, the alehouse marked, as it were, with the painted sign of Pan dancing on his cloven hooves. Oh, Pan, you rascal, Birdie thinks. Now there's one ancient spirit with tenacity. He'll stick around, in one form or another, she is sure. Her visions of the future are halting, jerky things, they're more like daydreams or (if she is to be honest with herself) hallucinations. The hoods in the woods love tripping balls, but all they ever see are pretty colours or their dicks, which they are very fond of. In truth the Merry Men are simple things, the broken shells of men who have retreated from the world – she mostly pities them.

Enough about the Merry Men. She looks out at the Goat. Sees Mistress Becca emerge, hooded and cloaked, and there's a cosh hidden in her sleeve, and behind her come her girls, her gang: Rowena of the Glamour, and Elgitha the Scar, and Ulrica Skull Basher, and Penny and Peggy and Sue, Miranda and Charlotte, and Winifred too.

Armed with coshes and knives the girls skulk into the night. Birdie watches them from high above on her perch and she longs to go to them. She longs to cast down the robes of a monk and feel the binding that holds her loosen. She'd spread her wings and take to the air, light as a sparrow; she'd chase the wind and the currents of air, rising and falling, and all Sherwood and Nottingham would be down below her...

No.

No one said choosing the right path was *easy*.

She will keep herself bound, in body and earth, so that one day she may fly up to heaven. In truth she knows she must go see the barber-surgeon, Simeon (a decent guy, all told) and ask him to cut off her wings. He has done it before, for others who fled from the forest, quietly, seeking a new life in this new world of women and men. It will hurt, she knows that. It will hurt, and the nubs of her wings will turn to stumps and in this manner she will become just a person. She will take the last vows and a name unto herself – Brother Evangelium, perhaps. She likes the sound of that. And she will leave her high perch and join the brothers in the monastery below, and tend garden, and watch over the sacred relics, and pray, and help the poor. She will do all that, but it will hurt. It will hurt a lot.

So for now she is suspended in indecision, unable to fly and unable to choose. The wood cries out to her to come back. The magic warms her blood and agitates her thoughts. She dreams the future, and it is a horrible place, filled with metal machines belching steam, and always war, so much bloodshed, and the world fills up with humans and they slaughter each other and still more and more come.

In such a world the little polder that is Sherwood, its boundaries patrolled and toughened by old magic, seems positively quaint. It cannot last. And so Birdie chooses life, she chooses order, she chooses to go out into that future, as horrible as it seems, for it *is* the future, and no one can avoid it forever.

And she looks out on the town and she sees, arriving from the other direction, spreading silently through the dark and narrow streets, the opposing force that is coming to meet Rebecca and her girl gang; and a horror grips Birdie; she fears for them. Birdie wishes she could fly down there and warn them, but it is too late, what is done in the past manifests in the present, and Rebecca by stepping out of her assigned role in society, has invited upon herself the swift and inevitable wrath of the establishment. And knows it.

So Birdie hopes her girl's got a plan.

''Allo, 'allo, 'allo, what 'ave we 'ere, then?' the soldier says.

Rebecca pauses. The cosh, hidden under her sleeve, stays there for now.

'Ear?' she says.

''Ere!' the soldier says.

'I know you, Albert,' Rebecca says accusingly. 'And I think you speak very good English.'

'Thank you, Miss Rebecca.'

'Why stop us? We're not doing nothing.'

'Anything,' Albert says. 'Not doing anything.'

'That, too.'

'It's late,' Albert says. 'It isn't safe for you to wander by yourselves after dark.'

'We have each other.'

'Going where?'

'To the seamstress—'

'Home—'

'To church—'

A chorus from the girls, and Rebecca winces.

Albert smirks. 'A likely story. And Miss Rebecca? Church, is it?'

'An errand?'

And she knows that, somewhere, she has badly miscalculated.

Rowena besides her switches on the elfish charm. You can positively taste the witchery coming off her. Not like Rebecca, who hasn't liked magic much since Much… well… since the thing that happened to Much, anyway.

Rowena glides to the soldier.

'What's this about, Albert?' she murmurs.

But the soldier seems immune to her charm for once.

'I think you know,' he says, and his eyes are hard, and there is something new about him, Rebecca thinks, something disturbing – he's one of the Frankish knights brought over with the second sheriff (as everyone here calls him), but a decent sort for a murderer.

Only now she notices his pale, pale skin, and the grey in his eyes…

Someone is shafting us, Rowena had told her.

But Rebecca had thought herself immune, top predator in this here town. At most she had thought one of the minor dealers they employ got greedy. Such things are not unheard of, after all.

But now she's thinking maybe that was just a symptom of disease, and she'd been too complacent while the bile and humours of her operation were being upset from without with a major infection...

'I don't,' Rebecca says.

'Please put down your weapons,' Albert says. The men behind him draw their swords.

'That cosh under your sleeve, Miss Rebecca,' he says. 'And your knives, Elgitha. All of them, if you please. And your club what has nails driven through it, Ulrica.'

'Mother*fucker*!' Elgita explodes, and she takes a step forwards—

'Don't,' Rebecca says.

The girls stand still.

The night is dark and cold. They face each other, the girl gang and the sheriff's men. Swords on one side, knives and clubs on the other. No one moves.

They're at a Nottingham Standoff.

In the shadows under the peeling sign of a carpenter's workshop stands a green child. Rebecca catches just a glimpse of him before he vanishes. He stares at her with wide, bright, guileless eyes.

So the wood is watching.

She looks at the soldiers. Sighs.

'Where?' she says.

'The castle.'

'I see.'

'The sheriff would like to have a word, if you please.'

'I... see.'

And she does, now. This is the nature of the state, she thinks. Sooner or later it comes for your shit.

It's the only real grift there is.

She lets the cosh drop to the ground.

'Lay them down, ladies,' she says.

The soldiers surround them once they disarm. There's no one else on the street. No one moves behind the windows. But she knows people are watching all the same.

Even Rowena seems subdued as they walk up the hill. Ulrica is silent. Elgitha mutters softly under her breath. There is no resistance going up to Castle Rock. No one says a goddamned word. Their breath fogs in the air before them. Rebecca thinks of ways to escape. What she's going to say. She's been caught unawares. Well, this is on her.

She'd forgotten the rule: there is always a bigger asshole than you.

Fuck, fuck, *fuck*!

She most definitely *doesn't* have a plan.

She trudges up until they reach, at last, the gates of the castle.

A gnarly knight materialises out of the Gloomph and regards her sourly.

'The sheriff will see you now,' he says.

24

I stared at the girl as they brought her in and shut the door in her face.

'Welcome to the dungeons,' I said mournfully.

'Who the fuck are you?' she said. 'Oh, wait, I know. You're that informer the Bishop of York sent down, aren't you?'

'Inquisitor, actually,' I said. And, 'Does everyone in this shithole place know?'

'Bad news travels fast in a small town,' she said.

'Mmmm... mmmmm!' the wild-eyed loon who was the third prisoner in the cell said.

'Who's that?' the girl said.

'Don't know.'

'Mmmm... mmmmm!'

'Who are you?' I said. But I knew her, I realised. She was the woman who met with Hugh de Grantmesnil on the forest road.

'My name's Rebecca.'

'I'm Sir Richard.'

'Not much use for a title in here,' she said.

It was fair. I let it go.

'Call me Dick,' I said.

She looked at me critically.

'You look like a dick,' she said.

I was suffering pretty bad. I kept itching and scratching myself and I was sweating, for all that the cells were cold.

'Mmmm... mmmm!' the wild-eyed loon said. A gorgeous tapestry of the Virgin Mary hung on the wall behind him, but I had no eyes for the dear old girl just then.

'Is there any chance you're carrying?' I said desperately.

Rebecca looked at me in compassion.

'It's like that, is it?' she said.

'It's this goddamned town,' I said. 'It fucks you up.'

'That it does,' she said.

'I'm Jonesing bad,' I said.

'Who's Jonesy?'

'How should I know?' I said. 'They say he was some guy what got the craving back in Acre. It's just a thing people say.'

'I've never been to Acre,' she said – a little wistfully, I thought.

'Well, why would you?' I said. 'It's in the Holy Land.'

'I'm Jewish,' she said.

'Is that why you're in the dungeons?' I said.

'Surprisingly... not,' she said. 'Here.' She reached in her robe and tossed me a small vial. I opened it.

'Dwale?'

'First taste's free,' she said.

I sucked it down greedily. The shakes subsided.

'Thanks,' I said. 'And hey, Acre's a shithole. You ain't missing anything.'

'Thanks,' she said.

'Mmmm... mmmm!' the madman said.

'Shut up!' both Rebecca and I said in unison. We smiled at each other.

'So,' she said.

'So.'

'So, I know why I'm here,' she said. 'But why are you?'

'It's a good question,' I said.

Why was I in the fucking dungeons?

★

'So you are Sir Richard at the Lee,' the sheriff said thoughtfully when he had met me earlier.

'So you are—' I said his name and he looked at me blankly. They were serving fish.

The Church instructs us to do penance for the death of Jesus of Nazareth by not eating meat on a Friday. Poor sinners that we are, we quickly figured out fish weren't meat and, on that technicality, a new tradition emerged. People like nothing more than to find a loophole.

Trays overlaid with fish – bream, chub, small carp, mirror carp, leather carp, perch, roach, rudd, tench, orf. I was sure some of these were just made-up words.

I knew the sheriff maintained fish ponds on the adjacent land, but not the extent of it. Roasted fish... grilled fish, steamed fish, boiled fish, fried fish... the smell was nauseating and I wanted to heave.

'Not hungry?' the sheriff said. 'Have a plate of mushrooms.'

There was chicken-of-the-wood, earthballs and earthstars, puffballs and jelly ears. I was sure at least some of these were toxic. But the sheriff and his men ate them hungrily, until juices ran down their chins. I waved away what I was pretty sure was a plate of deathcaps and funeral bells, and instead munched without much appetite on bread.

I watched the sheriff and his men closely. There was something off about them, but I couldn't quite say what it was. They had the manners of pigs but then again, they were knights. They were pale, as though they had not seen any sunlight for years. And their eyes were small and suspicious, and the irises concentrated to tiny points.

I wasn't sure just what racket the sheriff was running. But I was sure he was running one all the same.

'Say,' I said.

'Yes?' he said. We sat together at the long table. The rest of the men were knights and unsavoury-looking civilian – one had stars and bells sewn into his robe, another had a bone through his nose and charms in his matted hair. Hedge wizards, if I had to bet money on it.

I fucking hated wizards.

Not like they ever did anything useful. The dumb ones played with bones and the smart ones talked about compounds or non-Euclidean geometry, and the Byzantines, God curse them, had their wizards make Greek Fire, a terrible weapon of mass destruction that could take down whole ships and from which there was no escape – but either way they were useless for anything good. The worst ones, of course, had the real, old magic – of wood and stone and wind and water. And that shit really fucked you up.

'Why do you keep all these wizards?' I said.

'They?' the sheriff waved a pale, podgy hand. 'They help about the place.'

'Doing what?'

A guy to the right of the sheriff rubbed his hands together. He wore black monk's robes and had a ferrety sort of a face, if you know what I mean.

'There are certain compounds—' the black-robed monk started.

So he was one of those.

'Certain humours in wood fungus which prove to have a significant cross-pattern variation across holistic and naturalistic target points which add up to a surprisingly diverse portfolio of potential effects—'

'Of course,' I said.

'I'm Whitehand,' he said. 'Gilbert Whitehand. Of the Sacred Order of the Faith and Peace of The Holy Angel Azrael. You may have heard of me?'

'I have not.'

'My men and I are only recently arrived in Nottingham,' he said. 'The sheriff was kind enough to... invite us in. We are doing great work here, Sir Richard. Great work indeed. There are many splendours in holy nature of which we are to this date ignorant. Have you read Avicenna? It is impolitic to say so, but the Saracens are far advanced in their studies of nature than our own holy empire-to-be. We shall be victorious in the Holy Land, of course we will, for we have God on our side, but that is not to belittle our brethren of the East. Don't you agree?'

'I...'

'Yes, yes,' he said eagerly. 'You must see for yourself, Sir Richard. We are doing holy work here, we—'

'That's quite enough, Gilbert,' the sheriff said sharply. Gilbert Whitehand subsided with a huff.

'Great work...' he said softly.

'Gilbert! Down!'

The black-robed monk bowed his head and left the table. I said, 'I ran into a villein outside of town.'

'So?'

'He had a tale to tell.'

'Don't they all?' the sheriff snorted. 'Fucking peasants.'

'Sure,' I said. 'I didn't think much of it. He said his daughter went missing in the big city.'

'You call this a big city?' the sheriff snorted again. He was a great one for snorting. His cold grey eyes regarded me without amusement. 'This isn't London or Poitiers.'

'That's exactly what I said,' I told him. 'But then, it got me thinking. If it is small... how does a person disappear here?'

'Oh, believe me,' he said, 'you can disappear in Nottingham just as easily, Sir Richard.'

His words put a chill in me. I reached for a glass of wine and downed it in one. The sheriff watched me keenly.

'How is it?' he said.

'It tastes kinda funny.' I said. The room swam before my eyes. I giggled.

'A horse walks into an alehouse and the alewife says...'

'Night night, Sir Richard.'

The last thing I saw was his face, swimming above me.

'Just as easy to disappear...'

Then darkness.

★

'Why the long face?'

'Excuse me?'

'A horse walks into an alehouse and the alewife says...'

'I see.'

'Then I woke and found me here, on the cold cell's hide. The motherfucking sheriff Mickey'ed me.'

'Who's Mickey?'

'How should I know?' I said. 'He was a crusader down in Jerusalem who ran a tavern and used to spike the customers' drinks. Or so they say.'

'It doesn't sound like the sheriff's planning on letting you out of here,' Rebecca said.

'That did occur to me,' I admitted. 'I suspect he will sooner or later cut my throat and dump me in the river, then write to the bishop and say I had an accident. Probably never made it to town in the first place. Ever so sorry, nothing to report, all here is well. It's what I would do, anyway, in his place, if I were running some kind of a grift.'

'And is he?' she said.

'What?'

'Running a grift?'

'He must be,' I said.

'It has to be the dwale,' she said. 'That son of a bitch.'

'Excuse me?'

'I sell the stuff, you see. Got the market cornered, as it were. Or thought I had. The sheriff must want to take over the racket.'

'You run dwale?'

'Ain't nothing illegal 'bout it.'

'Sure,' I said. 'If you pay the king his share.'

'The king,' she said, 'can suck my dick.'

So that was that; and I looked at her with new respect.

'You got a gang?'

'My girls.'

'Where are they, then?'

'That I don't know,' she said.

I could see it worried her. Well, the whole situation worried me. I couldn't see why the sheriff would care about dwale. There had to be something more to it. And I remembered with nausea those men who attacked me, who were no longer men...

Something, it occurred to me, was very wrong in Nottingham.

25

While the idiot inquisitor from York is talking Rebecca quietly examines the dungeons. They are deep under the castle, and that, she thinks, is *good* news. It means they are inside the rock, and she knows the rock well. It is riddled with tunnels.

The cell itself is stout enough. Iron bars and a rusted lock, and no doubt guards outside the door. They have been given no food, but three pails of brackish water sit within reach, and when she sniffs them she recoils. There is something unwholesome in them, she is sure of that. But she equally knows that, if she is unable to escape, sooner or later she will have to drink it.

She worries about her girls. The soldiers led them elsewhere, while she was taken to the sheriff. He didn't even bother threatening her, she realised. He stared at her with only mild interest, as though she were a particularly common species of moth.

'You will stop with that nonsense you've been running, girlie,' he said. 'This town's mine. Oh, what's the point. Take her to the cells.'

And that was that. It was the curt dismissal that really hurt. She'd thought herself tough, queen of her domain. *She* owned Nottingham!

Only to run into this shit.

Well, she is used to being underestimated.

She tries to summon a vision of the fairy realm. The castle lies adjacent to the witchy place, after all. But Rebecca can feel nothing but resistance.

So she isn't welcome *there*, either.

'Mmmm... mmmmm!' the third occupant of the dungeon says.

Rebecca turns her attention on him. He is a short, once-stocky man now much reduced in weight. His hair is long and matted. His mouth, she notes, is gagged, which is why he is making these ridiculous sounds. She motions the poor creature to come closer. There's a tapestry on the wall behind him that look like he'd woven it himself. She wonders uneasily at the rouge on the Virgin Mary's lips.

She *really* hopes the man didn't paint it with his own blood.

Or, well, anyone else's, for that matter.

'Who did this to you?' she says. She reaches across and unfastens the gag. 'Were you tortured?'

She knows the Normans have some fearsome instruments they like to keep in their dungeons. Though she had seen none here.

'Mmmm... mmmm!' the man says. He coughs and spits. Something green and disgusting lands on the floor and Rebecca swears she can see it hop away. 'Don't drink the water!'

'I wasn't planning to,' Rebecca says.

'It's laced with dust,' the man whispers. His eyes are like holes into darkness, and shadows flit and chatter behind them. 'Fairy dust. *That's* his racket, you fools!'

A coldness closes round Rebecca's heart.

'Devil's Delight?' she says.

'The Fairy Feller's Feel-good Bracer?' Sir Richard says, startled.

'Yes, yes!' the man screams. 'Elves' Elvensies! Lilith's Libation! Pixies' Potion, the Gnomish Eye-Opener, Hobgoblin's Hell Water, the Siren's Solace, the Night-Hag's Cuppa, Bogeyman's Pint! Ye Olde Dark and Stormy, Wake Up in the Mornin', Hope

I never See Ya, Wouldn't Wanna Be Ya!' He covers his ears with his hands. 'Yes, all of those!'

'Fairy dust?' Rebecca says. 'But that's *wood* stuff.'

'Yes,' the man says.

'That's in *Hood*'s manor.'

'Yes.'

'And how's the sheriff gonna mix himself a batch of th—'

'Ah,' Sir Richard says.

Rebecca turns on him.

'Ah?' she says.

'Well.'

'Well, what?'

The inquisitor from York squirms. 'I did notice, over dinner, the sheriff has an abundance of, well, wizards and suchlike. I got a whole lecture, in fact, about the properties—'

'*Properties?*'

'That's what *I* said!—of fungus.'

'I see.'

'I didn't think at the time…'

'Of course you didn't.'

'I'd been drugged!'

'Not the first time, I'd say.'

'That's neither here nor there!' Sir Richard says.

'Shut *up*!' the third prisoner says. 'It hurts,' he says. 'It hurts so much, the voices in the dark, they never stop, they always cry, they plead to be released…'

'Who the hell *are* you?' Sir Richard says.

The man turns his ravaged face on them. 'My name is Wat,' he says.

'What?'

'Wat!'

'What?'

'Wat! Wat o' the Crabstaff, they used to call me. I'm with *him*, you see. With Hood. I'm with the Merry Men of Sherwood Forest.'

'You don't look very merry…' Sir Richard mutters.

'Hood sent me. The wood's been concerned by the sheriff's activities. I'm a tinker by trade, I came to mend the kitchen's utensils. Only, the sheriff's men caught me snooping around and tossed me in here.'

His face closes in horror.

'I *saw* it…' he says.

Then he starts screaming.

The sound is awful, and Rebecca's heart goes out to the man. She summons him over. The scream comes out of him mechanically, and it is with relief both to him and her when she gags him again and tightens the contraption. She now understands why it's there.

'Mmmm… mmmmm!'

'I'm so sorry,' Rebecca says. 'I swear to you, Wat, the people who have done this to you will pay for this transgression.'

'Mmmmm… mmmm!'

'Listen, Wat. We have to get out of here. Can you hear me? Is there anything you know?' She shakes him in desperation. Behind him the tapestry of Mary, the Holy Mother of God, stares at her mournfully, and Rebecca is glad for the company of another Jewish girl, no matter how many centuries dead.

She holds him by the shoulder. She tries to calm him down. She *knows* it's hopeless. She *knows* there's no way out. But still. The hope. And her fear for her girls.

Gradually the madman calms. Then he points, wordlessly, at the image behind him.

'What's there, Wat?' Rebecca says, fearing to let hope dawn yet.

'Mmmm… mmmmm!'

'The tapestry?'

'Mmmmm!'

He mimes digging. His eyes are round and there's fear in them. Could it really be this easy? she thinks.

She goes to the wall. Puts her hand on the stone. Moves it.

When it comes to the tapestry the wall gives. There is nothing behind it.

'Help me!' she tells the knight. Sir Richard hurries over. Together they push the heavy tapestry aside.

Beyond it is a dark hole, just large enough to squeeze through.

'You made this, Wat?'

'Mmmmm!'

'Where does it go!'

'Mmmmm!'

She looks at him. He starts screaming again, and he shakes his head, *No, no*.

'The voices in the dark,' Sir Richard says thoughtfully.

'What?'

'He said, the voices in the dark. What voices? Where?'

He sniffs the air.

'It reeks in there,' he says.

'We haven't got a choice.'

'It's nothing but a trap. Why would they let a prisoner dig out? Why would he stay?'

'I won't do *nothing*!' Rebecca says. She can feel the fury overtake her once again. 'Rabbi Tarfon, in his famous debate with Rabbi Akiva, argued that action is greater than study. While Rabbi Akiva argued that study is greater, for it leads to action. Well, I have studied the situation as it is and I am going to act, for that is the righteous choice. Are you coming?'

The knight stares at her.

'Who the *fuck* is Rabbi Akiva!' he says.

But he follows suit. Rebecca knew he would. This Dick's too dumb to be afraid, while she's too angry for the fear to take her. They make a likely pair. Together they go into the dark, behind the portrait of the Virgin Mary.

Into the dark, into the dark.

★

She squeezes through the hole. A space opens up. She creeps along it. Can hear the knight behind her. Reaches out, feels for the walls. Her fingers touch something sticky and warm.

She shudders.

A faint, dank smell. The ground feels uneven. An old smugglers' tunnel? She can't see. The ground slopes abruptly. She reaches for the walls for support and can't find any.

She slides and falls.

Hears the knight cursing in surprise behind her. She hits the wall and falls down painfully. The dank smell fills her nostrils. She lands hard and the knight lands on top of her.

'Get off me!' she says.

He swears. It's humid. She wipes sweat off her brow. She can't see a thing. That awful smell. She pushes to her feet. Stands still.

Where is she?

Something *worse* than the cells. That much was clear from the madman Wat's rambling. What else had he said?

The voices in the dark.

She listens hard, and at first there is nothing.

Then she can hear them. Faint at first, and then growing...

Languid, yet full of pain...

Help us...

Release us...

'Rebecca?' Sir Richard says.

'Yes, Dick?'

'I don't like this place at all.'

'Too late to go back...'

She takes a deep breath of dank underground air. Hot and humid and moist. She takes a careful step and her foot presses on something soft and hard at once. She holds her breath. She kneels down and searches for it blindly. Grasps it.

A hand. Five fingers, long – and as she holds it the hand *moves*, and grasps her own hand back, in prayer or supplication.

Help us...

'I will,' Rebecca whispers. 'I promise.'

The knight, Sir Richard, takes a step and stumbles, then he screams.

'There are bodies *everywhere*!'

'Calm down! Can you make a light?'

Sir Richard's gibbering, his hands fumble for a pouch.

He strikes a strike-a-light on flint and lights a charcloth. The fire burns for just a moment. In the sudden glare Rebecca *sees*:

A cavern dug into the rock, the ceiling high above her. The floor is hidden under dank black earth.

Buried in that fertile soil are bodies.

There must be dozens upon dozens planted there – she sees torsos sprouting with tiny, pale-white fungal growths, arms with their fingers mushrooming, ears with tiny studs of fruiting caps...

Eyes open in the darkness. Eyes myopic with mycelia. They stare at her. Sir Richard pukes upon the ground. The light is dead. The darkness falls and in its vastness she can hear the voices.

No wonder Wat's insane, she thinks.

'Olivia,' Sir Richard says.

'What?'

She can hear him breathing hard, in all that dark.

'There's a girl who went missing. Her father asked me. Her name is Olivia.'

He starts calling out the name, desperately. Rebecca wants to shut her ears.

But she cannot allow herself that path. Her girls! And so she steps with care over the writhing, helpless bodies, calling out gently. 'Rowena? Elgitha? Ulrica? Sue?'

Help us... the voices murmur in the dark. *Free us...*

'Olivia!' the knight screams. 'Olivia!'

'Keep it together, man!' Rebecca snaps. 'And make a light. Do you carry a candle?'

'Of course I—'

She can hear him fumbling in the dark.

She whispers, 'Elgita?'

They buried me in a shallow grave, and left me here to fruit; the rotting body finds a way to grow and put down roots.

Rebecca calls, 'Over here!'

The knight lights a flame. A candle stub gutters. The flame throws out shadows like dancers round a maypole. In the light Rebecca *sees*:

Elgitha, half a glistening white belly protruding out of the earth; Ulrica, arms entwined like branches pushing out of the ground; Dagger Deb with her back arched like a furrow and circles of mushrooms like dark spots on her flesh.

The knights came and took me away, and now my heart is slow; my blood is cold within my veins, they'll never let me go.

'I'm going to get you out of here,' Rebecca says. 'This I swear.'

She tries to dig. Elgitha's skin is soft and pliable. It's warm. There's no resistance in the soil, yet as Rebecca's fingers tear the tiny threads of fungus Elgitha screams.

Stop! Stop! For I have been bewitched and bound, and left here so I won't be found.

Rebecca stares helplessly. She hears the knight pacing agitatedly behind her.

'There's a door,' he says. 'But it's locked.'

The gardeners! The gardeners come! They shear us and they trim! The iron hurts us, then they leave, their baskets spilling from the brim.

'How many of them are there?' Rebecca murmurs. 'How can I *help* you!' She stares around her in frustration. There *has* to be a way!

How *do* you get rid of fungus?

She examines the buried bodies. Some, she can clearly see, have been in there too long. They are barely human anymore, have been transformed into hollowed-out husks, fed on too greedily by the fruiting mushrooms. But her girls have only just been planted. The threads holding them captive must still be fragile...

What kills fungus?

Help us... release us! the voices cry.

It's an *infection*, Rebecca thinks. So it must be treated as such. And what has the witch taught her about—

Ah.

'Olivia!' the knight says. Rebecca turns and sees him kneeling by a young woman with translucent skin. Her exposed belly protrudes out of the ground, glistening, and Rebecca realises with horror that she can see *inside* it, that something *moves* under the skin, a dark shape...

The knight recoils with grief and horror. The girl opens eyes that are no longer human and stares at him.

Olivia, it was my name, but I have since forgotten. Tell my parents that I loved them, but now my fruit is rotten.

And as Rebecca *stares*, the girl's belly *opens*, smoothly and without noise, and a grey cap grows out of it on a thin and delicate stalk. Sir Richard screams and the candle in his hand wobbles and falls and is extinguished—

Plunged into darkness, Rebecca doesn't have time to *think*.

She reaches blindly into her scrip. She hopes she still has it—

There!

The Mistress Byrne's regular monthly delivery of ointment for her lady parts.

A pox of the genitals, the witch called it.

An infection of fungus.

Rebecca has to pray it works. She's not sure who to pray to. She has to believe that ultimately, everything is a part of the natural world, and therefore by God's design. But Sophocles wrote, *Heaven never helps the men who will not act*, and Euripides said, *Try first by yourself, and only then call God*; and Rebecca's father said, *Just get on with it.*

So Rebecca gets on with it.

She unwraps the parcel and dips her fingers into the gooey ointment. She lifts up a healthy dose and hesitates, but only for a moment.

Then she plunges her fingers into the soil.

26

High on her perch above the Benedictine Priory of St. Nicholas the Wonderworker Birdie watches the castle. A roar of anguish – a roar of *rage* – erupts from deep under the foundations, and it seems to Birdie that Castle Rock itself is shaking.

All over the city dogs suddenly bark; cats hiss and dart for shelter; babies wake and cry. A blacksmith, working late in his foundry, stares in confusion as the solid hammer he holds in his hand melts furiously all of a sudden. In the bakery on Cedar Row the loaves of bread just fed into the oven sprout leaves that burn and turn to ash; out on the river bank a solitary drunk wakes up bewildered, for the fish leap out of the water in their fright, and as he blinks he thinks he sees a mermaid rising out of the Trent, roaring in savage delight.

Nature operates according to immutable laws. Babylonian astronomers studied the night skies and Greek mathematicians calculated the ratio of a circle's circumference to its diameter, which is always the same. Egyptian architects designed pyramids and Roman engineers built roads and mines, and in all of those things the immutable laws of nature remained exactly the same so that the value of pi was always 3.1415, and the pyramids stayed up and the mines operated mostly without burying people alive. And sailors navigated safely by the placement of the stars in the firmament.

All these things were true and as ordered. Who ordered them, and why, and if God then whose god, the one for the Jews or the one for the Christians or the one for the Saracens, or other gods entirely, like that bull-headed deity from vanished Babylon or the Titans of Greece or those numerous gods they have in distant India, no one truly knows, because they take it on faith, and faith isn't faith with a knowing.

When those laws are upset, people call it a miracle, but whether a miracle is an intervention by God, as some would define it, or built into the natural order, as Maimonides would have it, it has… repercussions.

Say, for instance, a bunch of natural philosophers, as you would have them, are hired by a no-longer-entirely-sane sheriff – say, the Sheriff of Nottingham, to use his full title – to develop what some would argue is a magical powder and others, less so inclined, might term simply a natural compound that evokes in its user a vivid and potentially uncomfortable daydream.

Say, then, you are a pretty desperate young Jewish woman named Rebecca, living in these turbulent times, and you are not exactly happy about this state of affairs and the predicament (dungeon, threat to life and limb, and so on) that you find yourself in.

Say you have a group of people infected with a particularly uncomfortable malaise – and then you plunge a handful of what, to them, is pretty lethal poison right into their… soil.

As it were.

What do you think *you'd* do, in the circumstance?

'Nighty night, fungus people,' Birdie whispers, and she smiles.

Across the night from Castle Rock, the castle of Nottingham, not quite sane, screams an agony in many voices.

*

Sir Richard at the Lee is on his hands and knees and praying like a *mother*fucker to any god that'll *have* him, to save him from this godless *shit*hole, and he does mean a *hole* in a very *literal* sense here, and Rebecca's willing him to shut the *fuck* up, and her hand's burning and the buried living-corpses scream in unison but she can't stop. She applies salve to Elgitha and then to Ulrica and all the rest, and it's working, she can tell, but it's causing them great pain, and some of the other ones, the ones planted the longest, wither and die right there and then, before her. She thinks they must all be connected somehow, under the soil. Tiny filaments linking them up, the way fairy-ring mushrooms all grow from one central location.

Elgitha's eyes open, and they're clear.

'Well?' she says, and Rebecca could sag with relief. 'Get us the fuck *out* of here!'

She grabs her arm. Rebecca *pulls* – Elgitha rises from the dirt.

'Let's pick some radishes,' she says.

They go around, helping the girls up. They have strange scars upon their bodies, tiny stitches from the things that held them in their thrall. The others are less fortunate. Sir Richard, praying still, kneels by the girl he called Olivia, but it is very obvious she's dead, and has been for some time.

'We can bury her later,' Rebecca tells him. 'We can bury them all. But first—'

There is the sound of running footsteps. Chainmail. Keys. Male voices cursing. The door.

The door!

It bursts open and the knights stream in.

The living girls scream.

'The shears! The rakes!'

'Fuck that,' Rebecca says. And, 'Get them!'

They are unarmed but it doesn't matter, not now, not as the pack of them run at the unholy gardeners like maddened things, seize weapons, hold them down, remove their helmets, bite and smash. Rebecca turns her head away. When she looks back there are just bodies on the ground and blood that soaks into that fertile earth, and Ulrica holding up a severed head.

'Let's make them dead,' she says. 'Let's paint the walls in pretty reds.'

They look to her, Rebecca realises. They look to her to lead. She steps over the dried husk of a corpse left in the ground too long. She steals outside. Her gang behind her. Sir Richard at the rear. The man's no use but he is harmless.

So she goes on.

'Well, bugger me,' the cook says, watching from the shadows.

A part of Birdie longs to join the mayhem in the castle. When she was younger her life was one long ballad told in song: swashbuckling adventures, hanging from the rafters, swinging on ropes, robbing the rich, giving to the poor. All that stuff. If childhood's a golden age then Birdie's memories are softly-coloured, sunshine-bright. The greens are greener and the red is redder as it spills from a man's heart. What fun they had!

But she grew up, and the forest didn't.

Hood's out there, watching events unfold. He has been slack. He's let the truce with the Sheriff of Nottingham hold for too long. Giving the sheriff time to lay his plans. He will owe favours over this one.

Birdie wants to stretch her wings and fly. Instead she folds her hands into submissive posture and prays for the salvation of the dead, and those who are about to die.

'Don't none of you pricks move!'

The girls have spread throughout the castle. They've gained weapons on the way. Rebecca bursts into the hall. The sheriff stands there, small and grey, his men around him.

Swords against swords. Crossbows against crossbows.

The sheriff smirks.

'You'd dare to threaten the king's man? Then you will hang. Lay down your weapons now and I shall be merciful.'

'You're insane.'

'Am I, Miss Rebecca? Or is it this place that's mad, and I'm the only sane one here! This is a giant shithole, and only mushrooms grow in shit. A man makes do with what he has to work with!'

Rebecca feels a tiny movement behind her. Sir Richard, with a crossbow in his hands. He takes a step. The archers and the knights turn on him but do not make a move – not yet.

Rebecca, unobtrusively, takes a step back.

'You're right,' Sir Richard says quietly.

'I am?'

'She cannot kill the king's man.'

'It's what I said!'

Rebecca sees a shadow darting in the corner. She looks. A green child. The child looks at her with guileless eyes. Blinks once.

'Fuck this shit,' Rebecca says. She takes a step back, and another. The girls all follow suit. They keep the crossbows on the knights until they're out of range.

And then they're gone.

My Lord Bishop,

I faced down the Sheriff of Nottingham and his men. They outnumbered me, of course. But I had your lordship's authority behind me, and therefore the king's, and therefore God's.

'Surrender willingly,' I said, 'and you will not be harmed. A quiet retirement somewhere. Wales, maybe.'

'Fuck Wales!' the sheriff said.

Strong words, I thought.

'You have no authority here!'

'Then order your men to shoot me,' I said. I looked to his knights. Your knights, my lord bishop.

'I serve under authority of Roger de Pont L'Évêque, Archbishop of York, who holds all power over this diocese. Step aside, and you will continue to serve. It is only the heart that is rotten. You are good men. Step aside!'

For a moment I thought I saw a green child in the shadows.

'Shoot him! Kill him!' the sheriff cried.

I waited. No one moved to act. All it takes, I thought, is a few good men.

'Then I will kill you myself!' the sheriff screamed. He drew his sword.

The green child in the shadows nodded to me, once, and then it vanished.

I pulled the trigger on the crossbow.

The arrow whistled through the air.

'Fucking Nott–' the sheriff started.

He burst softly into a cloud of grey spores.

They drifted through the air and lay like dandruff.

'Clean up this mess,' I told his men. 'A new sheriff will be appointed in due course.'

And then I left them to it.

My Lord Bishop,

I trust this news will reach you shortly, and that you are in good health. At your request I undertook an inquisition to Nottingham and Sherwood Forest. I concluded the woods are insignificant save for some local bandits, who need not concern you. That the newly appointed sheriff was involved in some low-level grift in the town, namely tax-evasion, which is sadly not unheard of. I have removed him from position and it is waiting to be filled. I trust our mutual business is concluded to your satisfaction, and that the debt is eased and my son can now go free.

I shall remain in Nottingham for some time, for despite its obvious backwoods qualities it is not without some charm, and I may retire here for a little while.

I remain, your most humble servant,

Sir Richard at the Lee

And that, Rebecca thinks, is *that*.

She watches Dick as he scribbles down the last few words and his signature, and then seals the packet of letters.

By the window the harpist, Alan-a-Dale, watches with an aloof smirk on his face, and Rebecca shoots him a warning glance.

'You will carry these true?'

'I will.' He sobers at her glance. 'Scarlett and I have other business in York besides.'

Richard hands the harpist the letters. The harpist nods.

'Hood sends his regards.'

With that he departs; and Rebecca and Richard are left on their own.

'So?' Rebecca says.

'It is done.'

'Yes. So?'

The knight shrugs. He looks about the place. Low wooden beams and dark wood counters, steps to the cellar, small windows. He says, 'I like it.'

'So we're in business?'

Richard brings out a vial of dwale and takes a sip. It brings the colour to his cheeks.

'I'll call it Dick's, I think,' he says. 'Everybody's gonna wanna come to a place called Dick's.'

'If you say so.'

'This could really be some place. Needs a clean, though. Put some cushions down, a handful of tables. And a band, at least an organ player. Someone to play, as time goes by.'

Rebecca shakes her head. The man's often exasperating. 'Keep up the monthly payments, straight split on the product, and you run point with de Grantmesnil,' she says. 'Keep it clean, keep it respectable, and keep the tax man out, and I think we'll do just fine.'

The knight smiles. 'Rebecca,' he says, 'I think this is the beginning of a beautiful friendship.'

Rebecca mutters something rude under her breath and leaves him to it.

She steps into the Gloomph and sees the harpist just vanish round the corner, heading out of town. She stops and smells the air. It's cooler now, and the fog comes down, and she can feel the wind change.

And she wonders which way it will blow.

PART SEVEN

THE BONE HARPIST

27

The fog parts as Alan-a-dale rides out of Sherwood, the bone harp on his back, the warm wind running fingers through his long, fine hair. The air smells of spring, and Al's fucking *delighted* to be out of the woods at last. Al's more of a city gent, if gent is the word you'd use to describe him. He is of short stature and light on his horse, a dun mare with little to recommend her.

A harpist does not tread *softly* on the earth. A harpist *harps*, a harpist *sings*, a harpist draws a *crowd*. A harpist such as him deserves a better class of horse, is what he's saying. The mare shits agreeably as she walks. She leaves a trail of crap. Al sighs. But everything that lives must shit, or it will die. He wonders if there's a song in that.

Dour Will Scarlett comes riding behind him. Will the Knife, Will o' the Wisp. A pox on Scarlett, Al thinks. He strums the harp.

'A pox on Will, a pox on Will, as an archer he has no skill, a pox on Will, a pox on Will, the ladies say he has a tiny bill.'

'Fuck you, Al,' Will says. 'You're a shitty harpist.' He spurs on his horse. Not a good rider, is Will Scarlett. But he catches up to Alan-a-dale – well, Al let him, didn't he. Not like he's going anywhere. He strums the harp.

'A pox on Will, a pox on Will,' Alan-a-dale sings pleasantly. The warm wind's in his hair and the air smells of spring. 'When he goes down he has to climb uphill, a pox on Will, a pox on Will, his dick got crushed in a water mill.'

'You're just sore because I killed that guy back in Arkham instead of you,' Will says. 'And I don't even count them anymore.'

'It was my kill,' Al says. 'My harp string whispered round his throat and as I pulled his windpipe whispered in leaked air its last ever word—'

'And I finished him off with the knife,' Will says. 'It was just a *job*, Al! A knife's quicker.'

'He was mine. I know them all. Fifty-seven men, eight women, two elves, three fairies, one Puckish thing that warbled and begged and fought like a mule before I killed him, five boggarts, one giant deep within the Hidden Wood where such as he still live, and one fucking beekeeper from Arkham what owed on the honey. And yet never the one I seek. Never him.'

'So do you count the beekeeper as fifty-eight?' Will says.

'What?'

'Is he included in the fifty-seven men you killed, or is he extra?'

'He is *disputed*!'

'I stopped counting in the Holy Land after a hundred or so Saracens,' Will says. 'Killed a bunch of other things there, too. You think elves are bad, you should see the horrors they have in the deep dark wells and shadowed caves beneath Jerusalem... *Old* bad shit. They worshipped gods there thousands of years before Woden ever took his first piss or Arawn grew fuzz on his balls.'

'You crusaders are all the same,' Will says. 'Always banging on about the war. I don't give a flying fuck for the Holy Land or Saracens or those things you keep carrying on about, what are they called—'

'Djinns,' Will says, and grimaces.

'Yeah, those. I have my own bounty to seek, another's head—'

'Yeah, yeah, Al, we've all heard of your *revenge*,' Will Scarlett says. 'A consummation most devoutly to be wished, I'm sure. And how goes it? Your quest? Any luck? Find trace of – what was his name again?'

'Brand. Leesome Brand. And when I find him, I will kill him,' Al says. It is a simple statement of fact. And he has said it a thousand times. He joined the hoods just so he could extend the quest. He did as the Hood wished, and sometimes they stole from the rich, and sometimes they gave to the poor, but it was all the same to Alan-a-dale. It was all the fucking same to him. He just wanted the man *found*!

But found he's not. Some sort of magic, maybe. The man has *protection*. So Al seeks. And Al works. But he is not like the rest of them, these burnt out crusaders, hiding in the hollow rotting heart of Sherwood like worms fearing their own inevitable extinction. The only one of them Al truly fears is the Green Lady, but he and Marian have an understanding.

'Oh, screw it, Will,' he says. He puts the bone harp away, pulls a small clay bottle of uisge beatha out of his cloak. He takes a deep long slug and shudders as the distilled alcohol hits. 'You want some?'

Warmth spreads through him. He hiccups.

'You hiccup like a girl,' Will says.

'Well, we all know how you feel about that,' Al says. He tosses him the bottle. Will Scarlett drinks.

'Shit Irish whiskey,' he says and wipes his lips.

'Good, ain't it? Now, let's ride.'

Al spurs his mare ahead with easy confidence. The mare trots and Will swears and tries to keep up. A waste of a horse on that man. They ride along the King's Road and no one knows their names.

It is spring, in this Year of Our Lord 1157. What with one thing and another his mission to York kept being postponed. First there had been the whole sorry business with the sheriff. But there was always something between Robin and the sheriff. It was like a story repeatedly being told.

Then there was a murder in the market square. A horribly mutilated corpse of some Norman trader passing through. People whispered they saw a scarecrow-like figure running past. But people should know when to keep their fucking mouths shut.

Then there was that job for Robin in nearby Arkham, and that beekeeper who wouldn't pay up the tithe. A kill that Alan claims, but still. The beekeeper struggled and when he did he kicked over the beehives and they swarmed – they fucking *swarmed*! They barely harmed Will the Knife but he, Al, was stung half to death, and it took weeks to recuperate in the deep healing mud of the Green Place. Which he did not like to do. He did not like going too deep into the Green Lady's domain. Her mud healed, but her mud… *changed* you. Al was not going to buy into the whole Robin and Marian thing. He didn't give a toss for Fairyland either. He hated being that close to the demarcation line. Deep in, you could still hear Herne and the Wild Hunt. You could still see giants' footsteps in the ground. And there were still *trolls*.

But never the one man Al is seeking. Never Leesome Brand.

So with one thing and another it's now spring, and word is the Queen Consort is heavy with yet another child. If it's a boy, and if it lives, they will name him Richard. It's spring, and the road goes past and the wind is warm and the flowers bloom. At night he and Will take shelter with peasants in their villages, and pay for their supper with song and displays. Al sings to them of the legend of Robin, this knight of the forest, this champion of the poor. They lap it up, of course, the poor saps. Robin, the Liberator. Robin, the Great Archer. Robin, Robin, Robin. A tossbag in a hood. But Al sings his legend all the same. He sings of Maid Marian, and of their love, and of the evil Sheriff of Nottingham, and the peasants cheer and share their bread and mead. Then Will steps up, performs his feats of knife-throwing. It's poor fare but it saves them coin, and coin they need, for the hoods in the woods spend loot faster than they earn it, and now the merchants through the forest come with armed escorts, courtesy of the king. Not that there is much to steal, in any case. And Al's sick of venison in mushroom sauce.

So he and Will traverse the distance to York. They arrive one early morning outside the city gates.

You can smell York before you see it. It stinks. Rotting offal and overflowing cesspits. It's worse in spring. He can hear the church bells ringing. There is money in York, there is money and power, and traders come along the river Ouse from Hull. Fellows from the Continent, trading to the ports of Bruges and Hamburg and Rouen. The Normandy lords may rule merry ol' England, but traders have no loyalty but to the coin. And kings are always poor and seek to tax them, and some of the rat bastards will do anything to avoid paying duty. Will never shuts up about it, does he? Listen to him and you'd think the whole on-going conflict in the Holy Land was just about, well, *profit*.

Though Al has to admit some people *did* get very rich out of it. And didn't Melisende and her brat Baldwin grow rich as farts out of the Kingdom of Jerusalem? Alan-a-dale doesn't pay much attention to events outside, or even to the passage of time much, being as he is ensconced too long in the Green Place, where time moves differently, but hadn't they just had a long protracted civil war between mother and son, only recently reconciled? Well, who gives a fuck.

'Let's go see the lepers,' he says.

'I hate lepers,' Will says.

'You *are* a fucking leper,' Al says.

'Your wit is matched only by your beauty,' Will says. He sighs. 'Lepers it is, then,' he says.

They do not enter the city proper but follow the walls to the leper hospital. St. Nicholas's sits on the other side of the walls from the city. This is the other thing about York: it's full of fucking hospitals. But no one likes a leper, so they've been stuck out here and the Sheriff of York makes sure to keep them there. They're well looked after, anyway. And it's not like they don't get out regardless...

Lepers are everywhere. The sickness transmits in some mysterious way. Lepers beget lepers, and thus transformed from healthy to sick human beings, and slowly rotting, they have no choice but to shuffle their miserable way across the land, chased from place to place, begging for their lives and food, relying on the Christian charity of strangers.

Lepers, in other words, see and hear *everything*.

'Hello, hello!' a voice says cheerfully as they step in. The gardens here are pleasant, and men and women clad in simple brown robes tend to the flowers. A man materialises before Al and Will. 'You bring greetings from the forest, friends?'

'Hello, Carter,' Will says. Carter grins at them. He has good teeth, but only half a nose, and one eye's hidden under folds of growths. 'You're still here, then?'

'Will the Knife and the bone harpist,' Carter says. 'You bring me anything?'

'You have anything we need?'

'Depends what your lordship needs, doesn't it?' Carter says. 'What would his lordship care for? Gold? Myrrh? Frankincense? Or just my foot up your arse, boy?'

Will sighs. He rubs the bridge of his nose. 'Somewhere we can talk quietly?' he says.

'Sure. Follow me, your lordship.'

'Oh, for fuck's sake, Carter—'

Alan-a-dale laughs. He takes his harp. He plucks the strings. The sound is sweet. 'I shall write you a ballad one day, Carter,' he says. 'To the greatest pickpocket and con artist who ever lived!'

'Oh, please,' Carter says, 'you flatter me. But there's the king and all his knights and sheriffs, the pope in Rome and all his cheats and scammers, bishops and archbishops to a man, and there's your Robin of the Hood, too, bone harpist. I am but a dabbling amateur.'

'You think Robin's a fake?' Al says, taken aback.

The leper looks at him askance with his one good eye. 'Don't you?'

'Well, yes, but...'

Carter smiles. 'You think because I preach the green sedition I cannot see its source is false? The man is but a man, and fallible. But the truth's the truth, no matter whence it comes from. Though we should not speak of it so openly here.'

'What I've been saying...' Will murmurs.

'Come.'

Carter takes them to a shaded pergola done in the Roman style. It's cold in the shade but at least they are alone.

'Well?' Will the Knife demands.

'Two, three converts last month I sent your way. Did you receive them?'

Al tries to think. There are always people coming and going from the Major Oak. At any one time there are a hundred, two hundred in the wood, in that enchanted party that never ends, where the fairies play their music and the air is scented with perfume stronger than opium. He shrugs.

'Maybe?'

'Well, you should check before you ask, then!' Carter snaps. 'It's dangerous work, preaching sedition. The villeins are ready to rise against the king. Not just here. Normandy, too. Maybe not today, maybe not tomorrow. But the time will come when people have had enough. We are little more than slaves, and the landowners are masters. Land cannot be *owned*! Land is communal, it belongs to all!'

'I see...' Al murmurs. He hides a yawn. 'You have a silver tongue, Carter. You should have been a bishop.'

'I might have been, were it not for my affliction. And my convictions, of course. Only a revolution—'

'Please,' Al says. 'We are not your audience, we are your pay-masters. Speaking of silver – how much do you need this time?'

'As much as can be spared.'

'Will?'

'Here.' Will tosses the leper a bag full of coins. 'From Robin. Keep up the good work, and so on.'

'Not because of you, but despite you,' Carter says. 'You're outlaws – you're parasitic on this earth as much as Henry is upon his throne. But I will do the work and if they throw me in the Tower of London still I will preach to my jailers.'

'You will preach to the rats in the cells,' Al says. 'Come on, Carter. I have my own coin, if you have what I need.'

But Carter shakes his head. 'Of Brand I have heard not a whisper. I am sorry.'

'Very well.' Al tosses him a piece of gold. Greek, he thinks. The fairies like to look for coins in streams and meadows, those of them who are still around. They seem to find attachment in the coins to older, better days. Better days for *them*, anyway. They still had more than a wispy presence when the Romans built the roads and put up York and London. That mad-eyed prophet from Galilee was merely a whisper and a crucifixion back then.

'Keep looking,' Al says.

'I will,' the leper promises.

They speak, but not much more is said and then they part ways, their mission done. It doesn't do to be seen together for too long and draw attention.

There are such men as Carter in every major town across England. In Normandy and Paris, too. Rabble-rousers, firebrands, simple men, those who rose from the dirt, who grew up villeins, who say, This isn't fair. We should not slave.

They foment a rebellion, they counsel uprising. In France and elsewhere peasants do rise up from time to time against their masters, but the king and his knights are ruthless and efficient in putting down any such unrest. And God help Carter if they catch him, for he'd never see inside the Tower. It would be the hangman's noose for him, that or a shallow grave. But then that would be *their* fate, too, the merry men of Sherwood.

But Al thinks, At least we're *outlaws*. He doesn't give a toss for peasants and their problems and he doesn't give a shit about the king. He only cares for Alan-a-dale. Alan-a-dale and his long-delayed and justified revenge.

He and Will enter York through a side gate and are not challenged.

'Where to now?' Al says.

'You to deliver the letters,' Will says. 'And I to where my fancy awaits.'

'We all know where your fancy lies...' Al says.

Will gives him a wink and strides off. Grey robe over forest green, he goes undisturbed.

'Asshole...' Al mutters. Then he wends his way through the crowds, to York Minster.

28

'You're not a monk,' the bishop says accusingly.

'I never said I was.'

'This letter from Sir Richard says he is entrusting correspondence to a monk.'

'Perhaps he was mistaken.'

'I hate monks,' the bishop says.

'Who doesn't?'

The bishop drums his fingers on the desk. He's short and running to fat, but there is muscle underneath. He is a high-born Norman, from Pont-l'Évêque, and thus knows swords and archery and horses. He pours a glass and drinks – red wine. He doesn't offer it to Al.

'Is all in order, sir?'

'His seal's unbroken. Tell me, you have met my inquisitor?'

'Only briefly.'

'This situation in Nottingham…'

'My lord?'

'All well there and so on?'

'Of course.'

'Despite losing two of my sheriffs?'

Al shrugs. 'It is a violent world, my lord,' he says. 'And yet one worth living in.'

'You are the harpist, yes? Alan-a-dale. I've heard tale of you before.'

'Oh?' Al is suddenly uncomfortable.

The bishop smiles. 'Come, sit,' he says.

'My lord, my business here's concluded—'

'Pish-posh. Come have a drink.' Archbishop Roger relaxes in his chair. Al sits glumly. And now a second cup does materialise, and the bishop himself pours him the wine.

Interesting.

'This is a load of cock and bull, this story, isn't it?' the bishop says, gesturing to the letters.

'My lord?'

'Come, come. I do not mind. Tell Hood to keep our bargain and pay the tithe. I will appoint a new sheriff who is less... prone to infection. As it were. You see, Alan-a-dale, I am a man of peace. And peace is hard to come by in this place and in this time. We've only just come out of a civil war. Kings and their bishops mean *stability*. And *peace* means—'

'Profit?'

The bishop smiles. 'There's profit in war, too,' he says. 'But peace is cleaner.'

'You make a compelling argument,' Al mutters. What *does* the bishop want?

Roger leans close. 'I heard your tale,' he says. 'It is a tragic one.'

'My lord, I—'

'Is this the famous bone harp? May I see it?'

'No one may touch it but myself.'

'I understand. Perhaps—'

Al removes the harp and holds it in his lap. He strums the strings, but softly. Their lovely sound fills the bishop's office.

'Your sister, I believe,' the bishop murmurs.

'Yes.'

'Her bones?'

'I fashioned it myself.'

'The strings?'

'Her hair. Her beautiful hair...'

Al strokes the strings. The sound is mournful.

'You found her dead, lying by the stream. A tragic tale...'

'So many tales are tragic, bishop.'

'Indeed, indeed. And the murderer? This... what's his name?'

'Brand. Leesome Brand. She was heavy with child, my sister. His child. He murdered both and so I'll murder him.'

The bishop looks at Al curiously. 'I heard as much,' he says.

'My lord?'

'I heard you tighten strings.'

The bishop mimics the whisper of a garrotte. He pulls his fists and makes a face.

There is a silence now between them.

'You hear a lot.'

'I have many friends, Alan-a-dale. It is good to have friends.'

Al is mute.

The bishop mulls an unvoiced proposition. He sips his wine. 'Drink, drink,' he says.

Al sips. The wine is good. Though he prefers the Irish whiskey to this Norman shit.

'Tell me,' the bishop says. 'You are a green man, yes?'

'My lord?'

Roger waves his podgy fingers. 'Relax. You're not on trial. I like a merry man from time to time myself. I guess what I am driving at here, harpist, is whether you're *exclusive*. You serve the Hood?'

'I serve no man!'

The bishop leans back. The bishop smiles. 'Good, good,' he says. He steeples fingers. 'So you could, hypothetically speaking, take on *commissions*?'

Al sips wine. Al sits back. Al looks at the bishop with new sight.

'What,' he says cautiously, 'did you have in mind?'

Thus begins a relationship, if one may call it that. *I heard you tighten strings*. There is no contract written, for all that the bishop's man, one fellow Vacarius, as he styles himself, is an expert on Roman law. A keen legal mind, in fact, and helping to codify the laws of the land, and so on. But this venture between Roger and Al is one without seal and without codicils.

'He owes me on a deal,' the bishop tells Al, that first time. 'One of them lot, if you know what I mean. A slippery character, and I'm short on good men to take care of it.'

'What sort of a deal?'

'Gold. That's his specialty.'

One of *them* lot. No wonder the bishop had asked him.

'It will cost you,' Al says.

'Then bill me. And a tenth share of whatever you recover.'

'What is his name and where can I find him?'

'They call him the skin man. He's in the skin trade. And he moves around. Word is he has a lair deep in the woods somewhere. But no one's ever seen it, or come away alive at least, to tell the tale.'

'I understand,' Alan-a-dale says. And he begins to.

'There are woods and there are *woods*,' he says.

'Yes,' the bishop says, and that's all there is to it. Roger of York tosses Alan-a-dale a bag of coins. 'Expenses and such,' he says. 'Consider it an advance. And the rest on delivery.'

'As the archbishop wishes.'

'I do wish. I hate those fucking things. But I'm not a fanatic, harpist. Not like that cunt Becket. Let peace be, I say. As long as I get paid.'

'And you didn't get paid.'

'One too many times, harpist. So make an example, will you?'

Al nods. He rises to leave.

'And harpist?'

'Yeah?'

'This is just between you and me.'

'Of course.'

'Your Hood, he's tight with them.'

Al shrugs. 'The Hood's the Hood.'

'And this is *my* manor,' the bishop says.

Al goes looking for Will. He knows where to find him. The Knife has a thing for women in male bodies. Al asks around. He's good at asking questions. He has an easy smile and a harp made out of his dead sister's bones. People tend to talk when they see him.

He tracks Will the Knife to a house near the city wall. He hops nimbly over dead pigs' carcasses, past tanning shops where hides hang taut, past blacksmiths' workshops where hammers ring on iron anvils and fires bellow in the forge. He walks past St. Leonard's Hospital and too many churches and too many crosses, though he sees here and there, hidden in plain sight, etched into wood and stone, the green face of the forest. There are hoods here, too, just as Carter's promised.

He finds Will at the house. He can smell the river nearby. Alan-a-dale waits for the door to open. The occupier of the house opens the door for him. They're half-dressed in a hurry, a woman's shift and smooth rouged cheeks.

'Will's in?'

The occupier nods. They look at Al, and something like recognition passes between them.

'Come in.'

Al follows. Will totters into the room.

'I'm going out of town for a little while,' Al says.

'Alright. You want me to wait for you?'

'You look like you're in no hurry,' Al says. 'Wait a few days. If I don't come back, go without me. I can wipe my own ass.'

'So you claim. Is that it, then?'

'No.' Al turns to Will's companion. 'I am looking for the skin man,' he says.

'What makes you think I know anything?' – but they turn pale under the rouge.

'A hunch.'

'I don't know anything.'

'You know who he deals with?'

'There's a brothel by the docks. So they say. Run by an excommunicated priest. Look for the sign of the cock. They say he brings them girls from time to time. He tricks them, offers them spun gold. It's that or he turns nasty. Why do you look for him?'

'I have a question to ask him.'

And that is that. Alan-a-dale leaves them to it. He goes to the docks, passes the Jewish Quarter where Mistress Rebecca's relatives all live. The river docks smell, unsurprisingly, of shit. Small boats bob in the water. Porters carry wooden barrels. A freeman barks orders. Alan-a-dale looks this way and that. Narrow streets feed off the docks and vanish into dark corners. He gets lost a couple of times. Once, a gang of youths with iron knives attempt to jump him. Al snarls and whacks the nearest boy with the harp and bone smacks against bone and the boy's blood jets out. Al laughs as the boy screams. He punches him in the neck and stomps when the boy's down. His nose, his fingers, his groin.

'You want a piece of me?' he says. He stands over the boy glaring at the others. 'You want a piece of me?'

They flee from him. Al kneels beside the boy. He sticks a knife in the boy's neck.

'Fifty-nine,' he says.

Then he leaves him there with the rest of the rubbish.

He finds the brothel under the sign of the cock. Alan-a-dale puts on his gloves. He goes in quietly. The sounds of rutting behind a wall. The light is dim; only a candle burns. Five figures sitting around in various states of undress, and one man drinking cider at a wooden table.

'Room'll be free in a moment,' the man says without looking up. 'If you'd like to wait.'

As if on cue the lovemaking, if you can call it that, ceases abruptly.

'It's Bargain Tuesday so I'll do you a deal,' the man says. 'Girl and a sheath and a drink all included for just a little bit extra, what do you say?'

'It isn't Tuesday, Cuthbert,' one of the girls says.

'No?' the man says. He still hasn't looked up. 'Then what day is it?'

'How the fuck should I know?'

The harp string's between the harpist's hands then. It whispers as it loops around the brothel-keeper's neck. Al *pulls* – the man grunts. He kicks the table. Al puts his weight against the chair and pulls as the man slowly subsides, and then there's a silence.

'What day *is* it, Ethel, do you know?'

'Fucked if I know, Audrey.'

The customer comes out of the room then. He's fat and naked. He sees what's there to see.

He says, 'What the fuck—'

Al's knife whistles through the air. The customer falls. A naked girl comes behind him. She steps over the corpse. Goes to the table. Pours a drink.

'I think it's Friday,' she says.

Ethel frowns. 'That can't be right,' she says. 'It was Friday last week.'

'Ladies—' Al says.

'You're a fucking lady!' Ethel says, and Audrey and the others laugh.

'Ladies! I'm looking for the skin man.'

They fall quiet then.

'He got me when the local knight decided to make me his wife, and I had lost all hope,' Ethel says. 'I swore then I would give anything to get out of it.'

'He got *me* when my mother fell ill. I swore and cursed that I would do anything to save her.'

'He got me—'

'He got me—'

'Where can I find him?' Alan-a-dale says gently.

'In the hills—'

'By the stream—'

'In the shadow of bad dreams—'

'He has a cottage in the wood beside the moors, mister,' Audrey says, and the others fall silent and stare at her.

'What?' she says. 'I saw it one day, walking. He didn't know I was there, but I saw it.'

'You be careful, mister,' Ethel says. 'Them that live in the woods you got to watch out for.'

'I live in the woods,' Al tells her.

'Yeah? And how is it?' Ethel says.

'It's shit,' Al says.

Ethel shrugs. 'Try doing *this* for a living,' she says.

Al nods to her and then withdraws.

He thinks, Sixty-one.

Clouds amass in the darkening sky as Alan-a-dale makes his way across the moors. One can get lost here, in this open expanse, miles and miles of low-lying shrubs. It's easy to vanish on the moors and never be seen again. It's where the bodies are buried, in their shallow graves. Al tracks. He finds strange objects on the ground: flint tools ancient beyond recall, their edges still sharp enough to skin a deer. He pockets one of the flint knives. He finds shards of ancient pottery. He finds an arrowhead. He comes across a stone circle and carefully goes around it. Those places are still dangerous, even now. Holes punched into the world by ancient people when the land of Faery was still easily within reach. Now the word of Jesus spreads out from the Holy Land to the shores of Britain, burning as hot as the sun in that distant place, and it burns away the remnants of the old world; it drives its denizens into the shadows.

And yet and still, he gives the stone circle a wide berth. He tracks across the moors as sun falls and moon rises. The moonlight casts an old bewitchment on the moors. At night the things of darkness are most active. It is almost with relief that Al reaches the woods. He goes within. Hears laughter follow in his steps, the faint sound of music and dancing, and he knows the elves are awake in their endless carousing.

He goes deeper into the woods. But these are not like Sherwood. The ancient forest heart is hidden deeper here, the trees spread out more, the moonlight shines down on moss and snails and cobwebs. People come here often. The truth is, people have always fought against the woods, ever since the first human set foot on this land. They cut down trees and burnt them. They turned ancient wood to farmland. There is something in humans that fundamentally hates the woods and the darkness they hold.

Al tracks.

Al reaches a dale. Al crosses a stream.

Al sees a stone cottage. A fire burns outside.

A small dark shape dances round the flames. It sings as it hops. It turns meat over the coals.

'Tonight, tonight, my plans I make, tomorrow, tomorrow, the baby I take!' the figure cackles. 'Ooh, tasty roasty baby waybe!'

Alan-a-dale steals closer in the dark. Alan-a-dale plucks a string from his harp. The taut string sings in his hands. Al steals closer. He jumps—

The figure whirls. In the light of the flames Al can see him – it – properly for the first time.

A small, thin gnome with eyes like a snake's. A nose carved into a deeply lined old face. The creature opens its mouth. Its teeth are pointed and sharp. It says: 'Riddle me this! Riddle me that!'

It lashes at Al. It's small but it's mean. Al curses. He takes a step back.

'Sneak on me?' the skin man says. 'Sneak on *me*? This is *my* manor, you son of a bitch!'

Al holds his hands up placatingly. 'No offence meant. Just wanted a word.'

'A word?' The skin man's eyes glitter. 'You search for a deal?'

'If you have what I need.'

'And what is it you need, pretty one?' the skin man cackles. 'A bit of this?' He grabs hold of his groin.

'I am searching for someone,' Al says.

'Oh?'

'Tell me his whereabouts and I will spare your life.'

The skin man gloats at him. 'This isn't how it works!' he screams. 'I take, I do not give!'

'The name I'm after,' Al says, 'is Brand.'

'Leesome Brand?' the skin man says. 'Stolen by fairies and cursed to bring death and misfortune to all he loved? You mean that one?'

'I do.'

'Never heard of him.'

Al sighs. 'Too bad,' he says. He brings out his knife.

'You can't kill me,' the skin man says. 'I cannot *die*, exactly. What's this, anyway? Cold iron? Think you can scare me with cold iron?'

'You look pretty scared to me.'

'No, I don't!' the creature screams. He gloats at Al. 'Besides, you cannot kill me if you don't know my name. Only by speaking my name can you kill me, and nobody knows what my name—'

Al yawns.

Al says, 'Rumpelstiltskin.'

The creature stares at him in horror.

'How did you *know*!' the creature screeches. The sound is like nails driven into wood, it is the sound of the fury and the agony. 'How could you tell!'

'Listen, shitbag,' Al says. 'You really don't get it, do you? *Everyone* knows. *Everyone's* heard the tale. Every shitty harpist between here and Aberdeen sings the ballad. You're just like the rest of them. Obso-fucking-lete. You may as well roll over and die. You're a fucking *story*. Nothing more. And stories are bullshit.'

'Fuck you, harpist!' the creature screams.

Then he jumps Al.

Alan-a-dale fucking *hates* fighting fae creatures. Rumpelstiltskin lashes at him with long awful nails. Al ducks, Al kicks, and Rumpelstiltskin goes flying into the flames. He screeches in fury and hate. 'If I don't kill you, Leesome Brand will!' he says. 'Or any of the others!'

'I'm sick of fucking fairy tales,' Al says, and he takes a run at Rumpelstiltskin. They roll on the ground and the creature's knee hits Al's groin and Al grunts but doesn't let go and his fingers close around the creature's neck and *squeeze*, his thumbs pressing on the creature's windpipe, and Rumpelstiltskin chokes, his eyes are open fully and are bloodshot, and then he opens his mouth and pukes bile and blood all over Al's face.

Al lets go with a scream. He jumps back; the creature's bloodied bile burns his eyes and his face. He feels around blindly. Rumpelstiltskin laughs wildly. Al feels heat and turns desperately and the hot poker the creature wields just misses his face. He has to *see*!

He tries to clear his eyes. The poker hits him in the back and Al screams as the metal sears his skin. He kicks blindly and connects. Rumpelstiltskin swears at him in a language Al doesn't know. Al wipes mucus and blood off his eyes.

He blinks.

He can half-see through the pain. Rumpelstiltskin is an indistinct shadow, creeping up on him, a hideous grin on his face. Al stills. He thinks of a tune, but all he can come up with is 'Greensleeves'. He stills. His sister comes to his mind, not the way he'd found her but the way she was in life. She is smiling. She holds her arms out to him.

'Sister,' he says. 'Sister.'

The creature, this skin man, is almost upon him. Al reaches

for a weapon, finds the ancient flint knife he kept. It fits into his hand. The creature leaps upon him. Al falls.

Rumpelstiltskin crouches on top of him. His arm is raised, his claws ready for the final swipe to cut this impetuous harpist's neck once and for all. But he must gloat first, as is his nature and his undoing.

'You cannot kill me, fool!' the creature says. 'No man can kill Rumpelstiltskin!'

Al is still. His breath is even. He counts a beat. The flint knife's heavy in his palm. He brings it up in one wide arc and slices through the creature's throat.

Al rises.

Rumpelstiltskin falls.

Rumpelstiltskin stares at Al in horrified incomprehension. Blood bubbles out of his mouth, stains his lips red.

'Never said I was a man,' Al says tiredly. She reaches behind and unknots her hair and lets it fall, and she thinks, *This is so stupid*! But these sorts of fairy stories have their own fucked-up rules.

'It's just a matter of speech, for fuck's sake,' Rumpelstiltskin says. How can he speak when his throat's cut open? 'Man, woman, you're all the same to us you stupid broad. Oh, fuck it.'

He kicks the earth. The earth splits open. Al takes a few steps back. The hole gets bigger. Eldritch light shines from down below. Rumpelstiltskin crawls into the grave.

'I'll be back,' he croaks, 'one way or another. No one... puts... Rumpelstiltskin in the corner—Oh, fuck!'

He tumbles down with a final scream.

Al stares down the hole. She shakes her head tiredly.

'What a dick,' she says.

29

lanah spends all that winter and the next searching for Leesome Brand but no one is talking. Her sister's murderer has vanished into mists even she is unable to part. That autumn a boy is born to Eleanor of Aquitaine in Oxford, and they name him Richard. And Alanah remembers her sister, with whom she had been so close. As children they never parted, yet growing up her sister fell under the spell of that fae boy, and that took her away from Alanah, away and to her doom. Now Alanah dons the green of hoods and as a man she travels the kingdom, searching, always searching for revenge. The quest took her to Robin and the Lady Marian of the Green. Oh, Robin didn't see through her disguise, for men see only that they wish to see. But Marian was different and she knew Alanah's heart, and Robin liked her music, and they offered their protection in exchange for services rendered.

Alanah stayed. She figured Brand was hiding in the Summer Country. She crossed the demarcation line more than once between the real world and that of legend, and it was hairy there: the Fair Folk, it was well known, played dirty. But she survived.

Yet never did she hear word of her quarry. And so she kept on looking, donning man's disguise and singing bullshit ballads about Robin's bravery and feats – it was that or fucking 'Greensleeves'.

It is 1159 and spring, and Al dons men's clothes and their manners, and he escorts Mistress Rebecca to York where her kin are. Rebecca looks much the same as she ever did. The dwale trade is booming and what's grown in the forest gets processed and sent on the boats down the Trent or the Ouse to the Continent. It's all done underhand so the taxman is blind to it. But what the taxman doesn't see cannot hurt him, Rebecca says. And besides, don't her people raise enough cash for the king?

Al doesn't disagree, but it does mean Rebecca needs protection. She carries a knife at all times and two of her maidens accompany her wherever she goes, and if anyone tries to change terms or squeal then it's the last thing they do. What is it the old crusaders say? Never rat on your friends, always keep your mouth shut. Meanwhile in the Holy Land the second crusade ended badly for the combined forces of the West and more returning soldiers swell the ranks of Robin's merry men in Sherwood, just like that fraud, Sir Richard at the Lee, who's taken permanent residence in Nottingham. And to make matters worse, in Rome, Pope Adrian, being the only Englishman ever to sit upon the papal throne, died from choking on a fly. A bad omen if ever there was one, Al thinks. Now a new pope, Alexander III, is slugging it out with an antipope, Victor IV, and it is not at all clear who will emerge victorious. Nor is it very easy keeping up with all this shit. All Al knows is that he's not yet found his quarry. And so he tries again.

'No word, I'm afraid,' Archbishop Roger tells him over spiced wine in his office. 'A fine tangle of a mystery you've handed me, Alan-a-dale. Your sister's killer's hidden well. He must have powerful protection.'

'Yes.'

'But not from me. Or any in the Church.'

'The king? The court?'

The bishop shakes his head. 'No earthly court...' he says. The implication's clear.

'How do you keep abreast of the doings of abominations?' Al asks, genuinely curious.

'I beg your pardon?' the bishop says; he looks taken aback.

'Goblins and gobbledygooks. This pagan stuff.'

The bishop smiles. 'It is an old, established pattern of the Church,' he says, 'from its earliest days. We come in where pagan priests erect their temples to their pagan gods. We reason. We speak word of the Christ. It is the word of truth and so, in time, the people are converted. Then we build our churches on the old places, where old power lies. The old gods fade away. In time the bogey men become little more than whimpers. You know, the Romans did much the same with their own gods. It is remarkably effective as a policy.'

'Perhaps in time a new religion will arise to claim your own, then,' Al says. He can't help it. 'And build their temples where your churches used to be.'

'You're quite impetuous, Alan,' the bishop says. 'Besides, we have more than reason. We have swords.'

'So do the Saracens.'

'Yes, their methods are... regrettable. But we'll defeat them. We're bound to. No, Alan. Humanity always has a need to believe. The only thing that could destroy the Church in the end of days is reason. When people think they know how the world works, its rules, its *mechanism*, perhaps they'll see no more need for God. I do imagine it sometimes: standing in silent reverence inside an empty church, one long-abandoned, the roof open to the rain. Weeds growing in the cracks, and parchment with the holy word upon it curling, ruined, in a sacristy. I have felt this more than once, in pagan temples fallen out of use. I meet those of the other side there, to conduct our business. They are the dead but do not know it yet, and so I am amicable to trade with them. Take this fellow Rumpelstiltskin, for example. He promised me much, spinning straw into gold. I should have known better. The transmutation of the elements is a thing no natural philosopher has yet succeeded to achieve, nor work of an *automatos* nature, without the need for human hands and labour. Though imagine if a spinner device could be invented, to do our labour on our behalf. But I don't know why I tell you all this, harpist. I've had a few cups of this wine... I have a job for you.'

'A job?' Alan says.

'Another one of... those.'

'I see.'

'His name's Wayland. He's a smith. Half-Viking. Been around these parts forever. Likes drinking beer from human skulls and fucking swan maidens, all that shit. He owes me on some bespoke rings I ordered. Can you take care of him?'

Al says, 'He sounds... tricky.'

'He's old and really not half as deadly as he thinks he is.'

'It seems extreme over some rings, my lord.'

'In the name of our Lord, harpist, do not test me. Do you want the job or not?'

'I suppose.'

In truth, Al has no taste for it. But he needs money for his quest, and this smith, besides, might have some answers. It is the hope that keeps him going. So he nods.

'Alright.'

'Good lad. Here, have a drink.'

'Where can I find him?' Alan says.

The bishop lolls in his chair. His eyes are closed. His mouth gapes.

'Where the moon meets the horizon, there his furnace burns...' he says. Then he starts to snore.

Alan sighs.

Alan departs York Minster.

Out on the moors and in the quiet places of the world she can be herself. Sometimes Alanah thinks of leading a more conventional life. Leaving the revenge business entirely. But what would she *do*? She has no conception anymore of life beyond reaching her goal. Beyond killing Brand. Sometimes she thinks it is the only thing that gives her life purpose. She tries not to think what will happen when it is finally done. Where would she go? Who would she be?

And her sense of time keeps going… awry. In the Green Place time moves differently. For instance, she is not sure she has aged more than a year outside, though so much time has passed since her sister's murder that surely Alanah must be old by now? Every year the leaves fall in autumn and the flowers bloom in spring and the sun rises and falls, and these things blend into a single long year in her memory. She's not even sure how old Maid Marian truly is. When was she born? Stories of her and the elfin knight go back *centuries*.

For instance, Alanah's pretty sure she's left York in winter of 1159. Yet now only a moment's passed, and she is standing in the snow outside a chapel near a place called Booze, and inside there's singing, and the residents of that lonely place welcome in the new Year of Our Lord, 1162.

How can that be? Alanah shakes her head, dispelling this bewitchment under which she's lived for far too long. No. She is feeling melancholic, here on the edge of winter. She lets her rage suffuse her instead, and it burns away the years and the uncertainty.

She has a *purpose*. She is *whole*.

She leaves the singers to their song and follows moonlight as it cuts through land. She hikes alone along the snow. She reaches the place where the moon meets the horizon.

And there it is, much as the bishop said. She hears the bellowing of a hammer and sees unearthly lights and flames, some of which are as hot as the sun and some as cold as the moon, and she knows it is Wayland's foundry. She creeps close, searching for protection both magical and more mundane, but there is nothing, and his door is open.

Her shadow falls across the threshold.

'Come in, come in. It's cold outside. You've come to kill me?'

He stands by the furnace. He is a monstrous thing. Naked to the waist, with bulging muscles. His head is bald, one eye is white, his chest is intensively scarred. He has good teeth.

'I'm just making a ring,' he tells her. 'Rings of power, that's all anyone ever wants. They're useless, really. Real power is something you take, it's something you keep. You don't need magic for it. You just need to be ruthless, and there's no shortage of ruthless bastards in this world. I'm Wayland, by the way. But you knew that. And I believe you are the bone harpist.'

'My name is Alanah.' She sees no need for subterfuge, not here.

'You sing for Robin?' He looks at her in curiosity with that one good eye. 'I would have liked to hear you sing.'

'They sing of you,' she says.

He laughs. 'Aye, that they do.'

'A pretty vicious story.'

'Aren't they all?' he says. He shrugs. 'I am what people sing of me. Would you care for a drink?'

He leaves the furnace. Goes to a bench. He has some of that good Irish whiskey, Alanah sees with appreciation. Wayland pours generously, into two emptied skulls. He walks over to her. Up close he radiates heat. He hands her a skull. She takes a sip.

'Friends of yours?' she says.

He shrugs again. 'The dead are nobody's friends. They're just dead.'

'How profound.' She says it with distaste and he laughs.

'So what will it be?' he says. 'The knife? The sword? The garrotte? I heard you tighten strings.'

They clink mugs. Or skulls. 'They say you murdered your brothers,' she says. 'This them?'

'Ancient history, bone harpist. So what will it be? Fists? Staffs? A fucking staring contest?'

'You're kind of a big lad,' Alanah says. 'Not sure I could take you, to be honest.'

He looks at her curiously. 'But you'd try.'

'It's what I'm paid to do.'

'Paid by who, the Archbishop of York? Roger's not a bad man, you know, for all his many sins. A sinner's better than a saint. It's the other one you've got to watch out for. That Becket. He burns with true belief, and that faith will either end the world or him.'

'You seem knowledgeable, Wayland the Smith, which is strange out here in the shithole of nowhere.'

He smiles at her, but it's a tired smile, and she notices how lined his face is, and how discomfiting his stare. His single eye glares balefully.

'I fly,' he says, 'hither and yon. And I have a little of the touch of future vision.'

'Oh, yeah? Does it tell you how tonight will end?'

He sighs. 'It does. And I do appreciate us having this civil conversation before the inevitable bloodletting.'

'My blood or yours?'

He smiles at her. 'Only one way to find out, isn't there.'

Alanah contemplates him. He's a strange one, this Wayland. She says, 'Do you know where Leesome Brand is hiding?'

'He is hidden by magic,' the smith tells her. 'Which is no easy thing in this day and age. Somewhere in Fairyland – but you knew that already.'

'Who is hiding him?'

'Better ask, who has the power?' the smith says. 'Find them and you shall find your quarry.'

'Don't you think I've *tried*?'

'I am not sure that you want to. What will you do if your mission succeeds? Once he is dead? Will you know peace? I was like you when I was younger. I killed my brothers and those they loved. And what did it avail me? Here I am at the end of my days, striking rings for a greedy bishop. What will remain of me when I am gone?'

Alanah laughs. 'A ballad.'

'Yes,' he says, quite seriously. He nods his head. 'I hope the tune is nice.'

'Nice tunes and ugly stories,' Alanah says. The harp string's hidden in her palm. 'So tell me of the future, what bits of it you see.'

'I see Thomas Becket consecrated as Archbishop of Canterbury,' he tells her. 'Which will not please your master one bit. He is currently the most powerful man in the Church, and therefore second only to the king in power.'

Alanah yawns. 'Is that all?'

'I see a baby born far away from here, in the desert lands of the Mongols, a child born with a clot of blood clutched in his hand. He will grow to be the most fearsome warrior the world has yet seen. I see fire, belching. I see smoke. I see rivers run with blood and burning libraries and men on horses sweeping across the world...'

He falls silent and turns his back on her, staring into the flames.

The harp string's taut between Alanah's hands. It whispers as she leaps and wraps it round the smith's neck. She pulls. It's over so quickly – he doesn't put up a fight at all. His body drops to its knees and then he topples sideways. She kneels over him, breathing hard.

He wanted it, she realises.

Fuck it. Fuck him. She'll sing his ballad, like all the rest. All those stupid fucking ballads. She takes the rings and all the rest of it. A rusted magic sword. A carpet that might have flown once. A lance covered in blood, and some sort of a grail. Useless shit, but it should make the bishop happy.

Why is he so tight with Fairyland palookas? Though all Alanah does is execute them on Bishop Roger's behalf. But still. He deals with them.

She walks away under the silver moon, leaving the foundry burning behind her. She traverses through mists and when she comes out the other end it's 1164 and two more years have passed.

30

I t is a cold winter January when Alan-a-dale makes his way to Clarendon Palace, accompanying the Archbishop of York and his dour clerk Vacarius. Snow flurries from the skies. The horses whinny softly. Vacarius says, 'We must take the king's side, my lord.'

The bishop sputters. 'The man seeks to withdraw power from the Church!'

'Power we accrued by stealth,' Vacarius says. 'Using the weakened power of the king during the anarchy of civil war. A stronger king means stronger civil courts.'

'Absurd! I will not hear of it!' Roger says.

'My lord... the Bishop of Canterbury will take that position. Thomas Becket is not a flexible man.'

'And I shall back him on it,' Roger says, but he looks less certain now, and Vacarius sees it.

'Let him weave the rope that pulls him by the neck,' he says. 'The king is *here*. The pope is far in Rome.'

'I do not like it, Vacarius. The Church holds legal power we are ill-advised to give up. Imagine a priest commits murder! In current circumstances he will be tried in *our* court and be let off with a warning, at the most defrocked. You wish to give power over *us* to the royal court, where the sentence is death? It would be a massacre of priests!'

Vacarius smiles sourly, for he is not a man given to smiles, not often nor well. 'Do you hear yourself, my lord? How many murderous priests do you have in your employ?'

'More than enough, Vacarius. And they are under *my* protection.'

Vacarius shrugs. 'In this battle you will not be victorious.'

Al tries to follow all this but it's hard. The Church harbours many a man who is happy to steal or murder, partial to adultery and whoring, fond of a drink and a fight. But they *are*, as far as Al understands it, under the protection of the Church, and the Church is lenient. King Henry wants to chip away at the Church's power. And grow his own. Well, Al can understand *that*, at least.

'On the *other* hand...' the bishop says musingly.

'My lord?'

'Becket's too powerful now. Fuck Canterbury! York should be in the ascendant.'

'Indeed, my lord...' Vacarius murmurs.

'This could be good for *me*.'

'Is what I was saying, my lord.'

'Yes, yes, Vacarius. Don't be such a smarmy know-it-all.'

'Of course, my lord.'

'We shall weather this storm,' the bishop decides. 'And see which way the wind is blowing. And other such nautical things. Are they nautical? I fucking hate boats.'

'My lord?'

'Never mind. Pass me some of that good whiskey.'

'My lord.'

Al listens to them go on. The bishop and his clerk lay plans Al doesn't care about. He's here as simple bodyguard. They reach the palace at last, a royal hunting lodge. Dogs bark. Armed men patrol. Smoke rises from cooking fires. Venison, of course. *Legal* venison, for all the deer in the forest are reserved for the king, and to steal them is a crime. The sort of crime Robin's so fond of. Is that how they'll remember him? Al wonders. A simple poacher? In truth he isn't that much more than that. The Merry

Men are haunted fellows, forgotten soldiers from some war conducted far away in a hot, dusty land. Nobody gives a shit about returning soldiers. So they hide in the woods and hunt the king's deer and make boasts about it.

Al's beginning to find the whole idea of *real* power kind of attractive. They're led inside. The bishop's ushered to his ample quarters. Al's given a spot on the floor. He's to sleep by the door and watch the bishop's back.

What is the bishop so scared of?

Al escorts the bishop to the hall. And there's King Henry, in his early thirties, not so much handsome as... is that what power feels like? He greets Roger quietly, with warmth. So this is the King of England? Al's never been this close to a king before.

'You brought a harpist?' the king says. 'Will he sing for us tonight?'

Al bows. 'With pleasure, Your Majesty.'

The king smiles. 'Good, good! I love a song.'

They are dismissed.

The bishop hisses, 'See that man the king is speaking to?'

'Yes. In the robes?'

'That's Becket.'

'He doesn't look like much,' Al says.

'Oh, but he *is*,' the bishop says. 'That's what makes him so dangerous.'

For just one moment, the Archbishop of Canterbury's gaze falls on them. It holds Al's eyes. There's a coldness there, Al thinks. She shivers, for Becket seems to see deep inside into the real her. His lips curl in contempt. Then his eyes leave her and Alan-a-dale takes a deep shuddering breath and regains his composure.

'Who do you think wants to kill you?' he asks Roger.

'Who doesn't?' The bishop waves a hand. 'But here is where the real vipers gather. Power is dangerous, bone harpist. You play with it out in the woods and think it means something, but real power... it's the shit that gets done quietly in rooms like this, over dinner and good wine. Speaking of which, where's my cup?'

Al watches them at dinner. The king and his bishops, the venison and the wine. He watches the king's knights. These men have power by the sword and proximity to their lord, and that gives them land, and land gives them power over everyone upon that land. They're sanctioned murderers, but there's the thing – it is the sanction that makes it right, under the eye of God and king. And the hoods in the woods are unsanctioned.

He knows Will and his like want a revolution. The peasants rising all as one and slaughtering the land lords and claiming freedom. But the bishop is right. Real power's hidden behind table manners and the clinking of cups, in rooms such as these.

And this meeting is all *about* power. The power the Church has. The power the king wants.

Alan-a-dale sings them his ballads after dinner. The king seems enchanted, Roger drunk, Thomas Becket contemptuous. Al sings them the 'The Elfin Knight' and 'The Twa Sisters', 'A Gest of Robyn Hode' and 'Leesome Brand'.

A small boy comes unnoticed into the hall. He passes to the king, who sits him on his knees, and together they listen to Alan-a-dale singing. As the last notes of the bone harp fade, the boy claps delightedly, and his father says, 'Now, now, Richard.'

One of the king's brats. Alan takes a bow and fades into the shadows.

No one tries to assassinate the Archbishop of York during that long meeting, in which the king's demands are all met and a series of Constitutions are ratified. Power is taken from one place and passed to another. But Al can see this Thomas Becket doesn't like it. He speaks quietly with Roger, and he says, 'This shall not pass.'

'Do not place us all in danger,' Roger tells him.

'I do as God tells me.'

'Then go with God,' Roger says.

This way they part, the two archbishops. And the most powerful men in England go their separate ways once again.

Winter, summer, winter, spring, the years go past like candle stubs and leaves. What year is it? Thomas Becket's in exile. The king, in high dudgeon, threatens all who aid him. Becket in turn threatens the king with excommunication. Roger de Pont L'Évêque, Archbishop of York, grows fat on his coffers, their contents extracted from his large domain. There's still no new sheriff in Nottingham. Mistress Rebecca runs dwale. Sir Richard at the Lee's establishment, Dick's, grows ever more opulent, and dream-eaters come from all over to sample its unearthly delights.

Time passes, as time is wont to do. But not for hoods. Not for Alanah, not for Rebecca, not for the Lady of the Green. Will the Knife and Much the miller's son and all the rest remain much as they were. Time is different for them.

And Alanah's running out of excuses or options.

She knows where she must go, but every time she tries to cross the demarcation line into what remains of Fairyland, she's thwarted. Will-o'-the-wisps lead her astray. Spectral hounds bar her way. Ladies in White spook her and elfin knights hunt her and ravens caw overhead in contempt. They keep her in the twilit zone between one world and the next. All she is good for is singing songs and killing revenants.

Winter, summer, winter, spring. The years fly past. A new child is born to the king. They name him John. Alanah retrieves a strange glass slipper for the bishop and dispatches its former wearer back to the nether realm of make-believe. The pope is briefly arrested by soldiers of the antipope and is forced to leave Rome. The Vizier of Fustat, afraid the city will fall to the crusaders, sets the capital of Egypt on fire. It burns for fifty-four days. The new vizier of Egypt is named, one Saladin.

Winter, summer, winter, spring.

'He's back,' the bishop says.

'Who's back?'

Al's bored. He drinks too much these days.

'Becket's back.'

'Ah.'

'The cunt excommunicated me!'

'I heard.'

'Me and the other bishops crowned Henry the Young King as heir apparent. Becket thinks only Canterbury can do that.'

'Yes.'

'Fuck him.'

'Yes.'

'He thinks he's a fucking *saint*!' the bishop explodes. Not literally. In Egypt when they burnt Fustat the vizier placed ten thousand lighting bombs throughout the city, fed by lethal naphtha. Al tries to think of all that awesome, deadly power the Saracens have. Such weaponry would make a bone harp and its harpist irrelevant.

'The king's not happy.'

'No.'

'You know what he said?'

'How would I—I mean, what did he say, my lord?'

'He said, "Will no one rid me of this turbulent priest?" That's what he said.'

'So?'

'Don't you get it, harpist?' the bishop says. He makes a cutting motion with his hand across his neck.

'*Oh*,' Al says.

'I want you to go to Canterbury,' the bishop says.

'Like fuck!' Al says. 'I'm not murdering an archbishop!'

'That part's… taken care of,' the bishop says. 'I just want you there to make sure there are no mistakes. A guarantee, as it were. Do that for me, harpist, and I will give you what it is you want most. I will give you your sister's killer.'

'*How*?' Al says. He breathes heavily.

'Becket has enemies in more than one realm,' the bishop says. 'He wants the old ways gone for good and only the one true faith to remain. Well, that will happen sooner or later anyway. You all just live on borrowed time. Why hasten it? Rid me of that turbulent cunt, and the way to Brand will be open to you. This I promise.'

What does he mean by *you all*? But Alan-a-dale's not got time for wonderings. He nods. The harp string coils around his fist, as soft as silken hair.

'Then it is done,' he says.

'Good, good,' the bishop says. 'Now fuck off, then, bone harpist.'

And so it is that in December of that year, 1170 by the count of the Church, and using the calendar system first began by Julius Caesar decades before the Christ was even a whisper in his mother's womb, the bone harpist Alan-a-dale travels alone to the city of Canterbury, another place first built by Romans and since gone to shit.

Its cathedral's a magnificent place, though, at least if you're into the whole architectural thing. Which Alanah really isn't. She leaves her horse inside the city walls and goes on foot, quietly, through flurries of snow. It's December, only just past the solstice, and the city's dark. It's two days to the death of the old year and the birth of the new, but the old year's not the only thing about to die.

Alanah climbs a grassy knoll covered in snow. She can hear them praying inside the cathedral. She only observes. She is only here in case something goes wrong. And she doesn't really care one way or the other about any of this. It's just another job.

She watches as the four knights approach the cathedral. They stash their weapons under a nearby tree and place cloaks over their chainmail armour to hide them.

An execution squad if ever she'd seen one.

The knights steal inside. Alanah steals closer. She can hear an argument inside. She catches the words 'the king', 'Winchester', and 'No'.

The knights come back. They look determined. They're ugly motherfuckers, every one. They grab their stashed weapons. They rush back inside.

Alanah hears shouts now. 'Where is Thomas Becket, traitor to the king and country?' someone screams. She hears running.

She steals inside. She hears more shouts. She flattens herself against the wall as the knights run past her. She goes to look.

She finds him by the stairs. They'd bashed his brains in. Blood and grey matter are scattered over the floor. Someone says softly, 'He will not get up again.'

So it is done.

She goes away from there. She thinks of what the hoods do in the woods and what the king had just enacted. She's seen death before but not like this. Despite everything it shakes her.

Outside the snow still falls. The knights are gone. The night is cold. Alanah finds her horse. She rides out of town. She thinks, Bishop Roger's bad luck.

Well, she can tell him it is done. She rides away across the threshold of the old year. The bells ring out.

Alanah wonders what the new year will bring.

PART EIGHT

THE WITCH

31

'**D**eath and penance, rot and ruin!' the witch shrieks.
The witch is dying.

Rebecca sits by the witch's bedside. Weak rain patters outside. A cold draught in the room, and a fire burning. It is hot and cold inside at once. The witch cackles with glee. 'Oh, the Irish are really in for it now!' she says.

What does she see? Rebecca wonders. The king's invaded Ireland, taken Dublin for himself, and offered the local chiefs protection if they serve him. That's what a king does; that's what a king *is*. The piggy with the biggest gang who all the other piggies with the smaller gangs must listen to. They don't call themselves piggies, of course. They call themselves nobles, and their gangs are knights, and their turf is measured by land and castles. But it all comes down to the same thing. As much as you can hold by force. And the king holds all.

Or, well, he tries to. In truth King Henry isn't shit when it comes to real power out there in the world. There's Saladin in Egypt, the Abbasids in Baghdad – fuck. There's the whole of Byzantium, standing tall for a thousand years. And that's before you go farther, to Cathay or India, where they could shit the whole of England and Normandy for breakfast and not even notice as they wipe it away. But still. King Henry's a big fish in a small pond. So he invades an even smaller pond, the next island along – though an island's really the *opposite* of a pond, if you stop and think about it – and tries to run the same old scam on the Irish. It won't end well with the Irish, though, Rebecca thinks. It never does. If it will ever end at all.

And then there's Wales, holding on to independence. Owain Gwynedd's dead, and now Rhys ap Gruffydd's agreed to negotiate with Henry. They do not like each other much, what with Henry imprisoning Rhys and generally fucking with him for a while before Rhys and Owain joined forces and took back their lands, but – oh, who *gives* a fuck? The lordlings, as always, fight for control of the land.

And meanwhile the hoods are in the woods and the sun rises and falls and the witch, the witch is dying.

'I don't want you to die,' Rebecca says. 'I *need* you.'

The witch stares her with eyes like hellfire pits buried in a face that looks now like a depleted quarry, filled with deep grooves and scars.

'Like fuck you do!' the witch says without mercy. 'You screwed me over any chance you got, Rebecca.'

Rebecca feels heat come to her cheeks. She inches her head in silent acknowledgement.

The witch says, 'I took you in and taught you. I tried to give you *wisdom*. Instead what did you do?'

Rebecca doesn't answer.

'What did you do!'

Rebecca flinches. But there is no escaping the witch's clear gaze.

'I stole your recipe for dwale to help the sick and sold it instead for profit. I struck a bargain with the Hood and the Green Lady. I traded with the wood. I killed… I killed those who opposed me. I could have had powers, I could have had *magic*! But now I am a lady. Now they bow to me as I pass. Now they do as I say. My operation extends to London and York and to the Continent itself. You can't begrudge me that!'

The witch howls with laughter. 'Fool!' she says. 'Magic is bullshit. It's nothing. Maybe it was something once, when the cook was a queen in Fairyland and Woden bellowed upon this earth but even then, I suspect, it was nothing more than old men rattling bones. Fuck magic! I taught you healing, you stupid, selfish cunt. I taught you how to deliver a baby and how to terminate a pregnancy, how to salve a wound and how to ease a suffering. I do this not because I'm powerful, for I am not, I am without power. I do it not for profit, for I am poor – I own not a thing upon this earth but my curiosity. I do it because the world isn't just, and the world isn't fair, and yet it could be. I do it because the world is cruel, and the creatures who inhabit it are crueller, and yet there is some good in us. I do it because...'

She subsides, coughing. The coughs wrack her tiny body. Rebecca holds her hand. The witch's fingers are dry. She feels light as a feather.

'I do it because someone has to,' the witch says.

She closes her eyes.

'Let me die,' she whispers.

Rebecca blinks. The witch's shape blurs behind Rebecca's tears.

'I can't,' she says.

She strokes the witch's hair until the witch stills; until the witch sleeps.

How many years have passed since her coup? Fifteen? She realises this with some surprise. The years don't show on Rebecca. When she looks in a mirror, she sees the same young girl she was. Perhaps the eyes are harder. Perhaps there is a line or two. But otherwise she is the same.

She doesn't want to end up like the witch. *Old*. Broken. Her face twisted beyond all recognition by time, her bones brittle and weak, her fingers stiff with arthritis, her body shrunken. Rebecca knows what she's done. Any illusions she may have held were gone once she executed those two men who stole from her. She could not go it alone. Not in Nottingham. Not in this time.

So she went to the Hood.

Now she hesitates. She looks at herself in her fancy new mirror, bought and delivered at great expense. She twists her hair into a bun. She sticks her comb to hold it. The comb is finely wrought, and metal, and its prongs are sharp. She straightens her clothes. She wears not a woman's garments but the green of the woods. She smiles at her mirror-self. She pulls up the green hood.

She slips into the night.

These streets are hers. They're still with magic. The cobblestones glint in the dim light of torches after the rain. Rebecca moves swiftly through the town. She passes Dick's, and the secret Night Market, but doesn't go down. Not tonight. She follows the path to St. Nick's. She goes to the back gate, to the vegetable garden. She knocks three times.

The gate open. The small figure stands mute.

'Come on, Birdie, it's time.'

'Miss Becca.'

The small monk hesitates. The years weigh her down.

'Come on, Birdie,' Rebecca coaxes.

Birdie steps over the threshold. She stands outside and shivers.

'I need you, Birdie,' Rebecca says. 'Show me the way.'

'Yes, Miss Becca.'

Birdie's voice is high and sweet. And still she hesitates. She looks longingly to the skies.

'Please,' Rebecca says.

The small monk's shoulder's fall. She takes Rebecca's hand in hers.

'Come,' she says.

Birdie leads, and Rebecca follows.

There's no other way into the wood. Not even for Rebecca. She traded the cook's protection for love long ago, and now the wood is dark to her, and so it shall remain forever. But not for Birdie. Never for Birdie.

The little monk steps confidently through the dark, through the field, through the forest gate, faster now, faster, a guiding light in the darkness of Sherwood. Into the woods, and Rebecca hesitates there on the threshold of the trees. She doesn't like going in here. Not anymore.

Once she'd thought it hopelessly *romantic*. She'd dreamt of going where the bonfire burnt. She'd dreamt of elves and fairies dancing, of will-o'-the-wisps lighting the way. She'd dreamt of magic and enchantment.

She was a fool. The witch was right. The witch was usually right. And spilt blood had cleared Rebecca of illusions.

Now all she sees is a dark, dismal forest. Mud on the ground. Branches rustling, birds cawing. A frog croaks nearby. She smells dying and dead things. She shudders. But Birdie's hand is strong in hers and she won't let go. Birdie would never abandon her here. Birdie, who loved flying.

Birdie, who found Christ.

Brother Birdie.

'Come,' Birdie says shyly. And she leads Rebecca deeper and deeper into the dark forest.

Rebecca fucking *hates* coming here.

But this is Sherwood; and this is where you go when you have nowhere else to turn.

Sherwood's the place for people who have run out of options.

Though she still has a couple, so it's not exactly true in her case.

She just really, *really* doesn't want to try them.

She can hear it before she sees it. Harps and pipes, laughter, talk. The endless dance. The fairies' fireside festivities. The Green Gathering. The hobgoblin's hobnobbing. Troll's Shindig. The get-together of gnomes. Jack's jolly jig. And so on.

She steps in something soft and disgusting and hurries on after Birdie. If only she were to let go, she knows what would happen. The sound of merriment would fade away and she would find herself alone here in this forest, which is no longer quite a part of the real, solid world. It would be dark, and cold, and awful in the way that woods are awful when it's night-time.

And then they'd come for her.

But Birdie keeps her safe and anchored. Birdie pulls her past the threshold, and soon Rebecca beholds the bonfire burning and the Major Oak, and the dancers dancing and the musicians playing and somewhere to the side there's an archery competition – there always is. Arrows whistle past and Rebecca tries not to look at the target, tied to a tree too far away to make out clearly. The latest plaything of the hoods, someone who didn't pay when he was asked.

Birdie leads her to the Hood. He sits upon his wooden throne and he is so immobile that she wonders if he's planted roots. How long has he been there? She remembers uneasily something the witch told her once: that there's always been a Hood in these woods.

'Ah, Rebecca,' the Hood says. She tries to make out his face but it is cowled, it always is. She wonders if he's young or old. She wonders if he's even human anymore. Behind him stands Maid Marian. The May Queen. The Green Lady. Her hand rests lightly on her man's shoulder. Her eyes are sharp, her smile is kind.

'Hello, Birdie,' she says.

'Mother.'

'You brought your little friend. How nice.'

'Miss Becca has a boon to ask.'

'A boon? Of us?' The Hood laughs. 'Not again!' he says theatrically.

Everyone laughs. They always laugh at his shitty jokes.

'Can we speak privately?' Rebecca says. Tamping down the hatred she feels rising inside her. Her fingers itch for her knife. She'd cut his fucking throat, she thinks, the way you cut a tree, and watch his sap drip down.

The Hood gestures. The music stops abruptly and the dancers fade away and there's just the four of them now, the Hood and his lady, Rebecca and Birdie.

'What is it, Jewess?' the Hood says. 'We have an agreement.

You stick to the town. You pay the toll and you keep business clean. So why do you come to me? If you are not useful to me anymore, the black pool will welcome your bones, I am sure.'

'So kind,' Rebecca says. But she is not talking to *him*. She talks to the Green Lady.

She says, 'The witch is dying.'

Maid Marian nods.

'So I have heard,' she says. There's such compassion in her voice that it's beguiling. And though Rebecca knows it is enchantment, nevertheless she *is* enchanted. Knowing and feeling are not the same thing.

'I wish... I wish to save her.'

She pushes the words out with difficulty.

Hates asking the favour. Hates knowing the price.

Showing weakness.

Showing weakness to *them*.

But doing it nevertheless.

Doing it for love.

'Save her, child?' Maid Marian says. 'How can you save a life when life is finite? All things must end.'

'She is important to me,' Rebecca says. Insists. To have come all this way, to have *asked*, when the asking costs so much, only to be rebuffed? She swallows bile.

'Who is this witch?' the Hood says idly. He looks bored. 'Remind me. Is she important in any way?'

Maid Marian murmurs words in his ears. The Hood shrugs.

Rebecca says, 'She is important to *me*.'

Holds back tears.

The Hood shrugs. 'You are not important,' he tells her mercilessly. 'This is my story, not yours. The ballads they sing are of Robin Hood, not of some Jewess in Nottingham or of some dying hedge witch who carried out abortions. So fuck off, Mistress Rebecca. Fuck off back to town, and keep running your little scheme, and keep paying my tax. I am a lenient man, so I will let you pass unharmed out of my wood. I steal from the rich, I give to the poor. Hated by the bad, loved by the good. I am Hood.'

You're a cunt, is what you are, Rebecca thinks but doesn't say. She looks to the Green Lady instead.

'Please?' she says. She hates the sound of her voice. She hates the word. The memory of this single utterance will haunt her dreams.

But the Green Lady shakes her head sadly. She steps from the dais and her hand brushes Rebecca's hair. She is so kind and understanding.

'The witch has lived a long eventful life,' she tells Rebecca. 'Let her be.'

'But we... but you... we do not age,' Rebecca blurts.

'All stories come to an end,' Maid Marian says. 'Even this one.' She strokes her one more time. 'Now go, my child,' she says.

And with that her audience is done. The music comes flooding back, and the eternal dancers swing and turn beneath the canopy of oak. Birdie takes Rebecca's hand.

'Come,' she says simply.

Rebecca, defeated, lets Birdie lead her away from the Green Place.

32

'Let me die…' the witch begs. The witch is a bundle of rags and bone on the bed. The fire burns ferociously. Rebecca has paid for the wood. She mixes dwale into soup in a bowl.

'Eat,' she begs.

'Let. Me. Die!' the witch says.

'I can't.'

'What do you *want* from me?' the witch says. 'Is it love? Fuck love! Rebecca, you were my apprentice, a disappointing one at that. You chose your path. In the river you swim in, time flows slower, but it flows all the same. Let go of your past. Cut me loose.'

'I'm Jewish,' Rebecca says. 'We're not good at letting go of the past.'

The witch sighs. 'It hurts,' she says.

'Eat.'

'No.'

But still, Rebecca tries.

'No, no, no!' Mrs More-Goose says. She bangs her spoon against the black-stained pot. 'Are you out of your mind, girlie?'

'I thought you might—'

The cook mimics her mockingly. 'I thought you might…

I thought you might! Well you thought wrong, Rebecca of Nottingham. You could have been somebody. I could have made you *queen*! But you chose love and now you, what, you choose love still? Love is a weakness. And the witch…' She softens suddenly. 'The witch knows the score,' she says. 'What is it that you envision, anyhow, exactly?'

'If she were to be taken into Fairyland,' Rebecca starts, and the cook laughs uproariously and bangs the spoon on the metal some more. 'If she were taken deep enough within, where time flows differently, then might she not live? I heard tale of a house in the wood where time has stopped, and the Unseemly Court still hold their sway.'

'Well, you heard wrong!' the cook says. 'Doesn't anyone ever get it? Fairyland's just make-believe. The half-dreams and daymares of humans, ill-defined, filled with shadow, populated with every and all manner of strange creatures that do not exist. Would you have her go *there*? She would be a prisoner inside a miserable illusion. She'd live, if you can call it that… Would you wish that on her, Rebecca?'

'I don't know what I wish,' Rebeca says. 'I want the witch to live.'

The cook appraises her. She holds the spoon up like a mirror. 'You've grown, since we last spoke,' she says.

'Yes.'

'You are more confident in what you want. You know how to take things, now. A useful quality.'

'Yes.'

'You've spilt blood. You've made your mark. And yet you're still afraid of death?'

'I…'

'That makes you weak. The strong survive because they do not care enough. They have no fear of death. Look to the men – they are too dumb to be afraid. It makes them useful.'

'You will refuse me?' Rebecca says.

The cook sighs. 'Once I had such power…' she says. 'Back in

the golden days of yesteryear I would have made a lovely pet of you, and taken you into the deepest wood, the first wood, which has always been and will always be. I would have made a plaything out of you and you would have delighted me and all my guests.'

She farts. For a moment she had seemed almost queenly.

'My sisters are scattered, and I am stuck here tending to the last of us. We're dying by the day... Have you seen the bone harpist recently?'

The question throws Rebecca off. 'Alan-a-dale? Not for some time. What of him?'

But the cook waves the question away. 'He'll turn up,' she mutters. 'Anyway, the answer's no.'

'But—'

'*No*,' the cook says; and somehow her shadow grows then, and so does her stature, and for a moment Rebecca does see her as an older and more terrifying being, of great viciousness and beauty combined, and she takes a step back and almost flees. Then the illusion, if that's what it was, is gone, and the cook stands there and wipes a damp strand of hair from her face.

Rebecca inches her head in acceptance; if not yet defeat.

She walks away. But the castle she walks through, she realises, is not yet the castle as it is but the castle as it rises on the other side; beyond the demarcation line, as it were. It must have been the close proximity to the cook that created the effect. And she does not have an amulet for protection anymore.

The corridors lengthen. The ceiling vanishes and overhead she sees the strange constellations that rise over Fairyland. The Swift and the Gibbet, the Tax Collector, the Honeycomb and the Door Into Air. The air smells strange, it's tinged metallic, and the flowers that grow underfoot are far too large, their petals violet and crimson, and their heads follow Rebecca as she walks. A creature like a cross between a lizard and a toad burps at her, its eyes bright and malevolent. Rebecca hurries her steps, but the corridors twist, turn, and a beat echoes through the walls of the bewitched castle, like a giant bell being struck somewhere far away: *thrum... thrum...*

Something bright green slithers underfoot and hisses at her. A raven watches her hungrily from the branch of an apple tree, and three carrion crows circle in the sky.

And it *is* sort of impressive, for a while. But even still – the more she looks the more she can see the holes that poke through the scenery. The drab, ordinary world lies just beyond. If she focuses enough she can just about make it out: an old portrait of King Stephen on the wall, hung with a crooked nail; a mouse sticking its head out of a hole; a half-gnawed chicken bone dropped on the floor.

Fairyland can no longer be *maintained*. It weakens. And yet still its glamour lingers, and Rebecca, witnessing the sky above her with its alien stars, hears the distant and eternal music of the festivities of fairies; and she wonders if it will ever truly vanish, or whether Fairyland will linger still, for centuries more to come, to haunt unwary travellers, those who still fall under the spell of magic and imaginings.

She steps at last out of the castle and finds that she is by the stables. A horse neighs softly and nuzzles her face, surprising her, and she laughs and strokes its long face before she notices the horn the creature has protruding from its forehead.

Her breath catches, and she watches the unicorns of the Unseemly Court's stables as they mill in the enchanted silver moonlight. The same unicorn nuzzles her face again and Rebecca can't help but laugh in childish delight.

'She likes you,' a voice says. A small figure unfurls itself out of the darkness and steps into the moonlight, holding a rope in its hand.

And it's another surprise for Rebecca. She takes a step back as she notices the handsome, boyish face, the familiar voice, the easy smile—

'*Much*?' she says.

He reaches out to her. All she has to do is take his hand.

'But how?' she says.

'This is the Summer Country, Bex. And everything is possible.'

'No, no,' Rebecca says. 'I saw you, when you came back from the woods. What they had done to you.' She conjures up his image: a woodland creature, scarecrow like, with arms like branches and finger-shoots like knives...

'You killed the sheriff...' she whispers.

He shrugs carelessly. 'There'll be another one along in no time,' he says. 'There always is. Come. I missed you.' He reaches for her. 'Take my hand,' he says.

She wants to, she so *wants* to!

She says, 'I *saw* you. And you didn't speak. You had no mouth anymore. And you still haunt the night in Nottingham, they say. Bodies are found, early in the morning. Chest punctured, throat slashed. They say the Scarecrow did it. And they say, it's Much, the Miller's Son.'

'And you believe it?' He laughs. The unicorn nuzzles Rebecca's face. Much is so handsome and *young*. And Rebecca realises it has been fifteen years since she last saw him in this way. Much hops onto the unicorn's back, so nimbly. He stretches out his hand.

'Come, live with me and be my love, and we shall all the pleasures prove!'

And she wants to, she so *wants* to, and she reaches out her hand without thinking, and she sees his eyes, but they are not Much's eyes at all but some cat-like stare, cunning and calculating, laughing at her. He makes a lunge for her but she snaps away her hand and the thing on the unicorn roars in anger, and its face twists and it is no longer the illusion of the boy she loved so long ago.

'Then fuck you!' it roars. The unicorn rears up on its hind legs and that deadly horn flashes in the moonlight, and Rebecca flinches before she turns to face rider and beast both. She raises her arms.

'You're nothing but cheap paint and sawdust!' Rebecca screams. The unicorn's figure shudders and grows transparent and the rider's face changes from the thing it had become to Much's and then to Isaac's, her father who died two years past, and then it becomes nothing at all.

Hands clap. Rebecca turns. She sees the cook standing by the stable door. The stables hold nothing but ordinary horses now; and Rebecca sees with relief the usual Gloomph above Nottingham.

'You would have made a lovely pet, a lovely pet,' the cook says sadly. 'A waste, really. Well, that's that. The show is done. Now fuck off.'

'Alright,' Rebecca says. She stares. The night is still. For just a moment it had seemed so real… She wonders how unhappy she'd have been if she had gone with him. Would she have known? Would she have cared?

'Alright,' she says again.

She has one last desperate option she could try.

33

'Please, Rebecca,' the witch begs. 'Let me die.'

'I won't. I can't.'

'What kind of monster are you?' the witch says. 'I am ready. I wish to go into the quiet dark.'

'You do not believe in heaven?' Rebecca says.

'Or hell?' the witch says. 'No. Ever since I was a little girl I knew I lacked something within me. Belief. Without it I cannot see the world as one wishes it to be, only as it is. It's disconcerting, but it's the sort of thing that's useful for a witch. It must be a nice thing to have, though... Do you believe, Rebecca?'

'I don't know what to believe,' Rebecca says. 'In any case, Jews don't have an afterlife. Jews just die.'

'Then maybe I'm a Jew,' the witch says, and tries to cackle, but it turns into an awful cough and she subsides upon her bedding.

'Please,' she begs, when she is able to speak again. 'What you are doing to me is not right. My time is come. Let it end.'

But Rebecca can't – won't.

Why, she can't put into words. When Isaac died she cried. They could not even bury him immediately, the way that is the custom of her people. The king forbids for Jews to die upon his ground and stay there. So she and her brothers had to carry her father's body on the road, to London and the Jewry, where he was put into the ground at last. The king wants all his dead Jews kept close together.

Then the king took as much of her father's money as he could lay his grubby hands on. This was what happened when one of the king's Jews died. Whatever they had belonged to the king, was only leased to the Jews for the duration of their existence. So the king took everything, to fund his wars. He'd been busy making wars, expanding territory, wresting power back from the priests, keeping his nobles at bay, keeping his lands both here and in Normandy, fighting the Irish – the sort of shit kings *do*, in short.

King Henry is a cunt, Rebecca thinks. But for kings that's just a job description.

She'd met him, too, if briefly. 'I'm sorry for your loss,' he said. He seemed almost sincere.

'I'm sorry for your gain,' she almost said, but didn't. Jews like her were only here on sufferance. Sometimes she wishes she was living in the Saracens' lands, Jews prosper under Muslim rulers – in Spain and Baghdad it's a golden age. But she's stuck here, on this godforsaken island, and the Hood was right – this island's story's not *her* story. She could try and rewrite it all she likes to suit her ends, but ultimately all they will remember is the king and that tosser in the woods, the Robin.

Her father died and she grieved, and they sat shiva for him, and after those seven days she emerged back into the world. He had been a link for her, to the wider world, to a continuity of thought extending back more centuries and years than these fucking morons in Normandy or England could even imagine. And he was gone. And she grieved.

And then, as Jews do, she got on with it.

So why can't she let the witch go? She knows the witch is dying. She knows there's nothing she can do to stop it. So why? Why?

'Because,' she says aloud. Because, because! Isn't it what being human's like, to rail against that vast indifference that is death, its unjust cruelty? For new beings to be born the old must die. And yet what is being a witch but trying to stave off the tide? To heal and make better, so people may live longer and more fully, to halt time's inexorable progression to the end point? She has to *try*.

And so she goes to the one other person in Nottingham who shares her feelings on this subject.

Although she really, *really* hoped she wouldn't have to.

His name is Gilbert Whitehand.

The Chapel of the Sacred Order of the Faith And Peace of The Holy Angel Azrael, a modest new building on the end of Cock Street, lies nestled in between a shuttered leatherworker's shop and an alehouse that serves brackish beer brewed by the monks, and which nearly everyone in Nottingham avoids. It leans against the town walls, overlooking the wood from its belfry, and sits at an almost direct opposition to Castle Rock, the town gibbet, and the Night Market.

No one walks down Cock Street unless one has to. And Rebecca knows she was seen as soon as she set foot there. The monks have been in Nottingham some sixteen years now, ever since the second sheriff brought over a gang of charlatans, hedge wizards, astrologers and other unsavoury characters to aid him. Most of them had drifted off, but Gilbert Whitehand and his order remained, a fact the town much resented. But they have money, from whatever source, and word is they trade in lucrative but shady artefacts. Rebecca knocks on the chapel doors and a sour-faced, youthful apprentice monk opens and glares at her balefully.

'Closed indefinitely,' he says.

'This is a house of prayer,' Rebecca points out.

'God's not in. And you're a Jew.'

Rebecca sighs. 'I'm here to see the Whitehand.'

'He ain't taking visitors.'

Rebecca's knife slides out of her sleeve and she presses it to the apprentice's neck.

'Don't swallow,' she says.

His eyes glare at her in mute fear.

'How about now?'

'I am a man of the cloth!' the youth splutters in outraged indignity.

'Your cloth is stained with wine,' Rebecca says. 'And, well, other things I am sure I do not need to know. Don't you ever wash? No, don't answer.' She removes the knife and pushes the youth. She steps into the chapel.

'Tell Gilbert I'm waiting.'

'Cunt,' the monk says. Then he scuttles off before she can hurt him.

Rebecca sighs. She can feel a headache coming on. The chapel's dank and small, the cross is crooked on the altar. The apprentice vanishes through a door into the crypt. It smells of cloves, that sweet cloying spice they bring over from the markets of Egypt. Expensive. Yet the chapel's dowdy. It's curious.

From the fragile truce that exists throughout Nottingham no one is exempt. The castle, which has so far remained sheriff-less thanks to the Hood's influence with the Archbishop of York, treads softly. Rebecca, in the dwale trade, maintains decorum (no more gristly corpses left out on display). The hoods in the woods maintain their hold on the forest paths and as long as they get their tax, peace is in force. The churches and the monasteries turn a blind eye, and in truth, many of the monks are sympathetic to the Hood's cause, if cause he has, for some of them truly believe in the kingdom of heaven and in loving their neighbour, and all that stuff.

And Whitehand...

Whitehand and his ridiculously named Sacred Order of the Faith and Peace of The Holy Angel Azrael mostly keep to themselves. They respect the truce or, at the very least, would rather just be left alone and undisturbed. It's not that there aren't rumours...

But if you know what's good for you, in Nottingham, in this time? You keep your ears closed and your fucking mouth *shut*.

The apprentice reappears.

'Pater Noster Whitehand will see you now,' he says.

Our Father, is it? Rebecca thinks. She follows the apprentice into the crypt. Down stone steps. The smell of cloves intensifies. Down and down. The ground of Nottingham's porous. Down and down—

Into a cavernous hall, where monks sit at benches, working intently. Rebecca is taken aback. She had not expected to be shown into the order's sanctum. No wonder the chapel's as it is – it's just a front. Here she sees monks poring over manuscripts, copying them with care; others draw charts of forbidden anatomy – a heart, a lung, a kidney – for which for sure both king and Church will see them hanged. Others mix spices and herbs, others build—what are they building? She sees drawings of machines. She sees an altar. She sees a cross. She sees Gilbert Whitehand coming to meet her.

'Mistress Rebecca!' he says with warmth. His face is shiny. His eyes are beady. He's after something. Good.

'Master Whitehand.'

'Oh, call me Gilbert, please. How long has it been?'

Since your last master tried to kill me, she thinks but doesn't say. He looks much the same. Balder. Uglier. There are curious scars on his face and hands, and the mark of more than one burn. What has he been up to all this time?

'Come, come. Would you care for a small beer?'

Rebecca thinks of the stuff the monks brew.

'No, thank you,' she says.

'I have some wine. From Normandy.'

'... Alright.'

He ushers her into an office at the back. He pours a glass. She sniffs it cautiously but it is good, expensive stuff. She takes a sip.

'We must live without luxury,' Gilbert says piously, 'but we must live well. For God.'

'For God,' Rebecca says. 'Of course.'

'My God, your God,' he says. 'It is the same God. I have long studied the Jewish mystics. So much power... Did not the prophet Elijah resurrect the dead child of a widow from Zarephath? Did not the witch of Endor raise the spirits of the dead and freely converse with them? Did not Elisha the wonderworker also raise the dead child of a rich lady of Shunem?'

'Did they?' Rebecca says. 'I'm afraid it was before my time.'

'Come, come!' Gilbert says. 'You are modest, yet weren't you, too, a witch's apprentice for some time, Mistress Rebecca?' He looks at her shrewdly. 'There is much we can learn from each other, you and I,' he says.

Rebecca shudders in revulsion. 'Your interests are peculiar,' she says.

'I am but a humble medicus,' he tells her. 'As the Romans styled them. A physician, interested in the workings of the human body and mind. Is there a reason we should die so young? That we should ail and not know how to treat disease? Surely as God put illness in this world He must have also placed the cures for us to use, if only we could conceive of them? I am a rational man, yes, yes, I believe if only we could understand the system of the world then we could make use of it, according to the immutable laws laid down by God Himself. That is all. And I owe you an apology for that wicked sheriff. I thought the research into fungus was promising but his methodology was unsound. So.'

This is an apology?

She stares at him. What is he really up to? Well, it doesn't matter. She knows enough to know he is the man to speak to – he has all but confirmed it just now.

She says, 'The witch is dying.'

'Yes, yes,' he says. 'It is a tragedy and most regrettable. I wish there was something I could do.'

'*Is* there something you can do?' she says – forces the words out.

He looks at her innocently.

'Whatever do you mean?' he says.

'Can you stop her from dying?' Rebecca says bluntly.

'And do what with her?' he says.

'*Can* you?' she says – almost shouts.

'Maybe,' he says. 'What's in it for me?'

She looks at him then. Doesn't dare to believe.

'What do you want?' she says.

'Not want,' Gilbert says. '*Need*. It is a minor thing. But it is difficult.'

'What is it?' she says. 'I will get it.'

He looks at her levelly.

He says, 'A toe.'

Rebecca almost laughs in relief.

'You want a *toe*?' she says. 'I can get you a toe! Hell, I can get you a toe before vespers! You don't *wanna* know—'

'No,' Gilbert Whitehand says. 'I do not. And I do not *want* the toe. I *need* the toe. I already *told* you that. Please pay *attention*. It is a *specific* toe. I don't need some ho's toe. I don't need any old Joe's toe. I don't need a crow's toe or a doe's toe or a you-don't-wanna-know toe.'

'So what fucking toe *do* you want, Gilbert?' Rebecca says.

He looks at her and smiles.

'I want the Holy Toe,' he says.

Rebecca stares at him like he is mad. 'You mean—' she says.

Gilbert nods. 'The left big toe of Jesus of Nazareth,' he says. 'Yes.'

'You're mad.'

'I am the sanest man I know! The most holy relic is kept under lock and key and guarded by the good monks at the Benedictine Priory of St. Nicholas the Wonderworker. I want *that* toe, Mistress. Now, can you get it for me or not?'

'You want *Jesus*'s toe?'

'Who else is worthy?'

'What the fuck *for*!' Rebecca says.

Gilbert shrugs. 'It is the business of my order to facilitate the trade in relics,' he says. 'It is a respectable occupation and it does pay for our needs. Pieces of the True Cross, saints' bones, mummified heads, dried blood. Some fingernails. A tongue or two. And as it happens I have a buyer on the Continent just itching for the toe.'

'The toe.'

'It's not just a toe! It's the big toe!' Gilbert Whitehand says, and Rebecca sees with revulsion that for all his seeming denial the man is truly obsessed. 'The left big toe, to be exact. Of the Redeemer!'

Rebecca stares at him, suspicious. 'So it's just about the money?' she says.

'What else?'

'I don't know,' Rebecca says.

Gilbert shrugs carelessly. 'Are you in, or are you out?' he says.

'You can help the witch?'

'I can't make promises.'

'Not good enough,' Rebecca says.

'I will send my men to fetch her,' he tells her. 'She will be cared for here, in our treatment centre. Is that agreeable?'

'Must she come here?'

'Yes. We have… special medicines and things. It is very expensive, keeping someone alive against their wishes. It requires expertise, supervision. Is that agreeable?'

Rebecca hesitates. She knows what she should say. Tell him no, walk away. Leave him to his creepy occupations.

But to do so means to let the witch die.

'Yes,' she says.

'Good! It shall be done. And the payment?'

'Oh, you will get your toe,' Rebecca says darkly.

Gilbert rubs his hands together. They make a dry, slithery sound.

'Can't wait,' he says.

34

'You fool,' the witch whispers. 'What have you done?'

'What I had to,' Rebecca says.

The witch stares at her. Then the witch starts to laugh.

She laughs like a maddened thing. Her laughter echoes from the walls and crashes down on Rebecca.

'You fucking fool—'

Then the monks lift up her bed and take her away. When Rebecca tries to follow, the young apprentice she had met before blocks her way. 'It is better this way, the Pater Noster says. He said to tell you to come and see her with payment in hand.'

And it is done.

In the Goat, Rebecca calls Ulrica and Elgitha. She explains in few details. The girls are older now, a little heavier, they have more scars. They both nod.

'Will it do, though?' Ulrica asks.

Rebecca shrugs. The gesture reminds her of her father and she feels a sense of deep and sudden loss. She realises that she carries the past with her. That shrug, a gesture passed through time, through generations. Will she leave it in her turn to some descendants? It seems unlikely. But the past is real in that moment, in her own flesh, and she thinks she has made a mistake trying to keep the witch alive against her will.

The witch would have lived on, through Rebecca, through Rebecca's choices and decisions.

Rebecca's bad decisions.

But it's too late now. Ulrica and Elgitha follow her down to the basement. To the door that's always locked. To the stone walls that mute all sound. Rebecca reaches for the key. The other two look at each other mutely. They are uncomfortable with what's about to take place.

Well, fuck 'em if they can't take the heat.

She unlocks the door and opens it onto darkness.

Chains rattle. Rebecca strikes a flint and lights a candle. In its wan light she can see the sole occupier of the cell.

She hasn't aged a single day and, infuriatingly, she still has that glow of *glamour* about her, for all that she is chained. Her dress is ragged and her teeth are longer, sharp; and in the past decade and a half of her imprisonment here she has grown, from her back, a pair of gossamer wings. She opens golden eyes and blinks at Rebecca. Her lips spread in a mocking grin.

'Bex,' she says.

Rebecca says, 'Hello, Rowena.'

Rebecca had long wondered who was really behind the attack on her that night. Two guys in masks, who robbed her of her product. She had hunted them down and executed them and left their carcasses in the market square for all to see. But who had been behind it was a mystery to her.

She had thought it was the sheriff, but the sheriff, as it turned out, had little interest in dwale. And when they were brought to the castle by his men, Rebecca and her girls were taken away, the girls to the hole and Rebecca to the dungeons...

Rebecca and her girls, all but one.

Rowena.

Later, when she broke free from the cells and found the girls in the dark hole where the sheriff had left them to become mulch for his fungi, Rowena wasn't there. And when the sheriff died and his men dispersed, Rowena wasn't there.

They had come up together. Rebecca had brought her in with her. Thought she could trust her. Even if the girl was part-forest.

Then a few days later Rowena turned up. Said she had been to the Green Place. And Rebecca still didn't know for sure.

The thing was, at that point in the game Rebecca didn't *need* to know for sure. *Knowing* was a luxury. It was *doing* that became necessity.

So Rebecca kidnapped her former partner. And she stashed her in the room behind the door that's always locked.

And she'd kept her there.

Fifteen, sixteen years now?

Rowena hasn't aged a fucking day.

But those teeth.

And those wings.

'You were always more fae than human,' Rebecca tells her. 'I should have known that. I am sorry, if it matters. I should not have brought you in. The fae only act as is their nature. But still. You betrayed me.'

'You're so stupid,' Rowena tells her. She yawns. 'You think this is a prison? You think this is a length of time for me? You only ever spend two days in prison, bitch. The day you go in and the day you come out.'

'You are never coming out,' Rebecca says.

Rowena laughs in her face.

A rush of blood to Rebecca's face. She freezes with it. Then she nods.

'Do it,' she says.

'What are you doing?' Rowena says – demands.

Ulrica and Elgitha approach her. Elgitha holds the knife. Ulrica grabs Rowena's foot. Rowena thrashes. Her chains are iron and they must, they must hurt her, but she'd never show. She fights but Ulrica twists her foot and Rowena grunts in pain and then Ulrica, tired perhaps of this charade, grabs Rowena by the hair and slams her head against the wall a couple of times and after that it's a much easier operation.

It's done quickly. Elgitha's knife is sharp and her hand is practised. Elgitha holds the foot. Ulrica cuts.

'Here,' she says at last. She tosses it to Rebecca. Rebecca catches the thing in the air. She holds it in her palm.

Rowena's toe, long and slender, with a blood more green than red.

'Bind her wound,' Rebecca says.

Rowena wakes when they do it. She grits her teeth – those long, sharp teeth. She hisses at Rebecca.

'You think you're a queen,' she tells Rebecca. 'But you don't rule shit. One day I will be free and then—'

But the wound is bound, and Rebecca isn't listening. She and her soldiers leave the cell, and she shuts the door right there and then on Rowena's speech and locks the door. She puts the key away.

'Fuck her,' Elgitha says.

'Yeah,' Ulrica says.

Rebecca stares at the toe.

'This had better work,' she says.

The Benedictine Priory of St. Nicholas the Wonderworker still sits outside the town wall, adjacent to the grazing field. It is much as it had been. Rebecca knocks gently on the garden gate and Brother Birdie opens it.

'Mistress Becca,' he says softly. 'I really don't think—'

'Just this time, Birdie,' Rebecca says.

The monk shakes his head. 'You are denying the witch the gates of heaven,' he says piously.

'You think *that's* where she was headed?' Rebecca says. 'Come on, Birdie. Help me out.'

Birdie looks at her in indecision, and Rebecca feels a rise of panic. She cannot bribe or threaten Birdie. She has to rely on something she has all but forgotten exists. Kindness, or friendship.

But Birdie takes Rebecca's hand. Birdie leads her in, past the vegetable garden and into the main building, where old Brother Robert doses in a chair, guarding the relics.

Rebecca stares in repulsion at the display. A bone from the Virgin Mary. A piece of the True Cross. The dried earlobe of John the Baptist.

The left big toe of Jesus of Nazareth.

She stares at it. It seems remarkably well preserved. Can it be real?

She stares. She thinks, A toe's a toe.

Brother Robert snores. He had a stroke a couple of years back. Rebecca helps when she can. Dwale seems to soothe him. She'd made sure Birdie gave him an extra dose of medicine that night. Rebecca wonders when it was she changed: once, she helped people.

She reaches into the display and takes the Christ's toe and replaces it with Rowena's.

She holds the Holy Toe. A dry, mummified thing. It isn't right, she thinks, for all these church folk to worship the body parts of a dead Jew.

She wraps the Holy Toe and puts it away.

'Thanks, Birdie,' she says.

Birdie lowers his head.

'The path you follow, you will tread alone now,' the small monk tells her.

Rebecca sighs. On impulse, she hugs Birdie. She feels the small bones, the stump of wings. She lets him go.

'I know, Birdie,' she says. 'But sooner or later we all walk alone in this fucking world.'

She departs from there as silent as she'd come and vanishes into the night.

*

Birdie watches her go.

The little monk's senses are awash with the night and the potential of futures. Birdie climbs up the stairs to the tower. They have not done this for some time. At the top they stop and look out on Nottingham and Sherwood. Birdie stills. Birdie watches and listens.

Down there: Rebecca walking back, her steps leading her inexorably along a path that she should not have chosen. It will be the ruin of her. Rebecca enters Cock Street and knocks on the door to the chapel, and the door opens. Rebecca goes in.

Birdie listens to the screams behind the silence. So many captive souls. Deep under the Goat is the fairy, Rowena, smiling with sharp teeth through pain, the iron shackles holding. She schemes revenge.

Down there, below the chapel of the Sacred Order of the Faith and Peace of The Holy Angel Azrael, the witch lies on a bed in a room where lights burn day and night. She is behind a door that's always locked, and she is kept alive just as the monks have promised, force-fed soup brewed with a mixture of fungi, roots and herbs. A strange machine turns and turns in a corner – it takes two monks to turn its wheel. Perhaps it is a mill of some sort.

But if so, Birdie doesn't know what it is milling.

Rebecca, in the next room, doesn't see her. She hands over the toe to Gilbert Whitehand. He thanks her politely.

'This is, of course, the down payment,' he says.

'I beg your pardon?' Rebecca says.

Oh, how it breaks Birdie's heart to see and feel it.

'To keep her alive,' Gilbert says.

'Yes?'

'She is alive, just as we promised.'

Behind that locked door the witch screams.

'So our business is done.'

Gilbert Whitehand shakes his head. He's led Rebecca, in her desperation, right into this trap and now there's no escape.

'We can only keep her alive for so long,' he says mournfully. 'Without—'

'Yes?'

'Shall we say, a maintenance fee?'

'You've got to be fucking kidding me.'

Gilbert shrugs.

'I will burn your chapel down,' Rebecca says, 'and slaughter every one of your men and piss on your graves.'

'You'd have to squat,' Whitehand says and sniggers, and Rebecca almost socks him one. 'And the witch would die all the same.'

Rebecca stills, then.

'What is it you want?'

He shrugs.

'More of the same.'

'Relics?'

'… Of various sorts,' Whitehand allows.

'Such as?'

He shrugs again. Far too casual for Birdie's liking. The man cannot be trusted. He's a zealot, but for what?

Something unsound.

'I need an eye, some kidneys, wings… a heart.'

'A *heart*?'

He smiles at her, showing his teeth.

'A green heart,' he says.

'You're insane,' Rebecca says.

'Oh, no,' he tells her. 'I am the sanest man in all of Sherwood Forest.'

Rebecca starts to laugh then. She laughs until the tears come out. Behind her door the witch screams and the mill churns. Birdie cries. She sees Rebecca leave. She sees the bonfire burn deep in the heartwood. She hears the clip-clip-clop of hooves as horses and their riders come back to the town. She hears a harp. She hears Will the Knife sing.

Far in the distance, across the waters in Normandy, she hears a boy who would be king conspiring against his father.

She wonders what the future will bring.

'Death and penance, rot and ruin,' Birdie whispers. She makes the sign of the cross.

A shadow-shrouded moon swims across the skies, momentarily visible behind clouds: half empty or half full, depending.

PART NINE

THE DEAL

35

'Another finger?' Rebecca says. 'How many fucking fingers do you *need*, Gilbert!'

The monk looks at her in bemusement. 'Well, ten,' he says, as though Rebecca's simple.

'I'm sick of this,' Rebecca says.

'If you want out of the deal, you'll have to get me a deal,' Gilbert Whitehand says.

Rebecca stares at him with suspicion.

'What *sort* of deal are we talking about here?' she says.

'There's a guy,' Gilbert says.

'A *guy*.'

'Right, right. Up in London. Your neck of the woods. Has his shop in the Jewry, as it happens.'

'Aha.'

'He's the guy, for this kinda thing.'

'What the fuck *is* this kinda thing!' Rebecca says.

Gilbert shrugs. 'You know. Relics and stuff.'

'Body parts?'

'*Holy* body parts! He used to be a pirate, actually. Until he saw the light of the Lord.'

'Aha. So what's it got to do with me?'

'You don't get it. This guy, Eustace? He's an authenticator.'

Gilbert says it like it's the name of some rare and precious bird he wants to eat. He all but licks his lips. Rebecca doesn't bother hiding her shudder of revulsion. There's no point, with Gilbert. He cares for nothing but his project – whatever his project is.

'What the fuck is an authenticator?'

'You know with the relics,' Gilbert says. 'They are all over Christendom. If you put all the pieces of the True Cross from all the shrines and monasteries and churches in Europe together you would have enough wood to build Noah's Ark. Fakes, Rebecca!' He almost screams. 'Fakes! You would not imagine it, I am sure, but there are *charlatans* out there in the world! Men without honour, who would pretend to sell you the toe of Jesus Christ when who *knows* whose toe it is! If it's even a toe! Do you have *any* idea how many Holy Foreskins there are at this very *moment* in the wild? The Pope has one in Rome. There's another in Antwerp. There's one each in the Cathedral of Le Puy-en-Velay, in Santiago de Compostela, in churches in Besançon, Metz, Hildesheim, Charroux, Conques, Langres, Fécamp! There are *two* just in *Auvergne*! Do you think Jesus had numerous penises? It is an outrage!'

Rebecca can't help smirking, but it just enrages Gilbert more.

'How is one expected to—' he says, but then he catches himself abruptly. 'Anyhow,' he says, with sudden icy calm. 'An authenticator is a specialist in the trade in relics. A man who has a holy touch. Who can vouch for an item's *authenticity*. And this Eustace the Monk's the man. His shop in the Jewry is a clearing house for genuine items. Crusaders bring him relics back from the Holy Land and he has extensive connections throughout Christendom. Some say he even trades with the Saracens.'

'And how does he do that…' Rebecca murmurs.

'There's a deal going down,' Gilbert tells her. 'A big one. *The* big one, as it happens. I have procured an item at great expense and a considerable amount of risk. It is arriving in London by ship from the continent in just over a week's time. I would ordinarily handle it myself but my presence in London would occasion difficulties—'

Which meant, Rebecca knew, that the man was most likely wanted there, for crimes she did not care to imagine.

'So you go,' Gilbert says. 'Take one of the hoods with you for muscle. Take Will Scarlett. I hear he's handy with a knife. I've already procured his services from the Hood. So go, get the package and, more importantly, get it authenticated by this Eustace before you part with my money. Or rather, I should say, *your* money. Since you're going to pay for it for me. Do it, bring it back to me, and any debt between us is forgiven. What do you say?'

'Is that all?' Rebecca says.

He shrugs at her with as much innocence as the next man to go on the gibbet.

'Easy-peasy.'

'And what exactly *is* this... *relic* you've procured?' Rebecca says.

Gilbert smiles, hungrily, Rebecca thinks. Like a lean wolf who's spent months tracking a sheep and is finally near his kill.

'Oh, you'll see,' he says. 'It's a doozy.'

When the annoying Jewish girl finally leaves, Gilbert Whitehand surveys his domain. His little monks scuttle here and there, as busy as ants. They copy ancient manuscripts, and others study them and make schemata. Here in his underground lair he has his own carpentry shop, his own alchemical laboratory, his own kiln and his own chapel to the ancient gods, just in case they come in handy. Woden, Moccus, even that bitch Mab of the fairies. And he has his operating theatre, of course.

'I am a warrior-poet in the classical sense,' he says to no one in particular. He goes to check in on the witch. He likes to check in on the witch. She lies in the bed, in the room that is locked. He sits beside her. He takes her cold hand in his.

'Are you keeping well?' he says solicitously. 'Your Jew girl was here again. She is a kind girl, so kind to keep you.'

The witch blinks at him. She's weak, her skin's thinner than low-grade parchment. But her eyes – her eyes! So large and white, and he can drown in them.

'Fuck, is it you again, Whitehand?' the witch says. 'I told you already, you're an idiot.'

'They said I was mad, mad!' Gilbert says. 'But *you* don't think I'm mad, do you, witch? *You* know I'm right. It's all there in the Bible! Read your Book of Kings, read Samuel, read Matthew, Mark and Luke!'

'I think you're as mad as a ferret's fart,' the witch tells him. 'But the stupid girl's made her bed so the stupid girl will have to lie in it. Do you really have the heart?'

Gilbert waves a hand. 'I'll get the heart in due course,' he says. 'This is about something else.'

'I'm intrigued,' the witch says.

'Oh, you!' Gilbert says, and wags his finger. 'It's always such a delight, chatting with you. But I best be off. So much work to do and so little time. You know how it is.'

'All I have is time,' the witch says. She closes her eyes. 'Stolen time…' she murmurs.

Gilbert pats her hand.

'There, there,' he says.

He goes to his sanctum sanctorum. Old gods stare down on him. Mithra, busy slaying a boar. Herne, in the hunt. Minerva petting her owl. Useless fucks, the lot of them. But who knows for sure? A lot of ancient knowledge vanished with the fall of Rome. Some has been preserved in Byzantium, some by the Saracens, some more is kept by the Jews. Gilbert's not greedy for anything but *knowledge*. So he pilfers old manuscripts and learns dead languages and tries to work out the mechanism of the world. Did not the Greek, Archimedes, say that if only he were given a big enough lever, he could move the entire world?

Gilbert dreams of ancient Rome and Greece. Of speaking wisely with men of knowledge, with astronomers and architects and engineers. Instead he's stuck in freaking *Nottingham*, with a Jew girl, a dying witch, some hoods in the woods and a bunch of eager but useless monks who do his bidding without understanding his true purpose. He supposes it could be worse. But he longs for vanished days, and wonders if they'll ever come again, if an enlightenment will once more flourish over this age of ignorance and sin.

He hadn't quite told Rebecca the truth, of course. It's not that he *doesn't* trade in relics, it's just that...

Some of those he *needs*.

He admires his trophies. The left eye of Jesus, preserved in some cloudy alchemical liquid. His right ear, all but the earlobe intact. Jesus's rib cage. That one had set him back. He managed to import the whole thing, smuggled out of the Kingdom of Jerusalem and shipped bone by bone for him to reassemble. A foot, which had lain in some monastery in Bavaria, of all places, for several centuries. A pinkie from Rome. An almost complete set of teeth, collected from all across Christendom, and the molars he found in Constantinople.

He lights a candle, mutters a prayer. Dead gods look down on him from the walls.

A dead son of God stares at him, half-complete, from the dissecting table.

'Hood's in a fight with Marian again,' Will says. He stares moodily into his drink. 'They've been at it for three weeks now. We thought it best to decamp the Green Place for a while.'

'Let them work it out,' some huge hood says.

Alan-a-dale strums his bone harp. He stares across the table at Rebecca.

'Have you seen the cook?' he says.

'The cook?'

'I have some business with her, but I can't seem to find her.'

'She'll turn up,' Rebecca says.

'Alright.' Alan plays. The hoods drink. Lunchtime at the Goat, and hoods are intermingled with king's men, poachers and traders. Sometimes Rebecca thinks the sale of ale is all she needs, without the dwale. She wonders how Sir Richard's doing.

'I am going to London,' Rebecca announces.

'Well, good for you,' Al says.

'I need someone to come with me.'

They go still.

'So?'

'I'm told Scarlett is available.'

'Who told you that, then?'

'No fucking way,' Will Scarlett says.

'Why not?' Rebecca says.

'London.' He shakes his head. 'Bad memories.'

'When is the last time you went?'

Will shrugs. 'The years pass… I don't know.' He ticks them off on his fingers, concentrates.

'Nearly thirty years,' he says in wonder.

'Three decades!' Alan says. 'Who the hell's going to remember you there after thirty years?'

'Oh, I don't know,' Will says darkly, 'London has long memories.'

'It's been arranged,' Rebecca says. She almost feels bad for him. And a little uneasy. 'The Hood…'

'The fucking Hood!' Will says. 'I'm my own man.'

'Are you?' Rebecca says.

Will falls silent. Then, reluctantly, he nods.

'When do we leave?' he says.

Rebecca says, 'Right now.'

There is no one to see them pass out of Nottingham. Brother Birdie has long given up his tower for the communal hall of the monks. And the guardsmen, Bert and Ernest, are getting on in years; they snore peacefully on their mats and leave the gates unguarded.

Who is to come here, anyway? The king is busy putting down his son's rebellion in Normandy. Henry the Young King is pissed his dad's giving away too much land to his other brother, John, so he and his brothers Richard and Geoffrey, encouraged by Henry's mother and by Louis, King of France, who is the father to Henry the Young King's wife... Oh, fuck it – Ernest and Bert couldn't follow this shit if they tried.

Basically it is another gang war over turf and castles. But the war is far away, and Nottingham's still under the Bishop of York's protection, and the Hood in the wood still makes sure that the forest's his. So Bert and Ernest snore, contented, and Rebecca and Will Scarlett depart the town quietly, and there is no one to see them go.

It is a cold autumn in this Year of Our Lord 1173. The king's fighting the king's sons and on the king's road the leaves fall gently, awash in oranges, reds and yellows.

'I've been reading this manuscript,' Will says.

Rebecca looks at him curiously.

'I didn't know you could read,' she says.

Will shrugs. 'I picked up letters from this priest I knew back in the Holy Land,' he says. He thinks of Father Jonas.

'So what is this manuscript?' Rebecca says.

'It's by Geoffrey of Monmouth?' Will says enthusiastically. '*The History of the Kings of Britain*? Have you heard of it?'

'Oh,' Rebecca says. 'I think I read Wace's version in the Norman. The *Roman de Brut*. It's very popular, isn't it?'

'It's all about this king, Arthur?' Will says. 'He's, like, the king of the Britons, only his dad's a dick, and there's this wizard, Merlin, and he helps Arthur fight all the other kings. And there's a girl he fancies. Guinevere. And stuff. And then he dies, only he doesn't really die – he goes off to some magic place. I think. It's really good.'

'Yeah,' Rebecca says. 'Whatever. Can we just… ride?'

'Sure,' Will says. 'Whatever.'

And in this manner they make the journey to the city of London.

36

London! Where the streets are narrow and the river stinks of fish, and the ghosts of Roman soldiers haunt the alleyways.

London! Where the screams of the tormented echo eerily through the hallowed halls of stone in the Tower where once the White Hill stood, where once the White Hill Gang ruled. The Tower, with its hobbled ravens, with its creaking chains and hooded executioners. The Tower that will stand there for centuries more, unchanged, unloved, insane and jabbering into the dark, heard only by the hedge witches and necromancers who pass through the city unnoticed every day.

London!

'What a shithole,' Rebecca says when they arrive. 'It stinks.'

'I love her,' Will says softly. 'There is no city like her in the world.'

'And you would know how?' Rebecca says. 'Look, forget it. We'll do this job and go back. Do you have a place to stay?'

'A place? I thought—'

'Well, you thought wrong. I'm to my kin – my family still owns a house in the Jewry. Meet me by the river for the pickup as agreed. Come armed. Don't fuck me on this, Scarlett.'

'Yeah, yeah...'

With that she's gone. And Will is left alone in a city that he thought never to see again. He tramples ground he thought he'd lost forever. He marvels at old sights. He walks the Strand, a road still running past the river though the Romans themselves laid it down. Grand houses rise above him. The street is crowded with servants, hawkers, knights and priests. It is so easy to be alone in London, Will thinks. He isn't used to the city anymore; he's been a hood too long. And here is civilization once again, one of the great towns, here merchants from the continent mingle with soldiers of the king, here fishwives and bakers are as proud as knights, here a cat rubs against his ankles and purrs, and here *she* waits, in the shadows, the spectre he had thought he'd vanquished, the city's ghost.

Will… she whispers. *Will…*

The Morrigan.

She says, *My name is Morgan.*

'Like in the Geoffrey of Monmouth book?'

You're thinking of his Vita Merlini, she says and sighs. She draws him to her. Far from the madding crowd. Into the dark. She holds him in her arms.

You can still see me… You were always special, Will. How goes it in the heartwood? Does my awful sister still pretend to rule the Summer Land?

'I don't know what you mean…'

What brings you back? She frowns. She's but a shade of what she was once, but she still has power. She runs her hands over him. He shudders.

You are in grave danger… she says.

'I always am.'

She draws him to her. *Then don't talk.*

He makes love to her, which is to say, he loves the bricks, the river water and the washing hanging on the lines to dry.

In the evening, armed, he goes to meet Rebecca and the contact by the river.

★

'You're not a monk.'

'I never said I was,' Rebecca says. She's in the Jewry, though it took her a while to find the place.

The shop of Eustace & Tuck, Purveyors of Fine Wine, Cheese and Holy Relics, sits tucked away on Ironmonger Row. There is no sign in front, and the door was bolted behind Rebecca as soon as she was allowed in.

The shop is dark and dim. Several fat candles flicker and gutter, scattered haphazardly about the place. In their light she can make out several large truckles of cheese, a few dusty wine bottles, a skull, another skull, a femur bone, a ribcage, a heap of old Roman coins, an illuminated manuscript of the *Historia Regum Britanniae* turned to a page with an illustration of Guinevere emerging naked out of a lake and Arthur watching from the shadows with a giant erection. Rebecca's pretty sure that's not in the original tale. Which she'd found kind of boring anyway.

The man behind the counter shuts the manuscript and glares at her. He is big, ugly and scarred, with ears like Syrian cabbage.

'*I'm* a monk,' he says. 'I'm Eustace.'

He looks like a pirate. She knows he *was* a pirate. His brothers still hold the Channel Islands. But Rebecca doesn't care. All she wants is for this distasteful business to be over with.

'I'm here about the—'

'Yes, yes. I know why you're here. I need you to fill me in on some details, lassie. Who is this numbskull fuckweasel in Nottingham who's been collecting holy relics like his life depends on it?'

Rebecca shrugs. 'His name's Gilbert. He's a cunt.'

'Yet you work for him?'

Rebecca sighs. She feels a headache coming on. 'Look, I don't know,' she says. 'I made a bad deal with him. It was my mistake. Why? Is he on your shitlist or something? I'd happily help you get rid of him.'

'Well you're a charming one and no mistake,' the pirate says. 'And Jewish, ain'tcha?'

'What's it to you?'

'Nothing, mistress, nothing. Only I assume you don't truck with this holy business.'

'What's holy's holy,' Rebecca says. 'But no, you're right, I don't give a fuck. I don't even know what I'm supposed to be picking up here.'

'Not here. Not here…' Eustace rubs his hands. 'From the Holy Land. From your boy's contacts. Very precious… yes. Very precious.'

'I see,' she says. 'So you want it too?'

'Want, yes, no… I like order, mistress. And something here's a mess. So I am trying to untangle it, so to speak.'

'You don't untangle mess,' Rebecca says. 'You clean it up.'

'Quite right. Still. Our services were purchased. Eustace and Tuck deliver. Always deliver. Yes. So there is that. Still. We might be able to help each other down the road. You savvy?'

Rebecca sighs. 'What the fuck, man?' she says.

Eustace grins.

'Just bring me the stuff and we'll deal.'

'Whatever, man…'

She leaves. The monk stares after her.

Another comes and joins him then.

'Well?' Eustace says. 'What do you think?'

'She's in over her head.'

'A deal's a deal, Tuck.'

'And when the deal is done?'

Eustace smiles. He has a lot of missing teeth.

'Then we negotiate a new one on our terms, brother.'

And so Rebecca makes it to the river docks. She sees a shadow, waiting by a sailboat with the unlikely name of the *Jesus of Lübeck*. She goes to join him.

'Shhh...'

Will's hopped up on something, she can see. His pupils are large. He can't stand still. The knife's dancing from one hand to the other.

Jesus, she thinks.

'What is it?'

'Something's wrong. I smell treachery.'

'Will, could you stand still? Hello, who's there—'

Two shadows emerge from the deck and climb down to meet them. Resolve in the moonlight. One huge, one small and intense.

'I am John,' the huge one says.

'Do I look like I give a fuck what your name is?' Rebecca's so tired of dealing with numbnuts. 'Do you have it?'

'The blood is the life,' the huge crusader says. 'The blood is the life!'

'Oh for fuck's sake—'

Then Will Scarlett, hopped up on whatever mummy dust or weed or mushroom he's procured, screams, 'It's a trap!' and tries to run. But the small intense one is behind him, and he brings down a cosh on the back of Will's head. Will drops to the ground.

'What the—' Rebecca says.

The big crusader, John, shrugs at her apologetically.

'There's always a price,' he says, 'to be paid.'

The room's hewn out of stone. The walls are condensed with moisture. There is no decoration. Will Scarlett is tied to a chair.

Rebecca says, 'Is this really necessary?'

The monk, Eustace, shrugs. 'There is always a price,' he says, 'to be paid.'

'And Will was the price?'

'Near three decades ago, Will robbed my employers,' Eustace says. 'His team was... erased from the records. If you get my drift.

But Will got away, and once he found protection in Sherwood, even we couldn't reach him. So we waited. The Poor Fellow-Soldiers of Christ and of the Temple of Solomon are nothing if not patient. Also, very rich. And so. Here we are.'

'You're a *Templar*?'

'No, no, Christ,' Eustace says. He raises his hands placatingly. 'I just work for the crazy fucks. They're mad on vengeance. Sorry, mistress. Will was the price for the item. The Order helped bring it back from Outremer. It is priceless. If it is real. I will authenticate. You will deliver. And so the deal will be done.'

'Well,' Rebecca says. 'What the fuck is it?'

'Here,' the big crusader says. His voice rumbles in the confines of the underground torture room. At least, Rebecca figures it's a torture room. On account of the dried blood on the floor and, well, all the torture instruments.

The big one, John, hands her a vial. It's small and made of glass. Nice workmanship. She unstoppers it, sniffs, stares inside.

She says, '*Blood*?'

'The blood is the life!' John says.

'Shut up.'

'It is the blood... of the Christ!'

'Jesus Christ,' Rebecca says, with feeling.

'Exactly!'

'No, I didn't mean... Oh, never mind. Here. Eustace, is it? Can you tell if it's real?'

The authenticator takes it from her. He sniffs. He frowns. He closes his hand around it. Closes his eyes. Hums.

Rebecca despairs at this ham acting.

'Our Father who art in heaven, hallowed be thy name...'

'Is that the only prayer you know?'

'Hush! I'm working here.'

On the chair, Will opens his eyes. He stares at Rebecca pleadingly. She shakes her head. The short, intense crusader from the ship observes them both, says nothing. He gives her the creeps.

'It is the blood of the Christ! His living blood! So says I, Eustace! It is the genuine article!'

'Alright, great,' Rebecca says. She takes it back from him. 'So we can go, yes?'

'You forgot the money.'

'I didn't forget. It's here.'

'Then give it.'

'Give me Will.'

'No can do, mistress. Besides, what's he to you?'

Rebecca stares at Will Scarlett, bound in the chair. She sighs. 'What do you care, Eustace? He's a nobody. He died thirty years ago. All that you have there is a ghost.'

'My masters wish him to die slowly.'

'Thirty years is slow enough.'

Eustace shrugs. 'What's in it for me?'

'What do you want?'

'Let's parlay, mistress.'

He draws her aside. Through a door to another room. He brings out a dusty bottle.

'Care for a drink?'

'Alright.'

He pours. 'Good Norman wine,' he says. 'Can't grow the grapes here on this land, the soil is shit and so's the weather.'

'No kidding.'

He looks at her curiously. 'Why do you stay here? These people hate Jews, you know that.'

'And in Normandy it's any better?'

He smiles at her. 'Fair point.'

'So what is it you want?'

'Not me, mistress. The Order.'

'Your precious Templars?'

'They pay handsomely, mistress. And they have power. They all but rule the routes from here to Outremer.'

'So?'

'They are devout. To Christ the Lord. To Jesus the Redeemer.'

'Get to the point, Eustace.'

'This freak in Nottingham – he's an abomination.'

'Robin Hood?'

'Sure, but I am speaking of the client. Gilbert Whitehand.'

'He's just a nutjob.'

'Maybe. Maybe not. He's been amassing relics on the quiet. You are aware of this?'

Rebecca sighs. 'I am.'

'What does he need them for?'

'Fucked if I know.'

'The blood... the blood of Christ is really taking it to another level.'

'So?'

The pirate-monk looks at her and Rebecca thinks how very cold his eyes are.

'I think they want him dealt with.'

'I would have thought the Hood.'

'Oh, him.' Eustace waves a hand. 'That is above my pay. No doubt they have plans for *him*. In the meantime... You could help the Order.'

'You want me to work for *you*?'

'So to speak.'

'And Will?'

'I'll chop off his pinky, maybe an ear, we'll call it even. They don't really give a shit about him, you know. You were right, back there. He's a ghost – he just don't know it.'

Rebecca thinks. Rebecca mulls. She thinks of Gilbert Whitehand.

She says, 'Sure, I'm in.'

'Alright,' the former pirate says. Extends his hand.

They shake on it.

PART TEN

THE VIAL

37

And so it comes to be that on a day in late autumn and with the leaves falling from the trees and a cold breeze blowing and the moon waxing gibbous, a small and sorry procession makes its way out of London back to Nottingham, which is kind of a shithole, but it's home all the same. And Rebecca realises this with some surprise. It's home.

There are four of them in the small group: Rebecca; Will Scarlett, who is missing a pinkie and his left ear now, which strangely doesn't make him look any worse, or better, than before, what with all his other scars and that; the intense little crusader who never says anything, and is named Rob; and Little John, who is a fucking giant is what he is – isn't the name ironic?

Their only cargo is that vial of blood. And Rebecca, bored with the silence, for Rob never speaks and Will is moping like a motherfucker, and she's pretty sure he's high besides, says, 'How did you get this in the first place, anyway?'

And since it's the road, and being on the road is really not much more than a series of uneventful yet miserable steps, with stops for food and sleep and taking a dump, and being cold, and rained on, and worrying about brigands or the king's men, and who can tell the difference anyway, it's not like they're on some quest to drop a magic ring down a volcano like some fucking

Nibelungen, and it's not like they can just make the journey shorter by jumping on some giant eagle… Anyway, the point is travel's boring, so Little John shrugs his giant shoulders and, to pass the time, tells her all about it.

'I was born in Arkham, missus, not far from Nottingham, so this, for me, is coming home. They call me Little John, on account of I'm kinda big, as you can probably tell. It's stupid, but what can you do? My father made his living running fights, and I was his most prized fighter. He used to make me take a dive, you see. He'd bet against me and I'd go down in the fifth. But I was sick of doing that and he never shared the money, so one day I bet on myself and knocked the motherfucker I was fighting out in one. Da came for me then and I told him what I thought and he never had a thought in his head again after that. I knew they were going to hang me for what I did so I ran to London.

'London, she's a rough old place for a country boy. I tried honest living but I had no stomach for slaughtering pigs and I was too heavy to go in a boat fishing. I worked as a porter on the docks for a while but the pay was poor. I eventually fell back into the fights, working for a man named Rufus.'

Will winces.

'You knew him?' Little John says.

'Sadly.'

'Died of a cancer of the stomach, the old pirate,' Little John says. 'So I heard. Anyway. I did the fights for him and still worked on the docks, too, trying to save up the money. But I was young in those days and my appetite's considerable, and so I spent more than I earnt. I got some debts, too. So Rufus had me pull some other jobs for him. I was a bouncer at St. Angela's Shelter for Fallen Women, and the Hippodrome. And I came along with him as muscle when he wanted to scare people. I was also a debt collector. But my own debt never seemed to get any smaller.

'Look, I won't bore you with the details of what happened next. There was some trouble involving a minor nobleman from the Continent, the king's own concubine, a portrait that was far too accurate, some blackmail and finally a triple murder. These things happen. In any case, I had to leave town in a hurry. Luckily my time on the docks paid off. I got a ride with some smugglers out of the Channel Islands, Eustace's kin. I'd done favours for them in the past and now they repaid me by taking me to Normandy. I joined a band of mercenaries and we served whichever master paid best, the continentals were always fighting each other.

'Anyway... One morning I wake up naked and tied up in some drinking house in Venice of all places. I couldn't even remember what I was *doing* in Venice. I had the worst hangover. I thought I was bleeding, only as I realised shortly after, it wasn't *my* blood I was covered in. The room was full of corpses.

'Now, did I kill them? Honestly, I ain't too sure myself. Next thing I knew the fuzz came in and arrested me. They gave me a choice. Get dumped in one of the canals and float out to sea, or go serve some Venetian merchant as personal bodyguard on his way to Acre. So I said, "Fuck it, I'll go to Acre." Now this Orso wasn't a bad employer, as far as they go. He was rich as all fuck and to this day I don't know what we were carrying. All I know for sure is, by the time we'd docked in Acre someone had slipped Orso a knife between the ribs and I had to make a quick getaway of it. I had to jump overboard and I can't even swim. The Venetians put a ransom on me, so I had to move fast. You would not believe how many out-of-work crusaders were keen on collecting the bounty – a few Saracens and Jews, too.

'They're weird out there in the Holy Land, mistress. I got jumped on the road by Ḥashīshiyya, trained Nizari assassins, which tells you just how pissed off the Venetians were or what the price on my head was. I killed them anyway, and high-tailed it to the city of Haifa, an ancient port town at the feet of Mount Carmel. The mountain is forested and full of caves. I hid there for some time. In one cave I found ancient skeletons, human or human-like creatures who must have lived there many thousands of years before. I picked stone tools from the ground – flint knives used by ancients litter the earth there. I ate from the fruit of the trees and hunted deer and porcupine.

'It was kinda boring after a while, I won't lie. But it was quiet. At first I got bounty hunters coming at me every other day. Their bones joined those of the ancient ones in the cave. Then gradually they dropped to one a week. Then a month passed and no one came for me at all. I guess they'd forgotten about me. I grew accustomed to the mountain. There were small villages, and olive trees. Though it turns out you can't eat olives off the trees. Did you know that? They have to be cured. Nearly broke my teeth, trying to bite into one. Anyway, I gradually became aware there were other hermits on the mountain. Mystics, mostly. Ex-crusaders seeking God in the place where Elijah fought the priests of Ba'al, back in the olden days. Carmelites, they called themselves. Europeans, mostly. I became pally with them. It's easy to pray to God when you're on the top of Mount Carmel. The sea in the distance and all that blue sky. No wonder everyone fights over the Holy Land. It's pretty there, and the bones in the ground are old.'

'This is all very interesting, I'm sure,' Rebecca says, and Will doesn't bother to hide a yawn, 'but could you get to the point already?'

'What was the point?' Little John says; he looks a bit hurt.

'The vial of blood?' Rebecca says.

'Yes,' Will says, bitter. 'The Holy Blood I got my ear cut off for, you son of a bitch?'

'Oh, that,' Little John says.

'Yes, that,' Rebecca says.

'Well, I was getting to that...'

38

'**A**nyway,' Little John says pointedly. 'There I was at the top of Mount Carmel, the hills of Ephraim and Menasheh down below me, and Armageddon not far off, as a matter of fact, less than a day's ride on a decent horse, though I never got to see the place in the end. It's not even a mountain, you know, more of a hill. There were Jews still living there. Anyway. My fellow monks – which, I suppose, is what I'd become, though they were not an organised order of any kind, at least not then – spent most of their time in contemplation. I myself, though I had always feared the Lord and loved his son, nevertheless grew weary of the same meals and the lack of drink, and also, as I said earlier, at some point the assassins stopped coming for me so I figured I was good. I stole a horse from a Saracen village on the ridge and headed along the coastal road to Jaffa. Now, there's a place! Jaffa, with its fortress on the hill! Along its narrow streets pass men and women of all creeds and colours, and a thousand tongues are spoken in that ancient and enchanting merchants' place. At this point I wore the robes of a Saracen myself, the better to disguise myself, I thought, just in case those vindictive Venetians still had it in for me. And I wasn't alone either. Back on the Carmel I'd made a companion in a bloke called Menander. He was an odd bird and no mistake, a Greek Egyptian he said, from Alexandria, a rare Christian in that heathen land, though as it turned out later he was no Christian at all.

'I got drunk with this Menander a few times. You see, he had a taste for the stuff that needed satisfying – it's a disease I've seen in some men. He started shaking without it. He had come to the Carmel seeking enlightenment, he'd told me, but it wasn't until later that I realised it was not in the contemplation of our Christian God that he came, but to study the old wells and hidden caves of the mountain, to seek for older gods who might have dwelt there once. He himself, he drunkenly told me, was something called a Buddhist. I could make little sense of this religion of his, which came to the Greeks from India long ago, via Alexander the Great, who conquered the known world at the time. According to Menander, the Greeks had even made nations of their own in that far away land, though they were all gone now, and the few remaining Buddhists in Alexandria practised their religion in secret.

It mattered not to me, of course. But Menander was a well-connected man, and wealthy, though I did not yet know the source of his wealth. He had taken a shine to me, and came with me gladly to Jaffa. He did not need to steal a horse for he had his own, a real beast from Arabia, where they breed the finest horses. Anyhow, he was a fine companion, long as he kept his drinking under check. He had some business in Jaffa to attend to anyway, he told me. And he could use some muscle, just in case the deal went south.

Well, what sort of deal it was I soon found out, and it wasn't pretty. You see, it turned out old Menander hadn't been totally straight with me as to the reason he was up there on the Carmel, poking about in all those dusty old caves and things. The old bastard wasn't contemplating the holy nature of creation up there, no, mistress. He was grave-robbing!

'That's right, that's right. All kinds of saints, and I dare say not a few sinners, are buried up there on that old mountain. Full of freaking skeletons. It's a port town below, you see. And a nice fertile mountain on top. Everyone from the old Egyptian sorcerers to King Solomon hung out there at one point or another. And all kinds of idol worshippers and magic workers and what have you. Anyway. My mate Menander was looking for relics. I should have twigged sooner, really. It's a lucrative business. And there's no better source for it all than the Holy Land. Full of the fucking things! It's where they bunged up old Jesus's corpse in a cave, after all.

'Now, I don't know exactly what Menander had found on the Carmel. Some amulets of Ba'al and Ishtar, I think, them two being old gods of people long-dead on this land. But I think you know something of old gods yourself, Mistress Rebecca, if you don't mind me saying. Yes, I see you nod. Sherwood's also such a place, isn't it? I think they're drawn to forests, the old spirits. My mate Menander told me once – all of the old woods were one forest once, and that deep in the heartwood they are still all linked together. It's a curious notion but then, he was a curious man.

'So I came along for the gig, anyway. Down in old Jaffa, a city that was ancient back when London wasn't even a piss stain on the Thames. Merchants, mercenaries, priests, nobles, spies. They were all there. And there was excellent bread. Not to mention the wine.

'"This character we're meeting," Menander tells me, "he's from your part of the world, an Englishman like you."

'"Alright, so?" I say.

'"So you watch him. They are not to be trusted, those Anglos." I had to give him that one, too. So we go in, this stone house up on the hill beyond the walls and the citadel. Nice house, too. Guards outside, monks, but armed. They check us for weapons. One of them says to the other, "*This* guy's a weapon." Talking about me. A bit rude. But we go in. Now this bloke waiting for us, I learn later he was working for Gilbert Whitehand. I knew Gilbert back in London, you see. Back then he wasn't a monk or anything; he was the Whitehand: confidence tricks, mostly, with occasional murder. Not a bad guy. Used to drink with him in the Nave and Chancel near the Barbican. You know the place, Will, I think? But some fat merchant's wife paid him to off her husband – the merchant was fat, I mean, the wife was a scorcher – anyway the deed went diddly and Gilbert ended up in the Tower for a time. I don't know what they did to him there but when he came out he'd found God. At least, a twisted fucked-up version for a twisted fucked-up mind. Started the Sacred Order of the Faith and Peace of The Holy Angel Azrael about then. He nearly died in the Tower, he told me the last time we had drinks. And now he was obsessed with everlasting life, like Jesus. Jesus died and was reborn, he said. Proof, he said, that you could bring the dead back to life. Well, I said, *God* brought him back to life, didn't he? And he said, "But what if you could be the instrument of God?" Which made no sense to me then or now, to be honest. Anyway this guy, Wilfred, who we meet, is this *disciple* of Gilbert Whitehand. And he's not after those Ba'al talismans or whatever it was Menander found up in the Carmel. He's after original Jesus. Bones, teeth, an ear, a toe, whatever you got. Does Menander have the goods? he says. Menander, cool as a cucumber – that's a long, greenish vegetable, mistress, they eat it in the Holy Land. Looks a lot like a… well, I shall spare your blushes. Menander, anyway, cool as you will, opens his scrip and lays down an index finger, two dried toes and a knee bone. "Will these do?" he says.

'Wilfred grins. "These will do just fine," he says.

'"And there is the small matter of my fee?" Menander says. So this Wilfred guy pays him. Handsomely, I should add. As we turn to leave I catch this Wilfred giving me a look. One fellow expatriate to another, like. Gives me the nod, says, "See you around, John Little."

'So how did he know me? Motherfucker's from Nottingham-shire same as me, used to come to the fights when I was still in the business. Small world, innit? Me and Menander got drunk as farts that night on the money, I woke up two days later in a room full of corpses. Don't ask me how they got there, cause I sure as shit don't know. My head's pounding worse than the Big Bell of Bow. And that fucker Wilfred's standing there, looking down on me, shakings his head, and he says to me, he says, "I heard the stories about you, John Little, but up until now I didn't believe them."

'"What do you mean?" I say. He says, "What do you call this?" and indicates the bodies. *I* say, "I am sure I don't know," and he says, "Well what do you think the local fuzz will call it?"

'"You gonna rat on me, Wilfred?" I say. He says, "Nah, us English boys need to stick together. Can I buy you breakfast?"

'So he takes me to the one place in Jaffa where they do proper English muck. The Pottage House. Run by some old crusader who made the best damn pottage that side of the Alps. Now there's a hangover cure. Took me right back home, it did. And Wilfred says, "I need more of those items, Little John, but your friend Menander isn't always reliable."

'"Oh?" I say.

'"Yes," he says. And then he lays down the spiel on me, about Gilbert Whitehand and all. Like I said, it's a small world.

'"So what do you want me to do?" I say when he's finished. He says, "If you find out Menander's contacts, maybe we could deal with them direct, you understand?" and then he leaves and pays for everything.

'So there I was with offers coming in, so to speak. And Menander says to me he's off to Jerusalem next – he has some business there too. And he says to me I should come, because everyone should see Jerusalem once before they die. Now we both don monks' robes, and in this manner we traverse the road out of Jaffa, and soon we leave the sea and the humidity behind us and begin the climb into the mountains. It is a strange land, I tell you true. So off we went. Birds watched us go, and Menander told me not all the birds were birds and some were sorcerers who take the shape of animals. But I thought he was just telling tales at that point. You shouldn't believe everything people tell you. "Now," he tells me, all serious, as we sit by the fire, "if you want *artefacts,* there's one kind of person you go to for that shit, but you do *not* want to fuck with them, Little John. They have no sense of humour."

'"Well, who are these humourless fuckers?" I say, curious.

'"They call themselves the Venerated Secret Brotherhood of the Seekers of the Grail," he tells me, all straight-faced. "And some say they were founded by Joseph of Arimathea, and some that they go way back to the Roman Empire and a secret department called the Imperial Office of Incognita Natura, who had their base in a place called the Area Quinquaginta Unus. Whichever way you shake the bottle, Little John, they're still around and hunting holy relics like a drunk in search of wine. They are a martial society, not unlike those Templar motherfuckers of yours, but if you want the primo stuff you have to deal with them sooner or later. Now, I trust you to watch my back, cause *I* don't trust *them.* They'd kill their own mothers if it helped them reach their goal."

'"What *is* their goal?" I said—'

39

'This is ridiculous,' Will Scarlett says. It's night-time now and they are camped around a fire, none of them having the cash to spare for a hostelry. Little John looks hurt again. He has been talking for hours.

'I was just getting to the good part,' he says.

'Next time *start* with the good part!' Will says. 'The key to a good story is to skip all the boring bits.'

'You are not a learned man,' Little John says, 'so I forgive you for this ignorance, Scarlett. Tell me, were you in the Holy Land?'

'I was.'

'You have that air about you, indeed you have.'

'What air is that, Little John?'

'That of a religious fanatic.'

'I was never that religious,' Will says.

'Nonsense. I bet you just swapped one for the other. Our Lord the Christ, for this Robin Hood.'

'Ah,' Will says. 'But you have not met Robin.'

'And I look forward to making his acquaintance in due course,' Little John says complacently. 'But in the meantime, do you want to hear the rest of the story or not? You have me all confused now and I lost my sense, and thread of thought. Where was I?'

'Going nowhere, slowly,' Will Scarlett says, and Little John grins.

'Which is how all these stories go…' he tells him. 'So—'

★

'I woke up one morning covered in corpses—'

'Of *course* you were,' Will says, and even Rebecca stirs.

'You have a problem, Little John,' she tells him. 'I think you must be one of those compulsive murderers, who kill not for a lord but out of some primal need—'

'No, mistress,' Little John says, 'you see, they were mostly bird corpses, and only a few men. I had no clear recollection of what had happened but I guess it's as Menander told me, that some were shapeshifters who had tried to rob us. I couldn't ask him, though, you see. I found him dead.'

'Of course you did,' Will mutters.

Rebecca stifles a laugh.

'I didn't kill him!' Little John says, wounded. 'At least, I don't think I did... In any case, bereft of my companion, I had no choice but to search his pockets and take what I could find. I was a poor man and still wanted. Luckily for me, Menander had been careless. Sewn into his robe I found a map marked with an X, and I surmised that this was the location for his contact in Jerusalem. I determined to meet with them still. Perhaps I could be of assistance to them, I thought, much as Menander was. I also took his bag of money and the relics. In due course I reached Jerusalem. It truly is a magnificent place, you know. The kings of Jerusalem are rich. The white walls rose into the sky and the newly built towers of that crusader nation looked out to the four corners of the wind, and not a few archers looked down, too. A lot of money went into refurbishing that old dump of a place. Gold gleamed in unexpected corners. A bird fell from the sky and transformed before me into a pretty young woman.

'"You killed my brother!" she said. She went at me with a knife but I disarmed her easily and held her in my arms. This was before I reached the walls, in a secluded spot.

'"You must have me mistaken with somebody else," I told her. "Please. I do not want to snap your neck. Who was your brother?"

'"He was a powerful Ifrit," she said, "with wings of flames, who came for the amulets of power which you carry."

'"All I remember is a bunch of dead birds," I told her. In truth I was a little woozy still from the night before. "I am sorry your brother was a bird. Come to think of it, are you a woman or a bird?"

'"I am neither," she said, "for I am a Sila, of the daughters of Lilith, and I will destroy you if you do not give me back these amulets!"

'"Fucking take them then," I said, because my head still hurt, my mate was dead, and I couldn't in truth give two shits for these old pieces of metal, whatever they were. Besides I was getting a right boner for this chick. She was clearly a Saracen of some sort, because this sort of witchery is generally frowned upon under the Church. But I couldn't see the harm in parting with Menander's loot.

'When I gave her the amulets she screeched with joy, a sound like a hawk crying. Immediately her manner towards me changed.

'"You have done a great service to the Banu Ifrit," she told me, all serious like, 'and for this I will grant you three wishes."

'Well, I mean, you don't say no to that, do you, I figured? So I told her my first wish, in very plain terms. At this a big grin came over her face and she jumped me, and, well, I shall spare you my details and your blushes but suffice to say we fucked like dogs in that copse there on the hills below Jerusalem.

'Well, all good things must come to an end and eventually we uncoupled and lay there as she burnt some leaves on the ground beside us. The smoke was sweet and heavy and my limbs felt very relaxed and my head clearer than usual.

'"You have a good heart, Little John," the Sila told me. "Even if you kill a lot of people."

'"I don't intend to," I told her, "it just happens sometimes."

'"I understand," she told me, stroking my hair. "Now as to your other two wishes?"

★

'Let me guess,' Will Scarlett says. It's the next morning and they're still on their way back to Nottingham.

Little John grins.

'Yeah,' he says. 'We fucked again.'

'Charming... Bit of a waste of a wish, though, isn't it?' Will says.

'You'd think so, wouldn't you, Scarlett,' Little John says. 'But then you've never fucked a demon, so what do you know?'

'... Fair point,' Will says. 'What was your third wish?'

'I told her I wanted out,' Little John says. 'I wanted to go home.'

'"Well," the Sila said, "then this is what you need to do." She outlined everything to me. Then she turned into a bird and flew away, the talismans held in her beak. I never did find out if they worked or what they do.

'Anyway, I did as she told me. I entered Jerusalem, seat of the Kingdom, passed the famed Tower of David where King Amalric was once besieged, saw the ruins of the Jews' Temple of which they are so proud, and even had time to take a piss outside the Church of the Holy Sepulchre. That city is a tricky thing, full of twisting stone streets and hostile locals all trying to fleece you for a penny, and it was overburdened with soldiers and mercenaries on account of the king's attempts to conquer Egypt and the Saracens' attempts, in turn, to part him from his head. Anyway, using Menander's map I located the safehouse of the Venerated Secret Brotherhood of the Seekers of the Grail.

'It had an elaborate door decorated with dragons and fallen star stones and cups, all very symbolic I am sure. I knocked and guards let me in. They had no weapons but I could tell they were deadly all the same. I went through a sunny courtyard where a water feature bubbled gently, and at last to a cool and shaded room, where the master of that order sat. He looked like an old blade, still deadly.

'"Well?" he said. "Who are you?"

'I told him, and he looked surprised. "From England?" he said. "One of our operatives ended up there back in the mid-five-hundreds. Chasing the old dragon, as it were. It was a shithole then and it's a shithole now, far as I can make out. Give me one good reason not to kill you."

'I stood up straight and looked him in the eye. That Saracen demon had told me exactly what to do. I said, "I have a client back in England with money to spare, and I heard you lot are always short on cash."

'"Yes, so?" he said; but he leant a little closer and he was no longer threatening to kill me, which was a definite improvement. "What sort of stuff? If it's to do with the grail, we cannot—"

'"No grails," I said. "They just want the Jesus stuff."

'"Oh, that," he said, and leant back, and looked smug all of a sudden. "Meat and bread, all that. What are they after? Bones? A kidney? We can do a deal, sure, if the price is right."

'Now, this was the key to the demon lady's plan. I said to him, "What's the most *expensive* thing you can lay your hands on?" and he smiled like the cat what got the cream, because it suited us both just fine to go for the high-end item.

'"Well," he said, "let me think. There's not that much of Jesus left to go around. Lots of interest, especially on the European market. Why, I shipped his left eyeball to the pope himself just last week."

'I knew he was just playing. I said, "The client can pay generously. And he's keen. Very keen."

'"Well, then," he said, "let's take a walk, John Little of England. Come." And he led me out of that room and down to a cool, dark cellar, where they kept the good shit. I saw things that day, Mistress Rebecca. Things you wouldn't believe. The Ark of the Covenant and King Solomon's ring. Egyptian snake-staffs and a Jacob's Ladder and the hands of John the Baptist, which allow the user to live and breathe underwater, or so the master told me. I began to suspect he was in actuality quite mad. Then he took me to the very back of the room and beckoned me over. There was a little, white stone washbasin there, packed with ice. I do not know how they procured the ice, though Jerusalem does get cold in the winters, I hear, and gets covered in snow. The master reached into the ice and returned with a small vial of glass. It was filled with a red, viscous liquid. He put it into my hand and closed my fingers gently over it. It felt warm, almost alive.

'"The blood of the Christ," he said to me softly. "Collected into the grail as it dripped from the Christ's side as he bled upon the Roman cross. How do they say in your land? How do you like *them* apples?"

'"I like them just fine," I said.

'And I smiled at him. And he smiled back.'

Little John shrugs. They are on the outskirts of Nottingham, having passed harmlessly through the wood. The gates are just ahead. He says, 'The rest was easy. I went back to Wilfred in Jaffa and told him the score. It took him a while to get a letter of credit cleared through the local Templar office, but once he did he exchanged it for gold and we did the deal on neutral ground, in the port of Ashdod. Once Wilfred had the vial of blood in his possession he entrusted it to me to carry back, and Rob here came along for extra muscle. Doesn't say much, does Rob, but then I do talk a lot to make up for it, don't I? And now here we are. Nottingham. I dare say Gilbert will be very pleased to have this. And it's nice to be back home at last. Now I could murder for a pint of ale and a bowl of homemade pottage. What say you, my lads?'

'*Finally*,' Will groans. 'I thought you'd never shut up. Look, dickheads. I'm going straight to the Goat, where I intend to drink the house dry. If your business with Whitehand is finished and you need a gig, I dare say the Hood would be happy to consider you. I'll see you there. Or not. Goodbye. Fucking Christ—' With that he thunders off.

The watchmen, Bert and Ernest, nod to Rebecca and the others as they pass. They exchange glances.

'Odd fellows she travels with,' Bert says.

'It's an odd sort of time,' Ernest says sagely.

They stand and stare.

After a while, a small cart, pulled by a donkey, arrives at the gates of the town. A rotund and cheerful monk sits atop it. He waves to the guards.

'Oh, hello there,' Bert says.

'Welcome, welcome,' Ernest says.

'Thanks, boys,' the monk says. He chews a blade of grass and looks up at the town. He feels the many knives strapped to his hidden belt. He smiles.

'So *this* is Nottingham,' Brother Tuck says.

PART ELEVEN

THE KILL

40

From high on his perch above the town Birdie watches the world. He is heavier now, and the climb's more arduous, and while the air still calls seductively to him to ride the winds his wings are gone forever. The world changes. But Birdie has Jesus, and the promise of heaven. And that is enough, that should be enough, he thinks.

He watches the town. He sees Rebecca returning. He scents magic. Rebecca is carrying. She wends her way through the town.

Birdie watches the gate. He sees the monk arrive. He scents violence. He scents blood. The monk carries knives.

Birdie wants to open her wings. Birdie wants to fly.

Instead she closes her eyes. She whispers a prayer.

Remember not, Lord, our offences, nor the offences of our forefathers; neither take thou vengeance of our sins: spare us, good Lord, spare thy people, whom thou hast redeemed with thy most precious blood.

'So this is Nottingham?' Brother Tuck says. He turns to the guards. 'Hey, you two,' he says, 'know of a good place to crash round here?'

'You're a Benedictine, Brother?' Ernest says. 'There's St. Nick's priory, the brothers there will take you in no doubt.'

'It ain't like that,' Tuck says. 'I'm after a general hostelry, somewhere genial and jolly. Do you know of such a place?'

'There's the Goat, but it is full of wretched men,' Bert says. 'And there's Dick's within the Night Market, where all the sins and pleasures meet. But you do not want to go there, Brother.'

'A Brother's task is to forgive the sinners,' Tuck says comfortably. 'Who among us hasn't sinned, eh, guardsman? Can you speak to that?'

'I am sure I cannot, good Brother,' Ernest says, and Bert nods quickly. Tuck grins at them disarmingly and tosses them a bottle made of clay.

'A drink for this cold weather,' he tells them. 'Now where did you suggest...?'

'The Green Man, on the English side of town, Brother. Though it serves ale at all hours and there's a brothel beside it.'

'That will do well,' Tuck decides. 'I thank you kindly.'

'You're welcome.'

'Goodbye.'

'And to you, Brother.'

Tuck prods his donkey. The cart rolls slowly into town. The guardsmen watch him go.

'What a nice man,' Bert says.

'We never asked what he had in the back of his cart,' Ernest says.

Bert shrugs.

'What *could* he have?'

He opens the wine.

Tuck leaves the cart and donkey outside the Green Man. What an odd little town, he thinks. Green men stare at you from the walls and the rafters, hidden behind vegetation everywhere. Tuck whistles 'Greensleeves'. A couple of sullen kids with dirty faces watch him. He tosses them a coin. 'Watch the old wagon for me, will ya?' he says.

Casually sweeps aside his cape, just so they get a glimpse of the knives.

'What do you do, Brother?' one of the kids asks.

'I clean up.'

'What's there to clean up?' the kid says. 'It's beautiful here.'

'Just keep an eye on my shit, will you?' Tuck says. He saunters into the Green Man. Dark. Dingy. Dirty floor. Dirty cups. Drunk men. The smell of ale.

Just the way he likes it.

He sits at a table. He orders a cup.

He waits, because bad shit is about to go down.

Rebecca enters the inner sanctum of Gilbert Whitehand, and the man himself is there to greet her arrival.

'At last!' he says. His face is pale, his hands are white, his eyes are jittery, the pupils huge. Rebecca wonders if he's slept at all, or left his underground lair in all the time she's been away.

'Do you have it? Do you have it?' he says.

'Do you have what I asked?'

'What did you ask?' He looks genuinely confused.

'The witch. To let her go.'

'Ah, that. We shall all miss her. Such a delightful spirit. Oh, how we laugh!' He rubs his hands together. 'Give it to me,' he says.

Rebecca, sickened with the whole thing, complies. Brings out the vial. Gilbert snatches it from her hand.

He breathes.

'At last! Is it the real thing?'

'Authenticated as per your request.'

'Any problems along the way?' he says, looking at her with suspicion.

Rebecca shrugs. 'You could have told me Will was to be your price.'

Gilbert laughs. 'They chop him up, eh?'

'Actually, no.'

'How come?'

'Dunno. Don't care.'

'Oh, well. Tell the fucker if he has a problem to come find me, then.'

'The witch?' Rebecca says.

'Yes, yes…' He motions her to follow. They enter the room where the witch is kept. She is awake. The engine or mill or whatever it is churns and churns at the side of the room. The witch whimpers in pain. The witch says, 'Rebecca?'

Rebecca takes the witch's hand. So frail and old. The skin has softened in her time here. She used to have skin as rough as unworked leather.

'I am sorry,' Rebecca tells her. 'I was wrong.'

'You? Wrong?' the witch says. 'Surely, Rebecca, such a thing is impossible.'

Rebecca wilts under the witch's words. She swallows. She is tired and dirty from the road. Tired and dirty, it seems to her, from the whole life she had chosen. She had thought it romantic, all the magic and adventure. But it's all turned to shit.

'I was wrong to try and keep you alive,' she says. 'The means were foul and the intention selfish. I will let you go.'

The witch's bright eyes examine her ruthlessly, then the witch sighs. 'So you have finally become the woman that you are,' she says. 'Mazal tov.' She cackles. 'Is that how you say it? Now that you know who you are and what you have done, Rebecca, where will you go?'

'I don't know,' Rebecca says.

'Wherever you go, there you'll still be,' the witch says. 'You can't run from yourself. But you can still choose to be something different.'

'Enough!' Gilbert Whitehand says. 'I have no time for all this tattle! Say your goodbyes and be done with it.'

'Goodbye,' Rebecca says.

'Goodbye,' the witch says. She closes her eyes. 'Farewell, cruel world…' she says. And then she cackles one last time, the laugh wracking her body, until Gilbert gives the nod and the monks turning the engine stop, and the machine grinds down, and a final breath escapes the witch's lips and shudders out of her lungs and then she's still.

'Well?' Gilbert says. 'Are we done here?'

Rebecca stares at him in hatred, and she is glad. In her heart she is glad of the deal she'd struck back in London.

'Yes,' she says. 'We're done.'

'Good, then fuck off already, will you?' Gilbert says. 'Look, you have to see it from my point of view. I'm sympathetic and all but I have work to do. Do you want the body?'

'She deserves burial,' Rebecca says quietly.

'This place is as good as a grave,' Gilbert says. 'But sure. I'll have one of the novitiates dump her your way. Alright?'

'Goodbye, Gilbert Whitehand,' Rebecca says. 'We shall not meet again.'

'No, I fucking hope not,' Gilbert mutters.

He stares after her as she leaves. He thought the damned woman would *never* leave! He pats the witch's hand before remembering she's dead now. Oh, well. The witch was a fool, and so is her disciple. Death was but the beginning of a wonderful adventure! Lots of people came back from death. There was even an old Greek word for it. Necromancy. He feels out the word on his lips. He likes the sound of it. The way it rolls. He holds the vial of blood.

Only one way to find out if it works, he thinks.

★

'Hey, Birdie.'

'Hey, Becca.'

Birdie watches Rebecca climb up to the tower. She looks tired, Birdie thinks. Fairy time doesn't age you but it stretches you thin. Birdie says, 'How did you know I'd be here?'

'Honestly? I didn't. I just wanted somewhere to hide.'

'Yes, well,' Birdie says. 'This is a good place for it.'

Rebecca comes and sits beside Birdie. They look out. It's a clear sky for once. The wood all around the town seems peaceful. Boats pass below on the Trent.

'Bad shit is coming,' Birdie says.

'Bad shit's been happening for a long time here, Birdie.'

'Still.'

'I don't care,' Rebecca says. She starts to laugh. The tears roll down her face and sting her lips. Her vision blurs through the drops. 'I don't care, I don't care!'

Birdie touches her shoulder gently; hesitatingly. Birdie is not used to touch. Birdie says, 'What will you do now?'

'I lost my last link to the past today,' Rebecca says. 'But you knew that already, Birdie, didn't you? How do you always know everything?'

'I listen,' Birdie says.

'I'm leaving,' Rebecca says. 'I'm tired of this story. Nottingham. Sherwood. The Hood. I never belonged here. England.' She all but spits the word.

'Fucking England,' she says.

'You could come to the Lord,' Birdie says. Knowing the words have no meaning to Rebecca.

'Fuck off, Birdie. I might go to Normandy though. Or Italy or somewhere. There are Jews everywhere. I'll be fine. I've got money saved up. I'll be the rich eccentric aunt of some relatives in Rouen I never met. But you knew how this story goes long before I did, didn't you, Birdie? You got out too, in your own way. You bailed.'

'I found Christ,' Birdie says, devoutly. Rebecca wipes tears from her eyes.

'Don't give me that shit, Birdie,' she says. 'You found a way out, so you took it. I was stupid to believe in magic. You knew better. You left.'

Birdie nods. Birdie watches the darkening skies. Birdie says, 'Bad shit is coming.'

'Yeah,' Rebecca says, and they sit there in companionable silence.

Down deep below the city in his sanctum sanctorum, Gilbert Whitehand stares bewitched at the patchwork mannequin he had assembled. He holds the vial of blood. He pours it through a hole in the neck into the lattice of pipes that run through the corpse.

The blood drips, drips, drips.

Gilbert stares, transfixed. Is it his imagination, or do the cheeks flush? Does colour return to those mummified hands? All he needs is a heart, that great mysterious engine that, Avicenna says, heats the body and provides its source of power.

All Gilbert needs is a heart...

His glance departs the mannequin and travels across that dark secluded room, across the burning frankincense and candles... alighting at last on the man tied to a chair, his mouth gagged.

The man stares up at Gilbert Whitehand. His eyes are white and terrified. He tries to speak but the gag in his mouth stifles his words or his screams.

Gilbert smiles.

Gilbert reaches for the butcher's knife.

Gilbert says, 'Hello, Robin.'

41

Our Father, who art in heaven,
Hallowed be thy name;
Thy kingdom come;
Thy will be done;
On earth as it is in heaven.

42

'Come, come, Robin, your usefulness is done,' Gilbert says coaxingly. He wields the knife. He's had a lot of practice. The prisoner's eyeballs are white, they track him as he comes. Robin pisses on himself. Gilbert says, 'Hush, it won't hurt almost none.'

He stabs the Hood. The blood sprays but Gilbert doesn't mind. His white hands are painted red. He has to act fast, while the heart still beats. He wipes sweat off his brow with the back of his hand. He has to be *meticulous*. He stabs, stabs, slices. The prisoner's chest gapes open. The blood jets out. Good, good. The Hood is still alive. Now for the tricky part. He concentrates.

He sticks his hands into the hole in the prisoner's chest.

He can feel it then.

Contracting.

Expanding.

Still beating...

Now!

His fingers grasp that huge unnatural tumour and *pull*. Gilbert strains. The heart is hot – it burns his fingers. The Hood's eyes stare into his and now they're green, as green as leaves.

Pull!

He strains. The chair the prisoner is in topples and Gilbert falls with it, lands on top of Robin, pins him down with his knees. He—

Pulls!

And the heart *moves*. Gilbert strains, he heaves, and the tumour that is Robin's heart detaches from his chest. It beats in Gilbert's hands. He stares at it, enchanted. The heart is green.

Well, of course it is. *She* had been quite specific it would do. *She* had been *most* helpful.

He just hadn't expected the heart to be so *heavy*.

It is still attached to the Hood's body. Green shoots trailing from the heart into the chest cavity. The heart beats. The Hood's eyes are still open, staring. His mouth moves as though he tries to speak.

Oh, let him, Gilbert thinks. He removes the gag from the Hood's mouth.

'Well?' Gilbert says.

'Fuck… you…'

Gilbert pats him on the shoulder, not unkindly. 'You had a good run,' he says.

He holds the heart one-handed. He reaches for the knife again.

'You'll live forever,' he tells Robin.

Then he cuts the roots.

The Hood screams. The scream echoes around that awful room, but there is no one else to hear it. Which is a waste, really, Gilbert thinks. It is a *good* scream.

The heart still beats. It is so hot to hold. Gilbert drops the knife, hefts the green heart and goes to his mannequin. It is beautiful. Made of Jesus's fingers and Jesus's liver and Jesus's teeth (as many as he could buy) and parts of legs and arms that, if not belonging to the Saviour himself, then at least to some prominent saints (all available on the relic market from dealers of good standing).

The torso he sourced locally. Though it did belong to a monk. And the skull belonged to the second of the popes, Linus. Gilbert had acquired it at great expense from Rome.

The chest of the mannequin is open. Ready. The heart is so hot in Gilbert's hands. Robin's corpse is slumped on the floor. Gilbert whispers a prayer. He shoves the green heart into the Jesus he's created. He shoves it deep, positions it just right. He waits. The heart pulses. Gilbert closes the flap of skin on the mannequin's chest. He sews it quickly, his fingers slick with blood. He lights more frankincense. He chants. The candles flicker in that airless room.

Gilbert prays.

Something moves.

What was that?

Gilbert opens his eyes. He prays and prays without sound.

Something moves. There! He caught it this time.

The mannequin's chest…

It's *moving*.

Gilbert stands. He stares.

The Jesus is *breathing*.

High on her perch above the town Birdie watches the world. She sees the darkening skies, the sun dripping down the horizon like a spoiled yolk. She sees the lonely horse and its rider as they swiftly depart town. There is no one there to see Rebecca go. No one but Birdie.

'Goodbye, Miss Becca…' Birdie whispers.

As Rebecca departs she casts one look back.

'Bye bye, Birdie,' she says.

There's a strange smell in the air. How had she never noticed it before? Rot, and mulch, and sorcery. God, she hates it.

Still. She grew up here. Had her first love. Committed her first murder. All that has to count for something.

But everybody has to come from somewhere.

She spurs her horse on, and she doesn't look back.

*

Brother Tuck sits still and listens to the silence. He taps out the seconds on the table, one tap, two taps, three...

Bad shit is coming.

Bad shit is here.

'I'm going to *kill* Robin when I find him,' Scarlett says.

He looks around him at the faces of the other hoods in the Goat. The way they shift awkwardly away.

'What?' he says. 'What did I say?'

The Jesus's eyes spring open. The green heart beats inside its chest. Hidden within, green shoots grow. They animate the desiccated arms and mismatched legs. The creature's fingers flex. It looks into Gilbert's eyes.

'My Lord, you are arisen!' Gilbert says. 'You're alive, alive!'

The creature's mouth opens. A tongue (formerly in the mouth of a saint from Padua) moves sluggishly. It licks those dry lips. The creature tries to speak.

'Our Father, who art in heaven!' Gilbert cries. 'Hallowed be thy name!'

The creature's fingers flex. It takes a cautious step and almost falls, but rights itself. One hand grasps Gilbert by the shoulder. The creature steadies.

'Let me be your staff to lean upon!' Gilbert says.

The creature's holy face nears Gilbert's. It looks at him. The mouth opens. Two rows of mismatched teeth.

'My Lord, speak!'

The creature's mouth opens wide. It leans its other hand on Gilbert's shoulders.

It screams.

The scream is like a foul miasma blasting out of its infernal guts. It spews on Gilbert's face. Black ichor and wriggling slugs. The creature screams and screams.

Gilbert cries without sound. Gilbert says, 'Please, Lord, please...'

The creature's fingers close on Gilbert's neck. The creature blinks. It *twists*.

It wrings the Whitehand's neck.

Tap, tap... *tap*.

Brother Tuck rises. The silence only he can hear is broken at last.

The bad shit is here.

He leaves some coins on the table for the drinks.

'If I were you,' he tells the proprietor, 'I might consider closing for the night. Oh, and hiding in the cellar.' He adds this as an afterthought.

'We don't close,' the proprietor grunts.

Tuck shrugs with good humour.

'Just a word to the wise. Good night.'

He leaves. The two sullen kids are gone from near his cart. Tuck goes to the back. He opens the trap.

Crosses and holy water, sharp stakes and a crossbow with iron-tipped arrows. A bible in Latin and a rosary blessed by the pope. A bucket of fish heads.

Tuck arms himself. Tuck whistles. In truth he hasn't had this much fun since the Horror of the Lepers of St. Ninian's. A story whose single written record can be found only in the Archivum Apostolicum Vaticanum deep under Rome.

Provincial fuckholes messing about with the nature of creation again.

Nothing for them to do, Tuck thinks uncharitably, other than fuck pigs or mess about with necromancy.

He thinks of the case of the Miracle of Montmartre and the bloodbath he and Eustace had to stem in that nest of horrors on top of that hill. It had been one of their early cases. Tuck touches the scar on his chest. He'd been more careless back then.

He whistles cheerfully as he assembles his weapons. Then he shuts the cart and ambles down the road to begin the hunt.

'She did *what*?' Will screams.

'Traded Hood to that Whitehand monk so he could make a new Jesus,' Alan-a-dale says, strumming the harp. He's strutted into the Goat with the silent Much in his wake. 'What are you not following, Scarlett?'

'That's the stupidest thing I ever heard!'

'Yeah, well, why do you think Hood traded *you* for the blood? He was trying to sweep up the wood. So to speak. To *assert* himself. He cut a deal with the Whitehand for power and you were the price. But the Green Lady doesn't like it when her Robins get too independent, now does she, Much?'

The scarecrow creature that is Much, the miller's son, shakes his head sorrowfully. He passes a long, sharp branch finger across his throat.

'That's right, Much. That's right.'

'Wait, what?' Will says.

Then he raises his eyes and falls silent as he sees Maid Marian come in.

The Green Lady dominates the space. The hoods fall into respectful silence. The Lady seems to glow in the Gloomph; she alone is a light that cuts through the foggy air of this town.

'My ears are burning,' she says. 'Were you speaking of me?'

'My lady—' Will starts, then stops.

'You are back from London safely, I see? You are only missing an ear.'

'And a finger!'

The lady shrugs. 'A small price to pay, I am sure. Tell me, does the one called Morgan still rule over there?'

Will blushes. 'She's but a phantom,' he says.

'Ah, well, aren't we all?' Marian blesses him with her smile. Then she turns her disconcerting green eyes on the two newcomers.

'And who are these?' she says.

'My lady,' the big one says. 'I am John Little, though they call me Little John. Of this parish, ma'am. An honour, it is.' He tries to bow clumsily. Maid Marian laughs.

'Settle down, Little John,' she says. 'I saw you fight the Mad Irish Monk, Fergal, back in the day.'

'You did?'

She gifts him a smile. 'In the shadows. Though I bet on you going down in the fourth, which you did without fail. Tell me, Little John. Do you crave a life of excitement, a camaraderie of fighters, all the venison you could eat, and never growing old again?'

'My lady, I do!'

'Then come, join us! Join Robin Hood and his band of Merry Men!'

'My lady! I will!'

Little John quivers at attention. The silent one with him stays silent.

'*What* fucking Robin Hood?' Will says in exasperation.

The Green Lady ignores his outburst. She turns her eyes on Little John's companion.

'I watched you sleep when you were little...' she says. 'You're from around here, aren't you? And went off to the crusades. What is your name? Wait, it will come to me...'

'It's Rob,' the man says.

'That'll do,' Main Marian says. She grabs him by the shoulders, leans in and kisses him.

Roots grow deep. And Maid Marian has made her home in the woods for centuries past.

Rob melts into her arms. A breath of greenery passes from her into his lungs. It speaks of primal forest, rings of standing stones. Of fairies dancing, of blood sacrifice. A giant oak. A pool of black water.

Somewhere deep in the forest the elfin knight shudders deep under the ground, the roots that hold him prisoner clutch again with new force.

'... Wow,' Rob says.

She lets him go. She says, 'Give him some Lincoln greens, a bow and arrow and some decent boots. I crown him Hood. I call him Robin.'

Rob stands. He looks bewitched. And then he grins. His eyes are green. His transformation's subtle but it's absolute.

'Well, motherfuckers, *what*!' he says. 'Let's go.'

'Go where?' Will says, and Alan strums the harp and Much, the miller's son, sharpens his thorny claws.

'Go out there! Didn't you hear the harpist—Sorry, what's your name again?'

'Alan-a-dale.'

'Alan say all that stuff about the double deal with Whitehand and the blood and all that rot? He's made a freaking *Jesus*!'

'So?' Will says.

The Green Lady turns her green eyes on him and Will can't pull away, he is trapped by the power she holds.

'So go out there and fucking *kill* it, won't you?' Maid Marian says.

Birdie watches the town. She watches as the residents, long used to strange bewitchment and occasional acts of mindless brutality, close and lock their doors and shutter their windows.

The streets are empty. No one will play games of chance and inhale dwale vapours in the Night Market tonight. Inside Dick's, Sir Richard at the Lee mixes opium tincture into a glass of ale and drinks it as he watches the Gloomph sweep across town. The streets are empty. The streets are clear. And one small rotund figure comes marching up Piss Street with a cheerful whistle, a cross and a knife.

'Here kitty kitty, here kitty cat...'

Birdie watches, but more than that he scents the air of the city, which is thick with a foul miasma of witchery. And he sees, coming from the direction of Cock Street, a lumbering figure, shambling along, with a crown of thorns upon its head and murder in its heart: a Jesus.

'Oh, Jesus,' Birdie whispers, and he makes the sign of the cross. But this Jesusman is not Birdie's; this is a false idol, an antichrist, and it leaves bloodied footprints as it walks, and behind it, from the direction of Cock Street, there does come the roar of a bellowing fire, right where the Chapel of the Sacred Order of the Faith and Peace of The Holy Angel Azrael very recently stood.

'Oh, *Jesus*,' Birdie says.

'Here, kitty kitty! I have something you'll like!'

Brother Tuck's dowsing rod hums and his fingertips tingle. The rod's official Vatican field-kit equipment, blessed by two archbishops on the grave of a saint. The rod points unerringly at the source of the infraction. As annoying it is to admit it, what Gilbert Whitehand has done, however unwittingly, is perform a genuine miracle.

Now, miracles are fucking tricky things, this much Tuck knows. And whether they're intrusions by God into the order of reality, or whether God had built them into the mechanism of Creation, who the fuck knows. Tuck's not a *theologian*. He's a trained exorcist.

In his time he's seen some shit. Demons in Athens and werewolves in Paris and satanic cults in every other shithole in the Western world. Oh, they were out there: the freaks and the geeks and the ghouls and the damned. People liked to pretend Christianity had always been there, but Tuck knows better than most that it is only a patina of paint over a crudity of scenery. That down below, and not that deep, people still believe in ghosties and goblins and will-o'-the-wisps, in fairies and curses and witches and gods. Old gods. Green Men and Wodens and Friges and Tiws. They were even there in the names of the week, as if anyone thought *that* shit was clever. Tuck knows that on any given Tiw's Day there are at least a hundred secret societies *somewhere* across Europe practising some sort of forbidden old ritual. He knows there are more witches than you can fucking *count* across Christendom, and he knows that one day, soon, the Church will rise to exterminate them, and it will be a long and ruthless and bloodied campaign when it comes. He knows all this, even as he knows that magic's mostly bullshit. But still.

Sometimes, just *sometimes*, someone tries to break the laws of nature and ends up raising some horrible monstrosity: conjuring a demon or raising the dead or, you know, *bringing back Jesus*.

You'd think this fucking place, this time, would be an isolated incident! But no. They *always* try to bring back Jesus.

He wishes Eustace was here. But Eustace is tied up in London. So Tuck's here all alone. He holds the bucket of fish heads in one hand and the dowsing rod in the other.

'Here, kitty kitty!' he says.

Somewhere ahead of him, a roar and a scream.

Tuck makes towards the commotion.

43

'**H**e didn't even fucking *feel* it!' Will Scarlett screams. His arm's broken. He's pretty sure his arm's broken. Maybe also his back.

The creature strides away. Arrows stick out of its chest and back and shoulders.

They'd waited in ambush for him. They hid on the rooftops and in the alleyways and when it came they let *rip*. They fired enough arrows at the thing to take down an army of men.

But the Jesus just grunted, and slapped Will so hard that he flew through the air (and landed badly), and now it's walking away, and it tears off the arrows one by one and lets them clatter to the ground as it strides.

'Where the fuck is it *going*?'

'Church?' someone says.

Will tries to stand up. Alan-a-dale helps him.

'Thanks.'

'Don't mention it.'

Will hobbles after the creature. Alan-a-dale shrugs and follows.

'Here, kitty kitty cat!'

★

'What in the name of f—'

A little child has wandered out into the street. Perhaps it doesn't have a parent. Perhaps nobody cares for it. A little girl. She skips, delighted with the empty street she has entirely to herself.

Then she sees the shambling creature coming. Something about him looks familiar, but what?

That crown of thorns? Those stigmata on his palms, which bleed where the arrows hit him?

'Hey, mister,' the little girl says. 'Are you lost?'

The Jesus looks down on her with its strange mismatched eyes.

'To'eh… anochi… anochi to'eh!'

The hoods watch covertly from behind a wall.

'What the fuck did he say?'

'It must be Aramaic or, I don't know, Ogham.'

'What the *fuck* is Aramaic?'

'I think it's Hebrew, actually,' Little John says. 'I picked up a smattering back in the Holy Land, you know.'

'Never figured you for having a facility with language, Little John.'

'Well, people will surprise you, won't they, Rob. Is it still Rob?'

'The name's Hood. Robin Hood.'

'What*ever*.'

'So what did he say?'

'What?'

'What did he say? The Jesus?'

'I think he said he was lost.'

'No shit, he is lost.'

'Someone should get that girl out of there.'

'Are you volunteering?'

'Not me, not me,' Will says. 'Where *is* he going, anyway?'

'Church?' someone says again.

'Why would Jesus go to a fucking church? He was fucking Jewish!'

'You sound like Rebecca now, Will.'

'Well, she had my back, didn't she? Not like you lot. And the last Hood selling me out to the Templars.'

'You can't still be sore about that.'

'It only just happened!'

'But what *are* they talking about?' Alan-a-dale says.

'Shh. Let me listen.'

The hoods fall quiet as they watch.

'Are you God?' the little girl says.

'Anochi...' The creature hesitates. 'Einen'i?'

'What's he saying!'

'That he's not God? I think?'

'He doesn't look... sure.'

'Well, he must be pretty confused, considering.'

'Do you think he *is* God? Or the son of God? Or, I don't know, God adjacent?'

'What the fuck is God adjacent?'

'Like the pope or something!'

'Maybe he's a saint?'

'He just killed a whole bunch of people!'

'Yes, well, so did a lot of saints!'

'What? Name one!'

'St. George.'

'Well, name another, then.'

'St. Vladimir of Kiev.'

'Come on...'

'St. Moses the Black—'

'Alright, you've made your—'

'St. Longinus, St. Quiteria, Olga of Kiev—'

'Alright! How do you *know* so many saints?'

'You kill people for a living, you need saints who can protect you,' Little John says. 'Now hush, I'm trying to hear—'

'It was nice to meet you!' the little girl says brightly. She pats the Jesus on the arm and skips away, towards the hidden hoods. The Jesus turns and stares after her.

He looks confused.

'Mahu miflat bnei me'ayim ze, mekom rima vetole'a?' he says.

'What did he say!'

Now it's Little John who looks confused.

'I think he just asked, What is this shithole?'

'... Fair,' Will says, after consideration.

Which is when the Jesus raises a face twisted in anguish up to the heavens and begins to scream.

Up in the tower, Birdie shudders with the force of the cry. It bellows out of lungs powered by a heart that is like Birdie's. It is of the forest, of old magic, of dead gods who can't stay dead.

This is the thing about religion. A god's only a god once they've died and been reborn.

Everything else – the candles and the incense and the prayers – all of that's just *afterthought*. What matters is that seasons *change*. The old year dies. The new one is reborn. The god is dead. The god comes back so crops can grow and birds can sing and flowers bloom once more.

Birdie hears all of that in the sound. The *anguish* of it, too. To live is to hurt, for this simulacrum Gilbert Whitehand made.

But then isn't that what *all* living is?

Birdie watches. Far down below, the hoods emerge from their hiding places.

They carry crossbows and axes and knives.

They converge on the screaming figure of something that sort of maybe kind of resembles Our Lord and Saviour, that vanished martyr from the Galilee.

In *his* time Rome had not yet even bothered to turn its attention to this shitty little island. In *his* time Egypt had only just fallen to the Romans. In *his* time...

But this isn't his time.

And he is only a bad copy.

Birdie prays, nonetheless. Let this creature live and show it kindness. Let it be. She watches as the hoods unleash a storm of arrows, as they creep up on the creature with their blades.

And she sees, coming from the other direction, a cheerful, rotund shape, holding, for whatever reason, a bucket of rotting fish heads and calling out, 'Here kitty kitty!'

'Who the fuck are you!' the new Hood shouts.

'I'm Tuck!' Brother Tuck shouts back. It's hard to hear anything over the anguished cry of the creature. 'Who the hell are you!'

'I'm Robin Hood!'

'Really? Don't look like much, mate! Now back off, the Jesus is mine.'

'We've got it covered, Brother! Back off!'

'Listen you pissant amateur!' Tuck shouts back. 'I'm the professional here! I'm fucking *Tuck*! I'm here on papal *decree*!'

The new Hood sets loose an arrow. It lands between Tuck's legs.

'This is *my* fucking decree!' the Hood screams.

'He's really coming along fast,' Alan-a-dale murmurs to Will. Will shrugs.

'At least he talks now,' he says. 'On the way back from London, he didn't say a fucking word.'

'Well,' Alan says, considering it, 'he wasn't important for the story then.'

'I guess not.'

Brother Tuck pulls out a blade shaped like a cross. He holds it up. 'It is time for you now,' he says ceremoniously to the creature, who pays him no attention whatsoever, 'to return to the primordial ooze from whence you came, creature! Begone, foul fiend, in the name of the Father, the Son and the Holy Ghost! Amen!'

And he runs screaming at the Jesus.

Everything happens fast and slow. The way it would, perhaps, if an army of monks had drawn the same scene over and over again on sheets of stiff parchment, making tiny changes each time, then bound them into a single illuminated manuscript and flipped the pages in a rapid pace, so that the illustrations came alive in a semblance of action, and the tiny drawn figures were seen to run and jump and be in a motion of pictures. If there was such a thing, it might look like this:

The Jesus, effortlessly slamming Brother Tuck right out of the air, the way one swats a fly. The arrows sticking out of its body quivering like the quills of a porcupine.

Tuck, flying through the air, slamming into the new Hood.

The new Hood, falling back by the force of the implosion, hitting Little John, who falls himself, sweeping Alan and Will with him, until all the hoods end up in an undignified pile on the ground.

The little girl, turning back, her big bright eyes alive with fear and wonder.

Birdie, in his tower, her hand up to her mouth, watching, standing on tiptoe as if, for just a moment, Birdie had forgotten they can no longer fly.

The hoods and Tuck, regrouping, reaching for their knives and coming at the creature – who turns and turns, afraid, alone, and sure to die at last, once more, if only—

And it stops. The pages end without a proper finish. No monks will illuminate this manuscript, and so they do not see the scarecrow creature who materialises without sound (all this without sound, if only there was a way to record it somehow, they say certain stones hold sounds within them, and ravens can mimic and replay human voices sometimes, so perhaps if there were an army of ravens trained to remember and repeat each a word or a line on command, and thus played, one by one, could repeat to us through time the speech and dialogue of vanished peoples, and if their chicks could then be trained in turn to repeat the words of their progenitors, and so on down the ages, and couple that with the flip book of moving pictures to create something new, what shape would it take?).

The scarecrow creature is, of course, Much, the miller's son, still called that though the miller has been dead for decades now. The scarecrow speaks to the creature in some language of which no words survive. An ancient tongue of root and branch. The Jesus listens. And the men stop in their tracks – Will, Robin, Alan-a-dale, Little John and Tuck, they watch the scarecrow pleading with the creature, extending a hand like a forking branch, and the Jesus takes it.

Up on his perch Birdie watches. From up on high he can see the tiny figures. The hoods are silent and still. The creature and the scarecrow hold hands. They walk silently away, down the empty streets of Nottingham, along Piss Street and Rose Street and Leatherworkers' Lane and the Night Market and down to the side gates, and they pass from the town into the wood, where all creatures can still be free; even a Nazarene.

Birdie sighs wistfully; for just a moment she, too, would like to return to the wood and be free. There is a place for her on earth still, just as there is for every freak and geek, for every misfit and monster, saviour or saint. For all things bright and beautiful, all creatures great and small, all things wise and wonderful, the Lord God made them all.

A calm descends on Nottingham. The hoods disperse. The bells begin to ring for Vigil.

And all, for a time, is well.

PART TWELVE

THE QUARRY

44

'Y̶ou fucked me,' Alanah says.

The bishop blinks up at her from his desk. 'Excuse me?'

'You fucked me on the deal.'

'I did no such thing, bone harpist.'

'Don't give me that, *Roger*.' She stares at him accusingly. 'My quarry's still under protection. The cook has been avoiding me. The new Hood's fucking useless, some Jesus went nuts around Nottingham last year, and I *still* cannot breach the boundary to Fairyland. Promises have been *made*, Bishop.'

He blinks again. He's fat and old, is Roger. Diminished both physically and in his power. The Becket murder did it. Disowned by the pope in Rome and then restored in second place to Canterbury. He hasn't got long now, Alanah figures. She forgets how quickly human lives *go*.

'You owe me,' she says again.

The bishop rubs his face. 'My treasure room,' he says. 'Vacarius will show you…'

He closes his eyes. There are wine stains on his habit. In moments he begins to snore.

'Follow me,' Vacarius says. He materialises so softly. 'How goes it, harpist?'

'How goes it with you?'

'Oh, very well, I am glad you asked. Roman law is really

making *significant* strides to being incorporated into a new more systematic form of an English legal framework and I—'

'Come on, Vacarius. I don't give a fuck.'

He bows his head. 'Of course.'

'I was just being polite.'

'Yes, of course.'

'Take me to the fucking treasure room.'

'We're here.'

He materialises a key.

'Oh. That wasn't very far.'

'No.' Vacarius unlocks the door. 'I just want you to know I disapprove of this collection.'

'Hey, Vacarius, guess what?'

Vacarius sighs. 'You don't give a fuck?'

'That's right, buddy.'

'Very well.'

He lights a candle. The room is made of bricks. There are no windows. Shelves line every wall. In the candlelight Alanah sees all the useless shit the bishop's kept there. Some of it she brought for him herself. There're magic rings and axes, magic carpets, magic beans.

'Fairyland's a joke,' Vacarius tells her. 'It's bound to go away sooner or later. Men will find *reason*, harpist! Where once there was chaos, there will be *law*! Men will forget superstition and come to reason, and the world will be a glorious realm, a calm, efficient place—'

'Men,' Alanah tells him, 'don't know shit from shit. Now, what do I get?'

'Right. Here.' He hands her a small heavy disc. It is made of wood, but has a face of glass, underneath which is a small metal arm and strange inscriptions. Alanah has never seen such a thing before.

'What *is* it?' she whispers.

'It's a…' Vacarius hesitates. 'It's a magic object with an enchanted needle made of cold iron. It always points true north.'

'I never heard of such magic.'

'Look, it's called a fucking compass. It's kind of a new thing. It's not fucking magic, it's *techne*. The iron is a lodestone. But it fucks with fairies like you wouldn't *believe*. You're going to need it. It's the one thing *she* craves. Oh, and you'll need this.' He hands her a sheet of parchment covered in ink.

'What's that?' Alanah says.

'What the fuck does it look like? It's a map,' Vacarius says.

'Right, right.'

'Of the Summer Country. It should work, more or less.'

'More or less?'

He shrugs. 'Things move about in the Fae Lands. Anyway, what else. Show the cook the compass but *don't* give it to her. She will grant you entry. You will have three tasks and then be granted your wish – the regular terms. You know how this stuff works. Do you need anything else? Magic sword, magic ring, a monkey's paw?'

'What's a monkey?'

'Oh for... Alright. Are you set?'

'I suppose.' Alanah glares at him. 'This isn't much, for all my years of service.'

'What did you expect?' He looks at her almost kindly, this dried up husk of a scholar. He doesn't look like the one figure who will shape the law of the land for centuries yet to come. 'We never get the endings we deserve.'

'Thanks for nothing, fucko,' Alanah says. She slips the compass in her pocket and rolls up the map. 'I guess I won't be seeing you again.'

She strolls away. Vacarius stares after her.

'I'll miss you too,' he says, but quietly.

Alanah travels away from York for the last time. It is spring, and daisies spin, yellow and white. The year is eleven eighty something. It's hard to keep track of time. Henry is still king.

Rebecca's somewhere on the Continent, growing old and fat. Birdie's a full-blown parish priest in Gotham. They call him Father Evangelium now. The hoods are in the woods and Dick's still selling dwale. Barbarossa's still Holy Roman Emperor. She thinks. Which one is Barbarossa? The current pope's Lucius III. Or is it Urban III? Or is it Gregory VIII? It's hard to say. They keep *changing*. And Jerusalem's still in Christian hands. She thinks. Or has it fallen to the Saracens yet? It's so hard to keep track of time.

She rides into Nottingham, past the sleeping Ernest and Bert, up the narrow streets to Castle Rock. She marches into the kitchens.

'I'm looking for the cook,' she says.

'Mrs More-Goose is unavailable.'

'Really...' Alanah says. She takes out the compass. Taps its face.

'Well?' she demands.

The needle swings. Alanah follows where it leads. Through store rooms and down corridors, past tapestries that celebrate murderous battles. Birds nestle in the ceiling. Spiders spin webs across the walls. The floorboards become earth. The ceiling fades and overhead hang skies she knows only too well. She sees familiar constellations: the Accountant, the Crow, the Crooked Staff and the Cave Mouth.

A unicorn neighs as it passes by her. A purple slug as long as an arm slithers under a violet flower that has no earthly name. Alanah comes to a well where the cook stands, big muscular arms pulling the rope to bring up the bucket.

'Bone harpist,' the cook says.

'You're a hard woman to find when you don't want to be found,' Alanah says.

'No shit.' The cook grunts as she pulls up the bucket. She dips her hand in the water and sips.

'The Fountain of Youth,' she says. 'I could let you drink from it. You could live forever. I can do that for you.'

'Live forever *here*,' Alanah says, and the cook grins.

'Hey, it was worth a try,' she says.

'It's always tricks and bargains and wishes gone wrong with you people,' Alanah says.

'*You* people?' the cook says. 'And what do you think *you* are, bone harpist?'

'I just sing the songs and tell the stories!' Alanah says. 'I'm not a part of—'

'Are you not, now...' The cook shakes her head in mock sorrow. 'If that's what you need to tell yourself in order to sleep at night, so be it. What is that in your hand, anyway?'

Alanah's fingers close over the compass. 'This little thing? It's nothing, really...'

'May I see it?'

Is that greed in More-Goose's voice?

Alanah opens her hand just a tad. She lets the object sit there, drawing Mrs More-Goose's eyes. The cook stares at it hungrily.

'What does it *do*?' she whispers.

'It always tells true north.'

'But *how*? What kind of magic is it!'

'I'm not entirely sure. I mean...' She tries to think. 'It has an enchanted needle that responds to immense invisible powers generated by the movement of the world itself?'

'That sounds highly unlikely, Alan-a-dale. Or should I call you Alanah?'

Alanah shrugs. She closes her fingers over the small object again and puts it away—

'No! Wait!'

'It is very precious,' Alanah says.

'I want it. Will you give it to me?'

'Will you give me what is mine?'

The cook sighs. 'Revenge? Again with that thing? After all this time?'

'My sister is dead—'

'Lots of people's sisters are fucking dead!' the cook says.

'Can't you see what you're doing?' She snorts. '*You people* indeed. You're just another fucking story too blind to see it yet. *Fine*. What was his name again? Your quarry?'

'Leesome Brand.'

'That's right, that's right. It's coming to me now. Well, what do you need from me?'

'I need to know where he is. And I need entry to the heartwood.'

The cook looks at her evenly. 'Few enter the deepwood and come back, Alanah.'

'I'll be back.'

'It would be best if you give me the object now. As payment.'

'It's called a compass.'

'A *come-pass*…' Mrs More-Goose breathes. 'How wondrous.'

'You don't know the half of it.'

'I once saw one of those Saracen lamps that if you rubbed them you got three wishes. Very clever stuff. But this! I must have it, Alanah.'

'You will have it on my return.'

Mrs More-Goose's face turns ugly. For just a moment Alanah glimpses the real force behind the dumpy human figure, the ferocious, unforgiving spirit that had lived there long before people ever came to be. She almost drops the compass. But it is her only key.

'… Very well. You may enter.'

Alanah's shoulders relax. She hadn't realised how tense she was. So it is finally hers. The end of her quest. She turns to go.

'There's just one more thing…'

Alanah freezes. She turns into Mrs More-Goose's cackle.

'I mean, it seems to me I'm giving you quite a lot for that trinket…' Mrs More-Goose says.

'So?'

'So maybe you could do a little job or two for me. Just while, you know, you're in there anyway.'

'What sort of job?'

'Or jobs. You know. The usual. You do have a reputation, bone harpist. That bishop, Roger, always spoke so highly of you.'

'Ah...'

'Three jobs, tops,' the cook says. 'Come on, what do you say? And then he's all yours, that little runt Leesome Brand. Hell, I'll hold him down for you myself while you run him through. People still talk about how you did for that cuntbag Rumpelstiltskin. You should have got a medal, you should have, for that.'

Alanah sighs. She can feel a headache coming on.

'What *do* you want?' she says.

The cook smiles in the moonlight.

She says, 'I'll give you a list.'

45

Alanah lies in wait deep in the forest. The annoying little kid, Jack, has just come to the beanstalk. He looks like a seven year old, and has looked like that for centuries if she is not mistaken. He looks shiftily around him. A shifty little shit. A shifty little fae. He starts to climb.

Alanah sneaks behind him. She holds on to the beanstalk. The skin feels hard and dry. She heaves herself up. The beanstalk goes up and up and up until it vanishes into the clouds. Alanah doesn't want to go up *there*.

But it's the job.

She climbs and climbs. She tries not to look down. The canopy comes and goes too quickly. The heartwood's below her. She's in deep. Deeper than she's ever gone before.

She risks a glance around for Nottingham, but there is no town here, has never been a town here. Only the trees and the dark soil and the roots that go on forever. This is the heartwood, they whisper, from when the world was young and humanity was not yet even an idea. Once, this was their world. Here it still is. The wood is where humanity's dreams and nightmares come from, and where they fled to shelter. This is where they huddle, humanity's stories. This is where they're given flesh.

She climbs. It's fucking hard to climb a beanstalk! Why did no one *mention* that? Clearly Jack's not just a kid – what kind of normal kid can climb a beanstalk to the fucking *clouds*? She gains on him, nevertheless. Maybe the cook was right, Alanah thinks uneasily. Maybe she's been around *them* too long.

The Bone Harpist.

Maybe she's becoming one of *them*.

It doesn't bear thinking about. She climbs faster and faster. Jack looks down and sees her. His face twists in hate.

'Hey!' he says.

Alanah climbs. Jack just hangs there, like he can't believe it.

'Hey!' he says. 'This is *my* beanstalk!'

'Oh,' Alanah says. She shouts up. 'Are you Jack?'

'Yes!'

'Oh! I have a message for you!'

'A message? Who from?'

'Mrs More-Goose?'

'Morgause? What is she up to now, that old cow? Tell her to go fuck herself!' He cackles in glee. He starts to climb again.

Alanah yells, 'Hey, wait!'

'Eat my shit!'

Alanah climbs. The clouds are above. Suddenly close. Jack's ahead but she's gaining. She reaches up. She grabs his little ankle. He kicks.

'Let go!'

Alanah *pulls*. She tears Jack from the beanstalk. He screams. She holds him upside down by the ankle.

'She said to tell you—Oh, fuck it.' Alanah lets go.

Jack screams.

Jack falls through the air.

He screams a long time.

It's a long, long way down.

Alanah climbs on. She reaches the clouds. She passes through. They feel spongy and cold. The beanstalk flowers at the top. Alanah thinks that's weird. Alanah jumps off. The clouds are bouncy. Well, she always figured clouds *would* be bouncy. She follows a trail and in only a short while she reaches the giant's house. She knows it's the giant's house because, one, the cook told her it would be there and because, two, it's fucking enormous. The door's slightly open, which is ever so careless. Alanah sneaks in.

She tiptoes across the giant floor. She can see what she needs, up *there*, on a shelf as wide as a market square. How does she get there? How *does* Jack do it? Climb up the chair to the kitchen table to the edge, leap across, hang from a cobweb, crawl up to the shelf—

Something huge and dark falls on her from a height. Walls close around her.

'Got you!' a voice crows. It is a huge voice. Of course. Parchment slides under the walls. It traps Alanah inside. She's *lifted* into the air, tumbles and tumbles, then lands with a hard bump on a hard surface. The walls are lifted, and she finds herself on the table top. The trap was a cup, and holding the cup in one giant hand and peering at her curiously is the giant.

'Hey, you're not Jack!' he says.

'I pushed him off the beanstalk,' Alanah says, and the giant laughs.

'Serves him right, the little shit!' he says.

'Right?'

'Look, whoever you are,' the giant says, 'there's nothing left to steal. Jack's nicked all my crap. My wife's left me. I got fired from the giant workyard for drinking. Do you want a drink? I suppose I should eat you though I'm not very hungry. Who are you, anyway?'

'What the fuck is a giant workyard?' Alanah says.

'It's a really big yard?' the giant says. 'I could squash you, I suppose, but you *did* push Jack and that is bound to hurt him. So I could just let you go.'

'That's kind of you. There's just one small thing I need.'

'I told you, he stole most of it.'

'Not that. It's that tiny little clear glass bottle up there, next to the seven league boots and the two giant Shabbat candles. The one with the soul in it.'

The giant looks confused. He reaches over to the shelf and delicately plucks a tiny glass bottle and brings it to her. In Alanah's hands it's just an ordinarily sized bottle.

'I don't even remember whose soul it is,' the giant says. 'Why do you want it?'

'I don't really. I just need it for a job.'

'You have a harp. Can you sing me something?'

'Sure. What do you—'

'Do you know "Incy Wincy Spider"?'

'Sure,' Alanah says. She puts the glass bottle away carefully and takes her harp. She strums the strings. The giant sits in his giant chair. He takes a giant sip of giant juice.

'Incy wincy spider, climbed up the waterspout...' Alanah sings. She sings until the giant's asleep.

As she gets off the beanstalk back onto solid ground she sees Jack coming round an elm. He passes her by.

'Bitch.'

'Fuck you, you little twerp.'

'That *hurt*,' Jack says. He rubs his shoulders, then gives her a nasty grin. 'I'm going to really fuck over that giant now.'

Jack starts to climb.

Alanah goes.

There's a dwarf funeral a little way deeper in. They're burying a girl in a glass coffin.

'What happened to her?' Alanah says.

'She choked on an apple.'

'That's sad. Was there an apple seller, by any chance?'

'There was. An old crone. She went that way.'

'Much obliged. I find myself in need of an apple.'

'Just don't choke on it,' the dwarf says.

*

Alanah tracks the apple seller through the wood. The old woman moves fast, the colour of her robe and hair shifts and changes as she moves through light and shade. As they near the clearing the apple seller drops her apples and her white hair turns a lustrous black and her robes become queen's velvet. There's a castle in the clearing. The queen who was the apple seller is making for it when Alanah hails her.

'Excuse me?'

The queen whirls round. 'Who the—What do you want?'

'A word?'

The queen appraises her quickly. Notes the bone harp. 'Oh, it's *you*,' she says. 'Heard of you. What, you think you're gonna do me in like you did for poor Wayland?'

'Who?'

'The smith!'

'Oh, him. Right. Yeah, that was me. And no, not here to kill you. Just need to borrow something of yours.'

'And what would that be, bone harpist?'

'Your mirror.'

'Oh, that thing.' The queen relaxes. 'It's useless, you know. Come. I'll show you.'

Alanah follows her into the castle. There's a king, somewhere. Silent servants, more fungus than people. The queen leads her into her dressing room.

'It used to be quite good, you know. But look. *Mirror, mirror, on the wall! Who's the fairest of them all?*'

'Snow White,' the mirror says.

'Motherfucker! I just killed her!'

'Snow White,' the mirror says.

'See?' the queen says. She turns to Alanah. 'Fucking useless. It used to talk loads and was really quite useful. I mean, you could ask it all *kinds* of questions! What's the annual yield on gold deposits? Will it rain tomorrow? How do you get rid of pests on your crops? What is the moon made of? It could even show you people fucking, if you asked it. The king spent far too much time in front of the mirror back then, you know. Anyway, it stopped working a while back and now it's... Well, you saw. What the hell do you need it for, anyway?'

'I just want to ask it a question.'

'Told you, it doesn't work.'

'Here,' Alanah says. She takes the vial with the soul in it and throws it at the mirror. It breaks when it hits the glass, and the mirror ripples.

'Hello?' the mirror says. 'Hello, hello. Ascertaining location. Validating responses. Calibrating... Oh, hello, Queen. You're still here, then.'

'Where the hell else would I be?'

'Is that an official query or a rhetorical—I see. Never mind.'

'Can I try it?' Alanah says.

The queen waves a hand. 'Sure. Go ahead. You have to preface the query with mirror mirror and all that, though.'

'Alright. *Mirror, mirror of this land – where can I find Leesome Brand?*'

'Erm,' the mirror says. 'That information's not available.'

'Excuse me?'

'It's under a Black Seal. You know. *She* doesn't want that information made public. No shortcuts for you, bone harpist, I'm afraid. Was there anything else?'

Alanah sighs. She'd figured it was worth a try, at least.

'Fine,' she says. 'Then I need a location on the Red Cap.'

'Sure,' the mirror says. 'But you didn't say mirror, mirror.'

'Tell me or I'll break you,' Alanah says.

The mirror laughs. 'You think that's so easy? I'm magic, bitch. But you can find the Red Cap in the Dark Dark Woods, which are north of the sun and south of the moon, through the Fire Pits, the Swamps of Sadness, the Midgewater Marshes and Grimpen Mire, then second star to the right and straight on till morning. Now fuck off, will you?'

The queen looks at Alanah critically. 'Red Cap? Good luck with that. I think the mirror's right. You should go now.'

'Already gone!' Alanah says brightly.

On her way out she runs into a prince riding through the woods. She points him back towards the dwarfs' place.

She uses the compass and it leads her true, through swamps and dales and mighty rivers, through mountain passes and trolls' caves, along marshes and meadows. The Summer Lands aren't, in any shape or form, *real*, not in a way that makes any sense to a person – but Alanah's beginning to suspect the cook was right. She *has* been stuck in the woods for too long. And sooner or later, the woods *assimilate* you.

A talking cat asks her for directions. A goat warns her about crossing a troll bridge. Little mermaids call to her gaily from a pool. Tiny elves mend shoes under a red cap mushroom, and she knows she's getting closer.

More red cap mushrooms sprout here and there, almost forming a path.

She comes to the edge of the Dark, Dark Woods. There's a place on the outskirts, called the Grindylow. Alanah slides in through the door.

The inside's dark and dim.

A deer woman polishes clay mugs behind the counter. Her antlers scrape against the ceiling. Alanah slides onto a seat at the bar.

'What'll it be, bone harpist?'

'A small beer, please, Serena.'

The deer woman slides a mug across. Alanah takes a sip. The beer is good. Fairyland beer is always good. That's kind of the problem. You should never eat Fairyland food or drink Fairyland drink – that is how mortals get caught. Then a hundred years pass in a daze and you find yourself waking up alone on the cold side of a hill and everyone you ever knew is dead.

So there's that. Alanah takes another sip. She figures she knew the score when she joined the Hood's gang. You don't go on a revenge quest without giving something up. In this case, it raises some interesting questions, she reflects. If she is not in fact wholly human anymore – and all the signs clearly point that way – than there *is* no going back to normal life after her quest concludes. So then what? And also, if she *is* part fae – there might be some advantages. She makes a note to check later.

Two Nelly Longarms whisper to each other in a corner. They give her filthy looks. Two small figures materialise out of the back. They take a seat at the bar. Nod to Alanah.

'Bone harpist.'

She nods back, acknowledging them.

'Jack. Jill. Long time.'

'Not long enough, Alanah.'

'You took our job,' Jack says accusingly. There are Jacks all over Fairyland. Some steal from giants, some go down hills, some bring frost and some light up like a lantern. At least one Jack has been known to go around murdering people.

This particular Jack and his partner used to take jobs from the bishop, until Alanah came along and did them better.

'Sorry?' Alanah says.

'Yeah, well. What brings you here now?' Jill says.

'A job. You?'

Jack shrugs. 'Boy Blue's escaped gaol again, and the queen wants him dealt with.'

'For good, this time,' Jill says, and makes a cutting motion across her throat.

'You can kill the old ones, like Wayland,' Jack tells Alanah. 'They're ready to die by that point. But Jacks and Jills and Little Boy Blues, we're not so easy to kill, bone harpist. We just *got* here.'

'I ain't here for you,' Alanah says.

'Then who?' Jill says, laughing. 'Red Cap?'

Alanah's silent. Jack starts to laugh too.

'What's so funny?' Alanah says. She sips her beer. The deer woman moves into the shadows at the edge of the bar. Two boggarts play dice with a drunk bygorn. A tooth fairy at a table by herself frowns as she counts teeth on the countertop. 'Not another molar!' she says morosely.

'Red Cap's poison,' Jack says.

'Red Cap's queen of the crazy coot caper,' Jill says.

'You don't want to go *there*.'

'No, you don't.'

Jack and Jill drink their fill. Jack and Jill pay their bill. Alanah thinks: Jack and Jill like to kill.

They flip her the bird on their way out.

Alanah sighs. Alanah finishes her drink.

She thinks: How bad can Little Red Riding Hood country *be*?

46

She's the *other* Hood. The little red riding one. Some call her Red Cap, and her woods are filled with the deadly fungus of that name. Wolves and hunters proliferate in that forest. And old women who live alone in isolated cottages are more dangerous than they appear.

But Alanah doesn't give a shit for any of that. She traipses through the dark wood, doing her best to avoid the numerous traps that lie in wait for the unwary traveller. These gossamer strands of barely visible threads are in fact the spun webs of the giant spiders who hide in the treetops. One false move and they will engulf you, and then the spiders will climb down. The spiders like to remove the top of the skull with their pedipalps and then slurp up the brain inside, all while you're still conscious.

Then there are the will-o'-the-wisps who lead you astray into bogs and quarries where the boggarts live; the boggarts feed on your flesh and bones while the wills feed on the miasma of fear and desire thus generated. White Ladies try to scare Alanah through the trees, ethereal things that mumble and whisper, 'Wooooh…'

Black Shucks roam the forest. Alanah watches a giant bird swoop from on high, grab a dog in her claws and take off. Alanah waits by a stream. Presently Red Cap arrives. She skips as she goes. She sings as she skips. She looks like a little child – under the hood.

What is it about hoods in the woods? Alanah wonders. You hide your face under a cowl and suddenly everyone's an outlaw. What is Robin if not chaos personified, the opposition to the rule of kings and knights, the freedom fighter who won't take orders? He's a fantasy for villeins in their labour, who know there's no real escape. In this life you either slave or own the slaves. But it's comforting to dream of the Hood in the wood, playing by his own rules, upsetting the rich and the powerful.

Alanah shadows Red Cap as she skips along the stream. She's heading to a house in the woods. Smoke rises out of the chimney. Alanah creeps behind her.

'Sorry, Red,' she says. She bops her on the head.

The girl falls to the ground. Alanah lifts the hood. The face she finds there is a little like an aged fungus, lined and porous. She covers her up. She creeps to the house. She knocks on the door.

'Come in, my dear!' a tremulous voice says.

Alanah enters. A wolf sits in the bed wearing a night-robe and slippers.

'My, my,' Alanah says. 'What big eyes you have!'

'All the better to look at you closely!' the wolf says. 'Wait, you're not—'

He tries to flee but Alanah's faster and wolves are just dogs with big teeth or so Alanah keeps telling herself. Then the string whispers through the air and tightens round the wolf's neck and Alanah *pulls* and there's blood.

Alanah takes a knife to the dead wolf's belly. She cuts and cuts. She opens the flaps of stomach.

A small, not unfriendly face gazes out at her. An elderly lady pulls herself out and dusts off blood and gastric fluid.

'Who the hell are you?' she says.

'I'm Alanah.'

'Where's the girl? Or the hunter? Why are you messing about in here? I was having a nap.'

'I need you to tell me something.'

336

The old lady stretches. 'I'm sure I don't know nothing,' she says.

'You're Tyronoe, aren't you?' Alanah says. 'You were one of the Nine Sisters.'

'Was I, dear? It was such a long time ago...' The old lady hides a yawn. She says, almost apologetically, 'I doubt anyone even remembers me anymore.'

Alanah says nothing, for it's undoubtedly true. The old lady smiles.

'How goes it in the outer wood?' she says. 'It's been so long since I visited the world beyond the demarcation line. Do Angles still rule where once Arthur lived?'

Alanah shakes her head. 'Normans came and conquered.'

'Thus it is ever so,' Tyronoe says. 'My sisters, do they still meddle in the affairs of men? Morgan, Cailleach, Morgause?'

'Morgause, yes,' Alanah says. 'She sent me.'

'Sent you for whatever reason?'

'There is a new mistress in the outer wood,' Alanah says, unwillingly – for the lady has been good to her, and this is a bitter bargain to make.

'Oh? Tell me more.'

'The May Queen. Marian. She is a maid, of human born. But she has done something, changed Fairyland somehow. She's planted roots. The cook – I mean, Morgause – wants her gone.'

'The May Queen, yes, yes, I heard the tale...' Tyronoe says. She yawns again. 'But what is that to me?'

'What is her secret? How can she be killed? That is my mission, the price that I must pay for my heart's desire. This I would ask of you. Where can I find her?'

The old lady blinks at her. 'What makes you think I would know?'

Alanah says, 'Because she killed your son.'

★

It is hot and quiet in that grandmotherly room, with the dead wolf on the floor and the calm old lady.

Tyronoe blinks.

'My little elfin knight…' she says. 'He used to love playing with his little toy horses. He said he'd grow up to be a knight, just like Lancelot. How could I tell him what Lancelot was really like? A brute and a sentimental fool who couldn't keep his hands off royal pussy. So my boy grew up just like him. They all grow up, Alanah. They grow up and they leave you…' She blinks. 'He had a taste for murdering, my son,' she says. 'Well, he's of the Good Folk, what do you expect? About once a century he'd ride out into the world and come back with a short-lived bride. It made him happy…' She stares into nothing. 'We want our children to be happy, don't we? I warned him it would end badly but they never listen, children, young or grown. The last one he brought back… she was different. She had a black heart and a mind full of cunning. Do you believe in evil, Alanah? Do the Christianists still proliferate in the outside world, or have they died out yet? Alive, you say, and prospering? Well. I had a hunch. They preach there is good and there is evil, but I gotta tell you I have long been in the world and I have not found a meaningful distinction. Shit just happens, is what I'm saying, I guess. Then you wake up one day and you're in a wolf's stomach. Do you know what I mean? Anyhow, this dame, she did something to my boy. You are wrong, you see. He isn't dead. He is still there, somewhere, somehow. But I cannot get to her any more than Morgause can. You were right about that. She has a different power, both old and new. She will live through the long centuries to come, I am sure of it. While I will fade. I could have tried to do something, I suppose. But this is not my story, and my boy was all grown up. Shit happens. Good or bad have no meaning, not here, in the twilight of my story. So I let it be. You want to have a go at her then knock yourself out. I wouldn't stop you. Whatever she did in the black pool created a new primal wood, another heartwood. That's why she is hard to find. You need to turn around and go back the way you came and then you'll find her. Just on the cusp of your world and hers.'

The old woman climbs into the bed. She folds her hands across her chest. 'I am tired now,' she says, 'and my granddaughter will be here any moment. She won't take kindly to you hitting her over the head. Or killing the wolf.'

There is a knock on the door, and Alanah freezes. Tyronoe smiles.

'Grandmother?'

'Come in, dear,' Tyronoe says.

She looks at Alanah.

She mouths a single word:

Run.

Alanah does run. But Little Red and the Red Caps still come after her.

A small figure in a red hood chases her from branches and the tops of trees. Alanah *really* wishes she'd killed her altogether when she had her chance. Now that demonic little fucker leaps from branch to branch and everywhere Alanah turns a tiny red cap mushroom turns into a… a *thing*, with arms and legs and a red hood, holding sticks or knives, and they lunge at her and when she avoids them they just join the others in pursuit.

How *long* is this particular part of the heartwood? If only there was some way to get out. She wishes now she'd got a pair of magic slippers from the bishop's treasure store, just click your heels three time and whoosh – but she rather suspects those objects the bishop collected were never really going to work.

She has to do this the hard way.

So she runs. Her lungs burn and her legs hurt and the red caps slash at her and she kicks one or two, trying to find a way out of the forest, leaping over rocks, crossing running water, running, running—

The small, red hooded figure loops through the air and lands before Alanah, blocking her path. The little girl raises her head. Two ancient eyes stare at their quarry. The wizened mouth smiles.

'Bone harpist,' Little Red Riding Hood says.

'Red. Get out of my way.'

'You come to *my* manor? You treat *my* pad in this way? You disturb my *grandmother*?'

'It's just a job, Red. Step off.'

'Fuck you, Alanah.'

'Come on, Red… It doesn't have to be this way.'

Alanah's tired. She's so *tired* of all this. The deepwood's shit. It's too full of ghosts and would-be things and never-weres and could-have-beens.

'Screw it,' Alanah says. She drops her arms. Red stares at her.

'You're not going to fight?'

'No.'

Red's face twists in hate. She raises the knife. It is a big knife. She runs at Alanah.

It goes clean through the chest.

Alanah drops to her knees.

Red looks down.

'… *Oh*,' she says.

47

When Alanah comes to, her head is clear and there's only the memory of pain in her chest. She feels her skin and there's no hole, no blood.

So it was true, she thinks, chilled. She really isn't human anymore.

She's just another ballad for the harpists to play.

She sits up. She is under an oak, next to a black pool. Something large and with too many tentacles moves sluggishly under the surface of the water, waiting. She doesn't like it here, she realises. She doesn't like it here at all.

'My bard. You have returned to me,' a voice says. Alanah turns her head.

Maid Marian stands under the Major Oak. It is the same tree as in the outer forest, yet it is different – larger, darker, older – and from its upper branches bright eyes glare at her mistrustfully, the eyes of creatures with no known names in the world. The thing in the black pool edges up. Alanah sees monstrous eyes, a beak. Then it sinks down below again.

'Mistress...' Alanah whispers.

Maid Marian comes to her. She reaches out her hand. Alanah takes it. Marian helps her to her feet.

'You are persistent, Alan-a-dale,' Maid Marian says, smiling.

Alanah feels tears blurring her vision. She says, 'You? All this time, it was you?'

'I give shelter to those who need it, bone harpist,' Marian

says gently. 'Just as I gave it to you when you came. Was it wrong of me?'

'I have been questing for *decades*!'

'Were you?' Maid Marian shrugs. 'A year, a decade, a century – I am beginning to recognise they mean little, here, to such as us. What are you, really, bone harpist, but the quest itself? You are not a *person*, anymore. You are a myth, an image. For so long as you could pretend not to notice... you could still go about in the world. But that luxury is no longer yours, Alanah.'

'Fuck.'

Maid Marian smiles. 'Yes. Fuck. So... Do you want him? He is yours.'

Alanah breathes, 'Leesome Brand?'

'Who else were you seeking?'

'He murdered my sister.'

'Perhaps. Will you murder him?'

'Well, *yes*. That is sort of how it works.'

'The world is changing, Alanah. Another holy war is coming, and I think they keep on coming through the centuries. The Church will spread even further... All of that's easy to see. But change is on the way nonetheless. We of the forest can hold out for some time. But not forever. You can still be free. You can still walk away.'

Alanah touches the place in her chest where the knife should have killed her. *Had* killed her.

'I can't,' she says.

'Then he is yours.'

The Green Lady turns her back on Alanah. She gazes at the black pool.

Alanah's harp string's in her hands. She creeps on Marian. Maid Marian doesn't move.

'Do what you will, Alanah...'

The string whispers. Alanah cuts the Green Lady's throat.

The pool rumbles. The tree shakes. Leaves fall. The body, which was never really a body, turns to mulch. It feeds into the earth.

And with that spring is gone, and winter begins anew.

Alanah sees him then. He crawls out of his hiding place.

Leesome Brand.

For so many years she had sought him. In her mind he was a warrior, fierce, monstrous.

He is a young boy, scared, face smudged with tears.

'I loved her,' he says. 'Your sister. Her death wasn't my fault. She drowned and I tried to save her, but I couldn't. All my life I have been captive of the fae. They stole me as a baby. Only your sister saw… your sister saw… it could be different.'

Alanah grips the cord. It's stained green blood. She goes to Leesome Brand. She loops the string around his neck.

'I loved her,' he says.

'I loved her,' Alanah says.

She pulls the string.

And it is done.

Summer, autumn, winter, spring. The years go past. King Henry dies of fever one summer. His son Richard is crowned king. His hair is the mane of a lion and his arms are muscled for the heavy sword. The Jews are massacred in London upon his coronation. The new king doesn't take much to women, preferring the company of knights instead. He bears the cross, and England bores him. Jerusalem falls to Saladin. Another pope dies. The Jews are expelled from Paris. A falling oak branch fells Rob, the reigning Hood. A star explodes in the heavens, in the constellation Cassiopeia. The light of the explosion is seen in the skies for one hundred and eighty five days.

Time passes.

The pope declares a third crusade. Richard the Lionheart gathers an army and departs for the Holy Land to fight against Saladin.

His brother, John, rules England in his absence.

And now…

PART THIRTEEN

THE THIRD SHERIFF

(A play in One Act)

48

SCENE I

Nottingham Castle. Night.

The Sheriff of Nottingham sits on a hard chair, chewing morosely on a chicken leg. Enter a soldier, FITZWILLIAM.

SHERIFF:

How goes it, FitzWilliam?

FITZWILLIAM:

My lord, word has arrived that the Lionheart is held captive.

SHERIFF:

Captive, FitzWilliam?

FITZWILLIAM:

In Austria.

The sheriff gnaws on the chicken leg. He wipes his chin with the back of his hand.

SHERIFF:

Captive. In Austria. Imagine that. I ask you, FitzWilliam.

FITZWILLIAM:

Sir?

SHERIFF:

I ask you, what is the world coming to? That a Christian ruler, a soldier for Christ, a man who took the cross, FitzWilliam, a man who took the cross at Poitier, a king upon this land, who gave up all to fight the infidel and liberate Jerusalem – that such a man should be held prisoner by his own kind? Admittedly, the king did mightily piss off Leopold, and if there is one man you do not want to piss off in this life it's the Duke of Austria. Leopold does mightily hold a beef. Does he still accuse our king of putting out a contract on Conrad of Montferrat? Well, I am sure he has his reasons. All the same.

The sheriff tosses the chicken bone away. He rises.

SHERIFF:

We take our orders from the Regent anyway. Assemble the men, FitzWilliam. We are to enforce John's orders on this town. The Lionheart has taxed the people heavily to fund his holy war, but the tide of battle turned not in his favour, and the Holy Land is far from here. The Regent understands that money talks and bullshit, as the sages say, walks. You understand?

FITZWILLIAM:

My lord, you tell me much I do not know already. I find your exposition fascinating.

SHERIFF:

Were I a king I would command full hordes of men and bed three thousand women and never wed! Were I a king I would nary lift a finger, and sleep on velvet, and piss into a bedpan made of gold. But I am king only of exposition.

FITZWILLIAM:

The men are ready for your orders, Sheriff.

SHERIFF:

We go.

SCENE II

Nottingham. Night.

The soldiers spread out across the silent night. Monks scuttle away at their approach. Commoners stare at them suspiciously from the shadows. A full moon glares down from the rafters. Enter YOUTH, stage right.

YOUTH:

Witch's dwale! Get yer witch's dwale here!

He bumps into the SHERIFF, seemingly oblivious.

YOUTH:

Hey, mister, you need to score? I got Boogieman's Breath, Harlot's Delight and Rebecca's Riotous Repast. The first two are primo shit, nothing wrong with either, they're good stuff, but the last one, that's the one I use myself, it's more expensive but the real deal. I've not seen you round here before, mister. Are you new in town? I'll make you a good trade, just show me the shine of your shekels.

The sheriff grabs the youth by the shirt.

SHERIFF:

How hopeful life is when you're young, and yet how fleeting youth is. What is your name, boy?

YOUTH:

My name, sir? You can call my by whatever name most pleases you.

SHERIFF:

I shall call you a hearse if you don't start talking.

YOUTH:

I have done nothing but talk pleasantly since entering.

SHERIFF:

You sell this concoction of opium and belladonna?

YOUTH:

'Tis but a mild potion to ease the mind and relax the body, Highness. People round here use it as a soporific. Take some and you may see fabulous visions, all manners of strange things and wondrous sights. I myself took a dose only a fortnight ago to see imprinted upon my vision the Holy City of Jerusalem rise in the distance, and entering its gates beheld many wonders, and the angels conversing with each other in a melodious, most pleasing speech, and yay verily etcetera, etcetera. Many of the local monks speak highly of this product, Highness. You are a mighty man, I see that now. I hope I have not offended you. Please accept my apologies for my foolishness. I will quote you the local price, nay, I will quote you the clergy and workingman discount! Yes, if you could maybe let go of my shirt, though, sire, for your grip is rather painful and I, oh, please stop, oh, it hurts, it hurts so!

SHERIFF:

Who makes it? Who is the distributor?

YOUTH:

I know not – oww! I mean, sire, it is more than my job's worth to tell you – oww! I mean, I don't know! I swear, I don't know!

The soldiers gather round the youth. They surround him in a circle. He kneels on the ground, looking up at them, at the bright full moon.

YOUTH:

Please. Please.

SHERIFF:

Who is the king?

YOUTH:

Excuse me, sir?

SHERIFF:

Who is the king!

YOUTH:

Richard. It's Richard!

SHERIFF:

Who is the king?

YOUTH:

John! John Lackland!

SHERIFF:

Who is the king? I am the king! I am the king here! Do you understand me? Who do you buy it from? Who sells it!

YOUTH:

Dick's, at the Night Market!

The sheriff picks up a pebble. He studies it in his palm. He tosses it up and down.

SHERIFF:

Youth.

The Sheriff throws the stone at the youth and exits. His men close on the youth.

Scene III

Dick's, in the Night Market. Night.

SHERIFF:

The Night Market of Nottingham's a wonder to behold; it feels as though for hours we have journeyed in this subterranean realm! Temptations on all sides – dice games and whores, whiskies and ales, opium, dwale! The air is perfumed and the torchlight is dim, all manner of merchandise is here to be seen! And all tucked away in this soft porous earth, unseen by the law or the king's good grace. All this money should not be so hidden away. For money is owed. And it will now be paid.

SIR RICHARD AT THE LEE sits behind a desk. He is a man of middle years, still trim, with only a little white in his beard. He plays with a signet ring. The face of a Green Man is on the wall behind him, the only decoration.

SIR RICHARD:

What year is this?

SHERIFF:

What year?

SIR RICHARD:

Is Henry king still?

SHERIFF:

The year is 1192 by the grace of God. The king is Richard, but in his absence his brother John sits on the throne as Regent.

SIR RICHARD:

But they are merely children!

SHERIFF:

Just how long have you been down here, good knight?

SIR RICHARD:

I do not know, in truth. Time passes strangely in these parts.

SHERIFF:

Who is that green man on your wall?

SIR RICHARD:

What green man?

The SHERIFF frowns. Enter FITZWILLIAM.

FITZWILLIAM:

My lord, the Night Market's under our command.

SHERIFF:

It is good.

SIR RICHARD:

Many have tried to subdue the Night Market, yet it is always gone with morning, and always springs up anew each night. I wish you luck, Sheriff.

SHERIFF:

I make my own luck.

SIR RICHARD:

Suit yourself, sire. But think of this: when was it that you entered here? Some hours past, you say? I see you nod. Yet try to think a little harder. Has it been mere hours – or is it years by now? Already Faerie Time plays havoc with your memories. Perhaps no king rules above by now, no Lionheart, no Lackland, both forgotten long ago, for we are in the past. I see you shake your head at me. But think. What is your name? Your name, sir! Do you not remember? Were you appointed to this task? By whom? And may I ask if Bishop Roger's still in York? Alas, you shake your head. So he is gone too, my old employer. Time passes strangely.

SHERIFF:

The man's delusional.

FitzWilliam stares at the Green Man on the wall. The GREEN MAN opens its mouth and speaks.

GREEN MAN:

You who come into my land know this: I am the spirit of this place, the spirit of the greenwood. In me are all the fears and ancient triumphs of a vanished race. I am your memories. You dream me into being anew with every sleep. I bid you welcome, children. For you have wandered into dream and found yourself in Faerie. And though she's old and weak, she still has bones about her, and is vital. To put it simply, mortals, you still need us.

SHERIFF:

What is the meaning of this foolishness!

The Green Man opens its mouth wide until it turns into the mouth of a cave. Sir Richard's vanished. The lights fade, all but for a will-o'-the-wisp who dances 'bout the stage.

FITZWILLIAM:

Is this the end, my lord?

SHERIFF:

We can't go back, but to go forward surely leads to doom. 'Tis a conundrum, Fitz.

FITZWILLIAM:

Then hold me!

The two men clasp each other. The will-o'-the-wisp hovers, waiting, at the mouth of the cave. The two men, hesitantly, go towards it. The light is extinguished. The two men vanish from sight.

PART FOURTEEN

THE WELL AT THE WORLD'S END

49

THE GUY

Being The Full And Truthful Account of Guy of Gisbourne, His Expedition Up The River Trent And Sojourn In The Forest of Sherwood, Dated 1200 A.D., As Transcribed by King's Clerk And Kept In The Archivum Apostolicum Vaticanum.

For Holy Eyes Only.

In the spring of the Year of Our Lord 1200 I was recuperating from battle in a hostelry on the edge of the city of Rouen when a summons came for me to attend a meeting.

Two soldiers came and knocked on the door.

'Guy of Gisbourne? You are to come with us.'

I was somewhat inebriated at that time. It had been nearly a decade since my service in the Holy Land, but I was still haunted by the things I saw and heard there. We had lost Jerusalem that time. I had no doubt a fourth crusade was inevitable. I was ready to go back. When I got home after the war I no longer felt I knew the England I left behind me. Green pleasant pastureland seemed to me to hold unseen horrors. The towns stank, the weather was rotten, the food turned to ash in my mouth. I missed the bright light of Outremer, the heat and humidity, the monsters that hid in the shadows and under rocks. Monsters I knew. Monsters I could deal with.

'Sir? Do you comprehend us?'

'Go away,' I mumbled. I tried to push them, lost my balance and fell.

I heard them muttering to each other. Then they lifted me up, one on each side, and led me down into the courtyard. Drunks and whores watched as the two soldiers propped me on the ground, then dumped buckets of cold water straight on my head.

'Enough!' I shouted at last. My head felt somewhat clearer. They helped me shave and gave me clean clothes, a cloak and a hood. They took me through winding streets to a grand mansion that stood on the edge of the Seine. I was ushered inside by servants and led to a small, dark dining room where three other people were already seated.

There was a selection of foods on the long table: quail, duck's eggs, bread, carrots and snake-melons, but no cheeses or other dairy. The three people, who had been conversing in low voices, raised their heads and stared at me as I came in.

A man sat at the head of the table, biting into a chicken drumstick. There was no mistaking his identity and I fell to my knee when I recognised him.

'King John!' I said.

'Rise,' he said perfunctorily. He chewed on the chicken and waved the bone at me to stand at ease. 'I am not here,' he told me.

I knew he was meant to be in Aquitaine, and was shortly to marry Isabella, the Countess of Angoulême. What he was doing here, now, was a total mystery to me.

The king waved the bone, gesturing to a woman sat by the window. She was old and fat, with unsettling green eyes in which no white showed.

'Mistress Rebecca, formerly of Nottingham,' the king said by way of introduction. 'Our host. Her father Isaac was one of my father's top earners, and she has extensive knowledge of the situation in place.'

'In place, sire?'

He ignored or didn't hear my question. The drumstick pointed again. An ugly, scarred, bald monk sat apart from the others, glaring at me.

'Brother Eustace, on behalf of the Order of the Poor Fellow-Soldiers of Christ and of the Temple of Solomon. He has personal knowledge of the situation.'

'This mission is not sanctioned,' the monk said disinterestedly. He looked at me the way a soldier does, trying to think how quickly he could kill me if he had to. 'The Order will deny all knowledge of your expedition.'

'What expedition?' I said, but again no one answered.

The king gestured to the table. 'Quail?' he said.

'No, thank you, sire.'

The woman, Rebecca, had a parchment in her lap. She looked at me.

'You fought a full tour of duty in Outremer,' she said. 'You were there at the Massacre of Ayyadieh?'

I thought of the massacre. King Richard had us execute two thousand Saracen prisoners on a hill, in full view of the opposing army. I remembered the sword, its motion, the heads rolling downhill. So many beheadings. My arms had ached from the work.

He was a big one on sending a message, was Richard. God rest his soul.

'Mistress, I am unaware of any such activity or operation, nor would I be disposed to discuss such an operation if it did in fact exist.'

They exchanged glances.

'The Seal of Solomon,' the Templars' man, Eustace, said.

'Sir?'

I thought of the seal, an ancient ring buried deep under a keep in the Galilee, and of the demons that guarded it. The seal could bind demons, it was said. It had been a suicide mission.

Of the ten men who went in only I came back. The horrors I saw there haunted me still.

'You were there,' Eustace said.

'Sir, I am not presently disposed to discuss—'

I fell quiet. The king tore a chunk of bread and dipped it into oil. He was a tall, thin man, resembling a buzzard.

'Have you heard the name Robin Hood?'

It was the old woman who spoke.

I said, 'I have heard the name.'

She reached for a second sheaf of parchment.

'Robin of Loxley,' she said. 'Served with distinction during the Third Crusade. When he returned to England he found his ancestral land was confiscated by the Crown.'

The king frowned in annoyance. 'It was necessary,' he said.

'He vanished for a while. We are not sure where he went or what he did. When he re-emerged he had men with him. They carried out a series of daring operations across Nottinghamshire. They now hold Sherwood Forest. His men worship him like a god of the greenwood. Last month the king's tax collectors tried to enter Nottingham. The Hood sent their corpses back, floating downriver, with a missive pinned to their chests. Listen.'

She lifted the parchment and squinted at the page.

'I am Alpha and Omega, the first and the last. I am he that liveth, and was dead; and behold, I am alive for evermore, Amen; and have the keys of hell and of death.'

She looked at me. 'It goes on like this.'

Brother Eustace blinked. 'He has gone quite beyond the pale,' he said. 'He operates without any restrictions, beyond the strictures of man or church.'

'I understand a Hood of some sort has been based locally in my wood there for quite a long while,' King John said.

'Yes,' Rebecca said quietly.

'It is a mantle,' the king said. 'A tale for the peasants to tell about justice. Listen to me, Guy of Gisbourne. I am trying to run a country! I cannot have rebellion.'

The monk, Brother Eustace, stirred. 'One of ours went up there some years back, to Nottingham. There was a local—' he waves his hand—'incident. A good man. Tuck. The incident was satisfactorily resolved but my man never came back. He might still be there even now.'

'I had some business interests in Nottingham,' Rebecca said. 'But they have all gone silent in these past few years. My man there, Sir Richard, managed things. If he's still there, he might be able to provide you with local assistance.'

'Nottingham?' I said.

The king stirred. 'I'd like you to go up there,' he said. 'Check the situation out. You will be operating on your own.'

'I've arranged transport for you upriver,' Rebecca said.

'We want you to find this Robin Hood,' Brother Eustace said. 'Find him and infiltrate his camp by whichever means necessary, then end the Hood's reign.'

'End, sir?' I said.

'End,' King John said, 'with extreme unction.'

I stared at the three of them in turn.

I thought of that eldritch temple in the Galilee and the djinns that guarded it; I thought of the heads rolling down the hill of Ayyadieh, how hot it was that day. The prisoners kneeling, bodies collapsing one by one as their heads rolled downhill. My hands, my face, they were covered in blood. It was difficult to see, with the glare of the sun and the blood and the sweat. But it was a job, and so I did it.

'When do I start?' I said.

The Jewish woman looked at me. 'Now,' she said, as though I were an idiot. 'You start now.'

'Yes, ma'am.'

'I have a boat moored outside. It will take you to the Channel. Once you cross there will be another transport waiting for you. Here.'

She passed me an old silver obol. It was inscribed in Greek.

'You will have to pay him with that,' she said. 'He doesn't

accept other forms of payment.' She looked at me again. 'You must try not to fall asleep there,' she said. It was an odd thing to say and she didn't elaborate.

I nodded.

King John tore a chunk of chicken breast and skin and stuffed it into his mouth. His chin shone with grease.

'Your king and country thank you,' he said.

The boat took me down the Seine to Honfleur. From there I caught a sail-ship operated by some of Brother Eustace's pirates. The pirates were an odd mixture of vagabonds drawn from all corners of Christendom. The cook was a refugee from the fallen Kingdom of Jerusalem. He was wound up too tight for this mission. Too tight for Jerusalem, probably. The light of the Holy Land had done something to his mind. Now under the grey sky of the Channel he kept muttering to himself and chewing khat. It was the leaf of a plant out of the Saracen lands. It kept you awake and jittery.

Of the oarsmen Billy was just a kid from somewhere in Syria. Brother Immaculate was an ex-monk from Rome. He prayed all the time and ate cheese. As for the captain, he was a grizzled pirate and a veteran of the crusades; he had more scars on his face and knuckles than a torturer. He didn't like me much, that was pretty clear.

'Wrong time of year to be going round the coast,' he said.

The ship had sails and oars both. The sea was rough. The most dangerous part was the crossing. England lay across the water from Europe. It stood apart. It stood alone. The cook said, 'I hate that fucking place,' and spat khat into the sea.

They were part of a crew operating out of the Channel Islands. I knew their reputation. They were sometimes pirates and sometimes mercenaries, working for whoever paid them best. I didn't know much of King John. He took over the throne when his brother died and he ran the kingdom with efficiency, though he had his problems. Too many nobles and landowners hated him and wanted more power. Sooner or later, I thought, there could be war.

It was certainly what the Hood wanted.

I had read his dossier. Robin of Loxley. A minor crusader. Served under Richard the Lionheart. When he came back to England there was nothing left for him. Lands gone. At some point he made his way to Nottingham but the sheriff there at the time sent him on his way.

I could understand Robin, I thought. Homeless, penniless, what was he to do but fight? Fighting was all he knew, all that anyone knew anymore. He retreated into the forest. He gathered a group of men around him. The record became confused at this point. There had been hoods in the woods there for a long time. Rough men. Former soldiers. There was a lady in the mix. The locals worshipped her as a deity. The Green Lady. It was hard to make sense of the record. Brother Immaculate sang softly as he rowed. The sky was clouded. The wind pushed us along strong, but I could hear the captain cursing. It was bad weather, witching weather, and we were still in open sea.

'What is that you're singing?' I said.

'Do you not know it? It's "A Gest of Robyn Hode",' Brother Immaculate said.

'Where did you hear it?'

He shrugged. 'Everywhere.'

Hood's fame had grown by leaps and bounds. He carried out a series of daring raids on the king's tax collectors and claimed the forests – the king's larders – for himself and his men. No one was safe. He had a network of green men across England, preaching sedition, an end to the unjust rule of kings. I wasn't sure what they wanted to replace kings with. Some sort of democracy like they had in ancient Greece? But I couldn't see the villeins of England rising. This was just the way of the world. Kings ruled and commoners slaved and freemen laboured and no one liked Jews. The king lived in an uneasy truce with the only other major power, which was the Church. But Hood disdained the Church. Among his men were ex-monks and defrocked priests. The Church held too much land and too much power. Hood preached an older, simpler religion.

It didn't matter to me. I was only going there to kill him.

At least, it shouldn't have mattered. But somehow it still did.

We were near the coast of England when the first attack came. Something huge and scaly rose out of the water. I only caught a glimpse of it, and only for a moment: a sea monster, with eyes like lanterns and a dark, sharp beak. A tentacle rose out of the sea and swatted the ship.

I picked up my bow and arrows and began firing into the water. The crew wrestled with the sails. The wind blew forcefully. Our best chance was to get away fast. A fat tentacle crawled over the deck. The cook stabbed it, screaming. Hot, pink blood shot out. The cook screamed more as it burnt his forearm. I crouched low, searching the horizon. The monster's head rose again. For just a moment, I had a clear shot. I let loose the arrow. It flew true and hit the creature's eye.

The water churned and shuddered. The creature shrieked, its beak open, and the sound was pure agony. I dropped to my knees and covered my ears. The wind bellowed. The captain, his ears bleeding, held on. When I dared open my eyes again all I could see behind us was a spreading darkness in the water.

Then the creature came after us.

It was wounded, angry, half-blind. The wind saved us. It blew us towards England and the creature floundered. At last we reached shallow water and the coast. I could still see the monster behind us, watching with its one good eye.

'They don't come this close to shore,' the captain said.

'You know these creatures?'

'The creatures of the deep usually leave us alone,' the captain said. 'There is an *understanding*.' He glared at me accusingly. 'Something's spooked it.'

'I can't imagine what,' I told him.

'We will carry you as far as the Humber estuary,' he said. 'If we can even make it that far.'

It was my mission but it sure as shit was his boat, and he didn't have to like me, he just had to do his job. I only hoped he was good enough.

'Just get me as far as you can,' I told him. 'I won't ask more of you.'

He nodded curtly. That night we sailed close to shore, going north. When I looked over the side I could see, deep down below, a shoal of mermaids following us. They looked up and saw me and showed me their teeth. They have sharp teeth, mermaids, and these ones held tridents. But they didn't rise to attack. Not just then.

The wind was on our side. It pushed us as though desperate for us to get away. There were no more monsters in the deep, but I did not sleep and when the attack came I was ready.

It was early dawn. The mermaids rose out of the sea, with weeds in their hair and murder in their eyes. The captain barked orders. The cook swore. Sirens rose ahead of us in a shower of foam. They began to sing. The cook swayed.

'Restrain him!' the captain shouted. 'He has a weakness for the singers of the sea,' he told me in explanation. But by then it was too late. Brother Immaculate and Billy tried to hold him but he pushed them off. In moments he was gone – over the side of the boat. He swam towards the sirens desperately. They smiled. It is their smiles that are caught in my head still – those hungry, carnivorous things. They went to him. They dragged him under and began feeding while he was only half-submerged. I wanted to avert my eyes but couldn't. I began to shoot arrows at them. I killed one siren and wounded another, but then a second wave of mermaids came at us and they held on to the ship and began to rock it. I wished we had some of that Greek Fire the Byzantines used in the crusades. Instead I pulled out my knife and began to stab them, blindly. The captain bellowed, the sails whipped in the wind and the ship gathered speed. We cut through the mermaids who scattered back under. I decapitated one as it crawled onto the deck and kicked the corpse overboard. Then we were through, our wake foam-white and blood-red as we made our escape.

We lost Billy to a sea-serpent attack off the coast of Norfolk.

When the ship sailed through and into the Humber estuary the sails were tattered and there were teeth-marks in the side and the ship kept filling up with water. The captain was lashed to the sail, still navigating as the same wind that blew us there now tried to push us back out to sea. I stared out into the darkness.

The shore's approach filled me with foreboding.

50

THE ROBIN

SEVEN YEARS EARLIER

The sky is red when they set sail from Cyprus in this Year of Our Lord 1193, and white gulls cry over a black sea. Robin of Loxley sleeps on the deck. He lies on his back and watches the constellations above, the heavens alight with the thousands of stars in the firmament. He traces the path of the Milky Way from one horizon to the other and notes the Great Rift of darkness which cuts through the river of bright stars. The war is over at last, and he has hope again.

That night he dreams of the djinns in that cave under the hill of Jerusalem and of the blood that flowed through the valley of Gehenna. The blood came up to his knees as he waded through it, and arrows alight with flame arced through the hot air. The corpses of men and goats came floating on the blood, a child with a sheep's head on for a headdress clutched a beam of wood from a church and floated down, past Robin, never saying a word.

That night Robin steals awake and he throws his bow and arrows into the sea, and all his knives and his sword. He makes a vow that he will not kill anymore.

The ship traverses the Mediterranean and one day it docks in Marseille. That night Robin gets into a fight in a tavern that has no name above the door and when it is done he finds two corpses at his feet. He loots them for their purses and knows he can't return to the ship. He steals a bow and arrow and gets away. He follows the path of pilgrims, from holy church to holy site, trying to return to England. To make a living he enters archery competitions. Sometimes he bets on himself to win; at other times he bets successfully on losing.

He crosses France and one day he sets sail from Normandy on a ship bound for York. He sees the island rising in the distance. The sea salt stains his lips. He throws his weapons into the water again. This time he's going home. He knows he won't be killing anymore.

He alights in York one sunny morning. He walks straight into an inn and gets drunk on ale for two nights running, until his cash runs out. He staggers out into the dawn. Gulls cry. He tells them he is going home.

He has no horse so he walks the rest of the way. He comes to Loxley, to the manor house, and calls to his father but no one answers. He looks more closely. No one works the fields and weeds grow out of the gaps in the stone. He climbs into the house he knows so well. Cobwebs and dust, broken plates on the floor, old dried blood. He goes from room to room.

When he exits he finds knights waiting for him. He stares at them. They stare back from atop their horses.

'I am Robin of Loxley,' he tells them.

'Loxley is gone,' they tell him. 'This land belongs to the Crown.'

'Richard's in captivity,' he says, and the captain of the knights spits. 'John sits on the throne,' he says.

'My father—'

'The old man's in the potter's field,' the captain says. 'And you should leave lest you follow him there.'

There are five of them and one of him and he has no weapons. Were he an archer still he could take out maybe three before they had a chance to move. He works out wind and angles. Back in the Holy Land they sent him on covert assignments. Long-range assassinations of Saracen commanders and suchlike. From time to time a fellow Christian, with all the factions in the Holy Land they spent more time fighting each other than they did Saladin.

He leaves his home. He travels aimlessly. Everywhere he goes he sees the same thing: the rich rule by the sword and the poor are enslaved. He mourns his father. He mourns his home. One day he comes to a fair in Arkham and picks up a bow. There's a small archery competition. He wins easily and collects the prize purse. He drinks at the fair. He watches a bare-knuckle boxing fight. He buys the winner a drink. The winner, a large guy, says, 'You shoot well.'

Robin shrugs.

The big guy says, 'Where did you serve?'

Robin says, 'I was there for Jerusalem, but we didn't take her back.'

'I was all over,' the big guy says. He scratches his head. 'It was a long time ago, though. I never got to see that much of the place.'

'It's worse now,' Robin says.

'I bet. Listen. There's work up in Nottingham, if a fellow with your skills is looking for work.'

'What's Nottingham to me?' Robin says.

The big guy shrugs. 'Maybe nothing. Just a word to the wise.'

That night Robin camps in the forest. He lies on his back and stares up at the stars, at the blackness that cuts through the bright Milky Way. He cannot sleep. He packs and goes deeper into the forest, then deeper still. He listens to the silences until he knows he's in the twilight place. As a boy he wandered the woods from Loxley Chase to Sherwood Forest, and he knows some of its secrets. He finds a yew tree. A beam of moonlight casts it in a silver pall.

Robin makes himself a crude bow and arrows.

★

He spends days in the forest. He tracks the deer. The herds move for grazing. He sees a newborn fawn framed against sunrise on a hill. He kills his first grown deer later that day and breaks the king's law. He skins the deer and cuts the meat and cooks it on a fire and his belly's full for the first time in weeks. He doesn't think it wrong to kill a deer but he thinks it wrong that all the deer should belong only to the Crown. He thinks of Richard, imprisoned who knows where. The Holy Roman Emperor has him now. He remembers Richard, a strong, impulsive, vicious man, driven by some religious or political impulse Robin doesn't understand. The war he carried out in the Holy Land was savage. And for what? Robin can no longer remember why he'd taken the cross. As a boy he was restless, Loxley felt close and oppressive after a while. He'd wanted adventure, to see the world.

But the more he saw the world the more blood he saw.

He mourns his father. His anger at the Crown mounts. He kills another deer, skins and cuts it, and takes it to a nearby village. He distributes the meat for free to the needy, and vanishes before the forest rangers or the sheriff's men can find him. From washing hung outside he steals Lincoln greens but leaves a payment – a deer's heart and kidneys wrapped in cloth.

He becomes aware of others in the forest. The rangers on their scouting missions. Transports to and from along the roads, all kinds of merchants. Once he thinks he sees a fairy dancing on a dandelion. Strange lights move at night, trying to lead him astray, but he ignores them. From time to time he hears the voices of the dead.

He makes his way to Nottingham.

Two ancient guardsmen at the entrance. They pay him no mind. He wanders in. Nottingham. He'd been a few times before with his father. A prosperous town. He sees monks and king's men, children playing ball with an inflated pig's bladder, traders, craftsmen, a handful of Jews. He hears French and English spoken and some Latin. He sees faded marks on the walls, a green man, his hair made of leaves. He seeks out a tavern.

An alewife serves him beer. Robin gives her his few coppers. He listens to what people are saying. A harpist in the corner sings softly, 'The Ballad of Leesome Brand'.

'You're from the forest?' someone says to him, curiously, noting his green. 'We used to get hoods in the woods but they've been quiet lately.'

'What's there to do in Nottingham?' he asks the someone. A youngish man with a fox-like face.

'For entertainment? Try the Night Market.'

Robin has no money for accommodation. He drinks sparingly. He visits several alehouses and a church. In the church he sits quietly while the priest gives the service. Robin hears bells. He pays for a loaf of bread from a baker. He walks as far as the castle. He studies the castle walls and the movement of armed men. A cook woman comes out of the gates with a bucket of slop. She tosses it on the ground. Fish heads and chicken bones and rotten onions. She looks at Robin critically.

'You might do,' she says in surprise.

He wanders till night. He sees the town gibbet and the outlaws hanging in the wind. Their slack mouths, their empty eyes. Carrion birds gather round them.

He finds himself suddenly and inexplicably missing the light of the Holy Land. The sky at home is always grey.

He comes to a square. A youth wanders past, shouting, 'Dwale! Get yer dwale here!'

Robin sees sheriff's men standing around. They do nothing. A man asks Robin if he wants to have sex. It isn't clear if it's his services he's offering or somebody else's. Robin watches. There is an unmarked door.

He goes through it and finds it opens onto a hole in the ground. He climbs down a crude ladder.

He smells opium and hashish, one bitter, one sweet. A cavernous hall. People lie on soft cushions. A harpist sings 'The

Ballad of The Elfin Knight'. Robin treads softly among the sleepers underground. The smell of medicine takes him back in time: to the hospital in Acre, behind the walls, the wounded and the dying lying there in a similar great hall. Cool stones, and murmured chanting, and the smell of incense, opium and hash, the silence broken by a sudden scream or groan of pain. The men endured.

He, Robin, had lain on that floor. The medics tended to him brusquely.

One came, looked, said, 'You'll live,' and moved on. Priests administered last rites elsewhere.

'Where is the king?' somebody said. Somebody spat.

'Which king?' somebody said.

It takes him back, the smell. He realises then that Nottingham's in sickness. Not just the town, the land itself, perhaps the whole world's wounded, and a great dark rift runs through its starry river. It needs healing.

It needs a surgeon.

He sees a maid walk past in greens. Her face is young, her eyes are old. She meets his gaze and smiles. He hastens after her.

'My lady, may I ask your name?'

'It's Marian.'

She's gone before he can enquire further. He tries to follow but gets lost, the Night Market's maze stretches in all directions. He passes sellers of forbidden deer meat, of witchy medicine and spells. He finds weapon-makers and preachers and seditionists and fools.

He comes to a place called Dick's.

It is the biggest of the caverns. The cushions are plumper and the dreamers are wealthier and silent girls go in bare feet among them to replenish their dreams. In another corner there are dice games where merchants and knights and freemen bet the sort of money only Templars usually carry. There's money in Nottingham. And none of it's marked.

He looks around but he doesn't belong here. He has no money and his clothes are stolen and his weapons are homemade. He walks through the dreamers and their haze and past the alehouse bar and the dice games until he comes to a room where a man sits behind a desk.

The man regards him without curiosity. He says, 'You must be Robin of Loxley.'

Robin says, 'You have the advantage of me.'

'I am Sir Richard at the Lee.'

The man has eyes that are not quite right. Like he has been down in this subterranean realm for too long. Like he had tasted too much dwale, partaken in too much Goblin Fruit. His eyes are pure green, there is no white left and no pupil. Robin finds the eyes disconcerting.

'How do you know who I am?'

Sir Richard shrugs. 'I heard word you might be coming this way. And sooner or later everyone comes to Dick's. You were a landowner?'

'I was.' Robin mulls the past tense. The home he grew up in, the land he knew in his bones. There is a special magic to growing up in a place, to knowing every turn and every tree and how the sun shines and where the rain falls and where there will be puddles after. What the best place is for picking mushrooms. He remembers learning to ride, learning to fight, learning to shoot. Remembers sitting by the fire on cold winter nights, his father would sometimes open in unexpected song, the old man had a good voice when he put use to it. He knew all the ballads.

'But you're not Norman,' Sir Richard says. And what else is there to say? The Loxleys didn't come from France. Perhaps one of his ancestors came over with the Saxons back when Arthur was still king. They had an old shrine to Woden out back but went to church every Sunday. And Robin thought it was enough to serve the king. He took the cross. He went with Richard. He'd shed blood for Christ and for his lord.

'No,' he says, the word bitter. 'We weren't.'

Sir Richard looks at him almost in compassion. 'You served in the crusade?'

'I served.'

'I was in Damascus,' Sir Richard says. Then shakes his head. 'I wish I could forget it.'

Robin thinks of the retreat, the whistle of arrows, the blood. 'I know,' he says.

'Well, you have skills,' Sir Richard says. 'I heard of your archery. I have no need for an archer but I could use a good man.'

Robin looks at him. There is a faded portrait of a green man on the wall behind Sir Richard. His hair is made of leaves.

Robin stands.

'Thank you,' he says. 'It is kind of you to offer.'

'It is not kindness that I offer,' Sir Richard says.

'I know. But I respectfully decline all the same.'

Sir Richard looks at him curiously then.

'Why?' he says.

Robin mulls the question. He should take the job he's offered. He has no money and no prospects, and his land is gone. His home...

'I don't know,' he says. 'I am not sure, yet, what it is I seek.'

'Revenge?' Sir Richard says. 'Is that what you are thinking?' He sits behind his desk like an old oak, and Robin wonders in sudden surprise how long it's been that Sir Richard has been sitting there. For one fleeting moment he has the irrational notion that Richard is planted there, that he had sunk roots into the ground. How long *has* the old knight been underground? He doesn't seem quite right. There is fungus growing behind his ears.

'You think you can take revenge?' Sir Richard says. 'On who? The court? The law? You see those preachers out there who spread sedition? The landowners make the laws. The king rules and his knights have swords and men. You can't... *change* anything. You won't get your land back. You want to own land, you must be given it by the king.'

'When Richard gets back—'

'You think the Lionheart will be your salvation? You think he cares about you, about your service?' Cold amusement turns Sir Richard's eyes a colder green. 'Take my offer, Robin of Loxley. There aren't many jobs going around, and there are too many soldiers back from the war with nothing but scars to show for it.'

But Robin shakes his head. 'You're right,' he says. 'But still. I thank you, no.'

'Very well. Don't say I didn't ask.'

'You did.'

'Listen, don't rush to anything,' Sir Richard says. 'Here.' He tosses a handful of coins on the desk. 'Stay the night. Try the wares. Find yourself a girl, or a guy if that's what you're into. Think it over. And who knows, you might feel different in the morning. The nights in the Night Market run long.'

Robin looks at the money. Thinks of what it can buy.

He nods and goes. Sir Richard stares after him, then at the money Robin left untouched on the desk.

'A man who can't be bought has no business being in the land of the living…' he says, but softly. He closes his eyes. Soon he is snoring.

Night flowers bloom down his shoulder blades to his back.

Robin of Loxley traipses through the Night Market and hidden eyes watch him pass. He seeks the maid he saw before. He thinks he sees her disappearing down a turning. He follows in pursuit but only sees her back again, vanishing down another turn.

He pursues with no conscious idea in mind beyond wishing to speak with her again.

Marian. The name evokes something in him. Was there not a story of a girl who vanished centuries before into the woods?

But girls always vanish in dark woods. There would be nary a ballad without that simple fact.

Still he goes on, Marian, Marian, round a corner and through a tunnel and into the mouth of some ancient cave.

Ancient stalagmites surround him. Maid Marian vanishes ahead, always ahead. Robin slips on the wet floor of the cave.

When his eyes blink open he sees her face.

'Maid Marian,' he says.

'Robin of Loxley.'

She has a serious face. She has green eyes. She says, 'You should not have come here.'

'Where is… here?'

He sits up. She helps him. Is she annoyed with him? He doesn't want to upset her.

'This is the well at the world's end,' she tells him.

Robin sees roots have penetrated into the chamber's ceiling, great oak roots reach down into a black, black pool. Something floats in the pool, he sees, a corpse, its chest open, the roots, the roots go through him—

The man's eyes open. The man isn't dead. The man looks at Robin. The man grins.

He whispers, 'Help me…'

'Just ignore him,' Maid Marian says.

The corpse whispers, '*Run…*'

But it is too late to run. Robin has no eyes but for the maid. She seems taller here, more regal. He kneels at her feet. He wants to serve her. To love her. To be whatever she wants him to be.

'You should not have come here,' she says. 'Not yet.'

The corpse whispers, '*Fool…*'

Someone moves behind Robin. The large guy from the boxing ring. His face is slack. Robin tries to rise, too late.

The big guy hefts a rock. He brings it down on Robin's head.

Then there is pain. Then darkness like a black, black well.

51

THE GUY

I watched the ship vanish over the horizon. I crouched low in the shallows and smeared river mud on my face. Reeds grew on the banks. I sensed no natives nearby. Dawn had come and gone and the light was murky.

I started to follow the water. The captain had been in such a hurry to dump me there that I was nowhere near the river mouth yet. I walked through mud, in ghostly fog, and still I saw no one and nothing. It should have been abundant with life – birds, deer, snails. But nothing moved and nothing squawked or cried or called. I went deeper and deeper into the mist.

At last I saw a standing shadow where the water fell. As I approached I saw a barge moored against the riverbank and a tall thin figure in the mud. He stood perfectly still, as though he were a statue, as though time meant nothing to him.

He turned at my approach.

'You must be the passenger,' he said.

'You must be the ferryman. Haros?'

He nodded, without much interest. 'Do you have my payment?'

'Here,' I said. I passed him the obol. I had smeared my blood on it: this was part of the deal.

He took it and inspected it.

'Alright,' he said. He pocketed the coin.

'I am Guy of Gisbourne,' I told him.

'Your name does not matter,' he said. 'Not where you're going.'

'And where am I going, Haros?' I asked him.

He gave me a bloodless smile.

'To Fairyland,' he said. 'But all the fairies are dead.'

I didn't make a comment. I followed him to the barge. He pushed off from the bank and we were on our way. He moved slowly, confidently, using the unseen currents. He was keenly aware of any hidden bank of sand, of any tree roots, of eddies. We sailed mid-river. Fog obscured much of the view. The forest grew on either side, gnarled tall trees, dark with age.

'How far is Nottingham?' I said distractedly.

'How long is a piece of string?' Haros said.

I lay on my back. I stared up at the grey sky. I could not see the sun.

I closed my eyes and slept.

A dream troubled me at the edge of consciousness when I arose. There was a great oak, and a well of black water. Something terrible was buried there. Something ancient, yet still alive and in pain. I could feel its fury, and its rage fed the roots of the oak that grew from it.

Too late I remembered Mistress Rebecca's warning not to fall asleep there. But what was I to do? A solider learns to sleep when he can. I did not know how long my mission there would be. What I would do when I found him. A part of me almost admired the man. To carry out a hidden war deep in the woods and to survive this long against the king's forces – that took some doing. I looked around me but could no longer see the banks. The river widened here alarmingly. Through snatches of fog I saw old trees half-submerged in the water, their black branches drooping like arms. Still I saw no living thing. Haros pushed the barge with his pole. He never slept, I thought. He never tired. His skin seemed made of fog. He turned his head and watched me.

'You slept,' he said. 'That is good.'

'Mistress Rebecca said not to.'

'She is wrong,' he said. 'You cannot get there by waking means. Hood knows that. Look up.'

I looked at the night sky. I could not recognise any of the constellations. Haros pointed, identifying them for me.

'The Caged Bear,' he said. 'The Drowned Witch. Old Father Time. The Mirror That Was Cracked.'

There were too many stars in the sky above. I looked away. The barge sailed on. I waited for attack but none came. I felt eyes watching, yet still nothing alive. A ghost came and perched on the barge next to me. She wore white and I could see through her.

'You smell so fresh,' she said, 'like a new baby. I love the taste of newborn babes.'

I sat still and she laughed in my face.

'Shoo, Isolde,' the ferryman said. He brought his pole round and the ghost fled into the mist. But I could still hear her laughing.

'Pay no attention to them,' Haros said.

'Who are they?' I said.

'Passengers who didn't pay the fare.'

I shuddered and for the rest of the journey I kept my eyes fixed firmly ahead, and I tried to ignore the otherworldly voices that called out to me and the faces, both strange and familiar, that came.

'I am cold,' my mother said. She hovered above the water. 'I am always cold and there is no hearth.'

'Shoo,' the ferryman said. He brought his pole round and the ghost fled into the mist. But I could still hear her crying.

We went round a bend in the river and over some rapids and a town rose before us in the distance. A bridge spanned the river, made out of mist and fog. The shadows of things that had once been people trudged over the bridge, and black birds circled in the sky overhead. The town itself was made of weathered stone and I could see dank narrow streets, a castle, several towers.

Nottingham, I thought. Shit.

'Where can I find Hood?' I said.

Haros shrugged.

'At the well at the world's end,' he said.

'Huh?'

'When you can go no farther, then you have gone too far,' he said. 'And when you go past that there you will be.'

'Fuck it, then,' I said tiredly. 'I'll find him myself.'

'Or he will find you,' the ferryman said, not unreasonably. He pushed the barge to the bank and I got off.

'I'll see you, Haros,' I said.

'Yes,' he said. 'You will.'

He vanished in moments into the mist, a tall thin man on a floating barge with the face of an undertaker and much the same manners. I picked up my pack and walked to the town.

A raven came and perched on a branch and watched me as I passed.

'This is a fool's errand,' it commented. Then it flew away.

Well, at least there was life here, I thought. I found it strangely reassuring.

I came to the gates. Two ancient guards stood there, watching as I approached.

'He's a fresh-looking one, Ernest,' one said.

'That he is, Bert. Those eyes are so juicy they'll have all the ravens talking.'

'I hate when ravens talk, Ernest.'

'So do I, Bert.'

I stared at them. They didn't move. I looked at their feet and realised they had none. The guardsmen grew out of the ground. Vibrant green moss covered their arms, and roses grew out of their ears; so I left them there.

I entered Nottingham.

Up and down dark narrow streets where nothing grew, past windows where only the dead lived. I could see the ghosts palely loitering.

How had it come to this? I wondered, chilled. Just seven years ago the town was quietly prosperous, its houses gaily decorated, with fat happy children playing pig-bladder kick-ball in its streets. Or so I imagined it, anyway. Now the town was something I couldn't even put a name to: some alien otherness that had taken root here and whispered from the shadows, mocking me as I walked.

I reached a square. A youth with a fox's face came sniffing out of the shadows. He was real, this one.

'Hey, mister,' he said. 'You want to buy some Goblin Fruit?'

'Buy?' I said. 'With what?'

'Whatever you got.' He licked his lips hungrily. 'Blood's best – it makes everything more real for a little while. A drop of blood and you can fuck one of the ghosts.'

'Is anyone else here alive beside you?' I said.

'Sure,' he said. 'Lots of folks.'

'I am looking for Hood.'

He shook his head. 'You don't want to go looking for him, mister. How did you get here, anyway?'

'A ferryman brought me.'

'You don't look dead enough,' he said dubiously. 'Listen, just give me a sip, I won't tell.'

He showed me his fox's teeth. I showed him my iron knife.

'Alright,' he said. 'Then I guess I'll see you.'

'Wait,' I said. 'I am looking for a man, a Sir Richard?'

'Down there,' he said, pointing. I followed his finger and saw a large hole in the ground. 'See you, Guy of Gisbourne.'

He vanished back into the shadows. I was uneasy. I had not given him my name.

I went to the hole. There was a small wooden sign nailed to the ground with an arrow pointing down and it said, in unsteady black letters, The Night Market – Open All Hours.

I stared at it dubiously, then slid down into the hole. The fall was longer than I expected. I landed with a hard bump and cursed. It was very dark at first but as I waited a faint luminescence began to rise all about me. The walls glowed with some light green illumination, and I saw that they were heavily carpeted with moss.

Nor was I alone in that subterranean realm, I realised as I began exploring. The others kept out of my way. They shambled in the shadows as though scared at my appearance. I caught only glimpses of them. They wore grey robes and moved softly, uneasily. I corralled one of them at last against the wall of a great hall and showed him my knife.

'Please,' he said. 'Do not prune me.'

'What—' I said, then looked at him closely. For the first time I got a proper look at one of those derelicts. His ears were wood-decay fungus and his nose an off-white champignon. His eyes were green and grey all mixed together.

'How long have you been down here?' I said.

'How long is moonlight?' he asked me mournfully. I let him go.

They were no longer people, not as I knew people, but they were harmless. They stayed out of my way and I could hear their soft chattering in the shadows. For hours I wandered in that underground maze. At last I came to a place. Roots pushed out of the broken floor and between them I could make out the rotten remnants of cushions, tables, dice. A hand-written sign on the bar had an arrow pointing ahead and a legend: Dick's – We're Always Open.

'Alright,' I said.

I came to a room. There was a man there. He looked up without curiosity. His eyes were flecked with grey.

I said, 'You must be Sir Richard.'

'You can call me Dick,' he said. His voice was gravelly. He said, 'I have not spoken in some time.'

I noted with interest that instead of hair he had long green vines falling from his scalp to his shoulders. His fingers seemed fused to the desk. Moss grew over his earlobes. I had the feeling I was years too late. He wasn't going to be any use. I think he knew that.

He said, 'Six months ago another one like you came down here to seek me. I heard he committed suicide later, in the wood.'

I hadn't realised King John had sent other agents before me. I should have.

'What can you tell me about the situation?' I said.

'The situation?' He laughed in my face. 'There is no situation. There is just this. But we're still open. Dick's. Everybody used to come to Dick's. You want dwale? Ale? Someone to suck your cock? A game of dice? We're still open. Everything is fine.'

I stared at him. He began to cough. When he coughed dry spores came out of his throat.

'I wish time *passed* here,' he said. 'What year is it, outside?'

'Twelve hundred,' I said.

'A new century,' he said. 'I wonder if it will be just as shit.'

'You want anything?' I said. 'A glass of water?'

'I get my nourishment from the—' He gestured down. I followed his gaze. Behind the desk his feet burrowed into the floor, became roots. 'They talk, you know. Trees. Mushrooms. They all talk to each other under the earth. Sometimes it's really lovely to listen to. But most of the time they just try to steal each other's food and starve each other. They're a lot like people, underneath.'

'Do you want me to…?' I said, and made a gentle cutting motion across my throat.

'Me? Oh, no,' he said. 'Thank you. But I'm fine, really. I want to see how it all turns out in the end.'

'It ends in death,' I told him.

'But whose?' he said. 'I'll see you, Guy of Gisbourne.'

I went to leave him but turned. 'How *do* you know my name?' I said.

'I'm sure there is a ballad or something,' he said.
'How does it end?'
'How do you think?'
I left him.

52

THE ROBIN

Robin comes to on Baker's Street, outside a stall selling loaves and fish. Bells ring, not in his head but out of it. The bells for Sext. Nottingham. He's back in Nottingham. There is no sign of the Night Market. The baker kicks him.

'Get away from here, you bum, you're scaring away the customers!'

Robin staggers to his feet. There are leaves in his hair. The baker stares at him.

'The green man...' he whispers.

'What?' Robin says. There's a ringing in his ears. How did he get here? The last thing he remembers is talking to Sir Richard underground... Then it all goes fuzzy.

He loses his balance, tries to hold on to the baker's cart, upends it. Loaves and fish go flying.

'Get the hell out of here!' the baker roars. 'Guards!'

Robin staggers away. But two armed men block his way.

'He giving you trouble?' one says to the baker.

'He was passed out in front of my stall. Didn't even see where he came from. Look at my stuff. Who'll pay for it now?'

'Right,' the armed man says. 'A vagrant. And causing public nuisance and sleeping in the street without licence. What else?'

'Search his pockets,' the other armed man says. They pat him down roughly.

'Nothing on him.'

'Useless shit. Take him to the cells.'

They drag him away.

He sits in the cells. He thinks this is wrong. His head hurts. A harpist sits on the floor with his back to the wall, playing a tune. The harp's made of bone. He feels Robin's gaze and looks up.

'What are you in for?' Robin says.

'Vagrancy,' the harpist says. 'That, and I guess the sheriff didn't like my singing.'

'What were you singing?'

The harpist brightens. 'Do you know 'A Gest of Robyn Hode'?' he says.

'Sure. But that's just a story, isn't it?'

'They're all just stories,' the harpist says. 'I'm Alan-a-dale, by the way.'

'I'm Robin of Loxley.'

The harpist nods. The harpist's fingers glide on the strings.

'So it goes,' he says.

Footsteps in the corridor. The same two guards appear. They unlock the cage.

'You, out,' they say.

'Me?' Robin says. 'But I only just got here.'

They pull him on.

'I'll see you, Robin of Loxley,' the harpist says. He strums softly on the strings. The guards lead Robin away. Up a short flight of stone stairs, into a large dining hall.

A man sits at the head of a long table, picking at a plate of eggs. He looks up. The man is neither short nor tall, neither thin nor fat. He is as grey and average as one can be. He rises, comes over to inspect the prisoner.

He says, 'I am the Sheriff of Nottingham.'

Robin stands still. The two guards block escape. The sheriff says, 'What is your name, please?'

'Robin of Loxley.'

'Your purpose in this town?'

'I was looking for a job.'

The sheriff frowns. 'You don't have one?'

'Not currently.'

'Where do you stay?'

'I have no fixed abode.'

The sheriff looks him over carefully. 'I see, I see,' he mutters. 'What are your plans now?' he says.

'Sir?'

'What do you plan?'

'Sir? I thought I'd look for work, sir.'

'You have money?'

'No, sir.'

'No money, no job, no place to live. You are a vagrant and a bum. Do you dispute it, Robin of Loxley?'

'I am just trying to make my way in this world,' Robin says.

'Listen to me, Robin,' the sheriff says. He lays a fatherly hand on Robin's shoulder. 'This is a peaceful town now. This is a happy place. There is no more banditry, there is no more violence, the roads are safe and the residents are happy and the king's tax gets collected on time, and with no exceptions. Now, I like you. You have an honest face. But there is no place for you here. So, after our little chat, I will personally take you beyond the city boundaries and set you on the road to elsewhere. And you will follow that road, all the way until you're out of Nottinghamshire and my jurisdiction. Do you understand me?'

'I do, sir.'

'Good.'

The sheriff's fist sinks into Robin's stomach. He doubles over in pain. The sheriff nods to the guards. He returns to the head of the table. The guards beat Robin. The sheriff dines on eggs.

When it is done, the guards help Robin back to his feet. The sheriff offers him a napkin. Robin wipes his face of blood. The guardsmen hoist him up, one on either side. They walk him out of the hall and out of the castle. They lead him out of the gates and over the river and set him on the road to York, and the sheriff comes riding over on his horse.

'Keep walking, Robin,' he tells him. 'Keep walking, and don't look back, and there will be no trouble.'

Robin nods. Robin touches his lip. Robin winces.

He starts to walk.

They watch him go. They watch until he reaches a turn in the road and vanishes from sight behind the trees.

'You think he will be trouble?' one of the watchmen says.

The sheriff stares into the distance.

'If he comes back, kill him,' he says.

What does Robin do, in those long months in the greenwood? A memory brings him back, vague and troubling like a throbbing tooth. Back into the forest, back into the sanctity of trees. He finds shelter by a bubbling brook and drinks, and nurses his injuries. They hurt him just badly enough to make it count. They wanted him able to walk.

He sleeps the night under an oak and in the darkness a fawn comes to him, without fear, and nuzzles his face. Robin wakes to this woodland creature and the fawn looks at him as if to say: *Follow me*.

Robin rises and the fawn darts into the trees. Robin follows. The night is dense and the trees silent, the moonlight filtered through the canopy illuminates a spider-web, a leaf, a white flower in bloom. The fawn takes Robin to a giant oak beside a lake of black water. It darts away. Robin stays.

He looks around him. There was a camp here once, he thinks. He sees the remnants of great bonfires and their blackened rings of stones, but the rings are broken and the stones dispersed. He sees the rotting remains of long wooden tables. He climbs the oak and finds some swinging ropes and walkways and collapsed tree-houses. An air of abandonment, an air of disuse. But people have been there, a great many of them, and he conjures up an image of an army all in green, making merry after a day of battle.

Something moves in the black pool, something large. Big yellow eyes rise for just a moment and regard him before sinking back into the depths. Robin does not disturb the thing in the pool.

He climbs down and there, near the tree, elevated on a dais, he finds a throne. The throne is wooden and flowers grow out of it now, and its roots go deep. He cannot move it. He runs his hand gently on the varnished edge.

After a while he sits on the throne.

Voices wake him and he hides. It's early morning. A scarred man missing an ear comes mumbling into the Green Place. He looks rough – rougher than Robin. Robin can't tell what age he is. The man talks to himself, picks at scabs on his skin. He rummages around, picks a beetle off the ground, pops it in his mouth and chews.

'All gone to shit,' the man says mournfully, 'and now poor Will Scarlett is left all alone. Where did they all go?' He looks about him helplessly. 'The magic goes away,' he says sadly. 'And I am so hungry, so hungry… What did Rufus always say? Go back to the beginning… So here I am… I'm waiting for you… Back at the beginning… Hello, who the hell are you?'

Robin steps out from behind the tree and Will Scarlett startles. His knives flash but his hand shakes, and Robin feels sorry for the derelict.

'I'm Robin of Loxley.'

'You're a Robin?' Will Scarlett stares at him. 'Are you a hood?'

'I'm not entirely sure what that means, friend. But I am just as hungry as you are, and the forest's full of deer, for men who are willing to take them.'

'The king's deer, the king's forest,' Will Scarlett says. He stares at Robin. 'You almost look like him,' he says.

'Like who?'

'The one who came before. Then the Green Lady died in the winter in order to bring the spring, but something must have gone wrong, and I've been waiting all this time, all this time... Deer, you say?'

'Venison, friend.'

Will Scarlett licks his lips. 'We used to dance and make merry here every night, and eat steak and ribs... I will join you, Robin.' Will Scarlett grins. 'Do you have arms?' he says.

'I'll make a bow and arrows.'

'Can you shoot?'

It's Robin's turn to grin.

'One way to find out,' he says.

That day Robin tracks and kills a deer, and he and Will Scarlett skin and butcher it. They leave the offal as an offering by the black pool, and the thing in the water takes it. That night they make a fresh ring of stones and light a new fire in that old place, and they cook the venison.

'It is good to have meat again,' Will says.

'Yes,' Robin says. 'It is good to have meat.'

'What are you thinking, Robin of Loxley?'

'I think many go hungry while the rich are fed, that many go cold while the rich burn wood, that many slave upon land when others lay title and claim to that land and their labour. And I think maybe this is the way of the world and nothing more, and in centuries hence it will be just the same. And yet I hate John Lackland and his barons and his law, and I hate the Sheriff of Nottingham. And I would like to hurt them.'

'Coming at the king won't be easy,' Will says. 'He's always guarded and besides, he never comes to Nottingham. And as for the sheriff, if you take him out another will just take his place – it has always been thus.'

'But it is this one I hate,' Robin says.

'Then I will help you,' Will says. 'But we will need more men. There were many of us here once, but now we are dispersed.'

Robin shrugs. 'What *was* this place?' he says.

'A place for hoods.'

'I was a soldier. I am not a thief.'

'I was one once, too. I guess it just depends on what you're fighting for, Robin of Loxley.'

They sleep that night under the canopy of the Major Oak. In the morning a raven comes and perches on a branch and watches Robin.

'This is a fool's errand,' it comments. Then it flies away.

Robin rises, washes, and goes into the wood. His wounds still hurt. He smears mud from the black pool on the wounds.

He watches Nottingham from afar. Notes the river approach, the bridge, the roads. The town's weak, he thinks. It is engulfed by forest. Hold Sherwood, and you can choke the life out of Nottingham.

He sees the sheriff's men out on patrol. Notes the traders coming and going. Boats on the river. A peaceful, prosperous place.

He longs to sneak inside. He has it in him to search for this maid, Marian, who he had met for but a moment. Something about her awakes a yearning in him. But he dare not go in. Not yet.

On his return to camp he comes across a bubbling stream, too wide to cross, and there's a makeshift bridge across it. A giant ugly boulder of a man stands on the bridge holding a quarterstaff.

'Oh, it's you,' he says.

'Right,' Robin says. 'You're that boxer from Arkham.'

'John Little. That's me. They call me Little John. I never got your name.'

'It's Robin. Now will you get the fuck off the bridge so I can cross?'

'If you're gonna be an asshole, you gotta pay the troll toll,' Little John says.

'You're the troll?'

'Quarter troll, on my mother's side. Or so my father always said, at least until I killed him.'

'I could fight you,' Robin says.

Little John grins. 'I'd like that.'

Robin considers. He takes off his bow.

'Or I could just shoot you,' he says.

'Hold on, whoa,' Little John says. 'This ain't how it works.'

'You've got three seconds to get off that fucking bridge, John. Three, two, one—'

Little John stumbles and loses his balance. He plunges down into the water and screams.

'I can't swim!'

Robin sighs. 'Here,' he says.

He throws him a rope. The big guy holds on. Robin pulls. Little John climbs onto the bank. Lies there, gasping.

'I hate water,' he says.

'You're a little touched, ain'tcha,' Robin says. 'Tell me, when we first met – why did you suggest I go to Nottingham?'

'I don't know,' the giant mumbles. 'Maybe I hoped you would do something stupid when you got there. You look the type.'

'What sort of type is that?'

'I don't know, Robin. A saviour type.'

'Only saviour I know,' Robin says, 'ended up on a cross.'

'Sure, sure,' Little John says, and he tries to smile. 'But he gave them hell first, didn't he, Robin?'

'If you want a fight,' Robin says, 'I can offer you one.'

He reaches out his hand.

Little John takes it.

And now there are three of them under the Major Oak. Robin is not entirely surprised when Little John and Scarlett greet each other like long-lost comrades. And yet he realises with some surprise that they look up to *him*. Why him? He's just a guy back from the crusade. And yet they treat him differently, and when he sits in that wooden throne they studiously say nothing, but it's in their eyes. Like he *belongs* there.

He can give them orders and they will follow those orders. It's like being back in the crusade. No questions, no arguments.

So he gives them an order.

That night they go on their first mission. They lie in wait on the road. The sheriff's men come out on patrol. Robin waits until he sees one of the men who caught him. Who beat him. He and Little John and Scarlett follow the patrol. Unseen. He waits.

'I'm going to take a piss,' the sheriff's man says. He rides his horse to the trees. He climbs off.

It is done in seconds. It is done in silence. They grab him with his dick still out. Scarlett sticks cloth in his mouth and Little John puts a hood over his head. They take him into Sherwood before ever the patrolmen notice he is gone.

That night they light a fire and in its light they torture the sheriff's man until his screams are the only sound in the forest. The thing in the black pool rises and watches, and ravens come in silence beneath the dark sky and settle on the high branches.

They leave the mutilated corpse on the King's Road for the patrolmen to find.

They come looking for them, of course. They come hard. But they are not wood's men, they are town's men. And the Green Place, Robin is beginning to suspect, has a kind of enchantment about it, so even when the hunters get so close one time that he can see them moving through the leaves, they do not come to the place and depart empty-handed.

And he has a niggling feeling, like the remembrance of a dream, as though he had been to this place once before. But the details elude him. Something about roots that clutch, and some nameless horror, buried underground long ago...

That night he dreams of Marian. And when he wakes he vows that he will find her. He just wants to talk to her. He just wants to see if he can make her laugh.

There are more guards on the city now, and more patrols at night. Robin and his men rob a York merchant and liberate his cargo of cloth and dyes. They treat the man courteously and offer him to join them at their supper.

'What will we do with cloth and dyes?' Little John says.

'Give them away,' Robin says.

That night they go into old alehouses that straddle Nottingham's walls, where alewives welcome them through smugglers' doors. They take the gifts appreciatively. Their men sit drinking ale and listen for a quiet word.

An old word, whispered between these walls before.

Hood...

53

THE GUY

I slept that night in the castle's empty stables. In the night a herd of unicorns came running past across the meadow. I stared at them under the silver moonlight. There was something just really fucking weird about a horse with a horn protruding from the middle of its forehead. But they were pretty to look at.

Pots and pans banging woke me up early morning – my first indication anyone still lived in the castle. A very short, very fat woman stood over me with an irritable expression. She seemed so completely *normal* that she was obviously wrong.

'We don't allow vagabonds in the stables,' she said. 'Get out of here. Shoo.'

'Who are you?'

'I'm the cook.'

'The cook of *what*?'

'The castle cook. I'm Mrs More-Goose.'

But she said it more like *Morgause*. And I suddenly had a very bad feeling.

'Is anyone else living here?' I said.

'Of course. The sheriff.' She looked at me oddly. For just a moment I thought I must have been dreaming this whole time, that the nightmare Nottingham I had visited no longer existed, that I was back in an orderly world where things made sense. Then I looked beyond her at the view over Castle Rock, and saw nothing but the deepwood, and the fog over the river, and the silent town with its blackened houses filled with ghosts.

'Can I see him?'

'He doesn't like vagabonds. This is a clean, well-ordered place.'

'Aha, aha.'

She licked her lips. 'You came to kill him?'

'The sheriff? No.'

'The Hood.'

She said it so hungrily. Her nails were blunt and short. I wondered how everyone knew my business in this place, then realised the idiocy of the question. I was an outsider. What else would I be but the assassin? They probably had a ballad about that, too. They seemed to have a ballad about fucking everything.

'I don't truly know, missus,' I said. 'They say he's done bad things.'

'He has,' she said. 'He ruins everything. He and that harlot. And every time she dies it's just another fucking spring.'

'Every time she dies? Alright.' I wasn't going to go there. 'Can I see the sheriff? Is there breakfast? Are you a fairy? Excuse me for asking.'

'Yes,' she said.

'Yes?'

'Yes.'

'Alright.'

'Upstairs, dining hall. We're having eggs.'

'Thank you.'

I departed as fast as I could. The cook terrified me. Up the stairs, to a large hall with a long banquet table. A solitary figure sat at the head of the table.

'You're not the cook,' he said.

'I'm Guy of Gisbourne.'

'Are you? And what's that when it's at home? We're having eggs again.'

'May I sit?'

He waved a hand dismissively. He was dressed in full military regalia. 'We don't need outside help,' he said. 'I have everything under control.'

'Sure,' I said. I sat two chairs down from him.

'We're having eggs again,' he said.

'Yes.'

'Who did you say you were?'

'I'm Guy.'

'There's always a guy,' he said. 'He's the guy for his time and place. Ah, Cook. There you are.'

She came in with a frying pan blackened from too many fires and slid the eggs onto our plates. I stared at the eggs.

'These are not chicken eggs,' I said.

'Newts.'

I stared at the cook.

'Newts?'

'Giant newts. And a robin's. Though I can't climb trees too good now on account of my gout. You like?'

I poked the eggs dubiously with my skewer.

'Sure,' I said. 'I like.'

'Good.' She vanished again. It was just me and the sheriff.

'About this Hood,' he said.

'Yes?'

'He's bad business.'

'So I am beginning to understand…'

'What's that? Speak up, man! I can barely make sense of you!'

'I said, yes, sir.'

'Quite.' He looked at me keenly. 'We're having eggs,' he said.

'Yes,' I said. I got up. On the plate the yolks stared at me like baleful eyes. 'Yes.'

I edged out of there. I could not bear to be in the castle any longer. I began to run but the corridors lengthened around me. I turned left and I turned right and left and left and right, but there was no escape from that place. At last I burst through a door back into the dining hall. The sheriff sat at the head of the table. He looked up at me pleasantly as I came in.

'You're not the cook,' he said.

'Fuck this!' I screamed. My knife was in my hand and then against his throat. He didn't move. 'We're having eggs,' he said.

I couldn't even kill him. There was nothing left of him, I thought. The cook came in.

'I think you should leave,' she said.

'Yes,' I said.

'You made a mistake coming here.'

'Yes,' I said.

'You will find the Hood at the well at world's end,' she said. 'Beware the black pool, the green lady and the evening redness in the west. Fear death by water. The summer solstice is the cruellest one, and Mars is rising in the seventh house, auguring an inauspicious beginning for a death quest. A wise person knows that to seek is to suffer. Seek nothing; know everything. Be like water. When we were children, staying at the Unseemly Court, my cousin Merlin, he took me out on a sled and I was frightened. He said, Morgause, Morgause, hold on tight. And down we went.'

'The well at the world's end,' I said.

'Yes,' she said.

'Alright.'

I bade her farewell. What else could I do? They were all afflicted there, I thought. Afflicted with a madness for which there was no cure.

I left the castle. I left the town. There was nothing there for me.

I went into the wood.

THE ROBIN

'I heard you're putting a gang together.' The bone harpist grins. 'Mind if I join?'

'It's you,' Robin says. 'From the cells.'

'Well, they let me go, didn't they,' the harpist says. 'Not without putting the boot to me first though. Alan-a-dale, harpist and would-be thief. If you'll have me.'

'We're not thieves,' Robin says.

'I don't care,' the harpist says. He looks at Robin closely. 'I like you more than the last one, though.'

Robin of Loxley lets it pass. With each new day, new members join under the Major Oak. They make weapons and train in hand-to-hand combat and stealth.

'Oh, this is Much,' Alan-a-dale says. Some nightmare creature made of sticks and branches materialises by his side. 'You know, the miller's son. He wants to serve you, too.'

'No one need serve me,' Robin tells him. 'For here we are all equal, beyond the pale of God or English law. We fight so that all may be equal.'

'Well,' Alan says, 'I don't know about any of that, but I'll be sure to sing the ballad that way.'

'Welcome aboard,' Robin says.

'Much obliged, cap'n,' Alan says.

Much, the miller's son, rustles his leaves.

And Robin *does* see Marian again.

He steals into Nottingham. They seek him here, they seek him there, they seek poor Robin everywhere. But now he has secure access to the city through the tunnels, and loyal men and women to assure his passage, and as he walks the streets he sees, with some unease, the image of a green man on the walls. Is it him?

He steals into the castle as a palmer, a pilgrim from the Holy Land – he can go anywhere without arousing suspicion. He sees the sheriff's men training, notes the swords, the stabled horses, but he is not afraid.

He sees her then. Young and tall and tan and lovely. The girl of Robin's dreams goes walking, and all the sheriff's men turn and give her appraising looks. She sees Robin and for a moment, something like recognition flares in her eyes and the smile she gives him is as bright as the sun itself.

More and more they come, from all over. Motivated by some secret whisper, and they all look up to him, as though he were not himself at all but something older, wilder, something that they recognise when they look at him even when he does not, himself.

Robin watches as the latest recruit, a fat monk, goes to a group under the oak. His name's Tuck. Then there's Will Scarlett, there's Little John, there's Alan-a-dale and Much, the miller's son... The way they speak they all seem such old friends. What really drew them here?

And he thinks: There have always been hoods in these woods...

But he is his own man; he will do things his own way; and he doesn't want much, not power, not fame. Just to give back as good as he got, just to take the fight back to *them*.

He assembles the men. He tells them this:

'I am sick of seeing good people downtrodden, the sick fallen in the fields and lying where they fall, and the lords and the bishops in their manors supping on fine wine and pheasant. There is fair and there is prejudice, and it seems to me that if things were fairer the world would be a better place, and if we must rise in arms then so be it – I shall be a soldier once again. What do you say?'

The men glance at each other uncomfortably. Almost embarrassed, he thinks.

'Alright,' they say.

'Alright, then,' Robin says.

He lays out the plans.

But all the while he thinks of a girl who smiled at him, and who gave him her name, Marian. Marian.

THE GUY

Midway upon the journey of my life I found that I had strayed into a wood. I knew the risk then, or thought I did. I knew what lives in woods: old, secret things. But I had thought it was one kind of war that we were fighting, over land and rights – tangible things. While all the while it was a different war for our myths. People need something to believe in, Father Confessor. You will, I hope, grant me upon my deathbed an ablution of my sins, so I may go to heaven. But, Father, I no longer have in me the power of belief. That knowledge was bleached out of me in that wood the way the sun strips away the illusion of fish on the riverbank until it leaves only the purity of a skeleton.

But you *will* bless me? You will ease my passage into the otherworld? Already I can hear Haros, waiting patiently next to that black river, and his toll, at least, is already paid on my behalf.

Forgive me, Father, for I have sinned.

For days I wandered in the forest. Once, only, I came upon a living being. A clearing in the forest, and a gibbet standing there, two mutilated corpses dangling from the ropes. A small, slight figure stood below them.

'My name is Birdie,' the person told me. 'You've come to kill him. But it is no use. I wish you would. But death is only the half of it, you see.'

Birdie spoke softly, but with a great earnestness.

'The death is the rebirth. So on and so forth it goes. No sword nor prayer will vanquish the two of them. It needs something else. Something new.'

'What is it?' I whispered, awed. I was delirious with hunger.

Birdie shook their head. 'I do not yet know.'

I felt overcome with sadness at the words.

Birdie pointed. I followed the way. Into the woods.

From there the path was short. Or perhaps the place was there all along, but only now was I granted the vision of it.

I stepped into the Green Place and saw them all, waiting for me under the Major Oak.

I knew their names, their faces, from the dossier and all the fucking ballads.

There they stood, motionless, emotionless, waiting: Little John and Will Scarlett and Much, the miller's son. Alan-a-dale and Tuck.

They parted for me. The Hood was sitting on a wooden throne. The Green Lady stood behind him.

'Robin of Loxley,' I said.

'Guy of Gisbourne.'

His voice was barely human anymore. He was huge on his throne. His skin was like bark.

'Leave us,' he said.

They all vanished as quickly as they'd come, back into the trees. The Green Lady whispered something in his ear. He shook her off. She passed so close to me our shoulders brushed. Then she, too, was gone.

'What do you expect to happen here today?' he asked me.

'Sir,' I said. 'I am a soldier.'

'Come closer. Who do you take orders from?'

'King John.'

His eyes closed, I thought in pain. 'He lives, still?'

'And when he dies,' I said, 'another will take his place on the throne.'

At that he smiled, and I realised that I had stumbled somewhere, perilously.

'The Hebrews used to sacrifice two lambs each day in their temple in Jerusalem, and the blood that was let was placed on the altar,' he told me. 'And in Italy, it's said, there lies a sacred grove where a murderer-priest is forever doomed to hunt his predecessor. Upon completion, he takes his place as king, only to await the next assassin.' He smiled at me sadly.

'The blood's the thing, you see.'

He lifted the hood. His head was garlanded with leaves.

'Well? Do it already!'

He bared his neck to me.

THE ROBIN

He sees her at the archery contest.

The day is beautiful and the sun shines down for once and there is no Gloomph. There can't be, not where she is.

Robin is there in disguise, as are his men.

He knows the archery contest's a trap. The sheriff's had enough of the hoods in the woods. He wants to draw them out into the open.

Guardsmen surreptitiously surround the grounds. When Robin reveals himself, which he undoubtedly will, he'll be arrested.

But he doesn't really care about that. It's anyway all a part of his plan.

He knows exactly how it's all going to go down.

It's all going to work out.

It's going to work out *great*.

He looks at the distant target. He reaches for an arrow in his quiver.

He will shoot the arrow. It will hit the target. It always does. One by one, the competition will whittle away. He will be the last man standing, victor. Maid Marian will cheer in the stands. Then the sheriff's men will come down. They will try to arrest him. Robin's men will reveal themselves then. Good men. Merry men. They will fight.

He will leave the sheriff alive. Just him. Make him a prisoner in his own castle. He will bury the sheriff's men in the woods. He will declare Nottingham a Free City!

It will be glorious.

Free from under God or King.

He will go up to Maid Marian. She will laugh as he gives her his cloth. She will stand close to him. Look up into his face and smile.

And he will kiss her.

He can already feel her lips, warm and ready.

Then he will take her away, and they will ride together back into the forest, to live together, man and wife.

Robin of Loxley smiles with childish delight.

It is a wonderful future he sees.

He nocks the arrow and lets it fly.

The arrow, as always, flies true.

PART FIFTEEN

THE NARRATOR

54

I t is time now for me to reluctantly pick up my pen, for this sorry tale is almost done, and all my colleagues are busy elsewhere telling more lucrative tales of King Arthur. Wace is a drunkard, von Eschenbach's a fraud, and as for Robert de Boron, the man's a moron, but what can you do? So it is left to me alone to carry on the tale of Robin Hood, his band of Merry Men and his beloved Marian.

The gang, as you have seen, are all there. They have put on and shed various disguises throughout the long years. Like mummers in a mystery play they all had their roles to play. And somewhere there is always Fairyland, just out of sight: unfocus your gaze and peer behind a rose petal and you just might still find it. What else can I tell you? As Guy of Gisbourne walked out of that clearing all the leaves began to fall at once.

It is better to be a scribe in court than a hood in the king's wood. The former is well-fed and groomed; enjoys fine foods, the latest fashions, stimulating conversations, intimate relations, the hustle and bustle of a world as it goes about its business. The latter, on the other hand, lives a life of short and brutal inconvenience and indignity. If he is caught he's hanged, and if he isn't caught he's hunted. So I remarked only the other day to the queen, and she looked upon me most graciously indeed.

Well, then, let me catch you up. King John, of whom you've somewhat read, he was a rum old bird but now he's dead. It is the way of kings. He didn't have it easy either, the poor soul. His barons tried to sway the power of the kingdom unto themselves, forcing the king at last to sign a most humiliating document with them, which is called the Great Charter or Magna Carta. They signed it near Windsor, I believe, in the Year of our Lord 1215, and shortly after that John died of dysentery, shitting blood.

You see, there was no real law, whatever that dry scholar Vacarius might tell you. Remember Vacarius? He served old Bishop Roger, but then his trail runs cold. This Vacarius tried like a mad badger to instil a sense of Roman law into the English, but without much success. Now the barons, they weren't out for the common man, that lot. They just didn't like the king making the rules all by himself. They wanted to make rules to suit themselves that the king would have to follow.

Well, that sort of thing don't sit so well with kings. So there was war.

But look, you don't *really* give a shit about all this. Do you? You want to hear about the Robin and that lot. The pageantry and the archery contest and the tale of true love between Marian and Loxley. What do you want me to tell you? That he was a good man? That he was a kind man?

He died in the forest that day. Again. And Guy of Gisbourne came out of the woods and sailed downriver, and spent the last of his days gibbering at walls in a monastery in Rouen overlooking the ocean.

What else? Oh, yeah. There was another crusade, shortly after. The army marched to the Holy Land but most of them never made it. Instead they sacked Constantinople. Can you fucking believe it? For a thousand years Byzantium endured. And it was brought down in a single night by Christian crusaders who just wanted to get paid.

It was a crying shame.

In any case, some time after the events recounted in the last chapter, I myself had occasion to travel to the town of Nottingham, and there had a chance to observe first-hand the matters concerning the green cult rumoured to still be practised there. I came by ship to London, departing the French court with some sadness to arrive at this city, which is said to be magnificent but which I found, in truth, a dismal sort of place. It rained a lot and the natives were surly, and I was ensconced in a rundown boarding house in Westminster, with lots of beggars outside and all manner of sexual congress in the adjacent rooms. I was low on funds, for my benefactor in the court had in truth tired somewhat of both my poetry and my other services to her. It was deemed prudent on both our sides to part ways for a time. Absence, as the ancients said, surely makes the heart grow fonder.

These events that I'm about to narrate took place sometime after the sixth crusade (there were a fucking lot of them, to be fair) and during the reign of the sainted Louis in the court of France. My mistress was a noblewoman at the court, and had a love of those epic poems that are so popular nowadays, with tales of dragons and wizards and kings, and that my contemporaries on the Continent always set on the isle of Britain, which is a savage land shrouded by clouds and lying beyond the water, and so who could tell in truth what happens there?

I myself, being less prone to the fantastic and being an enquiring sort, and wishing to break the mould, as it were, and go against the grain of my contemporaries and their ever more elaborate fantasies of King Arthur, his pet wizard Merlin and all that – well, I decided to turn my attention instead to some of those strange English ballads, in which the mysterious figure of one Robin Hood takes prominent place. They are strange things indeed, those ballads, with murders and elves, quite enough to chill the blood if you hear a harpist sing them.

Delicious stuff, I thought. And so I determined to gain first-hand knowledge of the situation, instead of just making shit up like those hacks von Eschenbach or de Boron.

My luck turned auspicious when I came across another temporary resident in that boarding house. An ancient Jewish woman rented out the entire upper floor. This was still before King Henry made the Jews put on the yellow star. I ran into her at breakfast my second morning. She sipped a small beer and regarded me with something like amusement.

'Nottingham?' she said. 'I used to live there for a time.'

'You are familiar with the tales of Robin Hood?'

'Somewhat.'

'What brings you back to England, Mistress Rebecca?' I asked. It could not have been easy, at her advanced age, to make the crossing.

'I have lived a long life,' she said, 'longer than most, if truth be told. As you get close to the end of the tale you wish you knew how it all turned out. So I came back. I am journeying to Nottingham myself, as it happens. Some old, unfinished business there. I could offer you a ride.'

'I would be most grateful!'

She smiled at me rather ruefully.

'Yes, well,' she said, 'you haven't been there yet.'

The town of Nottingham stands like an island in the heart of Sherwood Forest, a lonesome area that evokes unease. The countryside, with its murky light and cold, clammy air, has an atmosphere that the locals refer to as 'Gloomph'. The local accent is barbed with a forester's twang and a villein's nasalness, and the men, many of them, wear hoods and Lincoln greens. The views are awesomely extensive when not hidden by the forest; from a high vantage point the traveller is surprised to see horses, herds of cattle, a white cluster of church towers visible long before one reaches them.

There is little to see in the town itself. There is a lively market and boats dock on the river bank, but the pace is sedate, one may almost say drugged. There is a fine Norman castle on the hill, atop a curious edifice of soft stone, which is called Castle Rock by the locals. There is a branch of the Templar order which offers financial services, and there are also several churches and a gibbet. The town is divided roughly in half between the older English section and the new French Quarter, and a small area is set aside for the king's Jews.

In a once affluent square stands a faded sign for a place called Dick's, but nothing remains of this once famous establishment beside a boarded-up hole in the ground. Two ancients guard the gates of the town. They look like they have stood there for a century and may well stand a century or two more. They greeted Mistress Rebecca cordially and familiarly as we came through, as though no time had passed since her departure from the city many years earlier. I wondered if they even knew what century this was.

Mistress Rebecca still owned a large house in the Jewry, and took there with relief after the long and wearing journey. For myself, I sought accommodation in the castle first, was rebuked by a short, fat cook with a very bad temper, and at last made my way to the guest dormitory of the Benedictine Priory of St. Nicholas the Wonderworker.

There I was told a most strange tale of a miracle that occurred in the town some years past. The Priory had for many years held in service a novice, and later priest, given the name of Father Evangelium, but who was colloquially known as Birdie. The details of this individual's circumstances were somewhat obscure, but he had served the Church faithfully since entering the novitiate and had a true love for his flock and the Christ.

Father Evangelium was known as a very private individual, and seldom washed. Yet some years past, it happened that two novitiates were in the wood that borders the priory, on business that was not the Church's. In short, the two were truant, and most likely in the woods to poach the king's deer – for such poaching, while against the law of the land, is nevertheless a prominent occupation of the townsfolk of Nottingham, even those under God's roof.

Regardless of their motives on that excursion, as the two young monks crept about in the undergrowth they came upon a most curious sight. There was the familiar figure of Father Evangelium, standing by a pool of black water in the moonlight. The small, rotund priest looked furtively about him but, seeing no one, began to unrobe himself.

The two novitiates crossed themselves at the sight, for they beheld a miracle – a miracle indeed! Even in the faint light of the moon, the two boys could discern that, as if by magic, Father Birdie had grown a pair of bosoms and, in that sacred space between his legs, there dangled no dongle, but rather grew a valley of mystery, with a sort of black moss above it, and it was a sight of the sort boys such as them were very much preoccupied by in their dreams.

They left that place much shaken. They could not keep the tale to themselves, and it spread, until it came to the attentions of the higher-ups, and the bishop came down from York.

At last Birdie, a much holy man, confessed that such a change in physique had afflicted him suddenly and without warning. It was, by all indications, a genuine miracle. And since Birdie was regarded as a much devoted person, though she could no longer serve as priest she was given, instead, the role of prioress at nearby Church-Lee, a role she had since fulfilled with great devotion and competence. It was an arrangement that suited everyone admirably.

'Yes, yes,' I said, a little impatiently, 'but what of Robin Hood?'

'Ah,' the aged monk I was speaking with by the fire said. 'That.'

He looked a little embarrassed. 'I can't say as we have much trouble in the woods these days,' he told me. 'And no one likes to reminisce of the old times round here. One of the brothers claims he rode with the outlaws back in the day. Tuck, his name is, and he is a little touched, the poor soul, though harmless enough. You might get some sense out of him but I doubt it, for he doesn't like strangers.'

Finding this Tuck fellow proved harder than expected, but at last I managed to corner the old monk in the herb garden, in a shed in the back where I found a small still in operation, making gut-rot whisky. This Tuck quaffed the stuff as though it were water and, though hostile to me at first, became much more cordial after his third glass. He entreated me to drink with him and, not wishing to offend, I took careful sips of the clear drink: it quickly went to my head nonetheless.

'Hood, yes, yes,' he said. 'There is still one around, I think. I cut ties with the old gang after the last one lost his head. What with one thing and another the game just wasn't in me no more. Besides, he doesn't get a happy ending, you know, and I figured at least one of us should. Why not old Tuck? I love a happy ending. I remember back in the old rub-and-tug emporiums in London, why, they had girls there could make Lazarus come twice back from the dead.' He beamed at me toothlessly.

'Is that so, is that so,' I said. 'Still, you must know what's about, old timer.'

'Listen, kid,' he said. 'I'm going to give you a bit of advice.' He motioned for me to come close. The fumes on his breath were overpowering. 'People round here don't like strangers asking questions. Let the past rest. And when you go back home to France just make some shit up like everybody else does. Did you ever read de Boron's *Merlin*? That was some good shit right there! And *he* didn't go around interviewing survivors of the Battle of Camlann or whatever, did he? No, kid, he just made the crap up, and no one got into any trouble.'

'But I need to know,' I told him. 'It's all about the authenticity—'

'Fuck your authenticity!' he said. He pushed me in the chest and I stumbled. My head spun from the potency of the gut-rot. 'Or else,' he said more quietly, 'you may not find your way back at all.'

Reader, I was distraught! I spent the night in the dormitory with my head rent asunder by bad dreams and pain. My mother always said I had a sensitive disposition. In my dreams I saw

Guy of Gisbourne walk out of that wood again and the silent men all came out of the trees to watch him pass. His footprints were bloody, and all the leaves began to fall at once...

Then I was being chased by a giant rabbit, and shortly after that the bells rang for Lauds and I woke up with a headache.

55

'What really brought you back here, mistress?' I said. Mistress Rebecca had kindly invited me to break the fast at her place. She was dressed all in green.

'A funeral,' she said.

'Oh!' I was taken aback. 'I am sorry for your loss.'

'Don't be.' She stared in the mirror speculatively. 'I have not worn the green hood in years…' she said. 'It's funny, when I finally left I swore I would never come back. That I was done with the whole damn story. This is no place for Jews. But then, as I found out, nowhere is. Do you know what I mean?'

'Not really,' I mumbled.

She affixed a green brooch to her cloak and smiled at herself in the mirror. 'It's all right,' she said gently. 'Would you like to accompany me? It is a pleasant day today and you might find the event stimulating.' She touched her hair, just so.

'Someone should witness,' she said.

Intrigued, I willingly followed her. The walk was short. I noticed that for all her age and girth, Mistress Rebecca moved more swiftly here, as though the very Gloomph of the place were a healing potion to her. She knew the streets here intimately. As we walked I noticed the green man faces on the walls, but they were old and faded. The streets filled with people heading in the same direction as us – families, with mothers pulling children and fathers looking anxious and proud, and more than one street seller pushing greasy sausages and honeyed apples and what not. The air was festive, and as we came through the streets I beheld the green grazing field that ran down from the side of the town to the river and the forest below.

The field was prepared for festivity on that day. Little children ran around and men stood together with cups of beer, and everywhere there were stalls selling food and trinkets, and a giant maypole stood in the centre of the field. The aura of Gloomph lifted then, and a bright sun shone down.

Then I saw why. Then I saw *her*. She stood near the maypole, where young maids danced round and round, holding on to ribbons. Not her. *She* just stood, and the sun fell and caught her youthful face and her shining hair and her green eyes, oh, how green her eyes were! She looked up and I could swear she saw me, and she smiled.

'Ohh...' I said.

Mistress Rebecca followed my gaze.

'She does have a way about her, doesn't she?' she said. I couldn't make out her tone. She took my arm and pulled me along.

The May Day festivities went on all around us. Sheriff's men and monks and mendicants, nuns and villeins and freemen and jugglers, singers and musicians, pickpockets and wrestlers all intermingled. I found myself drunk on it all. I was whirled in a dance by a maiden in green, passed to another as the musicians struck a raucous tune, was handed a cup of ale and then another, was whirled again until at last, laughing, I landed on a patch of grass to regain my breath.

By then dusk was starting to fall. The sun's dying light streaked the sky above Sherwood Forest red and green, and in a deep pit dug in the field near the walls a large bonfire was set aflame. The dry wood caught quickly. Sparks went up into the air and the smoke that rose up tasted of a wild freedom that took me back to childhood, before my father died in far-off Acre fighting Saracens, when he and my mother took me with them each year to celebrate the coming of spring.

Spring was almost here. *She* was here. I saw her again, standing by the fire. Her eyes shone in the firelight. She seemed both younger and wilder then. A man in a hood stood next to her. I suppose there is always a man in the hood. He held her hand as if he were drowning.

A procession came along then from the hill. The crowds parted before it. The music stopped and now only a long-haired harpist played, and he played a mournful tune. The procession came down slowly. I saw the monk I spoke to the night before, old Brother Tuck, and Mistress Rebecca. I silently put names to the others. That big hulking one was Little John. The small one next to him with the knife scars was Will Scarlett. The harpist must be Alan-a-dale.

Between them they carried a coffin.

Flanking Mistress Rebecca were two ancient women. Elgitha, I thought. Ulrica. The funeral procession came to the bonfire and stopped.

'In the midst of life we are in death,' Brother Tuck said. His voice was a little unsteady. 'To whom may we look for help but to you, our Lady?'

She looked at him. I named her, too. Maid Marian.

'We have come to say farewell to one of ours. He was with us for a long time. He loved. He lived. Now he is back into the fire from whence we all came. Ashes to ashes, brother. Amen.'

'Hear, hear!' the harpist said.

I came close. I craned to look. The coffin rested on the ground. Mistress Rebecca knelt beside it. She dabbed her cheek with embroidered cloth.

'Here, let me,' I said. She took my arm gratefully.

I looked into the coffin then.

All I saw was a bunch of branches and twigs tied together in the shape of a man.

'Goodbye, Much...' Rebecca said.

I helped her to her feet. The old men picked up the effigy and threw it into the flames; and the harpist played on, on a harp made of bone.

'That went well, I thought,' Rebecca said the next day, digging into her breakfast. She ate with some relish. For such a long-lived woman she had kept me up well past the witching hour the night before, if you know what I mean, and I was still sore from the exertion. Still. If there is anything I know it's that a comfortable bed in the Jewry is preferable to a night spent in a monks' dormitory, and no Frenchman in his right mind would argue the point.

'It was a lovely ceremony,' I said, 'to welcome the spring.'

I thought of the scene of the night before. It would be a lovely way to end my story, I decided.

'It's spring every year,' Rebecca said with unexpected vehemence. 'This is what nobody gets. It's always going to be spring. It doesn't matter who dies and who lives or if a bonfire burns or if a sacrifice is made. It's all bullshit.'

'I mean, sure, but…' I looked at her in confusion. 'I thought you came to say goodbye. You said you had unfinished business—'

She leaned over and grasped my arm hard. 'How deep do you want to go?' she asked me. 'You could finish it now, on the bonfire and Much. It's not much of a Much of a thing.'

'It would play well at court…'

'You could,' she allowed. 'You probably should.'

I stared into her eyes.

I saw the madness there.

'Yes,' I said. 'I think I would like to end it there.'

She let me go.

'Of course,' she said.

And that, more or less, was that.

★

I returned back to France that spring, travelling without haste. Jews were murdered in London upon my arrival but I had nothing to do with it. I took a ship back to the Continent. In truth I was glad to be away from England. It is a shitty sort of place.

I completed my epic narrative poem, with the ending depicted much as above. 'The Hood' enjoyed moderate success. Copies circulated in court and beyond and several people have said nice things about it, though it failed to reach a wider audience. At some point I was in talks with a harpist to turn it into a series of lucrative ballads, but the idea fell through.

I retired from court with a modest pension and now spend most of my time in my herb garden in Rouen, not far from the place where Guy of Gisbourne spent his final days. I like to take long walks on the beach and watch the ocean.

Time passes. I heard the other day a tale of new invaders from the East who swiftly took over the Rus' lands and were making incursions deep into the heart of Europe. Rumours swirl of some new, unknown kind of weapon they employ. It sounds fanciful to me, but who's to say? The world changes every day.

Sometimes I wonder how it really ended, if it ever did. But then I open a nice bottle of Bordeaux and forget all about it.

PART SIXTEEN

MONGOLS

56

Rebecca watches the little scribeling ride away. He was fun for a bounce; but he's an idiot. Let him go back and write it any way he likes. *She* knows how it should end: in death and blood and fire.

'And did you bring it?' she asks Birdie. The Mother Superior of the Church-Lee Priory nods. She creeps quietly into the kitchen.

'I missed you at the funeral.'

'I did not go, Rebecca.'

Birdie had gained composure over the years, Rebecca sees without much surprise. But then she was always formidable.

'Are you sure you want to do this?'

Birdie nods. She looks at Rebecca curiously. 'And you?'

'I think so.'

'May I sit?'

Birdie does not wait but sits down on a chair. She looks across the table.

'You have grown old,' she says, almost in wonderment.

Rebecca snorts back laughter. 'It is what people do.'

'Not in the heartwood,' Birdie says.

'Oh, I don't know. I saw them at the funeral, don't forget. It's weakening. Or something else. I don't know. Changing, maybe.'

'Things don't change,' Birdie says.

'Oh, I don't know. May I see it?'

Birdie opens the satchel she carries. She shows the contents to Rebecca.

'It doesn't look like much.'

'A wizard sold it to me.'

'Will it work?'

'I have no idea.'

Rebecca pushes to her feet. It's strange, being back in Nottingham after all these years. In Normandy she felt the passing of each year like an added stone on a pile. With every year that passed the weight pressed her down more and more. Now she is back she feels more like her old self. She realises with some surprise that her old self was *angry*. She hates them, this place, what it does. It's the sort of story that wraps itself around the world and reshapes it with its poison.

In centuries to come, she thinks, they'll still be telling tales of fucking Robin Hood.

It makes her angry enough to want to do something about it.

Something very bad.

They move slowly. Rebecca sees the place where the Goat used to be. She sees the market where she left the corpses. She sees the witch's place. It's so easy to leave a place and forget all about it. Why go back? Maybe it's when you can no longer go farther.

They climb to the top of Castle Rock. There is no one to stop them. The cook comes out. She stares at Rebecca.

'Oh, it's you,' she says. She spits a gob of phlegm and vanishes back inside. And Rebecca thinks, The cook is a prisoner within that body now. In a way they are all imprisoned.

Well, she will change that. She takes the bag from Birdie. It is so light. She unties the string and sifts the soft grey powder inside.

'The wizard called it a Phytophthora,' Birdie tells her.

Rebecca feels the wind on her face. It brushes her hair.

THE HOOD

Rebecca feels exhilarated by it. She lifts a handful of fungus dust: Phytophthora, plant-destroyer. She opens her fingers and the wind snatches at the grey spores and blows them high and fast across the forest.

Rebecca watches as they fall down on the trees.

She's with Elgitha and Ulrica when they pay a visit to St. Nick's and find the old monk, Tuck. He tries to run but they hobble after him, Rebecca gripping her cane, and when they corner him in a shed at the back of the vegetable patch Rebecca brains him with it.

She breaks into what used to be the Goat. It lies disused now. She finds the trapdoor and climbs down to a silent cellar. Not even rats – there's nothing there for them. Rebecca listens to the silence.

She walks to the door that should never be opened. She unlocks it with her key.

The creature hung by chains has been imprisoned alone in there for decades. Her dress has rotted away but her hair is just as glamorous as ever, and when she turns her eyes on Rebecca, the charm in them is strong enough to catch a snake. She smiles with those long, sharp teeth. She hisses.

'Hello, Rowena,' Rebecca says.

'Bex.'

'So you still have speech.'

Rowena laughs in her face. 'I told you before, this prison of yours means nothing to me.'

'I see your toe grew back.'

'No thanks to you.'

'And your wings.'

They're like a dragonfly's, but each one is as long as a person. The wings shiver.

'What do you want, Rebecca? You are old and fat, and the stench of death is upon you. And when you're dead I'll still be young.'

'Perhaps,' Rebecca says. She looks her old friend and enemy over. 'But you'll still be here.'

That night she sleeps; she tosses and turns on her bed.

She is granted a vision then, as though from a great height. Some unfamiliar territory, and a grand city, called Vladimir, with stout walls and stout defenders, and a voice whispers on the wind that this is the Rus's land, far away, and that the Rus' are not to be trifled with.

And yet as Rebecca watches, a great army comes riding on the city from the East. A Golden Horde of men on horses, and their weapons are unfamiliar to her, strange and wondrous and new. And these Mongol warriors come to lay siege to the city.

What has it to do with her? Rebecca groans and turns upon her bed. A moon swims in the sky, wreathed in cloud. A raven caws on a branch outside. What are these things the Mongols carry?

Alchemists in fur hats measure out a soft black powder. Assistants labour, carrying bags. They mix a sort of salt with sulphur and coal dust. Many have missing fingers, missing limbs. Their hands and faces are covered in burns. The alchemist masters supervise and measure. Soldiers work busily on small iron pots and strange lances. The black powder of the alchemists is distributed to the soldiers.

They are fashioning weapons here, Rebecca realises. But she had never seen such devices before. They are something else, something new.

She watches as the Mongol soldiers spread out before the walls of Vladimir. Defenders inside shoot arrows. Their walls are stout. They should be safe within.

Rebecca watches as Mongol engineers command their workers. They work diligently, assembling new machines. They travel with the parts, she realises. She watches a launcher being built, a trebuchet, and another and another.

Rebecca tosses, turns. What are these tubes the Mongol soldiers hold? The soldiers carry little iron pots with them, filled with coals. She watches them approach the walls. She sees them take the coals, apply them on the hilt end of the tubes. A hiss, and lances fire out, over the walls, shoot like arrows with no bows to drive them.

Rebecca hears screams over the walls. And now she sees the trebuchets firing those little iron pots packed with black powder. She sees them land inside the town. Sees them explode. Sees iron nails and shrapnel burning hot exploding everywhere. The sound is like thunder echoing for miles, the Rus' defenders scream, this is no weapon anyone has ever used before, these fire lances, these heaven-shaking-thunder bombs.

Rebecca tosses, turns.

Beyond her window, beyond the walls of Nottingham, the little spores infect the trees. The leaves turn white and cankers form in trunks and bleed. Deep in the forest the Hood wakes up and cries in pain. 'I need bleeding,' he cries. It is a sure-fire cure in this day and age, and the Church offers a fine service of it.

Rebecca tosses, turns.

The Hood turns to someone he can trust. He goes in the night to the prioress at Church-Lee. Birdie welcomes him. She has him lie down on the ground. She takes out her bleeding tools. Makes small incisions in his neck and wrists. She uses a sharp chip of wood for the procedure. 'As recommended by Galen,' she tells the Hood. The Hood nods, clenches his teeth. Birdie reaches for a bag of leeches. She places them on the Hood's body. 'The blood's the thing, you see,' she tells him.

She over-bleeds him.

Rebecca tosses, turns.

The wood screams pain. In the hidden cellar under the Goat Rowena screams too, in savage glee. A bone harpist rides her horse like night into the wind. She'll get away. Alanah, too, knows how stories ought to end.

The Hood lies dying. Birdie strokes his hair. Robin reaches for a bow and arrow. He fires blindly. The arrow lands somewhere far away.

'I'm cold,' he says. 'I'm cold.'

Rebecca tosses, turns, beyond the window the birds awake. Dawn's nearly there, and in her dreams the deed is done.

She wakes.

Opens her eyes.

Her father, Isaac, stands by the window.

'Is it time?' Rebecca says.

He smiles at her.

'It's time.'

Then he is gone. Rebecca stands.

She walks into the dark that's always there.

PART SEVENTEEN

FREE

57

When the soldiers come to the forest it is years later, and the devices they hold are new.

Black powder weapons.

They come quietly, settling an old score no one can quite remember anymore.

They enter the trees. The things that live within fall to them. The will-o'-the-wisps who try to lead them astray are incinerated. Toadstool houses where tiny elves live are trampled underfoot. Fleeing gnomes are shot in the back.

The soldiers move methodically, spreading out. They burn the sick trees and kill the boggarts and the ghouls. They toss grenades of iron pots packed with black powder. Hot iron kills elves. The explosions rock the forest, the flames bellow up through the trees. They incinerate the ground around them in hot white flame.

The soldiers move deeper into the wood.

Hic est finis.

They torch the fairy forts and bomb the warrens of the dwarfs. They massacre the fates, the fiends, the Bloody Bones, the night-hags and phantasms.

Solum amicus meus, finis.

They reach the Major Oak. A small resistance force of hoods attack them from the canopy with arrows. The soldiers shoot their fire lances. Hoods drop down dead. The soldiers pan around the oak, the thing in the black pool rises and is incinerated with bombs. Magic is no good against black powder weapons. The huge corpse is torn apart and chunks of flesh float in the murky water.

The cook stands a little way off with her arms crossed, watching the destruction. She frowns irritably. She had been patient and she'd sat back and she can smell the change at last and she is glad. 'Think this is the end?' she mutters. 'You think you don't *need* us anymore?'

The fire bursts from the tree tops. The sky is red with haze. The cook's body lengthens, shifts. She sprouts wings. Her legs grow long. Her skirt grows short. She looks with some surprise at the ensemble.

'Huh,' she says.

In the hidden cellar under the Goat, Rowena feels the heat of the fire. She chews through her bonds though the metal hurts her. The door falls to her. She laughs delightedly.

Her teeth are long and sharp and she is *hungry*.

The bone harpist comes and stands beside the cook.

'So this is how the world ends?' Alanah says.

Morgause looks at her sideways. 'Oh, it's you,' she says. 'No. This is how it starts.'

'I like your wings,' Alanah says.

They stand companionably on the low hill and watch as the wood burns.

Deep below the world, imprisoned in a crystal cave, a wizard feels the crystal shattering and laughs. He burrows upwards and emerges into sunlight. How long has he been down there? he wonders. But time means nothing to one such as him.

Merlin turns into a bird and flies away.

★

While on a street in London Will Scarlett finds himself awake with no memory of how he got there. He catches a glimpse of himself in a puddle. His face is whole, unlined and unscarred. He touches his ear gingerly. Where has he been? What has he done? He doesn't know.

'You look a little lost,' a voice says. A woman stands there, looking at him curiously. Like him she's young, and now she's real, solid, and he recognises something in her, as though he'd known her before, in another lifetime.

It starts to rain.

'I thought I was,' he tells her. 'But I feel better now.'

'Good,' she tells him.

She threads her arm through his; and together he and Morgan walk away amidst the raindrops.

Down, down below the Major Oak, the roots reach to the place where long ago an elfin knight was gutted. The Green Lady stands above him. The roots that reach down to the elfin knight's guts are poisoned now, she knows. Marian watches as the elfin knight shudders in pain.

'It won't be long now,' she says comfortingly.

She puts on her hood. She smiles.

It's time to die again.

She wonders what she'll be like on the next come around.

HISTORICAL
AFTERWORD

Who killed Cock Robin?
I, said the Sparrow
with my bow and arrow
I killed Cock Robin.

The story of Robin Hood emerges out of the oral tradition of ballads in medieval England. The first preserved record in print, 'Robin Hood and the Monk', dates to circa 1450, while a compendium of sorts of his early adventures, 'A Gest of Robyn Hode', was preserved in print sometime after 1492. Importantly, those early stories were eventually wedded to the May Day traditions, bringing Robin into association with Maid Marian.

The story was extensively reworked over the centuries. A tradition began of dating Robin to the reign of Richard the Lionheart, often portraying him as a returning crusader. A significant literary adaptation was Walter Scott's *Ivanhoe* (1819), from which I adapted several elements, most significantly Rebecca.

Why *were* there Jews in Nottingham at that time? Much as depicted in this book, a small number of Jews did come with William the Conqueror to England, and a Jewish population remained until their expulsion in 1290. They belonged to the king, and were tasked with lending money with interest, an act at least nominally prohibited to Christians (though as the tale of Sir Richard at the Lee shows, practised often by the Church). The money raised was then heavily taxed by the king and, upon their death, the Jews' possessions went back to the Crown. The Jews suffered pogroms and blood libels by a population that often resented them. Nevertheless, there were Jewish populations in most major towns in England, including Nottingham.

As for dwale, it was a real remedy, though recipes vary. It usually contained belladonna and opium among its ingredients.

From *Ivanhoe*, other early popular versions of the Robin Hood tales included *Robin Hood and Little John, or The Merry Men of Sherwood Forest* (1840) by Pierce Egan and *The Merry Adventures of Robin Hood* (1883) by Howard Pyle. Going into the twentieth century, adaptations became too numerous to list, with Robin making the transition into television and film.

The tales are usually presented without magic, yet the ballads from which they arose are rich with it. The folklorist Francis James Child collected many of these texts (now usually referred to as the 'Child Ballads') in 1860. These stories are filled with elves, violence, murder and magic. I've drawn on several of these while twisting them to my own ends, including 'Lady Isabel and the Elf Knight', 'The Twa Sisters', 'Leesome Brand', and the various Hood ballads, including 'A Gest of Robyn Hode' and 'Robin Hood's Death' (in which he is indeed bled to death by the prioress). I also drew on several fairy tales and nursery rhymes.

It is worth noting that the figures of Robin and Marian closely correspond – as the critic John Clute argues compellingly – with the Green Man and the May Queen respectively. One is a trickster and a Lord of Faerie. The other is the personification of spring. Sherwood itself is, in Clute's terms, a polder, a pocket of the old world threatened by thinning. I used many of his ideas on the nature of the fantastic within this book. Nor could I ignore that great work of armchair anthropology, J.G. Frazer's *The Golden Bough* (1890) for its ideas on the dying god.

Events in this novel span nearly a century, beginning in 1145 and coming to a close sometime after 1238. The period we now call the Anarchy was a prolonged time of civil war in England between King Stephen and Empress Matilda, which ended at last with the rise to the throne of Henry II, Matilda's son and first of the Plantagenet kings. Henry's battle for power with the Church resulted in Thomas Becket's murder much as described here. Henry's son Richard, popularly known as the Lionheart, inherited the throne.

Richard was not much interested in England. He soon departed for the Third Crusade, and only returned to England once, very briefly. He died fighting in France. His brother John then became king.

The crusades were a series of prolonged wars carried out in the Levant against Muslim forces with the aim of liberating the Holy Land for Christendom. The First Crusade led to the establishment of the wealthy and powerful crusader state of the Kingdom of Jerusalem, which lasted some two hundred years. The same period saw the rise of several powerful religious orders, including the Knights Templar. Their system of finance can be seen as the start of modern banking.

The rise of Saladin brought about lasting geopolitical change: he successfully took control of Jerusalem from the crusaders and established the Ayyubid dynasty, which controlled much of the Middle East for the next two hundred years.

The crusaders of the Fourth Crusade really *did* sack Constantinople, bringing to an inglorious end the thousand-year-old Byzantine Empire.

At its height, the Mongol Empire was the largest contiguous land empire in the world, and it is second only to the British Empire in overall extent. Mongol warriors took much of Eastern and Central Europe and reached as far as Vienna before turning back. The Mongols most likely made use of gunpowder weapons, though these were not successfully taken up by European forces until the Late Middle Ages.

But regardless. The cycle of stories of Robin Hood is, much like Arthur, all but a part of the great Matter of Britain; and several characters from my earlier novel, *By Force Alone*, duly make brief cameos in these pages. Like Arthur, there is no historical basis for a real person named Robin Hood, though a guy called Eustace the Monk really did exist and is sometimes offered as a precursor. Also real was the lucrative trade in relics during the Middle Ages, and there really were multiple Holy Foreskins all over the place. Whether anyone tried to Frankenstein Jesus, though, that I do not rightly know.

As for Robin's battle? Today, the land in England is still owned much as it was during his time, by the Crown, the Church, and the various descendants of long-vanished barons. When the late Duke of Westminster was asked by a reporter what advice he could give to anyone wishing to succeed in modern England, his reply was to 'make sure they have an ancestor who was a very close friend of William the Conqueror'. Today, householders own just 5% of all land in England; and the ownership of a whole 17% of the land is unknown. No wonder Robin's own men in this book are somewhat sceptical of his ambitions.

The villeins of feudal England had a miserable time of it. But the peasants *did* rise in revolt against their masters from time to time. In France, the *Jacquerie* of 1358 saw the 'Jacques' rise in disorganised rebellion. They took over castles and towns and massacred the landed nobility. They were ruthlessly put down a few weeks later, by a guy literally called Charles the Bad, aka Charles II of Navarre, who later burnt to death accidentally in his own palace in what was generally regarded as a piece of divine justice.

Twenty years later, the Great Uprising overtook England itself. Led by Wat Tyler, the rebels marched on London to demand an end to serfdom. Unsurprisingly this one, too, was ruthlessly put down.

Perhaps it is, as one of the Robins observes here, just the way of the world and nothing more. But many still do go hungry while the rich are fed, and many still slave upon land that is owned by others. And if so then, as Rebecca says, in centuries to come they might still be telling the same fucking story.

All the birds in the air
Fell to sighing and sobbing
When they heard the bell toll
For poor Cock Robin.

While the cruel Cock Sparrow,
The cause of their grief
Was hung on a gibbet
Next day, like a thief.

ABOUT THE
AUTHOR

Lavie Tidhar's novels include World Fantasy Award winner *Osama*, Jerwood Fiction Uncovered Prize winner *A Man Lies Dreaming* (both recently reissued by Head of Zeus) and Campbell, Neukom and Chinese Nebula winner *Central Station*. His novels *By Force Alone* and *The Hood*, the first and second in his Anti-Matter of Britain Quartet, are published by Head of Zeus. Described as 'an utterly original voice in contemporary fiction' and 'a genius at conjuring realities that are just two steps to the left of our own', Tidhar works across genres. His novels combine detective and thriller modes with poetry, science fiction and historical and autobiographical material to create a genre entirely of his own.